Praise for John Hawkes and *Sweet William*

"Brilliantly realized . . . This is a tremendous, truly extraordinary novel." —*The Boston Globe*

"Hawkes has, through his equine hero, created an Everyman for human and animal alike. . . . *Sweet William* [is] by turns graceful and frightening—[it] remains a fully realized summation of one of the main fictional obsessions of a continually adventurous and challenging author." —*Chicago Tribune*

"A tour de force . . . So talented is Hawkes in his observations of the horse world, of what such animals—and by extension, any animals—go through . . . [that] we can't avoid a feeling of aware-ness in reading this novel." —*The Philadelphia Inquirer*

"When we look deeply into this creature's splendid, savage heart, we cannot help but hope to find our own." —*The Miami Herald*

"Compelling . . . *Sweet William* is a virtuoso performance, with William's voice rendered in masterful prose. . . . Hawkes offers a fascinating new perspective on the mix of instinct, emotion, reflex and reason that is the birthright of all intelligent life." —*Publishers Weekly*

"[Hawkes'] narrative is populated with first-rate characters and, most of all, a difficult yet sentient horse that finally achieves the grace of age-old wisdom." —*People*

PENGUIN BOOKS

SWEET WILLIAM

John Hawkes is the author of over twelve works of fiction, including *Second Skin*, *The Passion Artist*, and *The Blood Oranges*. He is a member of the American Academy and Institute of Arts and Letters. He is Professor of English Emeritus, Brown University.

Books by John Hawkes

Novels

ADVENTURES IN THE ALASKAN SKIN TRADE

THE BEETLE LEG

THE BLOOD ORANGES

THE CANNIBAL

DEATH, SLEEP & THE TRAVELER

INNOCENCE IN EXTREMIS

THE LIME TWIG

THE OWL

THE PASSION ARTIST

SECOND SKIN

TRAVESTY

VIRGINIE: HER TWO LIVES

WHISTLEJACKET

Plays

THE INNOCENT PARTY: FOUR SHORT PLAYS

Collections

HUMORS OF BLOOD & SKIN: A JOHN HAWKES READER

LUNAR LANDSCAPES: STORIES AND SHORT NOVELS

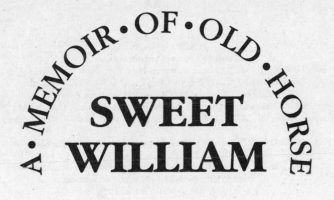

SWEET WILLIAM

A · MEMOIR · OF · OLD · HORSE

John Hawkes

PENGUIN BOOKS

PENGUIN BOOKS
Published by the Penguin Group
Penguin Books USA Inc., 375 Hudson Street, New York, New York 10014, U.S.A.
Penguin Books Ltd, 27 Wrights Lane, London W8 5TZ, England
Penguin Books Australia Ltd, Ringwood, Victoria, Australia
Penguin Books Canada Ltd, 10 Alcorn Avenue, Toronto, Ontario, Canada M4V 3B2
Penguin Books (N.Z.) Ltd, 182–190 Wairau Road, Auckland 10, New Zealand

Penguin Books Ltd, Registered Offices: Harmondsworth, Middlesex, England

First published in the United States of America by Simon & Schuster 1993
Reprinted by arrangement with Simon & Schuster
Published in Penguin Books 1994

3 5 7 9 10 8 6 4 2

Portions of this work appeared in somewhat different form in
Alea I, Conjunctions 15 and *17, Gulf Coast, Soho Square*,
and *O blek (The Burning Deck Issue)*.

PUBLISHER'S NOTE
This book is a work of fiction. Names, characters, places, and incidents are either
products of the author's imagination or are used fictitiously. Any resemblance to actual
events or locales or persons, living or dead, is entirely coincidental.

THE LIBRARY OF CONGRESS HAS CATALOGUED THE HARDCOVER AS FOLLOWS:
Hawkes, John.
Sweet William: A memoir of Old Horse/John Hawkes.
p.   cm.
ISBN 0-671-74057-1 (hc.)
ISBN 0 14 02.3616 3 (pbk.)
1. Horse—Fiction.   I. Title.
PS3558.A82S94 1993
813'.54—dc20   92-40125

Printed in the United States of America
Set in Garamond
Designed by Songhee Kim

For Sophie

A GENTLE WARNING

Browser beware. Pause while you may and reconsider. The horse's life that follows is not for ordinary lovers of the horse. Here are no extended passages in praise of this fabled stallion or that noble mare of ancient times, no heroism, no grand or even modest performances of horse and man and woman or favored child in competitions that exalt courage, good sense, grace on a large scale. All this existed in the past, does so today, and will in the future. But not here. There is good riding, classical riding, riding that is nothing less than spiritual. But not here. Here are to be found no well-ordered barns as mystical as temples, no honoring of the great tradition from which all horses spring, no luxury, and nothing whatever of professionalism. Here is no concern with success, with training the young, with good form, discipline, dedication to the rules and virtues of equitation, or with the general pursuit of good horsemanship from childhood to old age. Browser, if this is what you must have, go elsewhere. If convention and reassurance are what you must have, then stop and spare yourself unsettling surprise. But if you are not easily aroused to indignation, and if you are prepared to set aside familiar expectations, then persist, walk on, ride to the end, and in the adversities of this horse's life find yours.

·I·
SWEET
WILLIAM

The Days of My Youth

CHAPTER ONE

•

MY START IN LIFE BEING THE CRUELEST
EVER KNOWN TO HORSE OR MAN

I am Old Horse.

And I have been Old Horse and called Old Horse for longer than the oldest horse alive can remember. Born to glory, brought low, given a proper name, pampered, loved and scorned, trained and raced, maligned and gelded, sold repeatedly, kicked and bitten and beaten and tormented by fellow beasts and callow men until at last we met, Master and I. For our few months of life together we shared the silent music of arthritis, his and mine, the ignominy of gaunt frames and aching bones, the brief marriage of his innocence with my misanthropy, the unlikely collaboration of discarded man and discarded horse mutually revived at death's door—there you have the colors and thunderclaps of my long life.

For me there is still worse to come. No wonder I am called Old Horse.

There are those who say that the brain of a horse is no larger than the brain of a turtle, that the horse has no memory and, worse still, no intelligence. Little do such detractors know!

Distant sounds and long shadows swim inside this head of

mine, and clear sights and filmy scenes drift across my large and flickering eyes. A tree here, a bird there, a dung heap smoldering then and now, the voices of the children of my far-off youth, the sensation of Master's long bony hand against the flat of my neck, the clatter of frightened hooves, the scent of a mare, a large white house, a cool barn tangy with the warm smell of horses—I remember it all, no matter the size and weight of my brain.

When Master found me at the Metacomet Ranch I was only a skinny old horse, a frail and nasty bay—light chocolate-colored with black mane and tail—tied to a hitching rail with half a dozen other horses similarly forlorn but including that same black devil who only the day before had ripped open my shoulder with the last of his blunted yellow teeth. There I stood with my head hanging, my long neck swung low, my eyes bleary, my entire body aswarm with flies and sweltering under a hot sun and a western saddle bulky enough to carry the fattest Mexican ever to swing the burden of his unbearable buttocks atop a horse. A western saddle with stirrups like wooden boxes and a pommel the size of a man's fist! On my back! On the back of a Thoroughbred, though of course there were few who could have recognized the signs of my blood beneath my wretchedness at the Metacomet Ranch. Only Master saw me for what I was, and the sorry fact is that he knew nothing at all about horses when we met and learned little thereafter. Still, he could tell a Thoroughbred when he saw one. The Metacomet Ranch existed not in that dead sandy terrain once known as the Old West but in a rocky landscape of pumpkins, clapboard houses, abandoned cars, and the gales that come from that same dark ocean as the sunrise. *Ranch,* said the faded wooden sign. *Rides.* But that was no ranch, that hellish place, but only the final humiliation of my long life, the last and longest deception perpetrated by all those who have no love for the horse.

"That horse there," cried Master as soon as he saw me. "Who is that horse?"

"Him?" said the woman, a small wiry gray creature who looked like a man. "He's Old Horse."

"Old Horse?" said Master, approaching and reaching out to touch the long cut still bleeding on my shoulder. "Doesn't he have a name?"

"Oh," she said, raising her cigarette and sucking on the smoke that was as gray and abrasive as the woman herself, "his name is Hank. But everybody just calls him Old Horse."

"He's a Thoroughbred," said Master.

"Think so?" said the woman, shrewd enough to imply both ignorance and indifference. "He's gentle anyway. Easy to ride."

"He's a pure Thoroughbred," said Master. "I shall find him another name." And that he did.

But she lied, that woman. Never, never was I known as Hank.

My start in life was the cruelest ever known to horse or man. My birth was the death of me.

In the long long ago of all my years, the day of my birth, the season of my beginning, the tranquil scene of my earliest youth, are as clear as the yet vivid sight of my own long fresh face in the clear stream from which I first drank of those cool slowly moving waters that lent themselves to the name of our horse farm, Millbank. Some of us begin in poverty so severe that our small stars never rise but remain forever obscured in the pain and gloom of unrelenting denial. Some of us are born in poverty similarly abject, and yet, and beyond all reason, our small stars rise and rise with never a falter. Then there are those of us born to the best, to all needs totally yet modestly satisfied, in sweet circumstances that could not be more conducive to luxuriant growth, and our fiery little stars rise and soar across the heavens until they quite disappear from sight. Finally a sad few of us are born into this same soft nurturing world yet enjoy but briefly the rise of our stars, for soon, and no matter the harmony from which we have come, our swiftly rising stars abruptly fall, plummet, plunge for however long it takes us to become helplessly mired in lost hopes. My own case was such, my own star was, alas, of the kind that plummets.

Millbank was a horse farm small enough, modest enough, but

well enough appointed in tree and barn, field and flower, to prevent the slightest harm from threatening any horse or human on the place. The house was low, its encircling veranda cool and spacious, its white paint always fresh, and the barns too were white and clean inside, comfortable, warm or cool as needed, smelling of wood and straw and hay that was never dusty. The Gordon family owned our farm, lived there, treated every man and woman, young girl and boy who worked for them with that same reasoned benevolence that accounted for the enviable nature of the Gordons themselves. Jane and Jim were a fair-haired athletic couple in early middle age, whose daughters, Nana, Millicent, and Anna, reflected the beauty, good health, kindly temperament of the head of the household and his freckled wife. Those of us for whom Millbank existed, the bays and grays, blacks and chestnuts, stallions and brood mares and colts and fillies, were treated by the Gordons and their loyal staff with exactly the common sense and affection that every horse deserves. We of Millbank were of that fine blood yet flowing down to us in time from our original sires, no other than the Godolphin Barb, the Darley Arabian, the Byerly Turk. Even our ponies were the best to be found of the Connemara, the little Shetland, the Exmoor, the New Forest. And all of us, large or small, young or old, male or female, were attended by patient grooms, smart-looking stable girls and the occasional boy, as well as by trainers, farriers, veterinarians, and by the Gordons themselves. Each of the three girls had her favorites among us yet showed no favoritism. From the day of my birth, the heart that I won was that of Millie, youngest of those sisters and thirteen years old at the time.

But who at Millbank do I remember best? My dam, of course, Molly-Long-Legs, or Molly, the tallest and stateliest brood mare ever put to stallion in the covering yard at Millbank. Not for nothing was she named, since never have I seen a horse with legs as long as my dam's, so long in fact that at the withers she stood more than seventeen hands tall, or as tall as a six-foot man. But she was well proportioned, statuesque, no matter that her exceptionally long legs first caught the eye, and she was deep in the chest, broad and sculpted in the hindquarters, with a large head held always high except when she was nuzzling or nudging me or swinging her eyes about to see why I was so inconsiderate at the teat. She was a big bay, a grand bay, the mare most respected by our other mares and the quickest to agitate our stallions. She had been a great runner and had foaled a handsome crowd of winners before me. And no horse had a blacker mane or tail—the tip of hers literally swept the ground—or a coat of a more lustrous brown, so deep and shiny that Jim was forever saying that she looked as good as Viennese chocolate. And this horse, my gorgeous dam, was placid. Placid! For all her virtues, for all her rippling immensity and the spring in her step, still my dam was placid, even when being put to the most impatient of stallions.

I was the last foal she bore. I smell her still, I see her still, I hear the way she used to move about at night. What horse is ever so old as to forget his dam? Especially when she was a dam like mine?

My day, that day on which I was the only colt born into the community of privileged horses at Millbank, was one of the hottest and driest Molly-Long-Legs or any of the rest of them could remember. Hot and dry but sweet too, for no sooner did I appear, with all the family watching, than a soft breeze came out of the stillness. And the air, heavy that season with impending much-needed rain, was for my first hours and days to come dry, sweet, as if at the moment of my birth nature could not help but give me the freshest, purest air to breathe. Old Dr. Barker, the trusted veterinarian long employed by the Gordons, stood by but was not needed.

I arrived about midmorning with Old Barker and the Gordons watching and Sam, the oldest pony at Millbank, who possessed only cloudy sight at best and was stiff in his joints and had years ago turned gray, a diminutive old shaggy creature dearly loved by Molly, standing near my heavy dam as he did whenever the time came for Molly to drop another foal. The box stall was large, the sunlight came through an open window and lit the glistening straw and made it shine, as golden and translucent as the cicada's wings. A lark sang, Molly waited, paced slowly about the spacious stall, stood and waited. She raised her tail and held it there, a sure sign. She swung her head, looked behind her, patient but puzzled too, though over the years she had carried thirteen foals before me. Sam listened, gave her a nod, and then, precisely then, the waters broke, gushed forth; my hour was at last at hand. My dam, still standing, grunted as only the mare in labor can, and opened herself, and gently and firmly began to thrust me out. And the first human to touch me? Little Millie, who, with Jane's encouragement, seized my long thin protruding forelegs in her fists and pulled down, widened her eyes just as my newborn's head, about the size of that on the children's wooden rocking horse, came sliding into view along with my outstretched legs, head and face featureless, expressionless, slick and wet inside the tight membranes shrunken like a second translucent skin to my nose, my little jaw, my eyes, which were still sealed to the light and life of the world. Molly then lay down on her heavy side, gave another push, and now I was lying with my shoulders free, safe though not yet completely born, and Millie, young as she was, with her sweet fingers rent the membranes so as to free my nose, expose my nostrils to the breeze that now followed the shaft of warm sun into the stall. Sam nodded his old head, Molly whimpered in soft delight, and in another moment, another, out I slid as the Gordons laughed and nodded in approval, while the other mares and foals set up a distant welcoming clamor from atop the nearby hill, where they stood in the shade of the great oaks. My day, my hour, my introduction to serenity itself. And proud? Yes, Molly and the Gordons were all proud, but not half so proud as myself when my loving dam licked me and then prodded me to stand, tentatively, valiantly, with all my instincts already drawn to my mother's milk.

My name was Sweet William, though the papers attesting to my lineage are long gone and my very name was long ago unscrupulously expunged from the annals of horse history.

But I was born into bliss and lived in bliss for twenty-one days that seemed as long as a lifetime. It is to my everlasting despair that they were not. At least for twenty-one days we stayed together, Molly and I, trotted and cantered together in the cool of the early mornings, lived on the best alfalfa and the sweetest grass, despite the dryness of that summer, and drank from the brook and with the other mares and foals sought the shade of the oaks in the afternoons. I knew that I was Molly's progeny, blood of her blood, a long-legged lively replica of my huge and wondrous dam, and no matter how I frolicked with the other foals or allowed myself to be hugged and petted by Millie, who was forever appearing at the edge of this field or that and calling my name, her sisters not far behind her, still it was to my placid dam that I returned, not only to tug on the teat, and tug I did, but for the smell of her, the size of her, the reassurance I always knew in her presence that she was mine and I hers, as if her thirteen other foals had never existed. More than any other brood mare on the place, Molly swaddled the pains of labor in the glories of her maternal self. This was her character, her personality, to be the embodiment of that concentrated maternity found only in the horse, and during all the hours of those timeless twenty-one days it was from Molly's maternity that I was never far. Further, if I was born to bliss, as I clearly was, my very act of being born, of taking my rightful place at Millbank, brought still greater bliss since from the hour of my birth my presence as the newborn colt, and its significance, affected every horse and human on our sixty acres. The stable girls hummed to themselves, whistled, giggled for no apparent reason, and turned on their portable radios; Bob, the stable manager, spoke to his charges in a more calming voice than ever; the foals leapt about more gaily than they ever had before my arrival, while the mares took still greater pleasure in their young. Our stallions, whom I rarely saw, were in a constant and handsome state of arousal, though at that time there was not a mare in season. And up at the house a similar condition prevailed so that Jim, the stallion among the Gordon mare and fillies, as naturally I sometimes thought of Jim and Jane and their pretty girls, was heavier of flesh, keener of eye, more active yet also more contented than that always pleasant man had been before my hour, while Jane was fuller, more freckled, more flushed in her small face, even happier than usual. As for Nana, Anna, and Millicent, they could not keep away from me, though it was little Millie who loved me most.

The sound of lemon-colored grains of oats in a bucket, the song of the brook, the steady breeze that had blown since I was first able to breathe the air, to drink Molly's milk, to run, to try my voice, all the sights and signs of well-being that spread from Molly and me to our world at large, and above all my dam herself, placid handsome creature emblematic of everlasting equine life— it was time out of time, pastoral time as Jim drove the orange tractor in the distance and the ping of a horse's shoe on rock rang ever after, never fading in the warm light of day or darkening night.

Then, oh then, my star fell.

I awoke to my twenty-second day before dawn in a field still warm from the sun of the day before. And what, I wondered, was that dreadful sound? A moaning of such deep agony that I, struggling to my long legs, suffered throughout my being the electric intensity of pure consternation. It was Molly, as no one, least of all myself, could have surmised, Molly lying in a great dark heap on her side and moaning, now and again thrusting round her head to bite at her belly. I neighed my high-pitched cry of alarm. I thrust my head to hers, poked my nose against the great belly where the pain was lodged. I licked her, as she had licked me, I whimpered, I saw her eyes rolling in the darkness and the sweat standing out on her silken coat. She groaned again, a racking sound so foreign to my dam that I bristled and shivered in my fear. In the darkness immense shadows—other horses—became fitful, came close, backed away, disappeared, while I danced help-lessly about my dam.

There was a beam of light, Bob's voice, then later Jim and Jane squatting in the artificial light, talking as I had never heard them talk, stroking poor Molly's nose. She was brave, my dam, coura-geous as always, as restrained as she could possibly be, but these were not the pains of labor that filled her belly but rather those insidious sensations that could only end in death. For no reason my dam, in the full of her life, was about to die, if not now then soon. So much I knew. Jim's voice and Jane's were terse, grave, anxious as they knelt beside their most prized mare in that dreadful predawn darkness. She would die. She would. Not for her a tranquil death after a long life spent in the constant recognition of what she was, a mare. Not for her an old age spent amidst adoring females, horse and human, attending her, learning from her, valuing her until the end. Only this—her cries in the ghostly light, the beseeching sheen that glazed her eye, the sudden convulsion, the violent effort to eat her way inside herself to find the pain and devour it.

A thin bloody line of sunlight appeared on the horizon, and Molly's agony did not abate. Jane fetched my little halter, but I would not be led away. At last there was the sound of a car engine, and up the hill came a man we did not know, a mere stripling of a veterinarian, who, he said, was standing in for Dr. Barker, Barker himself being out of state. He was tall, he was heavyset, his hand was bandaged, bitten, he said, because he had not paid attention to a nasty fool of a stallion at the Hillsdale Farm. Not only bitten, he said, but two fingers broken. Just what he deserved, he said, for letting his eye wander when he should have been attending to business. He laughed.

Jane looked at Jim and he at her. The young man knelt and began to poke my dam with his good hand. His checked summer shirt was open at the throat, his blond hair had been shorn close with clippers, his blue eyes were cold, his voice was oddly arrogant for a veterinarian's. I smelled the cologne he had apparently dashed onto his unshaven face, I watched the way he touched my dam, pursing his lips as if about to whistle, and I loathed this man, loathed him, though he was here to help.

"Colic," he said over his shoulder.

"Yes," said Jim.

"But not your ordinary colic," said the man.

"What are we to do?" asked Jane.

"Put her down," came the answer, at which I would have

reared and kicked him, driven him off, young as I was, had Jane not held me.

"Good Lord," said Jim quietly, "do you know what this horse is worth?"

"And we love her," said Jane.

"Well," said the man, glancing down at my dam, who raised her head painfully, allowed it to fall. "The nearest clinic is five hours away. She'll die before then. And there's no saying she'd come out of surgery alive."

"Five hours . . . ," said Jane softly.

"Inhuman," said the kneeling man, "to make her wait."

"He's right," said Jim at last, and though I did not know specifically what that heartless veterinarian meant to do to Molly-Long-Legs, still I knew that her fate was sealed. The horse gods had suddenly and whimsically determined to strike at the good life of Millbank in which, until now, we had all thrived. And strike they did.

Down the gentle slope went Jane and I, without looking back, though twice I attempted to wrench free of the woman's firm hold, twice tried to swing round my head for a final look in the direction of Molly-Long-Legs. I smelled impending rain; the dawn was upon us.

"We shall miss her, Willy," said Jane in low tones, which, sad as they were, could not entirely conceal the voice that was hers, a voice generally as light and bell-like as a boy's. The breeze that had been blowing since my birth died down. The brass weather vane atop the main barn, a giant carriage horse with its legs full out in an eternal gallop across all the invisible points of the compass, was still.

Jane led me into the hollow-sounding barn and into the dark stall of what had been taken to be my auspicious birth, the same stall which Sam as if in premonition had refused to quit since that now seemingly far-off day. He raised his head, he looked at me. I saw that his dim sight was dimmer still. He made no effort to console me, since he had heard Molly's distant sounds of torment and was himself inconsolable. Courage, his own grief seemed to say, was something he counted on all young colts to acquire alone, and at only three weeks of age I was no exception. But was it courage I acquired at the time of Molly's death, or misanthropy? The latter, as my life will show, and proudly enough. Even in that distant past I stopped short in my grief and thought of my name, Sweet William, and then and there decided to deny the faith that my poor dam must have had in me and to become a full-grown horse who would be anything but sweet, a horse whose name would be only the bitterest of ironies. Then, in the midst of such musings, suddenly there came the sound of Jane's voice.

"Oh God," she said from a nearby stall, "my God," and never had I thought to hear such exclamations, such distraught tones, from our usually lighthearted Jane.

I went rigid; old Sam raised his shaggy head and listened.

Running footsteps, voices, among them Bob's as well as Jane's, coming, I thought in my newest grip of fear, from the stall belonging to a nervous chestnut mare named Misty Rose, herself on the brink of foaling. What was wrong? Why was Jane attempting to comfort Rose? What malevolence was invading Millbank? I heard a whinny that was clearly Rose's, and in my helpless coltish ignorance I turned to the old pony, who merely shook his head and once more slowly let it sag. Little did I know then, as I listened to Rose making her helpless sounds, that the brash young veterinarian was administering into Molly's bloodstream the barbiturate that would in seconds end her life.

"Little Will"—and it was Jane's voice, surprisingly enough, Jane who was once again taking hold of my halter—"perhaps we've found you a dam after all, Sweet Willy." Whereupon she led me out of Molly's stall forever and down the smooth brick aisleway a few steps and into the stall of Misty Rose, where Bob was waiting along with Rose. But what was this? What in the gray half-light did I see? Another colt, but a small flattened shape of a colt lying dead, I knew at once, on his side, the silvery membranes intact on his head and body, the silvery-whitish membranes of the sac, in which he was bound as in an elasticized translucency, making him look colder than he was, more inert, as if he were some mummified little creature freshly unearthed.

I looked, I started back, Jane held me and stroked my neck.

The grieving chestnut mare, the man, the woman, the dead colt, and in their midst myself, more baffled and horrified than ever, as if my own catastrophe were not enough. What would they do to me, this mare, these people, these strange and deadly instruments of the horse gods? I found out soon enough as man and woman enclosed me in the dead colt's dark corner, formed a screen between the two of us, the one dead and the other orphaned, and Misty Rose. While I waited, overcome in my first experience of amazement cloaked in ignorance and dread, Jane knelt beside the cold figure and began to free him of the afterbirth, to peel the glistening membranes from his flat and lifeless form. I was rigid, I was as cold as the dead colt himself.

Jane moved, and I felt something utterly foreign to my being against my neck, then across my back, and after a moment lightly falling onto my hindquarters, and then I comprehended the fact of what Jane was doing—draping me with the strips and pieces of the afterbirth of which she had robbed Misty Rose's stillborn foal. When I felt Jane hang the last cold fragment across my head, I thought I would drop flat to the straw beside the dead colt. I was shocked, I was humiliated. I stood there in my outlandish costume as mute as was poor Sam, garbed in his old age.

Silently Jane and Bob, who carried the body of Rose's colt in his arms, slipped out of the stall. I heard them leave, felt them disappear, heard the bolt thrust home in the stall door and the last of the footsteps fading down the aisleway. We were alone, unavoidably alone together, Rose and I, she the bereaved mare and I the outrageous impostor of the colt she had lost. Embarrassed? Yes, I was embarrassed and for the longest while could hardly bear to meet Rose's eye, for well I knew that I was no substitute for that small stiffened horse who would remain forever in both our minds. How, I wondered, could the big chestnut tolerate my ridiculous intrusion? Was I not, to her, contemptible? So I thought. And I felt like not only an impostor but a ghost.

Suddenly I remembered Molly-Long-Legs and was ashamed that I had forgotten my own dam.

The gray light deepened in the box stall where we were sequestered, Rose and I. I was only faintly aware of the silence filling the main barn and of the hay in the loft above us. A single small bird twittered somewhere in the rafters. I thought that I smelled the thickening scent of impending rain. I waited.

Rose was the first to move.

She had become aware of me after all. I heard the heavy single exhalation of breath that signaled her return from the remoteness of grief to consciousness of this place, this time, and of myself, my pathetic clownish presence in the farthest possible corner away from her, and signaled also her resignation both to her fate and to me. Then I heard the sound of a muffled hoof-fall, another, and knew that Misty Rose had turned and was looking down at me. I raised my eyes, I waited, she approached.

She was no dam of mine and I no colt of hers. Yet now she towered above me, the reddish-golden sheen of her coat a subdued suggestion of the light of sunrise in the darkened stall, and all at once she lowered her head and, from her loftiness and without so much as a single soft whinny of compassion, reached her great head toward me and began to do what I could not possibly have hoped she might. She pressed her nose against me and licked me and not only that but licked me with purpose. Yes, it was Misty Rose herself who licked her dead colt's membranes from my head and body, who turned me, gently pushed me, cleansed me with her warm tongue until for the second time in my life I bore no trace of the scent of the afterbirth. Feeling the last shred of it falling from me, aware of Rose's closeness and of her generosity, how could I have been anything but overwhelmed? And so I was and so much so that, without thinking, without considering what might have been dire consequences, suddenly and impulsively I swung my head and sought Rose's milk, found it, succumbed to the oblivion of the nourishment that was hers to give. I let myself go, I suckled, on and on with the feverish simplicity of the newborn colt, I who was already twenty-one days old. When at last I had my fill and my new dam the relief she needed, silently we stood together, savoring the first comfort we had found in each other. Then at last Rose, who was no sentimentalist, deemed it time to give me to understand what had happened.

Did I think myself unusual? Did I consider myself ill-used by our well-intentioned Jane? But what had stunned me was only a commonplace, Rose said, a superstition on the part of Jane and of humankind the world over, that the most obvious association of a stillborn colt and an orphaned colt might cause a grief-stricken mare to confuse the two and to accept the more readily the orphaned colt as her own. There it was, said Rose, and it was up to me to accept such well-meant human beliefs and practices, no matter how barbarous they seemed. I should consider myself fortunate and, further, more fortunate than many colts in my situation. Why, said Rose, men themselves knew full well the dangers of introducing the orphaned colt to the bereaved dam. Many a mare, she said, had in her grief and fury kicked and trampled to death a strange colt so crudely presented—and long before that colt had reached for the unfamiliar teat.

Here she paused, and I detected a hardness, even a threat, in Rose's tone and experienced a momentary apprehension, though I held my peace.

Further, said Rose, I should know that my own dam had always made Rose nervous, simply because Rose was in fact a nervous fiery chestnut and my true dam only a placid bay.

Here I felt a surge of pride but held my peace.

And then, of course, said Rose, I had none of the qualities of the little colt who was gone and could not possibly replace him. I was unfamiliar, Rose said, and in myself not appealing. Nonetheless we had made our peace, she said, and would continue on as we were. So I should consider myself doubly, triply fortunate, and so I did, knowing my place, knowing that I must not offend the only mare who could feed me, protect me, teach me, comfort me in her reluctant fashion, until I should become my own self-sufficient horse.

She gave me a remote but kindly nudge, and back I went to the teat.

A lull. A respite. A pause before the completion of my suffering, which, so far, had come down upon me with the roar of heavenly hooves and the speed of a garter snake slithering in pursuit of some helpless newborn rodent through high grass. I had been singled out. I was pursued. Attacks of misfortune come in threes, as the lore of horses tells us, and my third and cruelest blow was yet to fall. But in those first fewer than twenty-four hours that followed the death of Molly-Long-Legs and saw her burial, I experienced a calm, a peace, a freedom from apprehension not dissimilar to the days of pleasure I knew in my first consciousness.

We were turned out, Misty Rose and I, to join the other brood mares and their foals atop the gentle slope where they congregated in the shade and coolness beneath the oaks. Harriet and Henrietta, Kate and Barbara Bane and Jenny—they were all there, holding silent counsel in the midst of their young. The air was as laden with the palpable spirit of the female horse in the fullness of motherhood as it was with the warm moisture of impending rain. We were silent, we browsed and stood still, not a horse among us had forgotten the deaths of my dam and Rose's colt. Somber, yes, but tranquil, though I was alert and careful not to stray or drift too far from Misty Rose, who, adoptive dam or not, would make no concessions for a long-legged male horse she did not love and at the slightest excuse might well abandon.

I heard something, I pricked up my ears, waited. From below us, hidden from sight beyond the white fencing and behind the immense mulberry tree that faced the Gordons' house, there came the sound of men's voices, the heavy disordered sound of chains, the chugging and grinding of a backhoe, driven, I later learned, by Jim himself. I listened, as did the mares and other foals, though they betrayed not a sign of their awareness or interest in what was happening, and even I felt removed from that activity. Jim and several workmen were digging my dam's grave. Suspending her feet upward by the chains. Lowering her—too soon, too soon—to rest. I listened, I comprehended, still I turned away from that instant of vigil and back to Rose. Only a twitching along her flanks and a yellowish light in her eyes made clear to me her nervousness, her irritability at what those few sounds must have brought to mind.

The burial of a horse cannot be noble.

Silence. Resumption of those daylight hours.

Then the rain came down. It was the first rain of my life and began as a swelling, a gathering, a thickening of gray air that we could feel and smell. At the outset it was no more than a sensation that brightened our coats and colors in the darkness of never-ending hours, a burgeoning so undeniable and filled with promise that I could not restrain my elation. Through the leaves above us we began to hear it, the faint but unmistakable sound of falling rain, of dry leaves quivering beneath the droplets. Oh, what a pattering filled the wondrously complacent world of our mares! The smell of the rain grew stronger, increasingly we listened, harder fell the warm rain and darkened still more our coats and the light of this day. We had been secure before the rain, but how much more so were we now as the protective fall of the rain joined tangibly with the benign strength of the mares.

Down it came, and harder, and the boughs drooped under the weight of the leaves, a few birds as wet as ourselves took refuge beneath the oaks. The birds huddled together, and so did we.

In the summer months the horses of Millbank were allowed to remain out-of-doors throughout the night, even in the thick of summer rains. So it was now with the mares and foals. We were comfortable, we were uncomfortable, our dripping manes and tails and noses attested all the more strongly to the familial temperament in which we shared. What harm could come to any horse when the darkness was filled with such a reassuring sound?

New light. Another dawn. And the heaviest single rainfall in twenty years became no more than a mere dripping, an interminable trickling from tree, bush, gable, fence rail. The deluge was over, the restorative saturation of earth and beast complete.

Warm milk, wet grass, slow expectation passing from horse to horse.

But was I the only one among them to detect the telltale sounds that now I heard? Apparently. It was one thing to hear the lugubrious chugging of a backhoe, another to hear what no living creature could possibly expect to hear in a lifetime. My flesh tightened, my breath was stilled. I listened, cast a sidelong glance at Misty Rose. Nothing. Even my nervous foster dam was not sensitive to the all but inaudible messages rising to me—only to me—from that sacred place concealed behind the mulberry. Yes, the fresh earth that the invisible men had returned to Molly's grave was whispering in fits and starts, and for no other ears than mine. If I had been frightened in Rose's stall, how much more frightened was I now! I listened, doubted, suddenly quivered as it came again—a sigh of sorts, a declaration of weary pain, an appeal to blood. It was more than the soft earth responding to the weight of water. Much more. And suddenly I could not help myself and, after another glance at Rose—still nothing—tore myself free of the living mares and foals and, at a brisk and reckless pace, set off down the slope toward the death that lay at the foot of the mulberry.

By the time I reached the high white fence I was both bold and weak, frantic but defenseless too. I did not know what I had heard or what was happening in the secrecy behind the tree. But something was stirring, and I was in its grip. The white planking of the fence was wet and slick; I pressed myself against it and drew back, looked up, ran its length for a dozen feet, returned to where I had first paused. Now my trembling and rigidity were unbearable. And it was imperative that I make no noise, that much was sure, or as little noise as possible. What I was about to see was forbidden to me especially, yet was meant for my eyes alone. I was the secret witness to the eruption of secrecy. I wanted nothing more than to remain where I was, on my side of the insurmountable fence, yet wanted only to be transported to its other side.

The distant pinging of a pitchfork's tines on brick, the piping

of a small wet bird, Jane's sleepy voice carrying from an open
window in the white clapboard house—I heard it all, dismissed it
all, listened in longing and horror to that silken treacherous murmuring beyond the tree. Then I who had not yet so much as
hopped over a rock or bush swung away from the fence, stopped,
took its measure, and, with a brazen ability I did not know I
possessed, sped silently forward on my long legs and jumped that
impossibly high fence. I leapt, I soared, lightly and safely I landed.
And without a sound. I had surprised even myself, yet cared
nothing for my newfound talent. Little did it mean to me that I
had just proven myself the rarest of jumpers, so bent was I on
reaching the dense leafy protection of a giant rhododendron,
where I could hide invisible from the house but in direct line of
sight with all that lay beyond the mulberry. I took my place,
pressed in among the wet rubbery leaves, peered out.

A bed of roses, the lawn, the gravel path leading to the veranda.
And there at the foot of the mulberry, Molly's grave. It was twice
the size at least of a human's grave, and it lay where Jane had
demanded that it be dug, at the foot of her favorite tree and in full
view of the house. My poor dam's grave, and only an immense
rectangle of seething mud. And that, it came to me all at once, was
the horror. For it was churning, that muddy earth, was moving,
giving way to some terrible exertion in its very depths. This was
the sound I had heard, the agitation from which I could not
escape. Even as I watched, wet and shivering, jaws set, eyes
starting, heart aflame, suddenly a great hoof broke the surface,
poked up, atop a dripping foreleg thrust itself upward, kicking
this way and that, like some unnatural plant painfully and instan-
taneously flowering to full size. It jerked and twitched, that awful
hoof, then came another, and another, and the fourth, all flaying
the air and splattering the surrounding earth with watery gouts of
red mud. Molly was rising! Molly, my dear dam, was climbing
from her grave in the dawn light, heaving herself up, thrashing
about, and I saw her head, the clotted eyes and nostrils, the
haunches and the sodden tail. Up she rose, still blind, fighting for

breath—my dead dam trying desperately to breathe!—and staggered forth, free at last of the torn and gaping pit.

My agony was exactly this, that in my young mind my dam was dead while the sight before my eyes told me that quite to the contrary she was coming back to me. Alive. I feared her muddied figure, how could I not? To flee from it was my only thought. But that muddied hulk was Molly, and I loved her and might well have dashed forth whinnying in fearful triumph at her return. But I only hid and waited behind the rhododendron, because now the great spraddle-legged creature shook herself and weakly, valiantly, started forward. Horrified I watched as Molly dragged herself up the gravel path, reached the veranda, and with her front feet managed to climb the first three steps toward the broad space where the Gordons spent their summer evenings laughing and softly talking together. There, half up the steps, half down, helpless to either proceed or retreat, there in all her covering of cold slime stood the dripping figure of my dam. She could not have been more pathetic, more grotesque.

She made no sound that I could hear, or remember hearing. Yet in some way she must have called to Jane, because suddenly Jane appeared in the screened door, came out and, wrapped only in a cool negligee, found her favorite mare not dead and underground, which had been grief enough, but risen, assuredly, and now balked in the poor animal's efforts to climb the veranda steps and enter the house. The sight was a shock too great for our generally cheerful Jane. She screamed, she rushed forward without the slightest hesitation and flung her arms around Molly's neck. From where I stood, small Jane looked as if she too had climbed from Molly's grave, horse and woman bonded together in the gluey stuff of common clay.

Jim, dressed in nothing but pajama bottoms, which he was in the act of tying, came bounding and clattering through the screened door. He stopped short, surveyed the scene, stepped to his wife's aid. Then the children appeared. They cried, all three of them, while I gazed on perplexed, cowardly, and Jim, once

more composed, managed to back Molly down and off the steps.
There was confusion, weeping, little fitful cries from the girls. In
the course of it all Bob arrived, Jane wiped the mud from Molly's
eyes and nostrils, Jim reentered the house and spoke tersely on the
telephone. Molly remained on her feet minutes more and then
slowly sank to her knees, fell to her side. Jane squatted and
cradled the enormous head in her arms, still unmindful of the
wretched mud, and spoke to Molly, looked into her eyes, com-
forted Molly, sustained her, in the wet dawn loved Molly as only
one female can love another.

The veterinarian who at last arrived was neither Dr. Barker nor
the young man I had so disliked, but another sandy-haired person,
of a manner both businesslike and gentle. Jim and Jane conferred,
Jane still squatting and holding Molly's head, and then the girls
went back indoors, the veterinarian knelt down and, with syringe
and needle, ended Molly's life. There was a hush, an endless hush,
as the four adults spoke softly together. The light increased, the
air cleared; the veterinarian, having waited a suitable length of
time, as the young man the morning before had not, leaned down
to Molly and after several moments more pronounced her dead.

I started forward as if to rush headlong into their midst, then
stopped, aware that their heads had turned, and paused, wheeled
about, and, without thinking, once more charged the fence and
jumped.

"Oh, Jim," I heard Jane say. "Her colt!"

"For God's sake," said Jim.

"But, Jim," Jane said as in mid-flight I soared, "he can't jump
that fence!"

"But it appears," said Jim, "that he has."

And again I landed safely on the other side and in the world of
horses, where I belonged.

My cruelest start in life. My defeat. My victory. In the days that
followed I understood from Rose that Molly's second death, as I
had thought of it, was actually her first, and that what to me had
been incomprehensible was in fact something that did occasion-

ally happen, thanks to the carelessness of men. The fault lay in the unprofessional behavior of that callow young veterinarian we saw once and never again. He was to blame, as I might have known. Instead of waiting to be sure that the deadly drug had done its work and stopped once and for all the heart of the horse doomed by circumstance and man to death—which was the obvious and ordinary procedure, Rose said, since no one could be sure that the initial introduction of the barbiturate into the bloodstream would in fact be fatal, no matter how large the dosage—that young man had simply administered the heart-stopping drug and left poor Molly for dead. But she was not dead. Even beneath the earth her heart still beat, her life sank into a dormancy that could last for hours, as indeed it did. The earth was loosely packed on top of her; she needed only the scantest oxygen to breathe. She remained alive. And then of course the rains came, and the earth in Molly's grave changed density, liquefied, or nearly so, until all at once and bathed in rain-soaked earth my poor dam regained partial consciousness, refused the darkness, summoned the last of her strength, fought for life, in one terrified convulsion threw off her partial death, and, as I had seen, climbed from her grave.

It had happened before, said Rose, to other horses. And would again. With that her explanation ceased, and she fell once more to grazing.

But was I more consoled in the certainty that my dam was gone and that the grave beyond the mulberry would suffer no further violence, or in the certainty that no horse is safe? The latter, of course, the latter. Thanks to Rose, the dark seeds of my misanthropy were sure to grow.

CHAPTER TWO

THE DIFFERENCE BETWEEN MYSELF AND MASTER WAS THIS: THAT I WAS FORTUNATE ENOUGH TO LOSE MY INNOCENCE, WHILE HE WAS NOT

A training saddle, as it is called, is little more than an extended version of the racing saddle and, like its near twin, may be carried in one hand even by the slightest girl, which little Millie demonstrated when the time came. The training saddle is somewhat longer than the length of an ordinary sheet of paper, about as wide as the length of a man's hand, and, again like its smaller and lighter counterpart, swoops down on either side in tiny rounded flaps intended, it appears, to support the knees of a rider no larger than a child's good-sized doll or, better yet, the knees of some small manic anthropoid dressed in racing silks. No one is heavier than a jockey, nothing is heavier than the first sensation of a training saddle resting just behind the withers of a sensitive Thoroughbred. But I was in my second year before I was broken and finally knew and tolerated the impossible burden of a featherweight training saddle on my shiny back.

For all those intervening months—each a season unto itself for me—Millbank was spared any further mishaps or catastrophes. Tranquillity returned, the horse gods relented, retreated to the farthest of heavenly fields, gave up their wrath. Peace was ours.

Swiftly I acquired longer legs, more weight, greater height, until, by the time I had become a yearling, full growth was mine. I stood as tall as Molly-Long-Legs had once stood, and I was shinier than she, more handsome, and mine was the pleasure of perceiving how day by day the ever-increasing signs of my maturation—the strengthening of my shapely bones, the quickness and certainty of my every move, the total sweep of me—caused a corresponding increase in the special affection that Millie had felt for me from the start. There were changes, then, at Millbank, and all for the better.

I had become a yearling at the precise time that Jane gave birth to Ann, her fourth and final child. Without serious incident I passed my second January, still as free and pampered as the numerous new colts and fillies populating Millbank. Rose carried and dropped another foal at a time when, luckily for me, I was at an age to have no more need of her. Nana, the oldest Gordon girl, married a young equestrian of skill and means, whose family owned the horse farm adjoining ours. As for Millie, this period of timeless time saw no change in her height and weight. She remained as small as ever. But now this young girl, the one I most cared for in all the world, was at once the same Millie I had always loved and yet entirely different. She was nearly fifteen years old. Her upper body, no matter the loose T-shirts she wore in summer or the heavy baggy sweatshirts she wore in winter, had unmistakably assumed the endearing shape of the torso found only in small women. Except for Millie and the infant Ann, the Gordon girls were blond and as big as their father. Millie's hair was dark and now had turned a brilliant black and was fuller, wilder than ever. She was more shy than she had been but more assertive too; her child's legs, bared in the summer when she often dressed in shorts, had become the legs of a woman. Her full mouth was wide, her lips soft, her small face round, her color high, her eyes both quick and limpid in the sure knowledge of what she was—as much a young woman at the age of fifteen as I was now the almost totally ripened colt. Millie looked like Jane, talked like her in the same boyish hasty bell-like tones, sported on her little prominent cheeks Jane's freckles, and, to my personal delight, was if anything more good-humored than Jane herself. Certainly I never loved the mother as I did the daughter, though everyone, myself included, loved Jane.

All this time, as Millie and I grew up apace, I was ever mindful of one thing. My misanthropy. My bitterness. The humans around me and horses too preferred obedience, compliance, and docility to a mean temper and intractability. The world approved of good horses, and most of all I wanted the world's approval. To be admired, to be given preferential treatment, to be if anything more appreciated than the average horse—such was my ambition. Well I understood the power of my secret malevolence, and use it and to its fullest I surely would, but only when circumstances warranted what in its extreme form would prove to be my viciousness. When the time came that fortune once more treated me adversely, I would retaliate in small ways and large. But until then I would be well behaved, cooperative, trustworthy—or feign to be. I would come as close as I could to that fine line that separates a sensitive high-spirited horse from a malefic, downright dangerous horse. I would conceal my true colors, so to speak, as best I could. It goes without saying that there was nothing artificial in the nearly excessive love I felt for Millie, though she too soon tried my patience.

Adulthood was nearly mine; I knew myself to be the most highly prized and promising young male horse at Millbank. Then into my life came Harod, the black champion who was my sire and whom so far I have deliberately left unmentioned, along with Moggy, the yearling New Forest mare who, from the moment I first smelled and saw her from afar, was my equine Millicent.

In retrospect I have no idea how I managed to preserve my innocence for as long as I did. How, to the very brink of maturation, I was able to remain oblivious to the fact that I, like every other horse, had been sired as well as carried and dropped. How it was that I had not given a thought to the stallion to whom I owed my life. Had I been merely gulled by blissful arrogance into false security? Blinded by vanity to that male horse in whose shadow, like it or not, I lived? Was fear the cause of it all or self-absorption? Weakness or peculiar strength? Whatever the case, such was my condition: to be more susceptible than most to the vulnerability of innocence. So much for my resolve to live by my wits and willed restraint. So much for my faith in consciousness. At least my losses of self-control were short-lived.

A shiny day. A gray day. A misty day. A gray misty day in spring with the morning light refracted through a prism of cool wet air. A day of disappearing wintry colors both subdued and bright. A day on which the death of an entire season occurs. A day of change when merely to be out-of-doors was to experience the exhilaration born of one time of year giving way to the next. Snow was two months past, yet its scent was strong; dead leaves were turning green. The dampness was laden invisibly with melted snow and sunlight, wind and calm, and lay on everything it touched with the crystalline sheen of clear ice on still water. The surfaces of even the most dejected-looking tree or barn, animal or empty field, were rippling with life that was over, life to come.

On this gray day, when memories of the previous spring and the particularities of this day itself combined to swell my feelings of well-being, on this very day the contentment that had been mine in privacy was, all at once, no more. Innocuous moment. Half an hour of rude awakening.

I heard footsteps. I paused and, with a few strands of hay still hanging from between my lips, I turned my head, peered into the dimness, waited. It was the new girl, as I recognized from the smell of her and the sounds of the lazy way she walked, and suddenly I was certain that the new girl was coming down the aisleway for me. I was suspicious, I was on my guard. What business had such a girl with me? What business did she have at Millbank? She was large, she was big-chested, she smoked cigarettes and smoked them, as yet undetected by any person, here in the barn, where, as everyone knew and large signs clearly said, flames or sparks of any kind were forbidden. But this girl's voice was falsely cheerful, she was too familiar with horses and humans alike, mysteriously she spent a few days among us and then just as mysteriously and none too soon was gone, this nameless girl, this casual yet, I am still convinced, deliberate destroyer of my innocence.

"Hi there," she said in her offensive voice, and without the slightest hesitation entered my box stall, dared intrude into the comfortable space that was mine alone. Behind her the stall door stood ajar—had she no fear at all that I might bolt through that open door? My rope and halter dangled from her left hand.

"New shoes, big boy," she said and, calmly, infuriatingly, reached up, grinning the while, and plucked the last wisps of hay from between my lips. The gesture so surprised me that I did not recoil, though in the next moment I stepped aside and stared down at her with eyes that should have frightened her but did not. She began to whistle; back went my ears; and still she did not respect me as a horse that might not tolerate such trifling. I tensed myself and yet submitted to the halter when she raised it and hooked her arm around my head and, in her clumsy indifferent fashion, manage to buckle that leather thing in place. I could have bared my teeth, given her a quick nip, threatened her with all my weight, made one swift movement as if to kick, but I did not. Never had I been approached and touched by such a girl, and now I was both repelled and fascinated by her self-centeredness. Distaste was one thing, threats another, and harm or challenge this simpleminded full-bodied girl I would not. And yet and despite the strength of my forbearance, little did that girl know how much she risked when, in the next moment, she drew down my head, puckered her lips, and gave me a playful kiss on my broad nose. Shocking liberty! Unkindly kiss! And oh, what retribution that kiss would incur in years to come! For now, however, I controlled myself, stayed docile, though I could not help but wonder how anyone could be as insensitive as was this girl in her tight gray sweatshirt and tight jeans.

She led me out of my stall, again she whistled, meekly enough I accompanied her down the wide road in front of the main barn toward the building set aside for the farrier's visits. We heard the steady ringing sounds of his work. Already the girl's black hair was bright from the mist; I felt my own dark coat growing damp. All around us lay a sparkling wet world freshening moment by moment in the morning light. All was quiet, except for the girl's tuneless whistling and the rhythm of my footfalls, which matched the rhythm of the farrier's hammer. Then suddenly we heard a burst of disruptive sounds that reached us from the round barn-like enclosure of the covering yard. Men's voices, silence. A burst of squealing, more silence. An angry clamor, a muffled shout, a horse's trumpeting. I had heard such sounds before, and now, as then, they aroused in me instantaneous dislike. So I changed my ambling walk to a jogging pace, the quicker to reach the farrier, who was a kindly man, and the quicker to put the covering yard behind me.

"Hey," said the girl, "not so fast!" and gave a yank on my lead rope, stopped me, turned me, started us off briskly in the direction of the very place I knew we should avoid. It loomed in the distance, that building with its circular and windowless walls and domed roof, and again from its interior came the sounds I feared. I hung back; the impatient girl gave a short encouraging laugh and pulled me on. By now we were thoroughly dampened, the girl and I, and in passing I noted that the wetter the girl became, the livelier she grew, and the fleshier, and the more spirited. She glanced up at me, she winked, she gave another little tug on my rope. What, I wondered, was wrong with her?

Unnoticed we stood just outside the open doorway, unnoticed we watched.

"Wow," whispered the girl, "look at that!"

Well might she have so exclaimed, this mindless girl, though of all her disagreeable qualities it was her vulgar speech I deplored the most. However, for now I was as much the helpless witness as was she, and like her I stared with fixed attention at the scene in progress inside the covering yard and under its cluster of bright lights. But mine was a guilty attention, while the girl's was not. This, after all, was the second time I had spied on the activities

of one to whom I owed my life, and now my spying was unjusti-
fied beyond a doubt, a travesty I felt but could not understand. So
with guilty absorption I stood in perfect stillness beside the excited girl and watched what no horse should ever be allowed to
see.

In the center of the yard's soft deep carpeting of dark earth
stood none other than Kate, a bay matron I did not know well but
had always admired. She was a trim pretty brood mare of uncommon sweetness. Now the lovely creature could not move, stood
unnaturally out of her usual context of fields and foals, the pathetic object of what to me was a frenzy of senseless activity. She
was hobbled. Her left front leg was raised and sharply bent, and
from it long leather straps extended to her hind legs, where they
were fastened to huge leather cuffs around each ankle. One attempted step and she would fall. She could not move, she could
not kick or in any way defend herself. Spread atop her withers
was an ungainly oft-stained leather shield, the ugly thing strapped
in place like some monstrous parody of a saddle. It was a protective device, so that at least in the midst of this unwholesome
business she could not be bitten. Finally there was the twitch, the
small loop of rope twisted about her nose and affixed to a wooden
handle held by the traitorous Jane, as I thought of her this day.
No horse can bear pain applied to its nose, and Jane had only to
give the wooden handle the slightest turn in order to inflict on her
sweating charge the worst kind of pain. Kate's passivity was thus
ensured. Stand she must and stand she would—with raised tail
and dimmed and daunted eyes.

"See him?" whispered the oddly eager girl whom by now I had
quite forgotten. "He's your dad!"

See him? How could I not see him? Great jet-black frantic
stallion whose very urgency thwarted his own desire. Uncoopera-
tive to the two men, Jim and Bob, who wanted only to assist him
to accomplish the conclusion of what for me was his inexplicable
beastliness. There he was, struggling and straining against Bob
and Jim, lunging backward and attempting just as suddenly to
rear as the two men, more agile and wary, more serious and taxed

than I had ever seen them, applied their energies to hold and maneuver him, Bob with his chain-and-leather lead rein, Jim darting in to push the black stallion this way and that. So of course I saw him—the wet black coat, the thin lightning flash of whiteness down his nose, the wide eyes bloodshot in lust and terror. But "dad"? *Dad?* How dare the girl, I thought—what did she mean?—though naturally from the first I had understood conceptually that this very stallion was my sire. Throughout my days at Millbank I had seen him occasionally, briefly, from far off. I knew him, I knew that his name was Harod, after one of the greatest of all racing horses from the distant past. Yes, I was one of his progeny, but over some vast number of years he had sired as many as twenty foals a year on twenty mares, so that Harod's progeny were like chaff in the wind. Such was I, only a slight and worthless speck in the cloud of life that Harod had loosed on the world. Now he stood before me, immense, intolerable, and I before him, unseen, unknown, unacknowledged. And no word could have been less appropriate to the stallion I now secretly confronted than "dad." Sire he was, and in this instant the emotional shock of that truth went through me. Sire, handsome ugly sire.

"Come on, old guy," I heard her whispering. "You can do it!"

Desperation filled the covering yard, the captive yet receptive mare turning her head and eyes in mute appeal to the stallion, Jane's forehead as slick with sweat as were the foreheads of the men, whose task, of course, was dangerous. Most desperate of them all was the stallion, who, it became apparent, had taken an unreasonable dislike to Kate and now wanted to rush the mare, to kick her as well as to somehow vent that larger longing which I perceived but still denied to my consciousness.

"He's ready!" cried Jim.

The stallion gave fresh and terrifying voice to his demented instincts, as I thought of them, tossing his great head to the left, the right. His jaws were wide, his eyes were white. The sounds he made might have been coming from my own silent and constricted throat, so keenly did I feel the pain of his lonely trumpet-

ing. Yes, from my own torn and silent throat, and I listened in fear
and watched in horror as the stallion, finally positioned to the
rear of the mare, suddenly rose up like some greater-than-life-
sized horse statue come to life and, kicking and grappling with his
front legs and flashing hooves, propped himself for an instant on
Kate's haunches. Then he slipped, fell back to all fours, and Bob
leapt out of his way, Jim cursed. Then up again went the stallion,
hunching himself grotesquely atop the mare. His eyes rolled, his
tongue hung foolishly from between his brutal jaws, aghast I saw
poor Kate bracing her hindquarters beneath the weight of Harod.
But down he fell a second time, lathered in rage and ignominy,
then up again, Bob and Jim both pushing against his shoulders,
then down, then up, and this time found his footing and kept his
balance and stayed aloft on Kate like a ship on a rock.

"Hurray!" whispered the girl, and began to stroke my neck,
while Jim and Bob applied themselves to the task at hand. Yet
even now the destructive scene was incomplete, brought to a near
standstill in the center of the soft dark brightly illumined earth.
Harod clung to his post, half buckled over the stalwart Kate; the
eyes of the men were as fierce as those of the stallion; Jane's slight
chest was heaving; at my side the dampened girl was stroking now
my neck, now my shoulder, with increasingly insistent tenderness.
How I detested the sight of my sire lolling clownishly above the
patient mare, how I suffered the plight of the mare.

"Hold him!" I heard Jim say to Bob.

"Come on," urged the girl under her breath, "give him a
hand!"

And oddly enough, Jim, who could not possibly have heard
that girl, nonetheless complied. He stooped, he reached down,
swiftly and steadily he moved. I saw the sureness of Jim's grip, for
an instant saw the flashing of his wedding band beneath my sire.
Then Jim, suddenly quite calm, stepped away, and the mare
shuddered and the stallion heaved.

"In situ!" Jim said, laughing and rubbing his hand on the seat
of his britches.

"Good boy!" whispered the girl.

Bob grinned, Jane smiled, I watched, and still the coupled mare and stallion struggled. A tiny bird flew past us into the covering yard and alighted, immediately took to the air again and fled the scene. Jane wiped her face on her arm, glanced casually at Kate. I watched, I waited.

Then, "Done!" cried the girl in a triumphant whisper, and off slid Harod, more like some gigantic barnyard dog than a horse, and Kate slumped. Quickly Jane removed the hobbles. Bob turned my now completely docile sire and, as if nothing of any consequence had taken place, prepared to lead him off.

There was little else. Except that in the midst of the falling rain, midway between the covering yard and the outbuilding where the farrier waited, suddenly the girl tugged me once more to a halt and laughed, looked up at me. "You're cute," she said, giving a little yank on my mane, "just like your dad!"

Insipid innocence, despicable desire—that day I was caught between the two. And that day I denied the farrier, refused his care, kicked over his box of tools, impeded his work, until at last he gave way to exasperation and for the first time I found myself restrained by the twitch. Thus momentarily I was no better off than Kate herself had been, with the added indignity that in my case it was the nameless stable girl who held the twitch and, while I suffered such stifling, talked in her overly familiar way to the farrier, as if she had never led me to the covering yard nor seen what was now lodged in my brain like a sharp pebble in a horse's hoof. Offensive sight! Rude awakening!

For days and weeks I sulked and brooded, stayed aloof, refused my feed, knowing full well that such behavior was against my own best interests. Self-control was no longer mine. I was confounded, I could not rid myself of the smell of the girl, though by now she was gone, or of the recollection of the faintly coloring farrier with his mouth full of nails, could not escape the livid inglorious sight I had been subjected to. I envied the other nearly

full-grown colts around me: untroubled, the lot of them; I both
fought and welcomed this peculiar mood that was darker than
grief.

The weather cleared, grew both warm and crisp, thoughtfully
Jim came to my stall and ran his hand up and down my legs and
across my back, thoughtfully he and Bob would lean on a fence
and study me where I stood apart in a field. Jane too came to my
stall and once led me out for Dr. Barker's inspection. But if the
Gordons were concerned for my welfare, as indeed they were, it
was Millie who worried most for me in this bleak period of my
to them inexplicable malaise. She was present at each and every
unproductive consultation, sharing without a word Jim and
Jane's frustration; for hours she hovered in my stall, grooming me
or simply leaning against me, as downcast in her young troubled
way as I was in mine, silent for the most part, sometimes talking
to me or humming. She sat at my feet on an overturned bucket,
chin in her hands; she joined me in the upper field, leaning against
a tree and watching my indifference to the rest of the segregated
colts, as such we were, or my irritation at any of them who
attempted, consolingly or not, to approach me. My initial secret
shock was now the purest kind of petulance, and at this time the
only pleasure I took in life was causing the Gordons consternation
and making Millie as miserable as I was. Each dawn I dashed her
hopes that in the intervening hours of darkness I might have
returned to my former self, each night I longed for change and yet
determined that I would at all costs remain the sulky young male
horse I had become. At last, however, they deemed me fit for
breaking—a task that Jim naturally assigned to Millie.

Early mornings. Lemon-colored light. The pale green translucency of late spring. It began with nothing but the saddle pad, a
white rectangle of quilted cloth, innocuous enough when Millie
first appeared with it in my stall, small features set and eyes alert,
though the mere sight of that freshly laundered pad caused me to
stiffen and lay back my ears as I never in my life had done with
her. But I did not like Millie's sudden efficiency. I resented the way
her new maturity reminded me of that intrusive mysterious girl

who, intentionally or not, had brought about my gloom. And I did not like the implications of the saddle pad. After all, if I submitted to the initial stages of the training process, might not all that would then be required of me threaten what I assumed was the indestructibility of my present mood? Of course, I thought, and at once hardened my heart to Millie and showed her my teeth and looked down askance at what was only a harmless saddle pad and a gentle adolescent girl.

For days Millie came to me with that first piece of tack draped over her slender arm, for days I resisted the very sight of it in my stall. I knew what was coming, I anticipated the consequences in store for me. More than this, I knew that I was one of those horses that are unhappily possessed of a back as painfully sensitive to touch as an infant's eye to bright light. All my life I had been groomed by Millie, and lately she had groomed me still more thoroughly, languishing beside me, as I have said, and brushing me, combing out my lustrous mane and tail. She had a naturally light touch, she was innately careful, somehow she intuited that only the softest brushes were appropriate to my grooming. So not once had I flinched or snapped in her care, not once had she given me cause to return her kindness with any sort of rebellious behavior. Yet all the while I knew what she did not, namely that one harsh stroke of a brush on my back or the sensation of hard bristles instead of soft might send me into an uncontrollable spasm of resistance. Crude currying, rough rubbing—to me these simple matters could prove intolerable. Thin skin was mine, and because of it, present bad temper aside, I could kick, I could bite, I could cause injury even to someone I cared as much about as I did little Millie.

It was just as I feared. The first early morning that this quick yet sleepy-eyed young girl reached up and slid the saddle pad into place on my back proved disastrous. I felt the weight of that weightless thing, it seared my sensitivity: there might have been some large invisible cat straddling my back and digging in its claws. Intolerable indeed it was, and for the various reasons I have set forth, I would have none of it. I swung round my head, impossibly I attempted to snatch off that innocuous saddle pad with my bared teeth. I moved so violently that my ordinarily roomy stall became a space of dangerous confinement. I rubbed my side against the planking, I shook myself, I caused little Millie to leap nimbly away from my hooves until at last she retreated, bearing off the offensive pad.

Day after day she persevered, I persevered. She attempted to soothe me with her bright young voice, I scattered my bedding and kicked the walls of my stall. She cajoled me to behave myself, I stood still, breathing heavily and staring down at her with eyes that I knew were glassy with derangement. Against my will I refused to submit to hers. Like other colts of my generation at Millbank, I had been caressed and fondled since the day of my birth. But all that tactile affection meant nothing now, and I would not accept Millie's touch or the warmth of her breath against my neck or, and this least of all, the cruel and painful burden of the saddle pad and all it implied.

Then came the morning on which I went so far in my thoughtless irritability as to commit the single act that cannot be condoned in any horse in a stable. That is, in the midst of one of our hopeless contests Millie stumbled, lost her balance, did not manage to evade me, and in the instant I pinned her, as the expression goes, against the thick planking of my stall. I felt the energy of her little body trapped between my hot side and the heavy wood, I heard her gasp, I leaned toward the wood and, hooves rooted in fresh straw, slowly and deliberately pressed on, pressed harder, and savored both my meanness and that small girl's suddenly frantic struggle.

"Quit!" she cried, her angry voice muffled against me. "Stop it, Willy! Now! Let me go!"

I held my ground, she pummeled me with tiny fists, I prolonged the pleasure I took in her helpless wriggling, and all the while I knew that in the long view of things my physical power was in fact no match for her strength of mind. But no sooner did I step away from her at last and retreat to a far corner of the stall than Millie retaliated. Impishly, furiously, quickly she opened my stall door and snatched up my leather halter from where it hung on the outside of the door. And before I could so much as shy away or threaten her again with my sheer size and weight, Millie began to flail me with the halter. Her legs were spread, I saw a hard white knee through the usual rent in the threadbare jeans, her white T-shirt was damp with sweat and her black hair loose and wild. With my own halter this small person, the Millie I loved, beat me, slashed at me without mercy and without a thought for her own safety. I was surprised, I was mortified. How could Millie of all people succumb to such rage? I felt the blow of a brass buckle, in her aimless assault she struck me even about the head and eyes with the heavy leather. I cowered, dismayed at her deplorable performance. I trembled and accepted her every blow. I snorted, she cocked her head and swung again. The smack of leather against my hide, a sudden stinging as from an open cut. Unusual contestants, unlikely punishment. Her wide jaw was set, her lips were white; I thought that she would never stop. And yet when she finally paused in mid-blow and looked at me in what was unmistakable disgust and then flung down my halter and stalked out of my stall, her anger still unabated for all her violence, I knew that I had deserved what she had done and that the temper she had displayed was not a girl's but a woman's. Guilty, chastised, sullen, affronted—nonetheless I was elated to realize that now I not only loved Millie but admired her. In the next moment, in a rush of tingling sensation, it came to me that the hated saddle pad was still in place, and forgetting Millie as well as the beating she had given me, down I dropped my entire length to the bright glistening straw and rolled, thus ridding myself of the hated thing.

My first thrashing but not my last. And paradoxically—and is not my entire life a paean to paradox?—it was a thrashing that soon proved the glorious turning point in my maturation.

No Millie. Only an absent Millie. Gloomy isolation, hurt pride along with my other psychic ailments. For several mornings, then, she left me alone, stayed away, until I began to think that she had abandoned me for good. But no matter the thick suffusion of my recalcitrance, in my heart of hearts I knew that she would not give me up. And so came another and most special dawn, when I heard her entering the main barn—it was like a cathedral, so high did its white interior rise above our heads—and heard the inaudible tread of her sneakers down the aisleway, smelled her scent of fresh soap and freshly laundered jeans and shirt. She unbolted my stall door, stood looking up at me as if the painful incident from which I still smarted had not taken place between us. I was forgiven, I longed to forgive her in return. But no saddle pad? No saddle pad. I was puzzled when with her typical gentleness she cradled my lowered head in one arm and slipped my halter into place, led me in silence out of my stall and down the aisleway to the open air. My lead shank swayed between us; apparently she meant no more than to turn me out among the other colts kept separate from the fillies. Of course I welcomed though I did not understand this change in my daily schedule, and so followed her peacefully but warily as well.

Earliest signs of approaching dawn; a few birds singing; dew glistening on earth and wood and fresh green leaves. On we went down the back lane between rows of apple trees starting to bloom, turned up an incline toward the immense back field, which, I suddenly knew without looking, I was to have to myself. No intrusive fellow colts bursting with unfulfilled adulthood, only the natural teeming emptiness of four-thirty of a morning in late spring. I caught myself noticing anew the changes that had occurred in Millie's shape and the loose yet determined way she walked. An infant rabbit no larger than one of my hooves leapt across the lane, and whereas mere days before I might have shied and reared, kicked up my heels and thrown myself about, as if the tiny creature were some tight-bellied watchdog trespassing in the world of horses—brute animals to be feared and chased—now I merely continued quietly behind the girl who was leading me into a dawning landscape that was familiar and yet like no other.

More apple trees, a succession of white gates and fences, a glimpse of the brook after which Millbank was named, the rolling emptiness of the back field. And the farther we went, the more I was aware of my considerable height, my untried imposing stature, the lightness that was obviously mine on my long legs, the rippling of strong muscles in my chest and flanks and hindquarters. The tip of my dark tail swung to my springy rhythm; I was a young stallion whose handsome appearance, it suddenly occurred to me, belied his bad character. Yet surely the special solace of spite and mischievous behavior could not be so easily destroyed, and in reaction against the pride I had for the moment taken in my rare self I swerved, arched my neck, broke into an erratic jogging meant to convey defiance. But Millie paid no attention, and I subsided into reluctant enjoyment of the morning.

She turned me loose. I glanced once over my shoulder and trotted off until Millie was out of sight and the otherwise empty pasture mine.

After a few limbering minutes I slowed my pace and stopped. I listened, I relaxed into this uncanny state of things, I convinced myself of the safety inherent in a landscape in which, for some reason or other, or perhaps none at all, I was free to take my ease and to drift, to muse, to graze. I lowered my head, the grass was sweetened with a wet chill, I could hear the dawn still waiting to come to light on the horizon. I could hardly be suspicious or on my guard in a terrain of such tranquillity; I could not have been more my own center of attention. I forgot myself, I became myself. I heard my own footfall, my own breath. I moved on slowly, paused again to graze. I was both insignificant and monumental, was for once at liberty to eat my fill of the very world through which, unaccompanied, I moved. I could smell the apples yet to come, taste their wet bitterness as if I had eaten them before they had had a chance to come to life, to grow, to drop from the tree. All of the world's barns might have been empty, all the world's horses dispersed to distant corners, all the world of the horse rid at last of humans, who, from the time they first encountered and then captured us until now, have been the cause of our troubles.

A dawn for which no creature waited, one horse suspended in the absence of many. And it was not trouble that was in store for me but its opposite. Yes, it was joy that replenished my poisoned well that morning, the purest and least expected happiness, which, it goes without saying, I did not deserve, could not have anticipated, did not even want yet certainly could not deny once it was mine.

I stopped in my tracks, raised my head. I felt my mane and tail lifted by some sylvan current of air I could not feel. Something had changed, something was wrong, and all the alertness I could muster was no match for this intrusion. My being was concentrated in my distended nostrils, I breathed in the enigmatic smell. What was it? Where was it coming from? I filled my nose, my head, my lungs, my selfhood with this pale and disturbing scent. Without moving I readied myself for retreat or cautious progress toward its hidden source. Flight or investigation, alarm or adventure, which would it be?

Cinnamon. Pepper. Sugar. Blood. The longer I smelled it, the stronger that smell became, and the more tyrannical, the more alluring. All my senses were attuned to its promise; there was no denying the pungency of this living spice. Poised to flee, poised to advance, in eager indecision I stood rooted where I was, nose high in the air, nostrils twitching, head held as rigidly as the rest of me except for slight movements to the left, to the right, as dictated by the smallest variations in the direction of that ever-present scent. The sweet fuming breath of feed in a bucket, or the dark smell of algae on still water, or the intangible aroma of ripe grain in a field, or the smell of molten iron, or the salty smell of a long wet gash in a horse's shoulder, or the acidic smell of the fear that emanates from the flesh of certain humans in the presence of a hot-blooded horse—all this came to me now like a clear thread through the neutral atmosphere, and I sniffed, I savored what I sniffed, vaguely I thought of the eternal cycles of equine life. Then I heard a sound almost inaudible but as strong in its way as the smell from which it was inseparable—the sound of whinnying. The sound of another horse. The sound, I was forced to admit to myself, of a filly. In my mind's eye I saw the invisible creature standing as tall as myself and shining in colors as bright as mine, my twin but of the opposite gender and whinnying for no other horse's ears but mine.

Right and wrong, as always.

Off I trotted, reluctantly, and followed the smell and sound of her until over a gentle rise and down a greening slope I found her. But she was not a horse, not a racing Thoroughbred, not at all my match. What then? A pony. A New Forest pony to be sure, but only a pony. My spirits fell, though I did not know why they had risen in the first place, and in my disappointment I could only chide myself at having been afraid, initially, of this mere pony in the pasture adjoining mine. And could so small a creature be the source of such a thick and compelling smell? No, I thought, and yet beyond a doubt that smell was coming, incongruously enough, from her.

We were separated by two fences, hers and mine, running parallel as far as the eye could see, which is always the case, on a horse farm of any quality, with adjacent fields intended for the accommodation of colts and stallions on the one hand and fillies and mares on the other. The careful breeder of horses keeps the equine genders separate, a fact I had long and indifferently accepted but had forgotten this particular and peculiar dawn in spring. One seemingly boundless field for males, one for females, and in all this immensity only a single naive male Thoroughbred and a single New Forest pony of the female sex facing each other cryptically on opposite sides of the white fences. Of course there was no distinction between the grass in her field and the grass in mine, no difference in the air we breathed, or so my view of pastures and paddocks had always been, until now. But now the pony might have been standing ankle deep in blackened earth and I in golden wheat to my shoulders. Or hers might have been a field of vastly swarming bees and mine some swarthy acreage gone to dust, or hers a limitless stand of water and mine of briers. The very earth we trod, I realized in alarm, was forever changed.

Two white fences, then, between us. Tall fences. Sturdy fences. And not only insurmountable in themselves but in turn separated by a space greater in width than the length of a large lean horse. A formidable barrier, an unmistakable prohibition. The pony on her side, I on mine. Face-to-face. Silent. Motionless. Pressed against our respective rails. Gazing at each other with a raptness I had never until that moment known.

She was half my size but perfectly proportioned. She was a blue dun, which is to say a shiny bluish gray in color with a dark gray mane and tail, and her soft coat shone forth her pale lustrous colors, her little black hooves pointed straight ahead and appeared to have been lacquered by the hand of a loving child. Her head, despite its shapeliness, betrayed the soft-boned quality found in youth and in all the smaller equine breeds. She was short and light but strong. Her feet were well formed, her cannon bone was short, her back was desirably short and strong. Her eyes were bright, her withers were level with her croup, her thighs were muscular. No horse of ordinary stature could have been prettier in conformation than was this pony. Best of all, from her lower jaw and in sheerest coquetry, there depended a little fringe or beard of dark hair, which, as a natural adornment, could not have been more endearing.

She nickered. I whinnied lustily. She gazed up at me in mute appeal, grandly I gazed down at her. Primly she beckoned me with her entire being, pridefully I towered in the aura of her unaccountable adoration. I could hardly breathe, thanks to the by now hot and heavy smell of her, serenely she waited for me—to what? Crash headlong through those thick white rails? Jump them? Either way the task was all but impossible, yet either way, I knew, it was a task I could not fail to accomplish.

Again she nickered—appealingly, plaintively—and as if the better to reach me trotted off down the fence, drawing me with her almost step for step. She stopped and gazed at me, I followed suit. Back and forth we trotted in parallel frustration, pausing momentarily and moving on. Each time she turned I caught a glimpse of her little shapely hindquarters, the raised and flowing tail, the purpose that saturated the delicacy of her flesh and bone as the peach is saturated with its sweet juice.

Again we stopped and faced each other. Silently and with large
and lowered eyes she looked at me. She could not do more.

So off I trotted in a great half circle away from the double fence
raised against the fractious comportment of colts and fillies,
mares and stallions, and turned, breaking into my soon-to-be-
famous rocking-horse canter—a slow loping gait of the purest
power and containment—and then, unleashing all my latent energies, charged the double fence and jumped, rose up, higher and
farther than any other Gordon horse had ever traveled through
such hotly perfumed air. I flew, I soared, I overshot the pony by
some distance and landed, wheeled about, controlled myself and
stopped, waited, then trotted sedately to her side.

Trumpeting? Lunging? Pawing? Assaultive behavior typical of
the bestial stallion given his way? Not at all. Not a bit of it. I
wanted only to please the little pony, not to offend her.

She waited, I approached. Tentatively I touched my head to
hers, my nose to hers; she made a little welcoming sound deep in
her throat. With all possible consideration for her sensibilities and
well-being I turned, so that we were standing head-to-tail, no
matter the incongruity of our disparate sizes, and gently pressed
my length to hers as best I could. She made a small exploratory
gesture, again I heard the fluttering contented sound from far
within her fluted throat. Again I turned, she awaited me, gently
I nipped her silky neck, she nickered. On I went, courting my
small newly found companion, though it was she, of course, who
had begun in her diminutive fashion the resounding act of seduc-
tion. Then at last she turned, ever the proprietress of our relationship, and drew up and to the side her silky tail and, even while I
watched and forbore, too engaged to move, allowed me to share
the long moment of micturition that was, I understood, inseparable from the slick and pulsing rest of her. Then before my eyes she
braced her blue-gray hindquarters in a partial squat and turned
her head and looked at me, released me at last to action.

Up I went, fearful that my weight might be too great for her
little frame, though it was an unnecessary concern, and Moggy—
for it was she, of course—needed no hobbles, no leather shield to

protect her neck and withers. As for me, I needed no human hand to guide me.

The instant I mounted Moggy I became my own horse, possessor and master of new cravings, indifferent to how I might have looked to any horse or person who might have spied on our coupling. However, at the height of that performance it did occur to me that I, at least, was nothing at all like a wrecked ship snagged on a pinnacle of rock, and until its end was careful to keep my tongue in my mouth where it belonged.

We were allowed only three such mysterious clandestine dawns together. Three times I found her, three times I jumped and rejumped the double fence, three times we satisfied our instincts. I learned that Moggy was the newest Gordon acquisition, the finest of all the Connemaras and Exmoors and New Forests that Jim inspected in his search for little Ann's first pony. She listened patiently to my complaints. She nodded her approval of my misanthropy. We played, we pursued our passion, we reminisced, I about Millicent and Sam and Molly-Long-Legs and Misty Rose, she about an old bowlegged groom and a pretty child in a large straw hat who used to hitch her to a smart two-wheeled pony cart and drive her about beneath the shady elms. Once, during our second dawn together, she told me that we were not alone in what we did and that horses the world over defied the restrictive efforts of their keepers and, to be together, jumped inordinately high fences, or smashed them to bits, thereby incurring deep lacerations on their necks and chests and legs, and on occasion went so far as to couple through the rails of the very fences intended to keep them apart. Then she said that we horses must be ever on our guard against the wiles of men who, when it suited their interests, sometimes stooped to tricking horses like myself, stallions still fresh to the world, and older, more experienced stallions as well, into mounting artificial mares. I was shocked at what she said, especially this last, and yet admired her the more for her worldly knowledge and the candor with which she confided it. Moggy was not innocent, no matter that the old bowlegged groom had called her the most precious pony he had ever seen.

And so she was.

Elation. Exuberance. Confidence. My own horse, my old self. No wonder I submitted so readily to Millie. No wonder I did not take it amiss when, on the mornings subsequent to my introduction to adulthood, she stopped leading me to the distant field but rather resumed my training where she had left it off. The saddle pad? Nothing at all! Millie herself laughing and lying across me in order that I might grow accustomed to a person's warmth and weight? A pleasure! The training saddle? Insignificant! The bridle, the bit that felt like a wedge of iron in my virgin mouth? Mere novelties! I carried Millie astride me out-of-doors, I learned my gaits, I perfected my responses to Millie's faintest pressure as conveyed through hands or legs or her small buttocks on the saddle. And all the while I was intelligent, agreeable, never more eager to please and to display to Millie my new obedience. Not for a moment did I forget that it was to her that I owed my conjugation with the blue dun pony. Not for a moment did I doubt that sooner or later my good behavior would win my return to that pastoral remoteness where the lonely pony waited.

But it was not to be. Before I knew it, I was broken. Before I could help myself, my days on the Gordon farm were over, and I was torn from the arms of a tearful Millie and forced into a van that could carry fifteen horses—admittedly I did not go peaceably into that enormous van—and shipped off from Millbank to a training farm and thence to the track. No Millicent. No Moggy. Nothing in my immediate future but false hopes and then the threat of a singular and barbaric death.

Initially I too understood that adage, or thought I did, and subscribed to it. Do your best, it said, you have only one chance. Or, there is no other horse in the race to compete against, so outrun yourself. Or, nothing matters except the race you run, so run you must. Or, not to win, not for praise, running is its own reward. Or, the faster you run, the longer the distance and the shorter the time allowed you to complete the course. Faster! Faster! The selfless horse is the swiftest horse. Running is not possible without your rider, so obey your rider. And so on and so on, day in, day out, these adages came to me from every hand, an admonishment but more than that the very tone of the new life I thought was mine. Yes, I arrived at the track, a small establishment half a dozen highway days south of the Gordon farm, filled with unaccustomed vigor and anticipation, thanks, of course, to Moggy. I was fresh, I knew my speed, I listened to the older horses with deference and determination to excel. But quickly enough I discovered that the *one horse, one race* adage was nothing but the deceptive rhetoric of dull and mediocre oldsters, that it concealed rather than exposed the truth, that it reeked as strongly of conventional morality, which is no morality at all, as a poorly mucked-out stall reeks of ammonia. Yes, the blows that began to fall ever-increasingly about my head soon caused me to despise those oldsters and the shallow adage that even they did not believe.

I do not admire those who race, and would not race again if I could. The worthiest of horses is he who comes in last or falls. I put no stock in the promise of youth, in retrospect I do not admire the young horse that I once was. If I can recall with any pleasure the days when I was limber and when in the best of humors I could easily outdistance my jealous peers, I do so partly that my prime of youth may serve as the context in which the pain of my old age is the more acute. What was my youth if not the lie of my old age? I am not shod, I am not worth shoeing. I am gaunt, my flesh shrinks daily to my skeleton. My cheek teeth, the few I have, are worn and as soft as wood, while the remnants of my incisors protrude flatly and wretchedly from the front of my jaw. My wind is broken, my back sags. My suspensory ligaments long ago grew slack and useless, so that thanks to the wobbling of my ankles I can hardly walk, let alone be ridden. Pain is my favorite word. Each joint, each sickened and unresilient muscle, each of my more than two hundred bones is a source of pain. And my pain is so constant and so severe that the memory of my youth and athletic prowess in every way affronts my decrepitude. Complainer, laggard, miscreant—these admittedly I am. In a word, Old Horse. But I am not complacent, and the ammonia that rises from the filthy straw in which I stand is not a metaphor.

Spleen is the sustaining lyricism of those unlucky horses consigned at last to the abandoned paddocks of old age.

It was not mere coincidence that one of the only horses I ever loved was a pony or that throughout my life I never loved any but the smallest of girls and no woman larger than a small girl. The smaller the girl or woman, filly or mare, the more startling her capacity for thought as well as passion. That small, and able to think with the best of us! That small, yet more than able to accommodate and exhaust the carnal energies of even the mightiest male! What paradox could be more offensive to some, more pleasing to others? I have no explanation for this happy fact of my life: that the horse gods, whatever else, have always provided me with the most appreciative of miniature companions. To stand above them still taller and more handsome than usual, simply by sheer comparison, and yet to humble my princely stature to their diminutive existences—here was more than vanity, here was the antithesis of the complacent and condescending male. So I found small women, small girls, small horses wherever I went, though it never crossed my mind to seek them out. My predilection, which my fellows did not share, indifferent as they were to humans or at best scorning or disliking women and girls, while among female horses preferring those of heavy bones with rumps as large and round as moons, was only for the power inherent in vulnerability, the uncanny boldness latent in fine features. Such delights as I knew in youth were aesthetic. And I am essentially an equine aesthetician still.

In fine fettle, then, I arrived at Elroy Park. It was an agreeable place, a racetrack of no renown but exemplary of the highest standards and attracting to its freshly painted grandstand, with its flags and cupolas and pennants, only the most discerning and well behaved of enthusiasts. There were no brawls, no rowdy shouts, no dishonesty. The guards at the gates wore smart uniforms and cheerful smiles. The stable area, set apart from the track beneath tall trees, was safe and orderly. Elroy Park was a track intended mainly to try the mettle of beginners, and all of us allowed to make our debuts before its cheering crowds were worthy of that privilege.

Or, in my own case, more than worthy. Two factors augured well for my career at Elroy Park, namely that my reputation had preceded my arrival and that I disembarked into the midst of my fine-blooded peers already accompanied by Mary, the smallest and shapeliest rider of my career. Even as I made my entrance, so to speak, and clattered down the steel ramp of the horse van that had carried us in style from the training farm to this raceway, which I had dreamed about for months; even as I set hoof to earth early that crucial fall, more than ready to accept the challenge of Elroy Park, I felt the respect and envy of those other two-year-olds, who watched me from their stalls and who in advance knew me for the lanky favored unpredictable youngster that I was. With pleasure I soon discovered that more than half the riders exercising horses at Elroy Park that season were women, none of whom, it was soon accepted by all concerned, could compare in any way with Mary. She, among that handful of female gallopers, was the most childlike yet the most womanly, the most intelligent and the sweetest of disposition, and the prettiest and the best able to guide a difficult Thoroughbred around the track. I see her yet, standing beside Orville—her father and my trainer—dressed in the inevitable tight jeans and canary yellow shirt and little black cowboy boots and the crash helmet covered in yellow silk, smiling and sporting aslant the front of her helmet the raised racing goggles. No one kinder, no one who knew or rode me better, no one more honest or more receptive to horses and humankind at large. Small wonder that Orville, a short shrewd-eyed tobacco-chewing man and the greatest trainer ever to take my life in hand, rarely let Mary from his sight, though in fact the male exercisers at Elroy Park, big men mostly, who rode bareheaded or in baseball caps and wore long sideburns and went unshaven, generally treated Mary with the kind of abject deference they ordinarily reserved for only the oldest female members of their families, grandmothers and great-aunts and other aged matriarchs.

At Millbank freedom had been completely mine; at the training farm, where I had come under the care of Orville and Mary, I had lost a portion of that freedom in order to learn to run; now at Elroy Park suddenly I found myself propelled into a kind of freedom I had not expected, the freedom found only on the track itself, and yet contrariwise confined in a captivity more stringent than any I had ever known. Of course I had run at the training farm, and with Mary atop me and Orville watching us the while, and every now and again Orville had instructed Mary to let me run flat out, at my greatest speed, and she had done so, laughing as we sped by Orville, who looked impassive, as always, but whom I had nonetheless impressed. But such sprinting or breezing was not to be compared with approaching and entering and running on a racetrack on which a horse might be acclaimed or, more than likely, destroyed, for the sake of the race. I too wanted to run, to outrun my peers. At my first sight of Elroy Park, even with the grandstand empty, weeks before the beginning of the racing season, even then I intuited the dangerous freedom that would soon be mine. On the other hand, how did we maidens, as we were called—the term referring not to gender but to the fact that we had never raced—how did we and how did the few oldsters among us spend our days? In our stalls. Largely in our stalls. Locked away from fields, sky, trees, the very raceway for which, in our captivity, we yearned all the more, no matter the despair or pain or, less likely, the pride it held in store for us. What had I expected? How could I not have expected the obvious? Every morning from dawn until the approach of noon, each horse at Elroy Park was given his or her chance to exercise on the generally empty track. Twice around, if we were lucky, sometimes only once. Then a hosing down and back to our stalls. For the rest of the day and throughout the night. What else? The purpose of the place was to keep us fit, not to bow our tendons or exhaust us—except in a race. We were too valuable, too numerous, each too explosive in his or her own way—yes, it was only too apparent from the start that my competitors were nearly as temperamental and high-strung and unfriendly as myself—to be turned out into paddocks. If they had turned us out, our gallopers and grooms and trainers, we would have attacked each other and fought amongst ourselves until we were too bruised or lacerated or otherwise impaired to race. So except for those few minutes when they gave us our daily turns on the track, for no other reason than to maintain our fitness and well-being, what else could they, our keepers, do with us if not keep us confined? And confinement to a space measuring no more than twelve feet on a side enhanced desirably our desperation, as they well knew, to be on the track, to run, to run and nothing more. So we waited, pacing and turning or hanging out our heads in wait for unwary passersby. Woe to anyone so ignorant or careless as to pass too close—it took but an instant to drive forth our brute heads and bared teeth and to catch fast a shoulder, to strike a resounding blow to human ribs. But victims were as rare as accidents or other such diversions, and time our heaviest burden. The worst of our sufferers were known as "weavers," poor creatures who despite their lineage and prowess and perfect conformation could not contain their impatience and so swung their heads from side to side the day long and half the night. We were all stir-crazy to one degree or another, each in danger of losing his or her last shred of rationality. I fared better than most since Orville and Mary gave me more of their attention than they did the other Gordon horses in their charge, Mary tending me in my stall, Orville feeding me doughnuts—unlikely fare for a horse!—which he kept in large cardboard boxes outside my stall.

So I enjoyed my status as a newcomer, and a singular one at that, and for the brief period of my initiation into the life of Elroy Park I noted with the keenest pleasure all that was new to me and fresh and unfamiliar, from the proper way a wheelbarrow was positioned in front of a stall to the ingenious simplicity of the very design essential to the efficiency of a racing sable. Thus I heard a woman trainer complaining about a poor anxious fellow who had bought himself a talentless two-year-old and, without the slightest knowledge of horses or racing, was attempting to win a fortune. He would cause trouble, she said, for his horse or others. How did she know? Simply because when mucking out the stall of his ill-fated colt he had left the handles of the wheelbarrow pointing outward, so that any passing horse, especially a loose horse, might injure himself on those wooden shafts.

Our stable, like all racing stables, consisted of two long rows of box stalls back to back and roofed over so as to form on the sides and ends a continuous walkway, which, like a veranda, was on the one hand sheltered and on the other open to the world beyond. Those of us who were waiting for the day to pass and the night to come and another dawn to bring us our daily meager allotments of freedom could stand with our heads and necks protruding from the picture frames, so to speak, of our split stall doors, the top halves of which were generally left open and the bottom halves well bolted, and watch the passing of our more fortunate fellows on their way to the track or those on their way back to incarceration. How they pranced and pulled as they went by, their riders attempting to calm them by touch and voice or grooms restraining them with chains looped around their noses. How we impatient spectators kicked or jeered or whinnied enviously until they were gone from sight and we could only return to gnawing the edges of our stall doors or awaiting as best we could our next distraction. That covered walkway was constantly in use, and all those free to move moved quickly and with purpose. What confusion and collisions might have occurred had not the counterclockwise direction been long established! To the left was the rule, and it was unbreakable, learned early and soon innate. A horse is saddled from his left side, and mounted from his left side, and in a racing stable goes out of his stall to the left, and when at last he races he does so in the counterclockwise direction. The world of the horse, and especially of the racing horse, is sinister!

Dawn at Elroy Park. And each as startling, as exhilarating, as fraught with the most sportive kind of tension as the one before and, presumably, the one to come, though admittedly there was a difference between preparing for the racing season and that season itself. At three A.M., inevitably, I grew restive. At four A.M., while the heavens changed and the sounds of life accumulated here and there around me, I lost whatever patience I might have had. By four-thirty, when I detected the first scents and sounds of Orville and Mary emerging from the track's private cafeteria and rounding a far corner and passing through the parking lot and at last approaching that section of the stable where we six Gordon horses stamped and snorted in the row of stalls allotted us, my heightened energy was greater still, if such be possible, than on those long-ago early mornings when amorous desire and its relief attended me in the back pasture at Millbank. And using all my might, I let that energy be known to every living creature in Elroy Park until to the left and right of me and as far as either end of the stable, the entire host of two-year-olds set up an outraged clamor to still my own. Then into my din and racket came Mary, helmet already on her head and the familiar riding crop stuck jauntily into a tight hip pocket and poking up as high as her shoulder, a practice that was uniquely hers, and Orville, bearing his usual paper cup of coffee. Mary picked my hooves, tacked me up with the bridle and training saddle that were part of her own equipment as a professional, greeting me the while and chattering to Orville as she darted about me, under me, and behind me, readying me for the run that she and I were about to share. Orville watched, sipped his coffee, said nothing. Finally, in front of my stall and in the darkest shadows of that dawn hour, Orville, still silent, did Mary's bidding—"Hold him, Daddy," she said, and "Give me a leg up, Daddy"—though the three of us well knew that he was merely humoring horse and daughter alike, since no other man could see what Orville saw in a horse or had a temper as wordlessly violent as his.

Streaks of light, the first pearly ribbons on the horizon. The dawn air that smelled only of the night. The path that sloped away from the stable, the near rails, the tall oak that was a landmark midway between stable area and track. High on my back, Mary was as weightless as her saddle, and yet, as I had heard her say many a time, from the waist down her body belonged to me, and so it did and so I felt it as I jigged and jogged that first time toward the great dark oval of the waiting track. Comfort, then. Security. Anticipation. But what did I do as soon as I had carried Mary through the opening in the rails and onto that dark earth intended only for the hooves of Thoroughbreds? I stopped! Stopped short! Balked and braced my legs, raised my head, tried to see around the curving track, tried to see the very space of distance. I was afraid of that space, I felt an uncanny breeze lifting my mane, on my skin I felt the aura of Elroy Park, which, empty or nearly so, was nonetheless filled with the phantoms of former races.

There I was, standing on racing turf at last. Through the shredding curtains of that brisk dawn mirage, a fusion of fog and filmy light and dark shadows, I was able to make out snatches of white rail and the posts that marked off the quarters of the track, as well as the darkened shape of the grandstand, which was like an abandoned ship on its side. Immense, and not another horse in sight. Freedom. Challenge. Exhilaration. And yet I stood my ground and for the moment that was like no other denied myself the pleasures and perils of the course that was even now inviting me to run. Or rather, could not submit myself to those pleasures and perils no matter my readiness and pumping blood, and deepening breath. Why? Because I heard them, phantom horses of races already won or lost. Around the invisible turn, down the far side, endlessly—for that single moment—they bunched together in the triumph of forgotten races that would never end. Wreaths and burials, silver cups, the silent cheering of crowds long since dispersed or dead—indeed I shivered at this conjuring of past rituals in which all we racehorses shared. Then I shook my head, felt Mary's hand against my neck and the shifting of her slight weight as she leaned forward to pat my neck. Did she understand my immobility? Or did she merely think that I, poor creature, needed to take my bearings when first confronted with what would always be the uncertainty of the course? The latter, I sadly admitted to myself, the latter. In this case Mary was no different from exercisers or riders the world over, I no different from their horses. Sometimes—and this was one of them—the experience of the horse cannot be known to the human balancing on his back, no matter the love and understanding they share. But now the thundering sounds were gone and I was myself once more and turned, started off at a joyous trot as Mary bid me.

Suddenly a blackened shape ahead proved to be a horse and rider, and for me there could not have been a greater or more unwanted intrusion. What business had they in a world I had thought to be solely mine? We drew abreast of them, I saw that the horse was old, unkempt, an unblooded beast content to rest beside the rail—for what purpose I had yet reluctantly to learn—

and that his rider was a long-legged man slouching in a western saddle.

"Morning, little Mary," he said as we approached.

"Morning, JD."

"How's Orville?" he said.

"Mean as ever," she said.

"How's that horse of yours," he said as we began to pass.

"He has heart, JD, that's for sure," she called over her shoulder, while I, repeating to myself what I had heard, gave the old horse and his slovenly unshaven rider my briefest and most condescending glance, already rounding my back and cantering, feeling Mary standing upright in the stirrups and laughing, holding me in, guiding me around the treachery of hidden potholes and a long darker stretch of earth where only yesterday a black horse named Beacon Rock had fallen.

We swung wide on a banked turn; Mary shortened the reins and, leaning forward and in her sweet whispering voice, told me to slow down, to pace myself, that Orville wouldn't like it if we went too fast. Her warm calves were against my withers, and she had bent her upper body so that her round and cheerful face was closer to my outstretched neck. It was morning; clear light and the air of the new day were mine. Again our speed was quickening, my breath was deep, far ahead Orville was only a small black figure where he leaned at the rail and watched us through binoculars. I aimed for him, picked up my rhythm, hardly aware of Mary tightening her hold on my mouth. Oh, but I was aware of what she had said to the man she called JD. And I knew that a horse with heart was one of those rare horses who want to run, love to run, will run no matter the pain of the effort and—fatigue or no fatigue, shortness of breath, whatever—will always run still faster at precisely the moment their rider asks them to. And run until they drop. As for me, never in my presence had Mary referred to me as a horse with heart. Until now I would have said that no horse could have thought more highly of himself, could have been more vain, more confident, than the long-legged misanthropic two-year-old that I was. Now heart as well! Heart too! Well might

I have flown that day, first on the track, and fly I did as Mary settled closer atop me and, against her better judgment, gave me my head.

"Daddy won't like it," I heard her say again, and knew that nothing lay ahead except the empty track and the inevitability of still greater speed.

The faster I went, the lighter the four-beat sound of my gallop and the faster, it seemed to me, I could go and did, increasing my tempo with every stride, lengthening my every stride with each escalation of my tempo. Mary was crouching now—I could feel her—and had pulled down her goggles—I had felt that movement of her arm and hand—and was working her body in time to mine and humming—humming!—as if oblivious to the limpid violence of our exertions.

"Hey!" I heard the startled JD shout. "You crazy?"

But he was gone, and I had not so much as caught a glimpse of him. Nor did I catch my second glimpse of Orville as once more we approached the grandstand and I thought of him, looked for him where only seconds earlier he had stood at the rail, but saw that he was gone. And no sooner had that shadow of misgiving darted across the clarity of my growing speed than the joy of my impetuosity was dashed at its very height. Mere emptiness. The slightest possible sensation of nothing at all. One moment I was running at the peak of my self-absorption, the next I was thrown entirely off course, my greatest pleasure displaced by nothing less than panic. A flapping rein, a flying stirrup, and on my back that dreadful emptiness. Mary, it came to me! Gone! Like Orville, plucked from my back as he had been plucked from my sight. I had heard nothing—no gasp, no cry, no sound of her body landing on that fast track—and what I felt was not much more than nothing. Yet it was undeniable—Mary had disappeared, and I was riderless.

I tried to think, could not. I tried to slow my speed, could not. What worse than the absence of her guiding hands? Small hands that had, through reins and ring bit, touched my mouth with so delicate a power that the reins might have been attached to my bit by butterflies. Those hands were gone. The balance of her body bobbing atop me horizontally from yellow head to tiny rump like a bee on a pear, her slight balance that was analogous to mine—this too was gone. And I was without control, beyond control, potential victim of my worst and greatest speed. Fall I might! Trip over my own hooves! Break a leg! Suffer who could tell what painful or even fatal accident! I swerved, I was nearly berserk, my eyes rolled wildly in my frantic head, my ears were flat. How stop? How escape myself? And still as fresh as when I had started off!

Then came the voice.

"Whoa there, big babe!"

Instantly I swerved, instantly the ring of those words rang up others from some similar moment from my past. But which? Whose voice exactly? But where had this JD come from—for it was he, of course—and how had his aged mount managed a speed the equivalent of mine? How was this heavyset unwashed man able to speak to me as if from across a brook in an immense field in the quiet of a summer's day—softly, casually—when in fact we were traveling side by side at breakneck speed down the empty track? I could not account for JD's presence or manner or the way he spoke, but still I was a faster horse than his—I had to be!—and in a mere three strides could easily leave my improbable pursuer far behind. Now, I told myself, and felt myself easing into my next higher gear.

"Easy," he said. "Steady. Nothing's going to hurt you, babe...."

I heard him, hesitated, shot him a glance—and an uncertain suspicious glance it was. What proud young horse wants to hear the truth about himself? What creature of elegance wants to find his well-being in the hands of an obviously untutored man rocking deep in a battered western saddle on a pathetic old beast that stank, even at our speed and in the clear dawn air, of his own dung? On the other hand, what was I if not a fearful young Thoroughbred running away, as JD had made me see? If he had spoken contemptuously, if he had yanked on my rein, if he had cursed or yelled, then never would I have allowed myself to listen, to believe him and, this once at any rate, give in to common sense and obedience. But so I did. In days to come I heard strange stories about him—that he had once been a trainer and a prosperous one, that he had been known to calm horses given up as intractable by putting his mouth to one of their nostrils and breathing directly into their lungs. For now I merely heard the tone of his voice and submitted to JD and, with sudden relief, slowed at last to a walk.

He led me quietly back to Orville and Mary.

Orville took my reins from JD, saying nothing.

JD, for whom this incident was a daily occurrence and hence a commonplace, looked from the silent Orville to his silent daughter, thought better of speaking and turned his horse, returned at a heavy trot to his post on the track.

Orville held me, Mary undid my girth. Her left side, from shoulder to hip to ankle, was streaked and smeared with fresh dirt.

"Daddy," she said, and glanced at him.

She took the reins from Orville, removed my bridle, saddle, slipped the halter into place and buckled it. I tried to stand quietly for her but could not.

"Daddy," said Mary, "I'm sorry."

She led me onto the concrete slab, turned on the hose, filled the bucket, picked up a sponge.

"I shouldn't have let him go that way," she said, soaping me down, working as quickly as she could. I was still trembling. "You told me to hold him in. But it wasn't my fault I went off," she said and paused, glanced up at him, went back to work. "I never knew a stirrup bar to just rip away like that." She darted under my neck, sloshing the bucket. "It would take something like that to get me off. You know it's true, Daddy."

I shifted, kicked out harmlessly, swung my head, and stared at the silent Orville. He was standing behind me and to the side, white-faced, hands in pockets, soiled white shirt open at his throat. I recognized the mood as well as did Mary—he was containing himself. There was a distant shout, a nearby guffaw, a sudden curse. The sound of a truck, the sound of hooves, somewhere the high-pitched voices of two female riders. But Orville heard nothing, saw nothing, concentrating, as both Mary and I well knew, on his displeasure.

It was then that Mary, in her preoccupation moving even more swiftly and energetically than usual, stooped and lifted the bucket and, before she could stop herself, emptied it in a wide and misdirected arc.

"Oh, Daddy," she cried, dropping the bucket with a clatter. "Daddy!"

I tossed my head, sidestepped, turned halfway around, and stared at the now dripping Orville. His small black eyes were squeezed shut; the water had caught him full in the face and chest and trousers. My hooves clattered as loudly as had the bucket; warily and eagerly I watched him, waited for him to vent, at last, his famous temper.

"Daddy," Mary said, "I didn't know you were standing there like that!"

For a moment Orville stayed as he was, blinking, clenching his jaws, immersed from head to foot in the splash. He might have just come from under a shower, fully dressed. Then slowly, deliberately, making all he could of his false composure, he drew his hands from his pockets and wiped his eyes, his face, his ears, the top of his head. He flicked off the droplets. His shadowy chest hair was visible beneath the now nearly transparent shirt. Each casual gesture accused his daughter of the drenching yet passed it off. Finally he thrust his hands back into his clammy pockets and, still not looking at Mary, began to speak.

"This horse," he said, "is dangerous."

"Oh, Daddy," Mary interrupted in surprise, "he's not as bad as all that!"

"Dangerous," Orville repeated. "He's going to hurt someone or worse. He's going to cause us trouble and bring us disgrace. I know his kind. They're rare, but he's one of them. Mean. Mean as they come. None better, none worse. That's why I like him. But I won't put up with him, understand? I can see what you can't. He

needs to be ridden. He needs a smart race rider and a strong hand.
If you can't ride him, I'll put somebody up who can."

"I can ride him," Mary said.

Orville raised his eyes, turned his head, forced Mary to look away.

"I doubt it," he said. Then, "Next time, watch what you're doing."

With that he left us, striding off toward the truck in all the pride only a small man knows—his chin high and his trousers sticking to his legs.

"Willy," Mary said, skimming the water from my tight and tingling body with the sweat scraper, "my daddy's a hard man. He surely is."

But I was not listening. After all, it was my first morning on the track, and father and daughter had each flattered me in his or her own way, and both were right, though Orville's judgment of me was the less expected, the more pleasing. And I had betrayed Mary despite myself, and experienced JD's protection, which was why he would be out there every sunrise, as I now knew—in case of trouble—and taken my place in Orville's remembered string of savage stallions, though I had not yet displayed my savagery. To be loved, to be hated, such was my lot.

Beware of the dog, as the sign says. *Beware of the horse.*

A sound. A smell. The merest trace of sound, the faintest smell. Hardly detectable by any ordinary horse—a class from which I was obviously exempt in every way, from my size and character and quality of mind to my senses of, especially, hearing and smelling, both as torturously fine-tuned as my very skin. And no horse's skin was more sensitive to touch and temperature, more vulnerable to rashes, than was mine.

But that sound, that smell. Nothing to your ordinary horse, to me unbearable. But why? And which was the greater assault on my senses, the sound or the smell? It was impossible to say, just as, try as I might, I could not identify their source. Familiar yet unfamiliar. Minor irritation but as intense as pain.

It was morning again, another morning. And on the track and under Mary I had behaved myself. Nothing had changed, the stable was as clamorous as ever with activity, on the early-hour air the smells of our world—of hay, iron, leather, wood, oil— were as profuse as always, that wafting of odoriferous pleasure enough to mask, as one would think, the offending irritants. But were not for me. On the contrary, freshly returned to my stall as I was, I stood in my own impenetrable silence aware of nothing except the two new enemies to my peace of mind.

A sound. A smell.

They were reaching me from the stall adjacent to mine, which, for most hours of the day and night, confined the only other Gordon horse I could tolerate, a speedy little gray named London Bobby and known, of course, as Bob. Now Bob was sprinting on the track I had just quitted and his stall was empty, or should have been. Ordinarily I would have smelled his cooling-blanket folded on the stall door, the friendly scent of his droppings in the wet straw still to be removed. Yet now these odors were as nothing, were part of the contextual emptiness through which I was being pierced so suddenly and unaccountably by I knew not what—that sound, that smell.

I cringed; I thought that if I could identify these sensory assail- ants I might find relief. I pressed myself to the planking farthest from that thin wall separating Bob's space from mine, yet un- avoidably swung my head and neck precisely toward that parti- tioning through which I heard the sound and smelled the smell. Both were reaching their crescendo, and none too soon. I cow- ered, readied for attack. Then just as I thought I could stand no more it came to me, an explanation of sorts, for hadn't Bob himself and hadn't I made sounds and smells like these, only monumental, magnificent, forthright, strong and sweet to the nose and ear, admirable attestations to the naturalness of equine life? Similar, yes, but hardly comparable, this sound that was furtive, this smell that was poisonous, for the horse that passes water is majestic, while what I smelled and heard was from a source puny at best. But there I had it, passing water, and did this sudden knowledge—that in what should have been the sanctity of Bob's stall some creature who was not a horse was befouling my poor friend's space—provide me with the relief I sought? Not at all, and now a rising tide of rage swept through my pain. There in Bob's stall was no stray cat, no slinking dog. And then?

Exactly. Some man was passing water in Bob's stall and I, not Bob, was his victim, though soon enough poor Bob would get a whiff of that lingering violation. Yes, a man, I thought—as the sound subsided to a trickling and a mere rustling of denim, and the smell grew in rancidness—but more than that, a man, I began to suspect, who was not ordinary but one of the worst of them, as in the next moment proved to be the case.

A clumsy footfall, a heavy breath, a brutish sigh. Not a shred of doubt remained. Then I saw him.

Hoffman, as I should have known. None other. Having left Bob's stall as stealthily as possible, here he stood noisily readjusting himself in front of mine. He was short and squat, fat, obnoxious, an owner-trainer, so called, of half a dozen horses poorly tended on the other side of the stable. In fact he spent more time with Orville and the Gordon horses than with his own, though Orville all but refused to speak to the obsequious Hoffman, who, in turn, smothered Orville's reticence in torrents of nearly incomprehensible expressions of friendship. No one working at Elroy Park had a reputation as bad as Hoffman's for dishonesty, poor sportsmanship, unreliability. No one trusted the Foreigner, as he was called behind his back, and for good reason. He bullied his underlings, struck his horses, hired only race riders who had been barred from other tracks and should not have been allowed on ours. He stuffed his tight pockets with hard candies, which he was forever sucking, he waddled when he moved, he had white skin immune to tanning. His secret, which I had discovered early, was that he was afraid of horses and thus hated them, myself in particular. But worst of all, it was because of Mary that Hoffman attempted to ingratiate himself with Orville.

"Hey!" he said now in a deep and watery whisper and glanced to the left, the right, and again at me where I pressed myself to the rear of my box stall. The smell had not faded; Hoffman was still fumbling at his pants.

"You!" he whispered. "Long-legs! Troublemaker! Come over here—I give you a smack!"

I loathed him for his taunting, I loathed him more for what he had just done in my companion's stall. But I waited, watching him, judging the distance. He had tricked me before and had escaped me, laughed at me, and now I did not want to lunge at him again and miss.

"Coward," he whispered. "I get you yet!"

He put one of his fat white hands on my stall door and gave it a shake. But he was on his guard, quivering, wary. I waited.

"Dumbo," he whispered, "you just give dat girl a hard time. Dat pretty girl!"

I jumped, I grazed him, he leapt away with a little shriek and cowered, from a safe distance stood looking at me from under his upraised arm.

"Bluffer! Bluffer!"

But he turned, glad enough to be free of another encounter with Mary's favorite horse, and waddled off. At that moment, in the midst of blind frustration, suddenly I was overcome with a sudden and welcome urge and spread my hind legs, braced my haunches, lowered my flesh, and, with a gush, a roar, emptied my bladder in a sweet and acrid stream that felt as if it would never end. Steam rose, my pool spread, contentment was mine. Yet try as I did, I was not able to obliterate Hoffman's noxious smell. And the Foreigner bested me after all and soon enough, as we shall see.

"Little Mary," Hoffman said, as Orville walked away in disgust and I swung my rear end to the two of them, "I got something for you. Something nice. A hot one."

There was no need for me to look in order to see the proffered pink fist, the open palm, the red candy sitting in its glistening wrapper in his fat palm.

"Thanks, Bruno," Mary said—only she called him by his

Christian name—while I snorted at the kindness she could not keep from her voice.

"Makes tears," he said in his childishly happy voice.

I gave a kick, Mary laughed.

Inevitably there came that dawn when, returning from a vigorous and uneventful workout, proud of myself for having listened to Mary's hand and voice and basking in recollection of my hard-won obedience and hence blowing hard, bulging my muscles, perking my ears, listening to Mary's praise—"Good boy!" she was saying and patting my neck—suddenly I stopped dead in my tracks and sniffed.

Hoffman!

In drastically altered mood I bore the usual procedure, which, ordinarily, soothed me until I quite forgot myself and time. Mary removing my tack, the silent Orville assisting her. The hose, the soap, the towels. Oil. Cotton swabs. The delight of the classically formed young horse being cared for. But not now. Now I could do no more than grudgingly accept their ministrations.

"What's wrong with him?" asked Orville.

"Don't know, Daddy," Mary answered.

Hoffman! But where?

They finished; my mood was dark.

"In you go," said Orville, leading me to my freshly mucked-out stall and stepping inside, turning, expecting me to follow.

Balk? Indeed I balked. One sniff was enough; the fight that ensued was like nothing in Orville's long experience, as sense-lessly—to him—I pulled, reared, yanked Orville nearly off his feet, then bucked, swerved, set in motion a sympathetic staccato agitation in all the horses up and down our side of the barn.

"What the hell!" said Orville under his breath, Mary running to help.

They led me away, I ceased my struggling. They walked me, tried again. Refusal. More walking, more cajolery. In the end I submitted, of course, yet never again, for as long as I was at Elroy Park, did I regain completely my peace of mind.

Yes, that morning Hoffman had passed his water not in London Bobby's stall but in mine. And he was to do so repeatedly, as now I knew, but erratically, whenever he could, so that I was forever anticipating his contamination yet could never be sure when it would confront me, that fuming I could hardly breathe. Thus he had intuited a further and still crueler way to undermine my spirit. And the final injustice: it was Hoffman himself who owned the only two-year-old filly at Elroy Park to have caught and held the maleness of my attention. She was large and white, as tall as myself but heavier. She was aptly named Etruscan Glory and just as aptly known by everyone as Honey. I could not help myself, I could not resist Honey's frank announcement of her gender in her size, her proportions, the way she carried herself, the look in her eye, the strong and ancient mustiness of her perfume—Honey the big bland milky female, I the tall sleek lively male. She knew my feelings, she returned them. And this was not at all the romantic mystery I had shared so long ago with that other filly, whose name I had in fact forgotten. This was the lust that was mine only in maturity. But ignominiously enough, she was Hoffman's horse.

Had it not been for his filthy habit and choice of stall, I might have been spared. However, Hoffman was crafty, Hoffman was clever. One man pissing in a horse's stall—mine!—and for that I was doomed.

Exactly. A curious warping of an old tale. A twisting of tragedy. Even now, from the vantage of old age, from the distance of my more than twenty years of misery, still I am more sharply honed than ever to the sound of Hoffman's squealing rage and the sight of him rushing onto the track, fat as he was.

It was bound to come, that morning, how could it not? Bound to happen. My star was well on its way to sizzling extinction in a dark sea, the horse gods were calling unanimously for my ruin. Hoffman was their instrument, Honey their lure. Naturally there would come the morning when she and I would be out on the track at the same time, and alone, and our riders friendly toward each other and unsuspecting.

Exactly.

Mary and I were earlier than usual, as early as church bells, which was one of the few figures of speech Orville allowed himself, and we were the only horse and exerciser on the track, except for our guardian JD and except, all unexpectedly, for Honey and the boy who always rode her, Bud.

Mary greeted JD—a few words, a gesture—then slowly we approached young Bud on Hoffman's filly. Surprise, coincidence, good fortune, or so I thought. I had never been in such proximity to Honey, had never had the chance to be absorbed by the sight of her, the smell. This close she was larger and whiter and, despite her youth, more matronly of purpose than I had remembered, and when she gave me the briefest glance and nickered, I was beside myself and nearly broke stride, lost my footing.

"How's things?" said Bud, a boy of a mere thirteen years, who was nonetheless already renowned for his riding at Elroy Park.

"Can't complain, Bud," said Mary.

"Dating?" said Bud, staring off down the track, studying his horse. He was a head shorter than Mary and much younger than she, much lighter—he weighed no more than seventy pounds or so—and was wizened, serious, the opposite of Mary in every way, gloomy boy to her cheery girl, yet more the dried-out man than boy. His hands were immense.

"Oh, Bud," said Mary, "you know I never go out with anyone!"

"Too bad," said Bud.

On they chatted, that unsuspecting pair, and on we loped, Honey and I, and despite the naturalness of our appearance we were shocked, and equally so, at the ease with which we recognized the inevitable. How sudden was our mutual willingness to disregard racetrack protocol, horse etiquette, common sense, and all for the sake of the moment that—how well we knew it!—was but a breath away. Honey's eyes were large, lit to a liquid amber by all her body's declaration, and her nostrils were enlarged, flaring, red-streaked, glistening. She spoke to me, I answered, I smelled her syrupy secretions. Pheromones, genetic beckonings—

never had two horses succumbed to each other so swiftly, with so few preliminaries.

"Let's go," I heard Bud say through my distraction.

"Right on," came Mary's echo.

They meant to change pace, to pick up speed, to run. Honey and I exchanged fleeting looks of apprehension: it was now, we knew, or not at all. Now! The unthinkable!

She broke. I broke. I turned broadside to Honey and the startled Bud and stopped short, whirled, bucked as I had not bucked before. Up went Mary, down, just as Bud shot over Honey's head and, like some wounded bat, struck the turf, sprawled flat on his face. Commotion, whinnying, a tangle of dark legs and white. Catastrophe, imminent success! Once we had rid ourselves of our riders—despite their skills they were no match for the heat of the horse—there was no stopping us. Before Bud and Mary could so much as pick themselves up, Honey and I assumed our positions, went with not one false step to our purpose. Gloriously she braced herself, bravely I rose.

There were cries in the air, the sound of running feet.

"Stop!" someone shouted. "Catch them!" yelled another, though Honey and I were joined as though forever in one throbbing sculpture and were going nowhere. Then, finally, the voice I had all unknowingly awaited.

"Get off!" it squealed. "Leave her alone, fokker! You fokker!"

Too late, Hoffman. The deed was done.

But where was JD in this time of crisis? Why, at the far end of the track, it suddenly came to me, as I, contrite and spent, dropped back down into the chaos Honey and I had caused. Yes, our guardian, JD, and looking placidly the other way. But already a rude hand was snatching at my bridle, another at Honey's. What now except to rue that brief passion we had displayed in public for all to see?

Rue it I did.

Within the hour. Sooner.

If Honey and I had accomplished our purpose with all efficiency in the minimum of time allotted us, so too what followed—which is to say that no sooner had Orville taken charge of me in my joy and consternation, and begun to walk me with unfamiliar haste and an intention the more foreboding for being unstated, than I knew that retribution, whatever form it might assume, was already under way and would prove as swift and unavoidable as lust, its opposite. My complete docility, as Orville rushed me from the track, to the jeers and catcalls of the various grinning men and girls who had been witness to the escapade just past, was only a mask for my regret, which was sudden, and my anxiety, which was all at once severe. What, I wondered, would they do to me?

The worst they could, of course.

Luckily for me I had not long to brood on my immediate future, alone in my stall had hardly time to be amused at the congratulations I heard Bob softly offering me from the other side of our partition. Yes, Honey and I had achieved a mighty union. But what sundering would it provoke?

Men's voices. Footsteps. Orville, Doc Hanes, who was one of the old-time veterinarians at Elroy Park, JD. Not a sign of Mary.

In they came, grimly surrounding me in all my feigned innocence and sweetness of disposition.

"Causing trouble, eh?" said Doc Hanes, setting down his satchel and running his palm gently along my flank.

"Intractable," said Orville.

"Well," said Doc Hanes, "this may help."

"It better," said Orville flatly. "If not, we'll get rid of him."

Doc Hanes nodded, JD stroked my nose, Doc Hanes turned, knelt a moment beside his satchel. I did not startle at the cold syringe held upright in his left hand.

"Rompun," JD said.

"It works," said Doc Hanes. "We'll dope him a bit, then put him under. But just long enough to do the job."

That small good-natured man appeared to know in advance that I would not resist his approach, the touch of his hand on my haunch, the shot he was about to administer. And so I stood for him, placidly, and did not react in any way when I felt the needle. Nor did I resist what followed, but in fact welcomed the blurring of my vision, the hazy sense of well-being that began to suffuse my blood, my flesh, my consciousness. The mildest puzzlement, a faint and unfamiliar pleasure, and then I knew that I was beginning to droop, to sag, to sink into a horse's time out of time. Dimly I felt the jab of the second shot—the barbiturate, I later learned—with indifference heard the receding voices.

"You push, Doc," said Orville. "JD and I will ease him down."

So I yielded to Doc Hanes and leaned to the side, trusted my weight to JD and the tight-lipped Orville, sank until I was stretched out flat in a sea of straw. I thought of calling to Bob, of reassuring him, but could not. Submit, I told myself, submit. And down I continued, though my earthly self lay solidly on wood and straw, down in the longest and slowest possible descent until I came to rest in the very depths of my own darkness. But I was not alone. That darkness rarely visited by horse and never by man was now populated by shadowy humans and another horse—no, two!—and I was anything but passive. Could it be? Again? Had I not had enough of Honey? Had I not learned my lesson? Apparently not!

For I was my own new horse inside myself. And I was mounted—yes!—and not on Honey as I had just been but on another. Who? And now I was not urgent, not reckless, as, in the midst of a coupling that had had no beginning and, presumably, would never end, I savored my massiveness contained by my partner's and, so joined, speculated vaguely on her identity. But could I fail to know this mare beneath me or to recognize that great jet-black stallion skulking in the peripheral shadows around the scene that was mine? Harod, my sire, I acknowledged in passing, and dismissed him. And who else? Who the placid grateful mare if not Kate? It was she, of course. And I was no brute to her receptiveness but instead was her coequal in that singular and stationary statue that we horses are all destined to create. Not King Harod atop calm Kate but Sweet William instead. Yes, this was the case, and yet it caused in me no undue pride, only a fleeting shade of sympathy for my excluded sire. Was I in fact the prospective sire? I might have been, except that from this union there could come no issue. I understood, I was not aggrieved at the thought. Nothing in fact could disturb my prolonged tranquillity on Kate.

In situ! I remembered all at once and, I confess, with pleasure, as Kate and I pumped on like a lone ship pulsing across a purple sea, she the engine room—no, the entire ship!—and I the engine.

Never end, did I say? Oh, not a bit of it!

For in the midst of our quiet transport, and believing as firmly as any horse could possibly believe that I, all undeserving, had become the eternal stud horse, inseparable—literally!—from the eternal mare, I suddenly saw those faceless humans who had been lurking just beyond our sight and concentration come forward to a man and, arms outflung, soundless, speechless, crouching, darting about, close in upon Kate and me with unmistakable purpose. But could they? Did they dare? Had they the strength, the meanness of mind, to interfere with two great creatures so privately engaged? They did, they did! Yes, interrupt us was what they meant to do, pull us apart, leave us forever hanging, forever unfulfilled. So they laid hands on me, on Kate; ignoring them was impossible. They pushed, they tugged at the two of us, and I was slipping, losing my rightful place inside and atop the mare. Fight back? Resist? Of course I did, though first I clung to Kate with my wet forelegs and increased our rhythm, summoned my determination, tried to stay, could not, slipped off.

Brutal disengagement! Humiliating display of incompletion! Then I struggled against that ring of men—no faces, no voices— and attacked them, screamed, attempted to remount my Kate. Even as she faded, and the men too, all her spirit and substance dissolving forever before my eyes, I came awake, struggling, trumpeting my rage, my grief, my pain.

"God damn it!" I heard Orville say.

"I've got him!" said JD.

"Look out!" cried Doc Hanes, jumping to one side.

By now I was half upright, half down, my forelegs stiff, my

quarters still rooted heavily in the straw. What had they done to me? Did I not know? Yes, I knew, or knew increasingly in my returning consciousness and thanks mainly to the uncanny pain lodged somewhere beneath my silken tail, between my rear legs, at the nether heart of my haunches, the center of me. Yes, they had done their worst, and I could only struggle and fling myself about the stall.

"Some of them," said Doc Hanes with a gasp, "behave this way. But it's unusual," he continued between short breaths. "Ordinarily, when they've been kept under this short a time," he managed to say, dodging me and Orville and JD as well, "they're not violent when they come out of it."

"Violent!" Orville said, the scorn and anger all too evident in his cold voice. "I'll show him something about violent!" So saying, he did what he had never done to me in our many days and months together, and drew back his fist, and, small though he was, struck a blow to the side of my head that stunned me, rocked my entire frame.

I stood still, my poor head swayed. Orville and JD and Doc Hanes left my stall. And did I hear London Bobby voicing his concern through the partition? I did, but I could not answer. Gloom and despondency were my companions now, for now I was no colt, let alone prospective sire. The first horse ever to appear those myriad millennia ago was a tiny form of equine life no larger than a fox, and yet from him all the rest of us—genders, herds, breeds—emerged over time. And now, in me, the little primal fox was dead. Never would he reappear in any modern-day colt or filly sired by me. Never. Oh, he would continue on, reproduced endlessly and in endless variation, though in appropriately large size, throughout all the millennia of the horse. But never would I recognize myself in any day-old colt or filly born to mare. No twenty mares a year for me. Not even one. Never again. Between my hind legs there hung no future, but a void.

So it was over, brief ritual intended to tame me, to quench my fire.

There followed five days of peace or, more accurately, despair.

Or both. Five days of being left undisturbed, of listening moodily to London Bobby's low-toned attempts to cheer me with accounts of his mornings on the track and news of Honey, who, of course, was the laughingstock of all the horses at Elroy Park, though secretly envied by the fillies and all the more lusted after by the colts. Five days of languid inactivity and pain in the place where I felt most vulnerable. With me the while was Mary, sharing my despondency, pampering me, simulating London Bobby's good cheer. My best moments came at the beginning and ending of the day, when Mary would lead me gently onto the concrete slab and hose me down. I enjoyed the sensation of the clear water sliding down my coat in sheets, valued Mary's humming, the caress of her wet hands as she massaged me. Then the final gesture, for which I waited with faint anxiety and pleasure both. Lead rein in one hand, soft and sopping sponge in the other, a furrow in Mary's brow—her only thought was to spare me additional discomfort—swiftly she would step behind me, raise my tail, carefully thrust hand, sponge, and forearm between my hind legs as far as she could reach. Then pressing the sponge up under me as much as she dared, "Zoop!" she would say and draw back her forearm in one swift stroke. Then again, "Zoop!" and again, lightly, a look of concern and amusement on her round pretty face. With each exclamation and coursing of the sponge my hindquarters flinched upward in a reflex I tried unsuccessfully to avoid. However, the brief stab of pain was as unavoidable as the reflex, the relaxation that followed as soothing as the knowledge that it was Mary herself, none other, who touched and soothed the tender place of my trauma.

Zoop. Zoop.

But did my emasculation achieve its hoped-for effect? Orville must have thought it did, at least until my last and greatest explosion at Elroy Park—for in due course explode I did, revenging myself on the lot of them once and for all while at the same time incurring my ultimate disgrace, as sooner or later I knew I must. Patiently I awaited that opportunity. In the meanwhile, once my brief period of recuperation was at an end, I found myself quite the same horse as I had been before my gelding. Oh, I had my moments of disbelief, uncertainty, even grief. Nonetheless I had been deprived of my gender but not my identity, the loss of the one by no means necessitating the loss of the other, as most horses assume. I knew that in days to come I would forget what had happened and hence be unable to account for sudden listlessness, indifference, poor appetite. And there would be those moments when I would be the dupe of my former self and attempt to mount this mare or that, only to remember my new condition and fall back and turn away, defeated again as I would forever be. But for now I might have undergone no change at all.

My workouts resumed as if there had been no interruption in my routine: transgression apparently paid for and forgiven, Orville ready enough to test me again on the track. And I was the same horse as before except faster now, more consciously determined to do Mary's bidding and to justify the faith that I knew Orville still had in me.

In due time I entered my first race and, with Mary aboard, carried her to an easy win. That day, dressed in her spanking white britches and diminutive boots, fresh silks that made her look as bright as a maypole—that was JD's word—Mary could hardly contain the pleasure she took in our victory, and her vindication was mine as well. So the sum of my short but glorious career at Elroy Park: seven races in all, seven wins. But these were no ordinary wins, since in each race I ran, thanks to training, perfect timing, and a baffling ability that no one could quite account for, there always came the moment when Mary asked for my display of heart, whereupon I commenced that acceleration for which I became renowned, a proportional increase of speed that took us from where it began to the finish line in an upward ratio that was beyond reason or possibility and meant that I ended every race half again the number of lengths ahead of my closest competitor as in the race before it, my first victory being in itself by twenty lengths. Best behavior, best horse, best jock, as Mary now called herself. We took no unfair advantages, never blocking another horse's way, never bumping another horse, intentionally or unintentionally. We did not fight to win but merely won and in a manner unmatched by any other two-year-old in the history of Elroy Park. No crowd cheered for its idols as those crowds cheered for us, and many a person owed the fulfillment of some wildest dream to us. Wreaths and trophies, photographers. But it goes without saying that my every race was marred by some mishap or other. In my first, for example, I started to pass an already exhausted and clearly terrified bay colt—the same I had heard the woman trainer complaining about in my earliest days at the track, that talentless dull-coated two-year-old owned by the anxious man totally ignorant of the track, Thoroughbreds, horse racing—at the very moment the poor creature's two front legs buckled beneath him. Yes, I looked, I did not alter my acceleration, still I saw his two front legs break off just below the knees and, held in place by nothing more than blue brushing boots, flap about uselessly for several seconds until he crashed forward and down, legs flying off like bits of wreckage from a car crash. Few horses are exterminated on the track itself and in full view of the public, but that day that hapless horse was one of them. And still longer the season's list of calamities at Elroy Park—a disastrous and, as it turned out, fatal pileup on a turn; a rider's fall; more broken legs; death of one horse by heart attack. Still more. But from them all I emerged unscathed, undaunted, charmed victor as the crowd expected.

Exemplary behavior, perfect form. Yet in fact there was one place on the track, one point in time in the running of each race, in which I indulged my former and true self. The start of the race, the starting gate. Even in training I had learned that I could cause considerable trouble at the starting gate without doing any real harm. Here I could be as violent as I wished, as recalcitrant, and still no horse or person suffered, least of all myself.

"Oh, Willy," Mary would whisper every time we were led toward the gate, "not again!"

But it was always the same, and in fact it became my second trademark, along with my unheard-of acceleration. First to finish, last to enter the starting gate. Such was my way. All the others would be safely in their places, set and waiting, before the usual half-dozen men turned back to Mary and me, alone together on the track except for the faithful JD, and, all at once, summoning their courage, fighting their frustration, swarmed upon Mary and me and herded us roughly toward that one still empty place in line. And then how free I felt to resist them! What pleasure I took in taxing the patience of my peers, in delaying the race! I jigged and jogged in circles, to the left, the right, then suddenly backed off, just as suddenly proceeded calmly up to that narrow place crying out for my presence, only to swerve, at the last minute, and dash away and stop, leer back at my pursuers in all their fist-shaking anger. It was always the same, with variations, wasting all the time I could just short of disqualification. Usually I ended up with the crowd of men grunting and pushing until I was at last in place but with my hindquarters crashing down behind me, dragging, and my head in the air, poor Mary balancing atop me as best she could. Then came the bell, as always, interrupting the anger of my fellows and their riders, and up I leapt and off I shot—to win again. Curiously enough, the crowd cheered almost as strongly for the turmoil I brought to the start of the race as it did for the fleetness and confidence with which I won. My odds fell, my fame increased, there were no losers.

Rare horse. Phenomenal performances. Seven unprecedented victories.

Then ruin.

I won with ease, similarly I brought about my ruin.

One peaceful afternoon the all but forgotten opportunity I had been secretly awaiting was abruptly and without warning mine to seize—and I seized it. I failed to recognize the circumstances that one by one appeared and slyly arranged themselves so as to lure from the shadows no other than the figure of my own ruin, but appear they did: the peaceful afternoon itself, a passing burst of Indian summer, Mary and I alone in my stall. I could not have been feeling better in my horse's skin and was quietly drinking from one of my freshly filled water buckets; Mary was brushing my long tail. My lips rested on the cool surface of the water, I gave myself up to the pleasure of taking in the water with hardly a sound, hardly a movement in my long neck. Then Mary said a few words over her shoulder. I raised my head, droplets hanging foolishly from my cool lips.

"You better not come in here, Bruno."

Exactly. I might have known.

"Sure I come in," said Hoffman. "Why not?"

Nonetheless he hesitated, glanced about to be certain he was unobserved, then drew my stall door slightly open.

"The horse is harmless," said Hoffman in a thick whisper and with evident self-satisfaction.

"I warned you," said Mary with a shrug, a smile.

My first move was deft and undramatic. Before Hoffman could so much as graze Mary's arm with his half-extended hand, I shifted and planted my left front hoof on Hoffman's foot. Pinned him with all my twelve hundred pounds. I leaned on him, I remained as I was, I listened to the small bones breaking in Hoffman's foot. He went white.

"Off!" he managed to say, but nothing more.

Mary dropped the brush.

Then realizing that Hoffman was about to collapse from his anguish, swiftly and still without a sound I reared, and again using my left front hoof, I gave the Foreigner a good clip on his shoulder, thereby breaking his collarbone as deftly as any such bone could be broken.

"Orville!" Mary screamed. "Orville!"

But there was time enough to do what I meant to do. The stage was mine, the hour mine, Hoffman could not escape my stall or purpose, could not even cower at my feet, since now I clamped my jaw on his wounded shoulder and held him fast. Gently I shook him, slowly and steadily I closed my jaw, attentive only to the crunching sound I was able to extract at will from his shoulder. Laziest silence, purest sound. Hoffman did not lose consciousness, I saw to that.

"Daddy!" Mary screamed.

From Hoffman, as if in echo of Mary's cry for help, there came a sob, a groan, a sudden high-pitched wail so faint that it reached no ears but mine. I let him go, I struck his face sharply with the side of my head. A spurt of blood, an uncomprehending look in Hoffman's eyes.

"Gott!" he whispered. "Good Gott!" And glowering at me, he cupped a hand to his nose, clutched his shoulder.

On it went, a rib here, a shinbone there. I persisted, I paced my vehemence. I broke the nose already broken, reared before the stricken Foreigner and dangled my upraised hooves in his face. Then with a quick kick I cracked his sternum. I meant to harm him, I did him harm enough, while Mary wept and watched the entire spectacle, and through the silence Orville came a-running.

So I had my way and took my revenge, sparing Hoffman's life but not his person. For that, no more than that, my own career on the track was ended. Mary begged Orville to change his mind, aghast I heard his adamant refusal. He was exasperated, he said. What I had done, he said, was the last straw, the last pin in the cushion. He washed his hands of me once and for all, and that was that.

His speech was uncharacteristic, his decision—to me—unjust. Yet there it was. The next day I left Elroy Park forever. My only consolation was this—that each time I had won, poor London Bobby had lost. Seven wins, seven dismal losses. At the last minute, then, Orville decided to rid himself of London Bobby as well as me, and sent us off in the same van. Thus at least Bob and I remained together in disgrace.

CHAPTER FOUR

•

STANLEY & SON. PAUL J. GOOSSEN, MGR.
BOB'S DESPERATE HOUR

It was a dark night. A stormy night. There was rain. There was wind. The beaded trees were helpless but to accept their drenching. The pitch-black air was unnaturally heavy with summer heat. Not a light shone.

There was a road, a narrow road, empty and slippery, that went its way—somewhere—through the stormy night. There was a horse trailer and a pickup truck that pulled the trailer along the empty road. Inside the trailer were two horses separated by a shoulder-high partition covered in worn and tattered padding. Side by side in the cab of the pickup truck were a man, a boy, and a girl. A father and son. A girl. The father and son were large and fat. They were dressed identically in sweatshirts and tight jeans and western-style boots that proclaimed in every way that the boots were intended to be worn by large men or boys who spent most of their time on horseback. The son was indistinguishable from the father except for his hair, which was shoulder length and black and stringy, oily. And for the frightened look in his eye. The girl drove. She was a mere sliver of a girl, short and skinny, who always spoke in a high-pitched twangy whine. She was known as Sissy. The boy, who sat between the girl and the man, was Bo. The father, Stanley, sat to the outside, with his window down and the crook of his arm protruding into the storm. He spoke. He laughed. The father.

Two horses. London Bobby and Sweet William. Poor Bob, as I called him. Willy, as I was to Bob.

The trailer was small and decrepit, it lurched from side to side or swayed precariously on the slippery road, though we were moving at a slow pace. An uneasy pace. Feeling our way. It was darker inside the trailer than without, and the noise of the wind and rain was louder. The rain beat down upon the metal roof above our flattened ears like nailheads on tin. Directly in front of us was a narrow open window through which it was impossible to see or to glean anything of our whereabouts or of our condition except that we were making our way through the storm in darkness, without headlights. Between the narrow window and Bob's head and mine hung two hay nets stuffed with hay. But it was dusty hay, inedible. And how could we think of eating hay, poor Bob and I, when we did not know what was happening to us or why?

"Faster," came Stanley's voice above the sound of the engine and the rain.

A burst of Sissy's indignant twang in answer.

The sound of springs, the sound of metal. The roar of the storm through which we passed as through a tunnel. I lost my footing, fell to the side against the partition, felt Bob fall the other way and come up short against the trailer. The hay was old, there was no water, beneath our wobbling hooves the straw in which we stood, or tried to stand, was thick with half-buried horse dung dropped by other horses. A seedy carpet of uncleanliness, indifference. I heard Bob tugging on his lead rein, fastened short to a ringbolt. I swayed, fell back, my head jerked at the end of my own short leather rein.

There was a jolt, the trailer swayed out from under us, a wheel slipped off the shoulder, lurched back up and on again as Sissy struggled with the steering wheel and Stanley laughed and told her to go faster.

A shivering. A pounding. A swaying. On it went. Then stopped. Abruptly.

A long pause.

"All right," said Stanley all at once and in a voice that was loud, close to us, audible in every way but baffling. "Take them out. The little one first. He's easiest."

End of the road? End of the night? The storm? End of time? So it seemed, for indeed we had stopped, though Bob and I yet rocked and swayed on our unsteady hooves. Truck and trailer were standing still. Sissy had turned off the engine. And the wind had stopped, the last sheets of rain were coming down, abating, trickling.

Tense? Unnerved? Expecting we knew not what? Exactly. How else? We had braced ourselves against the erratic sensations of the drive, to each other had admitted our bewilderment. In days past, months past, we had been moved from stable to stable, barn to barn. We had grown thin, we had raced, I winning in my former way, Bob always losing. But now for time I could not count we had been kept idle, untended and, or so it seemed to us, for no purpose. It had been a long decline, a strange decline, though recently our feed had been increased, and we had regained most of our weight. Once again we looked well-treated enough.

There was a clattering of boots, a slamming of doors, behind us the ramp went down. Banging and clanging. Chains rattling.

"Hurry up," said Stanley from behind us, at the foot of the ramp. "Bring me that little horse."

Sissy scurried into action at the sound of his voice. Sniveling and whining to herself and moving as quickly as she could at the sound of a grown man's bullying voice, suddenly she appeared in the darkness inside the trailer with Bob and me, wiping her face on her sleeve and fumbling with Bob's lead rein, unfastening him.

"Come on," said Stanley, as a late squall hurried by overhead and rain fell in a burst and once again died to a trickle. "It's wet out here!"

"You heard him," Sissy said under her breath. "Back up!" She held Bob's lead rein short, gave his chest a push. Bob took one obedient tentative step to the rear. Another. He was ready, as always, to accept the worst, while I, for once, here, in this sagging two-horse trailer at the edge of a country road—nowhere, somewhere—was uncertain.

But not for long.

I waited, I listened, the space where Bob had stood was empty, from outside and below me came the sound of footsteps, fumbling, soft voices, and then, behind me, the ramp down which poor Bob had disappeared, backward, rose up again, clanged shut. I was alone, though common sense assured me that London Bobby was only feet away, a small gray horse standing in the wet darkness with a man and a boy and a girl on a country road in the aftermath of a midnight storm. But why? What sense was this? Why was Bob outside and I within? What were they doing?

I listened. Nothing. I tried to swing around my head, could not, of course. Restrained. Then suddenly in the metallic darkness of the otherwise empty two-horse trailer it came to me that what I was hearing was just that—silence. Prolonged silence. Significant silence. The kind of silence that cries out the very secrecy that it is meant to cloak. A silence more claustrophobic than confinement. A silence loud with the unnatural sounds that it conceals.

What were they doing?

But I had no time, I told myself, not a moment longer could I support this silence.

There is nothing more violent than an agitated horse who has broken loose in a horse trailer. And I was an agitated horse—for Bob's sake—and I was loose. The lead rein snapped with my first heave backward, I kicked and flung myself about, head and flanks and hooves, as if to topple the very horse trailer that contained me.

"Sissy!" shouted Stanley. "He's loose!"

"Hear him," came Sissy's whine.

"Get up there, then," shouted Stanley. "Stop him!"

A few indistinguishable chords struck on the banjo that was Sissy's voice.

Still I kicked and struggled, knowing that at least I was interrupting Stanley's plan, whatever it was, and sending far and wide my horse alarm through the night. But to see was my purpose, and see I must. To turn around. To thrust my head into the darkness and see for myself that Bob was safe—or not. So in the midst of my racket I drew my haunches to the left until they rested against the side of the trailer, then swung them to the right and in that single blow broke the fastenings that held the partition in place behind me. A crack of metal. Another shout from Stanley. And then, and just as Sissy crept up into the front of the trailer, I shoved aside the partition and twisted around, stood still, looked down upon the scene spread dimly beneath my eyes.

The blurred figure of London Bobby, patient as ever. The equally blurred figure of Bo, who was holding Bob. And Stanley— like Bo he was visible thanks mainly to his white sweatshirt—who was stretching wide the mouth of an immense transparent sack. I saw the plastic shape with which Stanley wrestled—it was form- less, wrinkled, glistening, collapsing about his hands and arms down there in the darkness—and instinctively, and without a moment's hesitation, I reared, I trumpeted a warning to poor docile Bob, and once again I kicked as best I could in that small space and gathered myself, readied myself to clamber over the top of the more than chest-high ramp and jump to London Bobby's rescue.

"Pop!" cried Bo, who rarely talked. "That one's escaping!"

"Sissy," shouted Stanley, "catch hold of him!"

"Cain't!" yelled Sissy shrilly.

"Why not?" shouted Stanley.

"Afeerd!" yelled Sissy.

"For Christ's sake," shouted Stanley. "Of what?"

"Smushing!" came Sissy's plaintive voice.

With that I ceased my struggle. In a trice I thought better of this attempt to liberate myself and so join Bob. Yes, even in the midst of my exertions I had heard her words, was thunderstruck by that pathetic thought. Harm the ragged little Arkansas horse girl, as Stanley called her? Certainly not. Crush her against the ringing wall of the trailer? Not for the world. After all, this hapless spidery person was only a frantic girl forever at Stanley's beck and call. And for all my tribulations, I trusted her. Intuitively. Furthermore, I told myself, I had already delayed the night's dark proceedings and would delay them more by compliance. Stanley had no choice but to remove me from the trailer lest I destroy it. And Sissy could not guide me down from the trailer without the help of the now thwarted Stanley and his frightened son. Thus I reasoned, thus I changed.

Violent horse no longer violent. Gentle. Perfectly safe. Turned himself around of his own accord. Head to the front, tail to the rear. Well and good. Surprising, but well and good.

More silence. A moment too much.

"Stanley," called Sissy, "you there?"

"Of course I'm here."

"His halter ain't broke, Stanley. I got a rope on him. And, Stanley? He's a right nice horse."

Vulgar expression from Stanley. Chains, dry hinges. A banging sound, ramp lowered. A small leathery palm on my nose.

"All right," she whispered, "you just back down now. You're a good boy!"

One awkward angular step. Another. My front hooves higher than my rear, my entire body canted steeply. A slow progress. A difficult progress.

"Take him down the road a ways," said Stanley, so close now that I smelled some sort of hot sauce on his breath, felt his heavy voice brushing my ear.

"But, Stanley," said the little Arkansas horse girl in surprise, "what's that . . . ?"

Then I too saw London Bobby. Poor Bob. Lying flat on his side. In the darkness. On a wet patch of country road. His gray color turned to silver, his coat wet, his tail stretched out behind him as it would have flown had he been galloping. For some reason Bo was still standing at his head and holding the leather lead that sagged gently upward into his fat fist. But Bob's head? His blurred and milky head? Even as I stared down at him it began to rain, softly at first, then harder. And was it possible? Drops of rain visible on London Bobby's head and upper neck and yet not on the rest of him? Droplets dancing and pattering on what I took to be a membrane stretched tight around his neck and head? *After-birth* flashed through my mind. Then *sack*. And could any horse alive still breathe inside such a deadly tissue shrunken about his head, his jaws, his nostrils? *No,* I thought. *Suffocation* was what I thought. Oh, they were trying to smother poor Bob to death, that swollen man with his own son for accomplice!

Sissy screamed.

"Pop!" shouted Bo. "He's after me!"

Whereupon Bo turned as if to run, as I thought he would, but to my surprise he stayed where he was and merely flopped to all fours beside London Bobby's silvery outstretched form. Flopped down and curled himself as tightly as he could into a fat and trembling ball, his head to his knees, his arms drawn protectively about his head, his broad defenseless backside raised.

"Pop!" Bo cried once more in muffled desperation as, for the second time, Sissy screamed and Stanley gave vent to vulgarity.

I meant to attack. I meant to spare not a breath of his life. I meant to kick Bo's head, arms or no arms, so hard, so swiftly that his round cowering body would become a lifeless sprawl. But I could not. For all my readiness, and even as I swung my haunches, turned, prepared to give Bo the one resounding mortal kick I had in mind, still I could not. After all, Bo's cowardly submission was a plea for mercy. And Bo's fear, as suddenly I knew, was as much of the father whose help he had called upon as it was of the retribution he expected and deserved from me.

So I turned on Stanley.

I wheeled. I clattered a few steps this way and that on the wet black deserted road. Then stopped. Stared at him. Suffered a moment of disbelief. Suffered a weakening of spirit. Thought of flight. Then thought of Bo, fleetingly, and thought of Hoffman, importantly. And recovered myself, reared up, dropped down.

Stanley loomed before me in the road. And Stanley was armed. He wanted nothing short of my life, as I had wanted Bo's. But with a difference, as I saw at once, since the murderous instrument that Stanley held athwart his chest had been fashioned in advance and for no purpose but to inflict what would look like accidental death on the second of the two horses he had meant to kill that night. One with a plastic sack, one with a pike.

Yes, it was some sort of pike that Stanley now aimed at me, a thick wooden staff pointed at its deadly end. Heavy, sharp, unbreakable. Now lowered in Stanley's grip and aimed at me. His face was animated, his eyes were on mine, his body was braced for the thrust that would drive home the point of the staff.

Bo cowered, Stanley prepared to lunge.

Where was Sissy?

At Elroy Park I had thought that I had met the worst of men in Hoffman. But Stanley, as I now knew, was worse than that. Injury, I had decided, was good enough for Hoffman. But injury, no matter how crippling, was not good enough for Stanley. Woe to the horse that kills a man—how often had I heard that admonition?—but I would kill Stanley, and not merely in self-defense, or Stanley would kill me.

Where was Sissy?

Surely the entire night was listening, tiny hidden birds quaking and listening, old barn owls awake and alert, listening, all domestic animals safe and warm, far and wide, all awaiting the outcome of this unnatural contest between man and horse. Earlier the living creatures had heard my equine bellowing. Now they heard the silence of my combative self filling the night.

It was an unequal contest, as weighted in my favor as had been my punishing of Hoffmann, and as easily concluded. There was an expectant light in Stanley's face, an eagerness more appropriate to amusement than to fatality. He crouched, he studied me, he was not intimidated by the awesome spectacle I must have presented to him there at the edge of the imminent ruination of his crude plan. But if I had reared again at that moment, exposing to Stanley my chest and underside, well might he have moved, as swiftly as any fat man could move, and been successful in lodging some considerable length of his murderous stick inside me. But I did not rear. Instead I did the opposite. I lowered my head and, eyes and jaws at a level not much above the surface of the road, began to swing my head from side to side, dragonlike. Thus throwing him off guard, I attacked him. And no sooner had he started back and lowered his pike than up I rose for a second time and towered above him like the invincible wraith that I was, though in flesh and blood, and kicked him with one front hoof as I had meant only moments before to kick Bo with one of my hind hooves—in the head. Down went Stanley, dropping his pike, with not a thought to plan, son, horse girl, and sprawled on his belly.

How was I to be certain that I had destroyed Stanley's life? Simply enough. By planting my right front hoof on Stanley's head. Then my full weight on my right front hoof. A smushing, as Sissy might have said.

That done, I swung around, all fear and agony, to face what I had assumed was a certainty—London Bobby already dead. The heat of his life already cold. Oh, but praise be to the horse gods, such was not the case! Wrong for once, and happily! For there, when I turned, were Sissy and Bo as well, both kneeling at London Bobby's head and together rending the last of the plastic, stripping it in long filmy strands from his eyes, cheeks, nostrils. And Bob was not at all a suffocated carcass, as I had thought to see him, but a living horse, a breathing horse, a small horse still surviving the snares of destruction that had been spread for us.

And Bo and Sissy? Two crouching figures ministering to a prostrate horse. And even as I held my peace and stood watching them, Bo, his plump face whiter and wetter than ever, made a small high-pitched nasal sound high in his head. Sissy answered. Another wordless sound from Bo, another answering sound from Sissy. Like horses. And then, in his softest and most uncertain tone, Bo spoke.

"Pop was laughing," he said. "Back there in the truck. He was laughing. Why?"

"Skully Equine Mutual. Said so himself."

"Don't understand," said Bo.

"Insurance," said Sissy.

"Still don't understand," said Bo.

"Kill horses," said Sissy. "Collect insurance."

A pause. A long pause. Not to be broken. Heads bowed, hands and fingers shredding plastic. London Bobby shifting, moving his head, looking up at them.

Soon he was standing. Soon we were once more side by side in the two-horse trailer and creeping onward through the passing night. Soon, near dawn, as we could see, truck and trailer were once more slowing down, stopping.

Slamming of doors. Footsteps. What now?

Again there came a metallic clanking, rattling, banging. Not behind us, as we might reasonably have thought, but at our heads, outside, below us. Then the slamming doors, the loud sound of the engine, the fading sound of the engine. Silence again.

So Sissy with the help of Bo had carried us off, far from the figure lying inexplicably on a country road, and then she had stopped. Uncoupled us. Abandoned us. Disappeared forever.

And so early that morning London Bobby and I were found— two horses locked inside a trailer left standing at the side of a road. A different road. A happier road by far.

Still, for all concerned, a mystery.

To this day the doubt returns. From time to time it still assails me. Was I mistaken? Was Orville not the man and horseman that I had thought he was? Did he consign Bob and me to that most unsuited racehorse owner in ignorance or, worse still, indifference? Could he have known what that ill-advised decision held in store for us? Impossible, I tell myself. Orville's way with horses was beyond praise itself. And Orville was thought by everyone to be as good a judge of men as he was of horses. Yet having thus insisted anew on the unassailability of Orville's character, I am immediately beset again by a single doubt. Once, that is, I had overheard my trainer telling Mary that horses are like women. In a crisis, he said, a woman screams, a man thinks. Horses and women are screamers, he said, turning and walking away, not thinkers.

At the time I dismissed what Orville had said as readily as did

Mary. Orville's eccentricity, I thought, nothing more. An affectation as harmless as his tobacco chewing, his doughnuts. But in the days and months that followed my departure from Elroy Park, those sorry words came back to me, and even now they remain my only clue. The man who could speak such words, I had to admit, is precisely the man who could dispose of two Thoroughbreds to a shady fellow bent on horse killing.

A reprieve, of sorts. A second chance, of sorts. Down the heat-stricken highway.

Yes, a second chance—not to race, as it turned out, but rather a second chance to prove ourselves adaptable to the conformity expected of the domestic horse, and hence to enjoy the care and security to be found in the horse's conventional submissiveness to men, to women, even to children. Yes, once more we were carried off into hotter days toward another horse establishment, unlike any we had ever known, in a vast acreage where nothing grew and the gentle earth itself was denied us. But could it be? A horse establishment in a city? Was there any way in which London Bobby and I might have heard of the very word—city—or in dreams or nightmares have stumbled upon this bare notion of the urban world? Certainly not. What horse could even dream of a city let alone inhabit one? But such was our latest and still more paradoxical fate.

We were taken away, one morning, from an unfamiliar farm near a small village—Harmony was its name, the hamlet closest to the scene of our rescue and in miles not distant from Elroy Park—and in another van, empty except for ourselves and a fat black horsefly, whose buzzing presence was an omen had we only recognized it as such, were transported from nature's landscape, intended first and foremost to sustain the life of the horse, to a city. London Bobby and I, like most of our kind, trusted in nature, believed in nature, and had but the sparest experience of so much as the motor vehicle, that first sign of the agglomeration of humans who denied themselves the horse. What then was the city if not by definition a denial of the precious fundamentals of the horse's life?

So indeed we learned.

Alone with the fiendish horsefly we lumbered on, while the heat inside the van increased and our spirits flagged. To the south, to the southwest perhaps, ever farther from Millbank, that place of our beginnings, which, given our aborted careers, had all but vanished from memory and imagination alike. We smelled the heat that gathered and shimmered on the highway, smelled sand, smelled the dryness of abandoned bones.

Finally, from all around us, came the sound of other vehicles. That sound increased, became the noise of traffic. Exhaust fumes filled the van's interior, overpowering its natural smells—our steaming dung, our heady sweat—and so strong at times as to drug the horsefly into long periods of stuporous frustration. The van slowed, on all sides of us pressed that horde of vehicles more felt than seen and kept in motion, it appeared, by little more than the erratic energy of their blasting horns. Hot concrete, brief glimpses through our narrowed louvered windows of occasional drooping palm trees, as anomalous to these humid city streets as we ourselves. Then, on this the third morning since our departure, the horse van stopped at last, sank down on collapsing springs, came to rest like nothing so much as an old and rusted ship grounded forever on a sandbar.

Thus our arrival—unmistakable, inescapable—and thus our descent into what might have been the source of new life but instead, from our first sight of it, defined itself as more of the same and worse. Much worse. A rural island in a city? An oasis for horses within the limits of some vast municipality in which horses could not otherwise survive? Such, no doubt, had been the original purpose of Goossen Horses, as it was called. Or had Paul J. Goossen, Mgr., founder and still sole proprietor of this establishment, known from the start that Goossen Horses would serve no ends but his own and thrive on nothing but the shallow interest the city dweller might take in the living horse stabled on what

would otherwise have been only a city lot laid waste beneath
truckloads of soft rubbish and tin cans? No better than this was
Goossen Horses. In fact, it was worse. Much worse.

Headlong down the shaky ramp we went, London Bobby and
I, head-to-tail—his to mine—prepared once more to greet with
eagerness—genuine on his part, feigned for his sake, on mine—
what lay ahead, yet not at all prepared for the sight reserved only
for the horse so especially unfortunate as to become the property
of Paul J. Goossen. And what a sight it was, as far from the
conventional stable as was city street from sylvan green. No barn,
no comfortable box stalls, no shaded paddocks with white fences.
None of this, but only an oval of hard unhealthy soil as large as
a football field, as Paul J. Goossen liked to say, roofed over in
entirety by a tentlike immensity of metal sheets riveted in place
atop rusted girders and ringed about by metal cages open on all
sides but overhead protected by the sloping edges of the gigantic
roof. Here, in the vast dark empty earthen area surrounded by the
ring of cages, Paul J. Goossen practiced his equitation and gave
instruction to what he liked to call his bevy of local high school
beauties, a few awkward girls who wore ill-fitting black helmets
on the backs of their heads and throughout their riding lessons
tittered uncontrollably at Paul J. Goossen's every move and word.
As for the cages, in them Paul J. Goossen stabled his fifty horses,
as if we were nothing more than beasts in a zoo.

The place was bounded to the west by a lot heaped high with
the crushed and abandoned bodies of old cars, to the north and
east by busy streets, and to the south by one small barren plot
fenced in with electrified wire—how we jumped away at the
touch of it!—in which we horses, a few at a time, were allowed
to view the open sky but made to bear the cruelest light and
intensest possible heat of that low-lying southern sun. It was
hateful, this small ragged enclosure of hot sand, the more so
when, on the other side of the strand of deadly wire, a group of
small boys gathered with bats, with balls, with great leather
gloves that deformed their hands, and played their mindless game
until, worn out and angry at each other, they turned to taunting

us horses herded together behind the wire. A few dying palms, a construction site, a warehouse wall, the mounds of cracked and sweltering cars, the small boys wearing duck-billed caps twisted sideways on their small shaven heads, and, at their mercy, us horses. And always the sounds of traffic and the guttural sounds of Paul J. Goossen shouting at the ineptitude of his high school beauties.

Thus it was that merely to arrive at Goossen Horses was to suffer its abrasive antipathies as if forever, without past or future, to be listless or sullen or rebellious according to individual temperament, afflicted down to the last horse of us.

Paul J. Goossen had his personal mount, of course, a tall white hefty mare part draft horse, part Thoroughbred, a vain old animal trained to the tricks and mannerisms of the performing horse. Trixy, as she was aptly named, carried herself with the contemptible false majesty of the circus horse—she had in fact spent long years in a traveling circus—and pranced about the otherwise empty arena with Paul J. Goossen on her back and her head held high as if from between her ears there still arose the artificial plumes that, in her former days of glory, she had worn. Fatuous creature, silly horse, bearing Paul J. Goossen through solitary high-stepping maneuvers that did no more than polish her rider's Netherlandish pride and affront and baffle the rest of us. But Trixy was her owner's horse, his favorite, as heavy a horse as he was a man, and on her he lavished all his attention and special treats and special feed, thereby making Mother Horse, as we called her, more insufferably standoffish than she might otherwise have been. As owner and proprietor of that impoverished center of incongruity Goossen Horses, Paul J. Goossen, Mgr., wore white britches and black boots and rode without stirrups and carried two long whips with which he teased and guided Mother Horse while the rest of us, no mean lot of horses either, since most of us were Thoroughbreds who had come off the track, looked on from our cages and scoffed. Many a morning in that hot summer Paul J. Goossen rode to our glum appraisal and to a scattering of applause that came from the sidelines, where a few of his young girls always stood and watched. And many a morning Paul J. Goossen acknowledged their marveling with silent smiles and then dismounted and handed his horse to one of the elated girls, and seized his ringmaster's whip and spent an hour or two haranguing this or that poor girl as she bounced around the arena on one of the few among his fifty horses that he had trained to undergo such mean, uncomfortable ordeals. It goes without saying that Mother Horse was not confined to a cage or allowed to accompany the rest of us into that ignoble open space raggedly defined by the electrified wire.

Sounds and smells of the nearby traffic. Rider and white horse senselessly performing. Shouts of the small boys. Netherlandish shouts of the Manager, followed by long self-satisfied silences in which, with his naked hands, he positioned this or that skinny girl's thigh and calf against the sides of the horse. Senseless, all of it, and senseless especially the empty days and nights of those of us ignored, still waiting for what we did not know, except perhaps for the training—a tedious merciless business—that would make us suitable to the needs of Paul J. Goossen, Mgr., and his girls.

Mother Horse's Brood, as we thought of ourselves. And not one of us who was not depressed.

So London Bobby and I, like our fellows, longed only to be uncaged, longed only for freedom, such as it was. Better that dusty plot and better to be jolted by the electrified wire and taunted by the miniature ballplayers than to suffer the dreary hypocrisy of all that lay beneath the iron roof of Goossen Horses. Better by far, though in or out there was no escaping torment. Or so it seemed and so we thought. Until all at once relief of a sort was ours, thanks, paradoxically, to the little boys themselves.

But oh, the horsefly's auguring! How quickly submission to senselessness proved preferable to relief when relief so suddenly arrived!

A hot day. A humid day. Overhead a thick gray layer of dense wet air that concealed the light of the sun but not its heat. A fiery sun, though invisible. And outside and as listless as the dying palms, London Bobby and I alone within the perimeter of the electrified wire that we were learning painfully enough to avoid. And the boys. On such a hot and humid afternoon, mightn't London Bobby and I have been spared the boys?

The hotter and wetter and grayer the day, it seemed, the more competitive the boys became. Now in that desolate silence they were shouting and tugging on their duck-billed caps and flinging down their bats and scampering like spiders around their diamond, as they called it, and throwing their gigantic leather gloves high in the air and rushing toward each other as if every last one of them meant to drop in heat prostration. But they did not drop.

Ripped and ragged shorts or faded pairs of swimming trunks that were much too small, even for boys this obviously young and underfed. Bare and bloated chests smeared with sweat, streaked with dust. Tennis shoes unlaced. Contorted faces, obscenities. Two packs of angry boys. Hate and chaos, chaos and hate. Relentless. Interminable. And all the while London Bobby and I hung our heads and suffered the heat and the noise of the scampering figures as best we could—ever careful to keep an eye on the boys.

Then boredom struck. As one, the two teams, as they were called, fell silent and, as one, dropped their bats and balls and leather gloves, turned silently in our direction. Uneasily Bob and I looked up.

"The horses," said the most brazen boy in a whisper, facing us and putting his hot and dirty hands on his hips.

"The horses," said another boy. A child's voice, a grown man's crafty mind at work.

London Bobby, head lowered to an itching hock, again raised his eyes, flicked back his ears. More warily than Bob I watched the pack of grinning boys. Then faster than I had ever seen him move, the most brazen of that group stooped down, scooped one dusty paw through the dirt and raised himself, spread wide his feet, clasped his hands together on his breast and, elbows as far apart as possible, eyes darting to the left and right, suddenly whirled in a vicious blurry circle and let fly.

Zing! went the pebble past the tip of Bob's right ear. We shied but held our ground.

"Strike!" squeaked one of the boys softly.

A pause, a gathering of intention, and then again the ritualized gyrations of the most brazen boy, and zing! this second pebble nicked my own left ear, and the blanketing cloud above us thickened, the heat came down. One of the little ballplayers made a sucking sound and turned to the side and hawked forth a gob of mucus, which made a faint puff in the sand.

"Horses!" shouted the brazen leader at the top of his lungs, and before London Bobby and I could so much as shy or flee, suddenly the air around us was filled with pebbles, with rocks, with stones, as every last one of those small sportsmen burst into random yet nonetheless concerted frenzy, stopping and snatching at the sand and rising and firing away with stones, with rocks, with pebbles. A barrage of vehemence, a hail of unavoidable pain. Never before had those boys so orchestrated their jeering, their shouting, their rock throwing, never before had Bob and I been the victims of such a pelting. In unison the boys cheered and whooped at their accuracy of aim. Stunned and mortified, poor Bob and I stood rooted for a moment more, dumb and even willing targets as we must have seemed to our attackers, while the air hummed and the swarm of boys pressed closer toward the restraining wire. Gone whatever final shred of fear they may have had of horses, fearless their slow approach. The most brazen of them led the way, urged them on, his torso slick, his faded tight red trunks bursting with the manhood his short life already promised, though in vain.

"Nags!" he jeered, and flung a bright fat stone in my direction.

"Nags! Nags!" shouted his companions, gaining strength and stamina with every rock they threw.

But then that most brazen boy went too far, and before my disbelieving eyes, and Bob's, he stooped low and scampered beneath the electrified wire. And with a swagger he approached and studied Bob and me with a mockery of mannish deliberation, and then discharged his meanest stone and struck poor Bob full in the face.

So of course I lunged, released into action by that final stone, and as the boy, startled at last, appropriately afraid at last, turned and darted back underneath the wire, a great cry of dismay rising up from his already fleeing fellows, in that moment I did the obvious and leapt the wire, London Bobby close upon my heels.

Mayhem. Shrieks and wails. A satisfaction keener than any I had ever known, Hoffman and Stanley-the-horse-killer notwithstanding. First I singled out the most brazen boy, bore down on him, cornered him, left him asprawl on his back, eyes closed, inert, duck-billed cap lying upside down and a yard or two beyond the spot where he had fallen. Dust settling on the most brazen boy, no longer brazen. Sprawled on his back as if still running. A childish smile on his face. A faint rouge color turning yellow. Then Bob and I fell to and took full advantage of our size, our speed, the terror that the mere sight of us now inspired in the rest of the routed boys. Leather gloves in the air, caps in the air, bats flying, screams of despair. Yes, we trampled those boys, Bob and I, and without regret, without the slightest twinge of conscience, until from behind us came the shouts, in his mother tongue, of Paul J. Goossen, Mgr.

But we were free, and we wasted not a moment but cantered out of the vacant lot and away from all those little ballplayers lying motionless atop each other or sitting up and softly weeping. Goodbye, boys!

Cantered off, slowed to a trot, two lively pleasure-bound horses ambling side by side down a city street. So much for Goossen Horses!

Cars stopped, horns honked, briefly we enjoyed the bemused or frightened surprise of those few pedestrians walking the sidewalks on that hot and humid afternoon. Shouting voices, angry brakes, as *clap-clop, clap-clop,* London Bobby and I trotted on past store windows and through intersections, indifferent to stop signs and stoplights and the rage of automobile drivers, who swerved to avoid us as we passed with no slackening of pace into and out of the turmoil that we left behind in those intersections. *Clap-clop, clap-clop,* as invincibly, or so we thought, London

Bobby and I made our steady way across the city and toward the horse country that lay, as we well knew, somewhere beyond. We were interested in all we saw—startled women, pointing children, hostile men—and we were confident that as effortlessly as this we would indeed traverse the city and gain anew the country. And we nearly did. *Clap-clop, clap-clop.*

In fact we trotted unimpeded and without injury through the worst of the city, though on all sides distant sirens began to sound, until we noted in passing that greater space was ours, that the air was drier, that tenements and traffic had given way to green trees and healthier palms and houses with tricycles and small rubber swimming pools abandoned on little squares of lawn. Silence, occasionally the lone child who squatted and gaped or rose and ran along beside us, calling excitedly to its napping mother. Peace at last. Signs, no matter how faint or artificial, of the countryside approaching. A slight quickening of pace, distant barking of a dog. *Clap-clop clap-clop clap-clop!*

Then from around a shady suburban corner came a police car. An indolent police car hardly moving through the heat of the afternoon. But moving nonetheless. Our nemesis. And carrying within it two burly sweating officers. No trouble in sight. Idling. Slow of reflex. And for all we knew, London Bobby and I, that car and those policemen might blindly cross our path, fail to see us, drive harmlessly off. But not if the horse gods had their way, as indeed they did.

Ahead of us crept the blue and white car, loudly rang the *clap-clopping* of our bright hooves on the otherwise empty residential street, and could we but have stopped, could we but have stilled the loud optimistic ringing of our hooves, could we but have broken stride, changed direction, slipped out of sight behind this white stucco house or that red clapboard house, could we but have managed all this, then the catastrophe that lay in wait for us all on that quiet street might have been avoided.

But before London Bobby and I could so much as collect our thoughts or change our course, suddenly the police car twisted about, lurched and spurted forward, jerked into reverse, backed up, stopped dead in the center of that residential street, with its hood toward one deserted sidewalk and its trunk toward the other. So it blocked our way, loomed in our path, at the same time that each and every one of its red lights and blue lights began to flash and its siren began to scream as if nothing in the wide world would ever appease its hysterical alarm, persuade it to return to silence, ever. And in that instant the two fat officers leapt from within, while a lone witness to this terrible affair, a grandmother aroused from couch and cardiac condition, burst suddenly onto the stoop of the red house, shouting silently and holding her ears.

I shall never know why London Bobby and I did not simply wheel about and retrace our steps at a gallop. But we did not, could not. Or rather, Bob did not. For it was Bob, not I, who in this desperate hour changed character, became the opposite of the mild-mannered horse he had always been and instead ran head-long at the very car he should have fled. The officers ducked down, Bob jumped. But in his misguided leap for freedom, poor Bob, who was no jumper, merely landed atop the car, forelegs hanging over its far side, hind legs over the near, lights flashing on and off beneath his belly.

Just then and unaccountably the siren gave a painful squawk and fell silent.

"Shoot him! Shoot him!" the old grandmother cried, still holding her ears.

Bob's screams mingled with the cries of the old woman and the astounded shouts of the policemen. As helplessly I stood by and watched, somehow Bob squirmed and twisted until he was lying across the top of the car on his back, legs thrashing feebly in the air, head lolling. The pitch of his screams grew higher, the lights were flashing, the grandmother was nodding vehemently, wringing her hands.

"You do it!" shouted the fatter of the two policemen.

"Not me!" shouted his mate.

"All right, then!" shouted the first. "I'll do it myself!"

The old grandmother descended from the stoop, came closer, while suddenly from the intercom inside the car a metallic disembodied official voice spoke to the missing occupants. And still the fatter of the two policemen struggled with his holster, while the distant sirens remained at bay and no crowd gathered. The grandmother's face went white, Bob writhed atop the car.

And then the shot. The explosion that filled the air. The echoing thunder, the policeman standing as if he would never move again, with eyes squeezed shut, feet spread, arms extended, the revolver gripped in his two white trembling hands. And there lay London Bobby draped forlornly, peacefully, over the roof of the car. And on the sidewalk, stretched out like a board, the grandmother. But it was still not done, though the gun smoked and a policeman cowered and a grandmother's heart had stopped. For no sooner was I convinced that Bob was dead than suddenly and slowly he shuddered and gave a heave, a groan, rolled slowly over, and in one long final act of volition slid down the windshield and came to rest, like some animal shot by hunters, on the hood of the car.

I stared at Bob. Three fire engines and a rescue truck and two additional police cars bore down upon us, and now the sun, all day invisible above the humid atmosphere, came forth, joined its merciless light to its oppressive heat. But it was not London Bobby's slumping shape that blinded me, but a different sight, a travesty of a different sort, a brief vision that persisted on and off the rest of my days. For all at once and before my eyes poor Bob turned from gray to white, began to swell until it was not Bob I saw athwart the hood of the car but rather a monstrous immensity of another horse, a white horse, yes, Mother Horse herself, consuming the scene of the accident, displacing grief, drawing closer to where I stood amazed, affronted, readier than ever to pursue revenge. Closer she came, larger she grew, flaunting her size, her whiteness, her self-confidence. But the great white haunch that she was now swinging as if into my very face, was it a mockery or a matriarchal offering or both? Closer still the white haunch, and larger, and there, tied to the thick dock of her flowing tail, a ribbon—a fat pink silk ribbon that rivaled in size and significance the mass of fresh plumes dancing atop her head.

So this specter of Mother Horse stood still and yet seemed to press upon me the smooth white roundness of her matron's haunch. I accepted it and slowly stretched forth my neck and opened wide my jaws and clamped them firmly on her snowy haunch, and hung on, waited, then relaxed my grip, drew back, studied what I had left like a youthful angry brand or broken necklace on Mother Horse's haunch. Droplets of bright blood, the imprint of my sharp teeth, the horseshoe shape of my resolve to remain and be at any cost myself, my own horse.

Then commotion came crashing back around my ears, and grief was mine.

Molly. Sam. Rose. Harriet and Henrietta, Barbara Bane and Jenny. Kate. Harod. Moggy. London Bobby. Honey. Trixy.

And more? Yes, more. Twice or thrice that number, to be exact.

Nipper, Chuckers. Turf and Nan, At-a-girl and Silker. Gambit. Pete. Goneaway. Lady Di. Miss O'Murphy. Pretty Polly. Yankee Peddler. Rivets.

Dead horses. Twenty years or more of misery. But who survives them? Who still stands at the head of that fair vanished roster? To be sure . . . ! None other than . . . ! That's right—Old Horse himself!

·II·
PETRARCH

My Days of Age

CHAPTER FIVE

A TALL MAN, A SHORT MAN, A HELLISH PLACE. OF HOW I WAS SAVED

A hitching rail, a few open-sided sheds in which we could take shelter in the worst of weather, and a corral of sorts—such was the Metacomet Ranch. A single aged oak provided patchy shade for that horse so fortunate as to be loose or tied to its trunk instead of to the infamous hitching rail. Beyond the corral, with its peeling paint and broken gate, there spread the eternal maze of narrow trails that we knew by heart and that wound and forked their way through endless stands of young and scrawny poplars where mosquitoes bred and stray dogs prowled. High on the ridge above us stood the storm-worn mobile home where lived the owner of the Metacomet Ranch. She was a widow, she was a grandmother. She was old and small, wiry instead of frail. She wore faded mustard-colored pants and heavy leather boots and a flannel work shirt no matter the season. She cut her own hair and cut it short. Her face was pocked and scarred and shrewd. Her skin was gray, her palms callused, her face wrinkled. She smoked cigarettes, she coughed, she laughed at herself while coughing. She openly disliked her little grandsons, Jeff and Gene. And no one could have been more contemptuous

of horses than that small tough-minded woman or more hypocritically friendly to the infrequent visitors who chanced to stop
at the Metacomet Ranch. "I'm Jo," she would say, greeting them
at the foot of the steep and dusty path and herding them with
sweeping arm in the direction of the wretched animals she
proudly presented as her plains horses. "Josephine, really," she
would add, "but everybody calls me Jo."

I remember Josephine. Well I remember her. For she begrudged
us every unavoidable chore demanded by our mere presence in the
bottom of that abandoned gravel pit, which is what it was, begrudged us every hour that she spent in sleet, in rain, in the hottest
days of summer, filling the old white bathtub with the sulfurous
water we somehow drank or carrying dusty bales of hay down the
path and into our clamorous midst. She drove nails, she hauled
the great dried-out western saddles from our backs at sunset and
heaved them atop us again at dawn, now and then she shoveled
away some of the manure that had long collected in the open-
sided sheds—and all this she did in a sullen and grudging manner
at best, with unconcealed contempt when her mood was darkest.
She shoved or cuffed us for no reason, she ridiculed our ugliness,
our intractable natures, our filthy state, for which she herself was
responsible. For days on end she left us entirely untended, except
by little Jeff and Gene, and then, suddenly, one of us would notice
her leaning against a corner of a shed and smoking, watching us,
that small enigmatic figure who might have been standing thus for
hours, taking her leisure or deciding what harm to do us next. The
mere sight of her picking up a pitchfork and swinging around and
facing us, advancing toward us, was enough to make the entire lot
of us fade back and then withdraw together to safety at the far
side of the corral.

I see her still, thin iron-gray woman who never wore a hat or
coat, no matter the sun, the hail, the sleet. I see her reaching into
a shirt pocket or pants pocket for one of her inevitable cigarettes,
and I see the flame cupped in her palms, smell the bitter smoke,
and I cannot help but wonder at the way she remained unchanged
while I grew old, and ask myself why I at least did not once turn

on that woman and inflict on her the injury she so well deserved for demeaning us, causing us pain, ignoring us. But in Josephine I recognized as pure and single-minded a human as I was a horse. In me she recognized a horse dissimilar in every way to the rest of her shaggy thick-featured animals, who, duns and buckskins that they were, carried on their flanks the ignoble brands of distant ranches as real as the Metacomet Ranch was not. Josephine recognized my blood, my past, the dangerous Thoroughbred abiding inside my gaunt and tortured shape. Most of all, Josephine disdained the Thoroughbred, that aristocratic horse of which I was a prime example, but she wanted no accidents, no serious complaints, and so she paired me only with those young men she judged at a glance to be big and brash enough to hold me in or, shouting at the tops of their lusty lungs, to stay on my back if in fact I ran away, which occasionally I did when boredom and exasperation became too great to bear. So I was less frequently ridden than my fellows, since such young strapping braggarts, who rode mainly to impress the girls who joined them on the trails, appeared but every now and then at the Metacomet Ranch. On the other hand, greater boredom was of course the result of my restricted use, while at the same time Josephine lost no chance to let me know that if she made allowance for my essential difference from the rest of her horses, she also considered me the most deserving of her contempt. She did not like horses; among her own she disliked me most. Yet in the depths of her distaste she unavoidably acknowledged my existence. Human spleen could not deny horse spleen, and vice versa. Such was the curious truce between us, achieved by mutual recognition of the strength we shared in negativity. It was a respect of sorts and prevented me from venting on Josephine the calculating rage I had discovered in my youngest days. After all, Josephine was no match for the men on whom I had revenged myself in my youth. In fact and at the very end of my dreary days and decades at the Metacomet Ranch, Josephine did at last bestow on me one act of kindness—as we shall see.

. . .

A hot day. A dusty day. Or rather the hot and humid daybreak of such a day. Seven or so horses, myself included, already tied to the hitching rail. Already saddled, already victims of the settling flies. Listless, necks long and low, heads hanging. Horses filmed in air too dense to breathe. What day was this? Had night preceded it? Day without night. One day, all days. The very smell of us hanging in a cloud around our ankles. Only an eye opening, an eye closing, a hopeless shifting from one cocked hoof to another, betrayed the life that was left in us.

I sagged, I kept my eyes either closed or cast down, refused to reveal in any way that I was not alone at the rail. But I was not alone, as I well knew and as the horse beside me knew. I cared nothing about the others joining me that dawn, but I could not deny to myself that next to me stood none other than Billy, a big black devil and the only horse at the Metacomet Ranch who was my enemy. And it was not chance that saw us tied side by side this dawn of all dawns, not the typical randomness in which we lived and died at the Metacomet Ranch, but rather Josephine's individual turn of mind that had so placed us inseparably together. She might well have tied Billy to one end of the hitching rail and me to the other, as common sense would have dictated and anyone else would have done, since our rivalry had been long-standing and in one dismal vainglorious moment had once more erupted. But not Josephine. Not for Josephine to keep apart two horses who could hardly tolerate the smell, let alone the sight of each other. Quite the opposite. For just as I was the least favored of Josephine's mastodons, as she called us in the brightest of her unpredictable moods, so Billy was the most favored. Furthermore, only the dusk before this particular dawn we had attacked each other, Billy and I. What else, then, but to tie us side by side when this day broke? So Josephine had tied us and left us. Such was her mind.

Yes, attacked each other. Viciously. With all the energy we had been able to muster. It had not been much, and our fighting had been short-lived. But we had inflicted on each other a goodly portion of the damage we had meant to inflict. Billy, oddly enough since he was a massive beast and the stronger of us two, had incurred the worst of it, though his skin had remained intact. Bruises for Billy but no open wounds. Whereas I had come off scot-free. Not a bruise anywhere. No injury at all save one, the gaping gash in my shoulder.

All night it had slowly oozed or freely bled, this jagged open cut as long as Billy's sullen jaws were wide, and now, despite the numbness and anger inside me and the general thickening paralysis of still another dawn at the Metacomet Ranch, now I felt the pain that sat on my thin shoulder like some exotic bloom. At least it was a new sensation that warred with the itching that beset me, the aching in my bones and joints. There was a fly testing the fluids of my left eye like a bather at the edge of a stagnant pond. My own filth and the filth of others caked me in a hard and crusty second skin. And as all horses and most humans know, the horse has a greater antipathy to uncleanliness than most sentient creatures, humans included, and is particularly vulnerable in his skin and organs to the malignancy of even such a supposedly ordinary substance as dried sweat. For the horse the all but invisible salt of his own secreted sweat is a deadly irritant, which is merely one example of our special need for sponging, bathing, hosing down, once we are subjected to domesticity. Neglect the horse for only a day, and all this inescapable pathology begins its life. What then of my once thin skin and its proneness to rashes? I need not say. And what of that dark and swampy area concealed as if forever beneath my tail and between my hind legs? Or of the open sores buried under the bulk of the old western saddle that weighed me down? I need not say. But no wonder I welcomed the clear distracting pain in my shoulder.

I dozed, I regained consciousness, the fly was long immersed in his pool, I heard the squeaking of Billy's saddle though he had not moved. The sun was rising, I noticed that old Ben, who had gotten loose as he often did, had not even sought the shade of the solitary oak but instead lay on his side fully and indifferently exposed to heat, to light, his belly dusty and distended and revealing not a sign of that aged quarter horse's breath. Old Ben asleep? Old Ben dead at last or merely exhausted like the rest of us? Who could say?

Then unannounced, without warning, suddenly little Josephine came clumping down the path, and at the hitching rail there was a stirring and once again we who were tied at that rail were back in time. Uneasy horses, woman undaunted by the heat. Even Billy must have wondered why Josephine was returning to us at this by now late morning hour, since no car had stopped and ordinarily she kept to herself in her mobile home.

"Well now, Billy," she said, coming up to him as if the other half-dozen horses, myself included, did not exist. "Look what Old Horse has done to you. Poor Billy."

Slowly she walked around him, with obviously feigned concern she felt his lumps and bruises, lifted one of his hooves, let it fall. Then she stood facing him and, as if deep in thought, carefully she lit one of her noxious cigarettes and studied him, furrowed her brow in apparent commiseration, ran her fingers through the thick black tangle of his mane. As for me, I glanced at them, I listened, but was not deceived. Excluded, yes. Ignored, yes— which surely was the significance of the attention Josephine was spending so pointedly on Billy—but not deceived. Oh, I knew her well, I had learned early never to trust the look on her face or the way she moved. She was slow-witted and yet full of duplicity, indecisive yet determined. Whenever she made up her mind she was indomitable. So it was not like Josephine to indulge herself by lavishing sympathy on one of her horses the more blatantly to disregard and spite the other. The very way she frowned and puffed on her cigarette told me that she was thinking and fumbling about in her hardheaded widowhood for a plan. But what did she want to do? What would she do?

As if in answer, and still without giving me so much as a glance, she flung down her cigarette and turned on her heel, retraced her steps up the path to where her mobile home was propped on cinder blocks in a sea of weeds. There it was, a decision, and seeing the purpose all too evident in her disappearing form, I knew that she would again return and soon. I waited, my suspicions grew, and sure enough and in no time at all she was back, pleased with herself once more and confident.

"Well, Bill," she said, turning her back to him and facing me, speaking over her shoulder, "Old Horse is just a troublemaker. Maybe this time he's gone too far."

Uneasy? Indeed I was uneasy, since just as I had known, it was not Billy who had been the object of Josephine's attention all along, though even now, standing as she was beside me and threading her needle—yes, she was now armed with thread, with needle—she was careful not once to meet my eye. Now, certainly, I was not ignored—far from it! Now I could not complain of her indifference. For what was she about to do if not sew up my cut? Precisely. With a shock it came to me, with a shock I understood the decision she had hit upon by chance, I thought, and not by any exercise of reason. If she had left my cut alone it would have healed or it would not have healed but become a livid source of infection. Why not? Horses had died before me at the Metacomet Ranch and would die again. And had my cut healed of its own accord into a long and ugly scar, that marring would not have mattered to Josephine or to any of her callow young visitors to the Metacomet Ranch. Equine aesthetics were no concern of theirs. Yet Josephine had taken it into her head to sew me up—from cruelty? from kindness? I could not say. Had I been wrong about her all these years? Perhaps. Perhaps not.

"Bill," she continued over her shoulder, "I think we've had enough of this old guy. Don't you agree?"

Squinting, pursing her lips. Drawing that length of black thread through the eye of the needle. Face once more composed, expressionless. Needle as long as her finger, black thread dangling. I saw her wrinkled hands, I saw her small clear eyes cast down steadily, I smelled the bitter smoky smell of that old lonely woman.

"Yes, Bill," she said, still speaking over her shoulder, "this time we may just have to get rid of Old Horse. That's what we might just have to do."

So saying, and though her words had nothing whatever to do with her actions, she squeezed together the flesh of my open

wound and thrust into me the glinting needle, pulled through a
limpid flowing loop of that thick black thread. Billy gazed at us,
I winced, the pain that bloomed on my shoulder turned bright
scarlet. But I did not resist my benefactor, if such she was, neither
kicked nor jerked away but rather set my jaw, braced myself,
determined as I was to conceal my pain and shock from both that
little ministering old woman and the black horse so pleasurably
engrossed in watching.

Another dispassionate jab of the needle, another long looping
of the thread. And then, bright needle poised for another thrust,
she paused, without a qualm interrupted her sewing, and, no
doubt meaning to address some further thought to Billy, glanced
once more over her shoulder. Prolonging the pain of this procedure? Unaware of the droplets of my blood in the dust? So self-
absorbed as to be oblivious of this her severest mistreatment yet
of a helpless horse? Or another example of her cruel turn of mind?
One or the other, obviously, and still I did not react but called
again on dignity, forbearance, strength, though against my will I
was quivering.

Now and all at once, before she could speak to Billy or resume
her sewing, and as if this morning were not already intolerable
enough, from the top of the path there came a shout, a laugh, the
pattering of little boots, and down the path ran Jeff and Gene into
our midst. Schoolbags banging, breathless in their good humor.
But stopping short at the sight of us—well might they have—and
drawing near in curiosity grown abruptly cautious, subdued.

"Grandma," said Jeff, a skinny boy whose family resemblance
was stronger than his brother's, "what are you doing?"

A jab. A tug on the thread.

"Can't you see?" said Josephine after another pause. "I'm
sewing him up."

"But why?"

"Billy bit him."

"I like Old Horse," said Gene, the smaller and gentler of the
two.

"Well, you shouldn't," said Josephine promptly. "He started it. He always does."

"But, Grandma," said Jeff, "doesn't it hurt him?"

Another jab. Another tug.

"Of course not," said Josephine. "Old Horse can't feel anything."

"Grandma," said Gene slowly, "are you sure?"

No answer. Question unworthy of an answer. Billy watching, small boys watching. At least three stitches already taken, countless more to go.

"This thread," said Josephine, "isn't really thread. It's fishing line. It belonged to Grandpa."

Boys' turn to refrain from answering.

"He was a terrible fisherman," she went on, yanking at a suddenly stubborn knot in the thread and pausing, giving way again to some stray distraction. "I never understood what he saw in horses."

"But you like Billy," ventured Jeff.

"He's not as bad as Old Horse," said Josephine. "I can't stand Old Horse. Maybe . . . maybe I'll get ahold of Ken Handy."

Silence. Silent boys, silent horse. My silence profounder than the boys'.

Oh, here was something new, a course of action it had not once occurred to me that she'd stumble on. But obviously one thing had led to another in her dark mind, pleasing her, alarming me, disturbing the boys, silencing all four of us. Ken Handy! Might she in fact turn me over to Ken Handy? I had seen him once, plump ageless man naked except for rubber boots and overalls and canvas cap. One sniff of him was enough to frighten the best of horses, but his round slack face and vacant eyes were more frightening still. His only interest was in selling the carcasses of the horses he slaughtered. Why, it was common knowledge that the slaughtering inflicted by Ken Handy was not humane! Now, in a mere word that she had not intended to say, had Josephine consigned me to Ken Handy? Dislike, distaste, reasonless contempt—agreed. But could she so despise me as to have my life destroyed? I shuddered mightily, from head to tail, and fell still. Gone my pain, forgotten the needle, the thread, the jerky exertions of that old woman's hand. What was left for me except gloom and apprehension? What indeed?

"Poor Old Horse," said Gene, though I was so cast down as to be all but deaf to his small boy's voice.

A final tug, Josephine pulling out her pocket knife, snipping the thread, tying it. The sound of a match, humid air filled all at once with smoke. Job well done. Satisfaction. Contentment. On my part oblivion to everything except Ken Handy. But not for long did it last, this longest moment of my long life.

Two puffs only, Josephine! Cease your gloating, Billy, and cheer up, boys—for suddenly, in a mere swish of Billy's tail, relief was mine, while Josephine became only Josephine and Ken Handy no more threatening than the grim little grandmother herself.

"Hello!" called Master—yes, it was he!—and "Hello, down there!" called Ralph—it was he as well—and down the path strode the most unlikely pair ever to intrude into the misery of the Metacomet Ranch. They were a tall man and a short man, a tall man older by far than myself or Josephine, and a short man in the fullness of what was obviously a horseman's life. The first, gaunt and white-haired in his extreme old age, was dressed in a threadbare black double-breasted suit as if he had come directly from some old-fashioned place of business to our gravel pit, while his companion, who meant to be deferential but was not, was dressed in riding boots and britches. Age had shrunken the tall man inside his suit, a horseman's vigor swelled the squat figure of his companion. The first wore a blue silk polka-dotted tie and, protruding from the breast pocket of the black suit coat that hung on him like a listless sail, a white handkerchief, neatly folded. In the hatband of his shapeless putty-colored cap the second and much younger man sported a poppy, long dead. The first approached us ingenuously, with the friendliness of purest innocence, while the second grinned in slyness and hardheadedness. The old man was the wolfhound of the pair and as such towered, foolish and angular, above the companion who was as small and solid as a bloated wineskin, all brawn and biceps and bulging hams.

"I'm Harry," said Master, smiling down at Josephine, "Harry of Hidden Hall. And this is Ralph, who, as you can hear in his speech, is from the country of the green. Irish, that is. I would have him no other way."

Silence. A long pause. Small boys hiding happily behind the grandmother. Grandmother staring up with ill-concealed dislike into the gaunt and eager face of the tall intruder. Ralph a few steps to the rear of Master and grinning and shaking his head unobtrusively, the stocky brute already miming his mockery of Master and attempting to ingratiate himself with Josephine.

"Well," said she at last, "what do you want?"

"A horse," said Master promptly. "I am in the market for a horse."

"These horses," said Josephine just as promptly, "are not for sale."

"I am looking for a horse with a kind eye," said Master, proceeding despite Josephine's adamant answer, "and with what we call a brainy head. You understand. And I require him to have a long sloping shoulder and a deep girth and big clean hocks, well let down."

Josephine stared, Ralph shook his head behind the old man's back and winked.

"This," said Josephine at last, "is private property. And I've told you, my horses are not for sale."

"All right," said Master, "but I shall just have a look."

And off he went, striding on his long legs to the far end of the hitching rail, where he was at once engrossed in his critical appraisal of Josephine's mastodons. From afar I watched him as he stooped, scowled, stood back, cocked his head, and held his chin between thumb and forefinger as if scrutinizing masterpieces hung on a wall. From the outset I had been convinced that Josephine would finally submit to Master and that Master would be successful in his quest, thanks to Josephine's craftiness and greed and his own foolish persistence. But would I be the horse to catch and hold Master's attention, or would his impatience drive him into hasty infatuation with some other wretch tethered at the hitching rail before he had so much as cast his eye on me, Old Horse, where I stood waiting last in line? I did not know, so I fretted in self-torment while Master busied himself in exercising his equine judgment and Ralph betrayed poor Master in his deep confidential brogue to Josephine.

"You with me?" said the small stocky horseman, thrusting on Josephine all his brash confidentiality. "His name's not Harry. There is no Hidden Hall. He's daft, you see. He's never been on a horse in his life, he doesn't know a thing about horses except for what he's got from books. It's the reading that's turned his head. He's correct about my nationality, but all the rest of it's just fancy. I'd humor him if I were you. Incidentally, what are you doing with these sorry-looking jades?"

"My horses," Josephine answered, "are my business."

"No offense," said Ralph, grinning still more broadly, "but I'd send the lot of them to the knackers if I were you. Of course I don't mean a word of it. Just joking."

Perhaps it was Ralph's black boots, well worn and swollen tight to the thick rounds of his calves, or perhaps it was the aged pair of canary-colored britches stretched unabashedly about all the creases and bulges of his fat loins and seat and thighs, or the chest that matched in massiveness the legs and seat, or the whole of his redheaded aggressive stance—for yes, his hair beneath the cap was of the traditional flaming Irish red in color—not to mention the pleasure he clearly took in rudeness, the sheer energy that flickered from the black pupils of his eyes or the weathered shiny brown of his round face or the deep throaty sound of the brogue he so obviously enjoyed in his own ear—but whatever the cause, Josephine suddenly reached for one of her cigarettes, patting this pocket or that, and despite her age and station as grandmother and owner of the Metacomet Ranch, lit her cigarette and exhaled a great cloud of smoke and colored slightly beneath the mellow grinning steadiness of Ralph's gaze.

"I don't like joking," she said then, the faint flush deepening in her shallow cheeks. "I never joke."

"Don't you now," said Ralph in his softest, most musical tones. "And what about these lads here? I can see they're lighthearted little fellows for sure. But tell me, what's your name?"

"Josephine," came the answer, in a gentler voice, "but I'm known as Jo."

"Jo," said Ralph, visibly holding the sound in his mouth. "Now there's an interesting name for a woman."

Small boys instinctively alarmed. Grandmother diverting her unaccustomed nervousness into puffs of smoke, a spell of coughing. Horseman enjoying the effects of Irish manhood on aged widow of stature even shorter than his. Hot sun bearing down upon us all, the stench of pathetic horses rising into the heat of the sun. Pain of all too recent stitches flaring up in my shoulder. Yet still in the midst of my immediate distaste for the burly horseman, whose meanness and hypocrisy I had recognized at first sight, now in my misery and anguish at least I knew for certain that Josephine would abide by Master's wishes, though I knew more clearly than ever that she had been exercising her crafty ways and had meant to dupe the old man all along. Not one horse at the rail, myself included, was worth buying, and at that moment and inwardly I both admitted and denied my worthlessness.

"That horse there!" cried Master, whose sudden reappearance surprised us all. "Who is that horse?"

"Him?" said Josephine, obviously irritated by the tall man's return. "He's Old Horse."

"Old Horse?" said Master, dusty from his long slow study of my ugly peers. "Doesn't he have a name?"

Master approached me, frowned, reached out a long and bony finger and touched my still wet wound.

"He's injured," said Master, frowning more deeply.

"Vet just sewed him up," said Josephine. "He's as good as new."

"He's a Thoroughbred," said Master, stepping away and casting upon me a look of purest admiration.

Josephine feigned ignorance and led him on.

"Well, Ralph," said Master, "what do you think?"

Ralph laughed, tipped his cap to the back of his head; the dead poppy shook and nodded and grew bright red in the sun. I stiffened and Josephine looked up sharply at the sound of Ralph's laugh.

Again Master approached me. "I've never seen a kinder eye," he said. "Do you see the splendid size and kindness of his eye, Ralph? A gentle horse of good disposition."

"Nonsense," scoffed Ralph. "He's an old devil and as mean as they come."

"Not so old," said Master.

"Ha!" said Ralph. "I'll show you!" And stepping forward, he seized my upper lip, squeezed it, caught hold of my jaw, and with all his strength pulled back my upper lip, exposing my poor teeth, or what was left of them, and more besides. I rolled my eyes, I struggled to pull my head from Ralph's tight grasp. "And what did I tell you?" said Ralph, gripping me all the harder. "Look at his teeth. But you can't fail to see that number there, tattooed inside his upper lip. It's the year he first went on the track—do you see it?—which is to say that he's more than twenty-two years of age. And broken down? Ah, he's broken down for fair!"

"Stop!" said Master shortly, before Josephine could intervene. "Desist, Ralph. Leave him alone."

Ralph obeyed, Josephine maintained her angry silence. I took a step, surreptitiously shook my head, testing the violent wrenching I still felt in my jaws.

A long pause. Hard breathing. Men struggling to retrieve their lost composure. Woman still angry.

"Ralph," Master said then, in his gentler tone, "look at his short back."

"And his silly long neck," said Ralph.

"But the flag, Ralph, by which of course I mean his tail. How long and full it is. A sure sign of friendliness in a horse."

"You'll find he can hardly walk," said Ralph. "Look at the pasterns."

"Ah, but the ribs," said Master, "wide and round behind the girth."

"He's skin and bone," said Ralph, "and not much bone. You'll never get the weight back on him."

"No, Ralph," said Master with a smile, "he's broad in the second thighs. And ah, the muscles between the second thighs are full and firm."

"We're not looking at the same horse," said Ralph.

"Perhaps not," said Master.

"Anyone knows that an overly long and foolish-looking neck is an indication that the horse in question has no wind," said Ralph. "Besides, a horse is not an automobile."

"My point exactly," said Master.

"Well now," said Ralph, with another wink at Josephine, "perhaps you'd like me to try him out. I'm sure this kind lady will oblige."

Whereupon Josephine objected, this time aloud, and, dropping and stepping on her cigarette and glancing angrily at Ralph, declared that she was not in the habit of selling her horses but, in this case, would make an exception, provided, of course, that the price was right. But if they wanted Old Horse, she said—my ears standing forward and my eyes brightening—they must lead him away now, as is, without taking any more of her time. Otherwise, she said, she had work to do.

At the end of this speech, surely Josephine's longest, Ralph laughed, flatly and rudely, while Master nodded and rested his long thin hand on my neck.

"Make no mistake, Ralph," said Master, "this is our horse."

"You'll rue the day," said Ralph.

Thus began the dickering, and thus in mere minutes I discovered that I had value after all and listened as, thanks to Josephine's cleverness, my value soared, shockingly, so that even Master, for the briefest moment, appeared to suffer a dimming of that boyish self-confidence which, until now, had been his. But he recovered, to Ralph's evident amusement and disgust, and, with pen and checkbook and formal handshake and gracious bow, the latter catching Josephine quite off guard, concluded his business. As for the owner of the Metacomet Ranch, for once she had met with good fortune, a fact she could not conceal. Yes, Josephine allowed herself to smile and, pocketing her check, told Master that he was going to love his horse.

"That I am," replied Master, "though my horse must have a new and more appropriate name."

"Now then," said Ralph, suddenly all brusqueness and good humor, "we'll be off then, if this lady will just remove that outlandish saddle from the poor animal's back."

"No, Ralph," Master answered, stroking my nose, "you do it."

As simply and swiftly as that the deed was done. When Master himself began to lead me up the path and out of the gravel pit, I summoned the tattered remnants of my self-control and did what I could to walk on steadily, without much wobbling in my ankles and showing hardly a sign of the pain that was more than ever plaguing my long legs—all this to give the lie to Ralph and prove to Master that, for short distances at least, I could walk and, yes, even trot and canter as well. The joy of my rescue, for so it was and long overdue, was marred only by the presence of the Irish groom, as Master called him, for from the beginning I understood that Ralph's true nature was well concealed in the mantle of his Irish charm. Ralph's dislike of me, I thought, was as great as or greater than Josephine's. If Master owned me, I reflected, Ralph was my keeper. Ahead of me stretched days of attempting to accept the eccentricities of the one while guarding against the persecutions of the other. How like the horse gods, I thought, to tarnish the pleasure of my rescue with the promise of daily new afflictions yet to come. Nonetheless, I told myself, in these first days I would exert myself to return the affection of the demented elder and to suffer without complaint the provocations of the Irish groom.

Walk on! I exhorted myself. Enjoy old age!

At the top of the path I stopped for an instant, swung round my head, and looked down at the four-legged shades in the depths of that hot pit. From far below the small boys waved. Josephine stood peering up at us, hands on hips, head tilted backward, fresh cigarette fuming lazily from between her lips. As I watched, old Ben, without a glance in my direction, suddenly hauled himself to his feet and dragged himself into the coolness beneath the nearby oak.

Good luck, Billy. Goodbye, Josephine. So much for you, Ken Handy.

- -

CHAPTER SIX

•

TWO HORSES MAKE A HERD. MASTER RIDES

- -

For the young horse fortunate enough to have been born into a stable conducive to his well-being, there is no greater pleasure, in his early days, than waking to find himself freshly centered in security yet also freshly attuned to everything that is unfamiliar. He cannot but trust the stable of his birth, yet is so new to this place of nurturing that what he does not know adds instant color to his unquestioned and unchanging trust. The life of the young horse, of that colt or filly born into such circumstances, is simple and yet enchanted as well. However, such a creature owes his enchantment not merely to the love of his dam or the skills of his keepers, or to the order inherent in good barn management, but to an instinct reaching back in time to the very genesis of our species. I refer, of course, to the herding instinct, that uncanny force that draws the individual wild horse to his fellows—for protection, initially, and for the propagation and hence preservation of the herd. Stronger than blood, stronger than spirit, some vital urge akin to the deepest and most familiar of all such urges—such was the power of the first horse's herding instinct, and so it is today. Put two horses in farthest corners of a wide and empty plain, and they will find each other and come together. Ride us down a country road, and we will do our best to bunch up, to bump each other, to find proximity between rumps and heads, noses and tails. And which of us has not been ridden out all day and worked hard, sweating and foaming around the bit and growing weary, less willing to respond to our rider's commands, when, turning toward home, we quicken suddenly, speed up, slough off fatigue, and, no matter how obedient or tired, try to thwart our riders and run away, if possible, back to the barn? Not a horse among us who, at the end of day, can resist a headlong plunge back to the barn—and not merely for feed, for water, for the comfort of our familiar and darkening box stalls, but because the herding instinct is still as strong in the domesticated horse as it once was in his wild forebear. For the domesticated horse the barn is the herd. For the young domesticated horse the barn of his birth is inseparable from his first hours of awakening to the day that is his by rights but also his to discover. And no matter how the young horse grows or how far afield he is taken, each successive barn in that horse's life will reflect the first, nostalgically or painfully as the case may be. Of course we grow beyond our beginnings, of course we lose sight of that earliest time in which, tranquilly and without question, we were meant to be. Nonetheless there is no horse alive who does not expect to come full circle, to find that this or that new barn where he is to be stabled is in fact the barn of his birth. Rare is the fulfillment of that expectation. But of necessity the promise of that fulfillment, or need of it, lies just on the other side of every gate that leads to this or that next horse farm, which we hope will prove to be our first and our last.

This, then, is what it means to say that the Metacomet Ranch denied the very birthright of all those horses kept there and hired out for rides. Only a barest shred of the herding instinct survived at the Metacomet Ranch. Hence our despair.

For obvious reasons I did not expect much more from Ralph. A new life, yes, or at least a different life. A life that had been denied me for one decade, then two. And good of sorts would come to me from Master, for all his illusions and eccentricities, of that I was reasonably assured. And despite the resistance and apprehension that Ralph had inspired in me with his first words, thick with the falsity of his hearty brogue, and despite the vehemence with which he judged my weaknesses, my ugly shape, scorning rather than making allowance for mistreatment and my old age, still Ralph looked and talked like a horseman. So I was elated to be Master's horse and freed at last from the Metacomet Ranch.

However, I had no high hopes for my new stabling. Ralph cared too much about himself, I thought, to care for horses. Even from what I had already seen of him, how could I hope to find in a stable belonging to Ralph any other horse or horses who would not greet me with a contempt as virulent as Ralph's own? Whatever I anticipated in my new stable, I was not prepared to be pleased, certainly not to be unduly pleased, never to find my nostalgia awakened or my long-dormant herding instinct suddenly, fully, vividly aroused. Not for me to discover in old age that flush of self found only beyond the freshly painted white wooden gate that leads to the past.

How wrong I was! How agreeably surprised! Since all that I could not have considered possible proved true.

Imagine, then—a green and yellow countryside of trees, elm and oak and the slender birch, and pastures newly mowed and here a small pond clear and fresh and there a low and mossy wall of fieldstone made by untutored farmer-artisans in a time long past. No arid gravel pit, this vista, but rather an open landscape of both wild and cultivated growth, a rolling sometimes wooded world in harmony with itself, which draws and frees the eye instead of confining it, a wide and airy sight sweet with the scent of Indian summer light. So far so good.

But then imagine a gate—an old wooden gate unpainted and hastily repaired, and a dirt road worn and washed with deep ruts and gullies and sudden holes, and at the end of this road, itself a warning of sorts threaded across the countryside just seen, two wooden buildings and three or four old horse trailers in various states of disrepair. And a lone paddock, a dunghill, a dreary stand of evergreens, a clothesline strung between two shabby pines and sagging beneath the weight of a few shirts and a broad white pair of undershorts. And what is this place if not the horse farm that belonged to Ralph? My heart sank at the sight of it.

Sank, but then rose up again, for there was more.

A tractor, for instance. Once green, now gone to rust, still functional. And a woodpile. And cats. Many cats. And the two wooden buildings, one small and the other large, both barns as it turned out, and though the larger of the two was used for nothing more than storage, at least the small barn was occupied, as I quickly discovered, and by man and horse alike—horse below, man above. So there was life in the smaller of those two barns, and inventiveness, since Ralph himself, as I was momentarily to learn, had converted the hayloft of the smaller barn into a few rooms in which he could sleep and thump noisily about and cook and keep himself warm and dry and live peaceably enough in seasons both harsh and fair.

But there was more than this. Still more. In the paddock.

Yes, in the paddock there stood a horse, an aged horse, a mare, as I knew with my first breath of her, an old Appaloosa mare who was nonetheless smooth and plump, round and substantial, compact and bright with the youth she still retained despite her years. Her coloring was dark except, of course, for the hindquarters, which, typical of the Appaloosa, were a milky white splotched and spattered with spots of the same bright black color that covered the rest of her. She was generous, she was tractable, of that sweet disposition for which her breed was famous. And on that first afternoon when Ralph unloaded me and Master, still incongruously clothed in his black business suit, stood by and worried, this mare was watching me—intently, patiently, invitingly. And what was there for me in that moment? A stab of disbelief, a pang of unworthiness, and then, thanks to Clover herself, for such was her name, and thanks to the horse gods, my second decision of the day—to disregard my infirmities, to overcome the sorry picture I presented, to allow myself the full pleasure of the handsome mare's kind regard. And so I did, and at once there was revived in me the ghost of my lost gender, the shade of the little primal horse long dead in my loins. Shyly and triumphantly I felt him stir, roll over, struggle to resume the stormy life that was his, while Clover watched and I luxuriated in her approval.

"Look there," said Master. "They like each other!"

"The old bugger," muttered Ralph in reply.

"Please, Ralph," said Master softly. "I dislike offensive language."

"That you do," said Ralph, turning me sharply away from my first long sight of the mare, who was Ralph's own horse and the pride of his life. "I quite forgot."

Clover, then. Myself. Two horses that made a herd, as Clover and I already knew. And no others of our kind to plague me or that I might plague. Despite decay and carelessness and dereliction, here was habitation of a sort. A gift of place? A gift of equine companionship at last? So it seemed.

But for all that pleased me in my first impression of Ralph's farm, and all that put me on my guard as well, it was not until dusk of the day of my arrival, when Ralph led Clover and then myself into the warmth and shadows of the little barn that was now to house us both, that I recognized the full extent of my new life.

There were four box stalls on ground level in that small barn, two to a side and end to end, the two rows separated by a wide aisleway newly surfaced with earthy clay. There were cobwebs, there were wormholes in the rude beams, there were cats on the beams, overhead there were a few unshaded light bulbs so sweated over with dust as to cast only the softest light on the life inside this little barn, which, until now, had sheltered no horse but Clover. For as long as she had been Ralph's own horse—a considerable number of years, as it turned out—Clover had occu-

pied the box stall farthest from the entrance on the left-hand side
of the barn. Hers was the brass nameplate gleaming on that stall
door, she it was who filled that stall with her gentle shape, drinking quietly from buckets that were always freshly scrubbed and
eating with uncommon restraint instead of ripping her feed tub
from the wall or scattering her feed about her stall, as some horses
do and as I know. In the gloaming, head and neck protruding over
the top of the stall door, thus she stood waiting when Ralph led
me into Clover's presence. Yet even in that moment promise
turned temporarily to disappointment. Naturally enough, I had
expected Ralph to lead me into the stall adjoining Clover's and to
allow me the pleasure of her closest proximity. But instead and as
I should have known he would, no sooner had I set hoof to clay
than Ralph yanked on my halter and put me into the box stall
nearest the entrance on the right-hand side of the barn. Diagonally opposite from Clover! As far as possible from Clover! Yes,
there was a mean streak running through that man's jolly green,
a sullenness that belied the twinkling eye, the lively brogue.

"Ralph," said Master, still trailing after us, still watching my
every move, tall and gaunt and more incongruous than ever inside
the barn, "shouldn't you put my horse beside your own?"

"Not a bit of it," said Ralph, flinging me a flake of hay. "I've
a good mind to leave him out in the paddock anyway."

"No, Ralph," said Master softly. "That wouldn't do."

A cat shifted, another leapt from sight, the hay landed in a
corner of my new box stall beneath the two freshly filled buckets
of water hung from ringbolts in the wall and—that hay—softly
exploded in a puff of sweetness that promised me a sustenance
that I had not known in years and that I could ingest at will and
intersperse exactly as I wished with long slow drafts of the cold
thirst-quenching water. Protected, roofed over, provided for—it
was a luxury that inside my bony head stirred dim figures and
shadows of . . . what? Some former time, some earlier day all but
forgotten and yet, yes, returning, even as I stretched down my
long neck and buried my mouth in the hay and ate my fill. But as
I indulged this new yet vaguely remembered luxury, still there was

the nagging presence of Ralph's mean streak, the faint certainty that in the very act of stabling me he meant to keep me as far as he could from Clover.

Hay of the finest sort. Light brown, light green. A good nose, as they say, fruit of the field. Cold spring water in buckets that did not smell of sulfur or other vileness, as do buckets that are left unclean. And darkness. Darkness gathering inside our barn. Old Horse absorbed as not for years in replenishment. Nagging thought hardly nagging at all. More concerned with eating than with new companion similarly occupied. Sounds of chewing, mine more audible than hers. And so engrossed that I paid scant attention to Ralph's return and Master's, or to the sounds of Ralph preparing the evening feed, or to Master's quiet well-mannered voice when he told Ralph that he, Master, would himself toss my portion of the evening feed into the large clean tub suspended near my buckets of cold water now half drunk. Thus one pleasure was followed by another, dry grasses all at once displaced by two full quarts of golden oats, the pleasure of the oats overshadowing by far the pleasure of hay as I thrust and rummaged and munched away at the shiny oats that Master himself had heaped into my feed tub.

Footsteps overhead. The smell of cooking. The scraping of chair legs, the murmuring of voices, the sounds of cutlery, running water. Then silence. Silence above, the silence of approaching satiety below. Feed tub empty, hay devoured. Head raised, a tentative exploration of the stall that was mine, another half-hearted nosing of the empty tub. A long night for the freely roaming cats.

But what of me? Was repose the sum of satisfaction? Was I content to lounge away my first night in the Irish horseman's barn as dreamy and mindless as one of Ralph's furry cats? Is this all it took—freedom from harm's way, a spacious stall, the unaccustomed heaviness that follows relief from appetite—to lull me like any other brute beast into mere lassitude and thankful acquiescence to the long night? It was not. Of course it was not. In my narcissism, in the avid filling of my shrunken belly, I had forgotten—yes, forgotten!—Clover. Now, of a sudden, I could only think of the patient and no doubt wakeful Appaloosa.

There was a moon, there was dusty darkness. The feeble artificial lights were off. Above us the two men, for Master was now to live with Ralph, were snoring. And diagonally across from me stood Clover, head turned in my direction, wakeful indeed, patient.

All at once the dim sight of her, and our closeness and yet separation, were for me unbearable. I kicked! I kicked again! I smashed first one and then another of my unshod hooves against the planking, I bucked as best I could, I pranced in place inside my stall, threw myself head-on at the rattling door, sent my empty feed tub a-flying, and all the while screamed as I had never screamed before. What a clamor it was, a racket fit to bring down the barn.

Lights, of course. Ralph in his nightshirt. Ralph cursing. Ralph subduing me with a convenient short thick length of wood.

Darkness again. A moment of peace. But I would have my say that night, and nothing would stop me, neither my own bruises nor Ralph's obscenities nor the terror of the hissing cats.

Repetition of Ralph in his rage.

Repetition of equine violence.

Lights on. Lights off.

On it went, while the placid Clover waited and the barn shook.

"Ralph," I heard Master clearly say at last in a lull in the terrible noise I was making, "I can't stand it. You must do something."

Which Ralph did, of course, since from the start he knew full well what was wrong with me and how to quiet me, and finally, thanks to sleeplessness and Master's pleading and what promised to be the longest shattering of any night ever known in a well-run stable, Irish or not, Ralph had no choice but to admit to himself that his stubbornness and meanness were no match for the herding instinct of Old Horse, as I was still named.

Down he came again, fuming and muttering, cats crowding about his bare feet and legs, and, as any reasonable man would have done from the start, he moved me from the box stall I was battering into the box stall adjoining Clover's.

Lights out. Silence descending. Sleep returning. Peace and harmony restored. That night I made no more disturbance.

Between Clover's stall and mine the pine boards of the wall that separated us rose not up to the beams above our heads but only so high that between the top of that wall and those ceiling beams there was a space, a fair space, a space sufficient so that we had merely to lift our noses and sniff a bit, to search the empty space and so with little effort find each other's noses and, upon recognition of that soft sensation of our touching noses, stand quietly with heads upraised and enjoy to the full the soft and yielding intimacy that we had so soon and so easily attained. Now and again one of us would draw away, step back, look up, and in the moonlight see the very nose and lips that our own had blindly probed but moments before. Thus throughout the night we stood touching, and nickering, murmuring to each other in the long pauses in the breathy expressiveness of our attraction—Clover and I, two old horses regressing to the ways of youth.

And what did we recount to each other in the stillness and tenderness of that long shadowy and sometimes moonlit night? Our lives, of course, or such essential facts and episodes of Clover's life and mine as could be voiced in the confines of one sleepless night and that accounted in main for the horses that we were that night. Merely telling my own litany of misfortune aroused in me anew the buried anger that had so long been mine, though it was quickly quieted by Clover, who here and there, now and again, interrupted my narrative and stopped it, changed its course by the sheer intrusion of her good sense and the brief sounds of what was nothing other than devotion. She listened to my recollections of Millbank, the first that had come to me in that long interval in which I had passed from youth to age—and it was no coincidence that I could think again of Millbank this night, here in this stable, fed and watered and mantled as I was in the aura of Clover's presence. I dwelt as best I could on past kindnesses, and even without Clover's prompting I myself had wit enough to suppress what I began all at once to remember of this female horse or that one who, unbidden and unwanted, trotted suddenly forward out of the dark past. Then a detour, another shard of memory, again the erupting temper that I could not control, but then again my companion's soothing interruption until my narrative of sorts was done and I fell silent, calmed once more by my good fortune into accepting the life that I had not expected or deserved or desired—quite the contrary. It goes without saying that to my emotions Clover offered calmness, and that after my long story, Clover's was short and unassuming.

There had been a child—nameless—the child's riding instructor—Ralph—and the child's first horse—Clover in the shiny prime of youth. The child had been devoted to both Ralph and her horse and, from their earliest days together, had promised to grow into an exceptional young horsewoman, much to the satisfaction of the proud father, who wanted nothing more than to spend his days watching his daughter in the ring or on the cross-country course on Clover.

Time passed, the little rider grew, all at once the child became a girl. And then? Lost interest. In what? In riding, in horses, in Clover herself. And why? Because of the very nature of girlhood, baffling at the outset, soon defined. No more equestrienne but rather, and in her place, nothing but a single-minded girl obsessed with . . . exactly. Infatuation. Career defeated by gender's bodily dictates. Unthinkable betrayal of all concerned.

Thus and like the fall of an ax the proud father gave way to rage and sent the daughter off to school and sold her black and white horse to the by then not so young riding instructor with the head of flaming red Irish hair.

And, Clover told me then in the waning night, from that day to this she had belonged only to the bachelor Ralph—for Ralph had always been a bachelor, Clover said, and remained one now. Why, she murmured in the grainy darkness, there was no man of moods more violent and disharmonious than Ralph, and no man more interested in female riders than Ralph, though in all this time no girl or woman had ever set foot in the rooms above our

heads. Of course it was true, Clover added after a thoughtful
pause, that occasionally Ralph disappeared with one such girl or
woman or another—his riding students or riding companions, as
Clover had seen for herself—into their parked automobiles or
into the cab of Ralph's pickup truck; even, upon occasion, into
one of the old horse trailers parked about the place, which made
no sense to Clover but there it was. Nonetheless, and despite the
time Ralph also spent showing this woman or that girl the ancient
bridles and halters and saddles he kept for sale in the other barn,
which was not at all used as a barn, he in fact became increasingly
adept at keeping his own house and practiced in the art of cooking
for himself. Why, continued Clover, many a day had Ralph descended to work in the barn still wearing a long grease-bespat-
tered apron over his shirt and boots and britches. Yes, he was a
man whose manly attributes were tempered by his womanly
ways. As for the sweet aroma of the pies he baked . . .

But here, of course, Clover sensed my growing restiveness and
ceased and waited for me to put by my irritation and to thrust
high my nose once more to hers. As I did.

So we returned to communing, she and I, barn and cats and
even our own life stories once more forgotten as if there had been
no night, no past, as if the new day were not already breaking
around us like gentle waters against the rock of oblivion. Spiders
hung motionless in webs suspended from the rude beams above
our heads; there were no listeners to the distant hermit thrush and
chipping sparrow. In the ebb and flow of our stillness the sounds
of our shifting hooves, Clover's and mine, were indistinguishable
from the sounds in our throats.

And then?

Laughter! A man's laughter! Ralph's, of course. And what
could have been ruder, more shocking, more incongruous, more
destructive of a tender mood, than this burst of apparently senseless laughter crashing down upon us from the rooms above? It
faded, that laughter, stopped, and then without warning struck
again sharply, brutally, rising and falling in pitch and volume. We
listened, Clover and I, shamed and horrified we lowered our

heads and drew apart, no matter the planking that stood in all safe solidness between us. My loins tightened, the ghost of my little primal horse retreated, fled, was gone. Now, all but swallowed in the ugly swellings and subsidings of Ralph's laughter, there came down to us a murmuring, a demurring, the patient slightly offended sounds of Master, of course, attempting to still the unseemliness of Ralph's Irish merriment, which had already shattered the morning beyond repair.

Footsteps. The roar of the barn door sliding open. Sunlight. It was Ralph, still chuckling to himself, still giving way, suddenly, to further paroxysms of cold humor. Laughing he went to work, chuckling and laughing he flung fresh hay into Clover's stall and mine and, quite unaware of what he was doing, as it seemed, tossed us our morning feed, all the while possessed by his hideous and unaccountable amusement. Then, in the next moment, there appeared to us the puzzled object of that amusement. Master, of course, following the shaft of sunlight into the barn and, tall emaciated sunlit figure that he was, trailing after Ralph and talking, trying to pit the voice of reason and chagrin against Ralph's laughter.

"Well," said Master nobly, "I can only think you mean to ridicule me, Ralph."

"Not at all . . . !" Ralph managed to say, convulsed again, his generally florid face now as bright red as his carrot-colored hair.

"What then?" said Master helplessly.

"Nothing!" shouted Ralph through another spasm.

"But this behavior is insulting, Ralph," said Master sadly.

"Nothing of the sort . . . !" said Ralph, staring at Master and starting in again.

"Well then," said Master, "please stop."

"Kindly meant . . . ," said Ralph, his lips wet and eyes bright. "Can't help myself . . . !"

"But you must," said Master.

"I can only say," said Ralph, laughing outright in Master's face, "I can only say . . . that you look the part!"

Gales and torrents, then. An Irish storm.

Master waited in the sunlight, then found his chance, spoke on.

"Ralph," he said quietly, "these clothes belonged to my grandfather."

"Wonderful!" shouted Ralph, choking on a great bubble of Irish wit. "Wonderful . . . ? You look like a true horseman indeed!"

"Thank you," said Master.

"Harry Sir," said Ralph then, struggling to contain himself and dragging out the second word as he would in saying *slur* or *surly*, "in all my life I've not seen such a getup on any man. Fit garments for the master of Hidden Hall!"

"My grandfather," said Master, his self-confidence returning, "was born and bred and lived all his days until the age of ninety-two in your own country, Ralph. Your own country. The original Hidden Hall was his. And I am Irish too, you see."

"I tip my hat to ya!" shouted the Irish groom, stamping back out of the barn to take the air and catch his breath.

To all this Clover and I were mute witnesses, standing as still as horses carved in stone, heads hanging over our stall doors, anxiously watching and listening to Master's humiliation. There he waited, narrow shoulders stooped, thin arms at his sides, a ravished specter of foolishness and pride. Ralph, I knew by now, was a peculiar man but not irrational. In Ralph a fit of mirth would have cause enough and, further, serve in one way or another his general injurious disposition. So Master looked the part, as Ralph had said, and Ralph's laughter was more than justified. And what had Master done to deserve such a spate of Ralph's derision? He had changed his clothes, quite obviously, forever, or so he thought. No longer was he wearing his black business suit and polka-dotted tie but in their place had donned the attire of another age, when stables were as important to human life as the enormous stone houses in which those idle forebears of Master dwelt. Yes, Master was now garbed in riding clothes, as Ralph had said, and would remain so dressed to within hours of the very end—his or mine, as the case would be.

Riding britches. Worn and faded twill britches too large about the waist and flaring out from either thigh. Ancient britches of a military cut, a patchy forest of dead moths. And boots. Old black leather boots with brown cuffs at the tops, and cracked, dried-out, smelling still of the past fox-hunting exertions of the Old Gentleman, as Master sometimes called his grandfather, and so ill-fitting and so loose at the tops, where they should have been tight enough to refuse admittance to so much as the tip of a finger between leg and leather, that even the sweetest of child riders would have had to giggle and point at the sight of them, as in days to come such children did. And what had he strapped to the ankles and heels of those disastrous boots? Spurs! Long pointed tarnished affairs whose merest touch to the flanks would drive off any horse alive—let alone myself—and leave Master flat on the ground, where in fact in days to come he often lay. Finally there was the coat, a long dark heather-colored riding coat that was meant to be neatly tucked and fitted tight to the waist but was instead as loose as a sack, with buttons missing and one sleeve torn. And to top it off, to complete the picture of Master, who, once and for all, had donned the garb of his grandsire's elegance in the hunting field, as he clearly thought, there sat on his head—a shade too small, of course—an old black velvet-covered hunting helmet that looked all the sillier for the rakish angle at which misguided Master had cocked it atop his head, and there hung from his limp left hand a long bone-handled whip, which some-how, somewhere, had lost the long leather thong that once had curled and coiled into the midst of ravenous rapacious hounds.

So Master waited in the sunlight. And he was not smiling.

In the meanwhile, and controlling himself with a mighty effort, Ralph had returned to his chores and his charges, Clover and me, and, still shaking his head, had removed Clover's water buckets from the ringbolts where they hung on the wall of her box stall and had washed out those two buckets and filled them and re-turned them to Clover's stall. It was then that I first experienced firsthand one of the abrupt and violent changes that Clover had warned me often occurred in Ralph's moods, since one minute he was obviously still preoccupied with the pleasure he had had at

Master's expense, doing his work from mere habit, while the next he was there at my side in a rage.

"You bugger!" he shouted, striking me a terrible blow on my injured shoulder and contorting his face, spreading his thick booted legs, drawing back his great meaty fist in readiness to repeat his first assault, which in itself had left me stricken with fear and so rocked off balance that I was in risk of falling. "You filthy, filthy old bugger!"

"Ralph!" cried Master, rushing into my stall to stay Ralph's arm. "What's wrong?"

I had recoiled, of course, pressing myself as if into the very wood through which from the other side I could feel poor Clover's concern and the heat of her body, while Ralph stood facing me and so distraught and discolored that he looked for all the world unable to breathe. His laughter had not robbed him of half so much breath as had his wicked, wicked display of bad temper.

"If it's one thing I can't stand," he said finally, his brogue reduced to a near whisper, a mere tattered and strangled remnant of its usual hearty and melodious self, "it's a horse that befouls his own water!"

"Oh my," said Master, deeply distressed and as shocked and puzzled as I was. "What can you possibly be talking about, Ralph?"

"Can't you see?" said Ralph, now in low ragged menacing tones. "Can't you see that your miserable horse does not know his head from his tail? His mouth from his arse . . . ?"

"Please, Ralph," said Master weakly, "no crudity. . . ."

"Crudity?" exclaimed Ralph, the shout beginning to return to his spent and angered voice. "Can't you see that this filthy, wretched animal has shat in his own drinking water?"

"Good Lord!" exclaimed Master, alarm and incomprehension clouding his long thin kindly face. "Has he really? . . ."

"He has," said Ralph with obvious satisfaction. "Look for yourself."

"But, Ralph," said Master, without moving, "how could he?"

Here there was a long pause, as the sunlight grew warmer and brighter inside our barn and Ralph pinched together his white lips and slowly swiveled to stare long and steadily at Master. He frowned, there was a twitch in his lips, to my horror and Master's it appeared that his rage was fomenting anew, gathering itself to explode once more like a head of steam from an engine. But when next he spoke he did so in slow measured scornful tones and in a voice that suddenly sounded quite normal, except for its faintest gleam of sarcasm.

"By turning around," he said, his cupid's mouth beginning to curl, "that's how!"

"But, Ralph . . . ," began poor Master, stopping short as he saw the look in Ralph's eye.

"Listen to me," said Ralph then. "It's not unheard of. Once in a hundred horses there will be found that single peculiar beast with this filthy habit. . . ."

"But why?" Master managed to say.

"Who knows?" said Ralph. "How could anyone account for the fact that in barn after barn of healthy wholesome horses there is suddenly one sly ugly animal with this disgusting predisposition? He must like it, of course. He must derive some sort of filthy pleasure from being different from other, normal horses. Maybe he likes the sound. How's that for an answer? Maybe he thinks so highly of himself, or so little, that he just likes nosing aside the globs of his own excrement in order to suck into his peculiar mouth the fresh water he's already tainted with his own waste. Damned if I know. But I'll tell you one thing. I'll not stand to have one of his sort in my barn!"

"Ralph," said Master softly, "you go too far. Too far, Ralph."

With that, and as Ralph drew himself up to reply, Master took a step or two and glanced down to inspect for himself my buckets, which hung from their ringbolts innocently enough, as I thought, at about waist high on a man.

Throughout this brief and strange ordeal I not only cowered as close as I could possibly get to Clover, from whom I was undeniably separated, but made not a sound and waited in honest and innocent and, yes, frightened puzzlement for what might happen next. For in truth I saw nothing wrong, though it was true enough, as only I could know, that never before had I so much as thought of doing what had driven the fastidious Ralph into such a rage. After all, for nearly twenty years I had drunk my water, and water none too fresh at that, from nothing more than the old rusted bathtub that Josephine had filled when she felt like it, that bathtub that was not only incongruous but communal, drunk from by every other shambling ailing horse at the Metacomet Ranch as well as myself. No, I had never once had the impulse to leave my personal mark in that bathtub. And what if I had and the other poor devils had followed my example? That surely would have been enough to offend even myself. No, it was only during the night just past, when there was space that was mine and two clean and freshly filled water buckets that were mine alone, that now and again, in the moonlit darkness, I had found myself marking the rhythm of the communion that Clover and I were sharing and, without thought, without awareness, turning and adding a small private pleasure to a larger. And from time to time I drank too, from those very buckets that I had made additionally mine, and if anything, the taste of that water was even sweeter, thanks to my thoughtless doing, than it had been when drawn from the pipe and hydrant that went to Ralph's well. Regression? Perhaps. Unusual? Perhaps. But whose business was it, after all, except mine?

So there was basis enough for my mystification and hurt that Ralph had reacted with such cruel violence at my naturalness, and demeaned me in Clover's presence and caused me to suffer one moment, two moments, of guilt, of shame.

"Well, honestly, Ralph," said Master quietly, interrupting my self-justifying meditation, "it does not seem to me as bad as you say. A few dark-golden shapes in clear water, Ralph. You wouldn't object to a fresh stream flooding a field of grain, would you?"

"Christ!" exclaimed Ralph, and Master drew back and prepared for the worst. "In this barn," he continued, once more in even, menacing tones, his voice then abruptly rising, "I shall have no perversion! Do you hear? No perversion! From either you or this offensive animal that I have agreed much against my better judgment to help you to keep alive. Do you understand?"

Master, who was as chagrined as I was, knew enough to resist no further, and nodded.

"Harry Sir," said Ralph, his brogue relaxing along with his breath, though the *churl* and *surly* sounds were still audible in the required word of respect he always tacked onto Master's name, "I have made you a bargain and I shall stick to my bargain—within limits. I shall teach you what you want to learn, though in all frankness I think the endeavor's foolish if not hopeless . . ."

Here Master demurred.

". . . and accompany you where you want to go, within reason and if you are capable of even climbing upon a horse's back, which I doubt. . . ."

Now Master remained quiet, accepting his humbling and mine.

"But in this barn," Ralph continued in still more brutally measured tones, which brooked no misunderstanding, "and in any matter having to do with horses or horse people, I am the authority, the sole authority! Do you understand? And Hidden Hall or no Hidden Hall, you are nothing! Nothing at all! Do you understand? No more, in fact"—here Ralph brightened, suddenly and scornfully inspired—"no more, in fact, than that horse's turds in those buckets!"

Now Ralph stopped, clearly pleased with himself, and smiled broadly and ran his florid hand through his flaming hair and stared at Master, as if daring Master to offer so much as one word of objection.

"Well, Ralph," said Master after a long pause and misguidedly encouraged by Ralph's smile, "when do we start?"

Ralph grimaced and then smiled again and said, "As soon as you learn to tell a horse's head from his tail!" Whereupon he left us, climbing to the rooms above, from which there soon wafted down the smell of coffee.

When Ralph returned, hot and steaming cup in hand, making an obvious show of offering Master no such restorative drink, which Master sorely needed, he merely pointed to a broom in a corner and told Master to see if he could learn to sweep up the scattered straw and hay from the aisleway, after which Master was going to learn to do my buckets, as the expression went, since he, Ralph, would never touch my filthy buckets again.

It was not but a few breaths later, alas, that I next disgraced myself in Ralph's eyes.

As follows.

After Master had dutifully swept the aisleway, frowning in concentration the while, man and broom similarly tall and thin and stiff, and after Ralph had led Master through the rudiments of doing my buckets—sniffing them for the telltale smell of sulfur, the clearest indication that a horse's water is not fresh, and carrying the buckets outside to the old-fashioned iron pump, emptying them, scrubbing them thoroughly with a stiff brush, refilling them with the clear spring water that gushed from the pump, and then returning them, with great exertion, apparently, to their places on the wall of my stall—it was then that Ralph decided to introduce Master to the art of grooming and hence led me from my stall into the aisleway, where he enjoined me to stand as he affixed to either side of my halter the crossties, as they were called, two ropes that hung from additional ringbolts, high on two of the upright beams facing each other across the aisleway. In this fashion I was both held in place yet free to move, within reason, as I chose to—a few steps forward, a few back, rump with all the latitude in the world to swing this way and that, and my head, above all, reasonably unencumbered, so that I could fling it high, if I so chose, or down, and from side to side, as I could my haunches. Of course there was nothing to prevent me from kicking, if that feared impulse came upon me, and—most important—nothing to prevent me from snapping at the hand or arm or shoulder of that person attempting to care for my hooves and tail and mane and coat, or, in the language of the barn, to tack me up, though heaven forbid that I should ever snap at Master or even Ralph.

The instruction began.

"This," said Ralph, "is the currycomb, and this the hard

brush, this the soft brush, this the pick with which you must remove the earth and possibly pebbles from the hooves of your horse—once, that is, we get him shod. After all, we don't want this horse of yours going lame"—here a thoughtless laugh since I was already lame—"but for now his toes are so long and his frogs so nearly obliterated that this part of the discussion is merely academic. . . ."

"Frogs?" said Master.

"We'll get to that," said Ralph, "in due time. Now then," he continued brusquely, "when you walk behind your horse, stay close to his quarters, for the closer you are to him the less chance he's got to kick you. . . ."

"Kick?" said Master.

"Yes, yes," said Ralph impatiently. "A horse needs room in order to kick. That, I should think, is obvious."

So it went, as Ralph talked and Master watched and listened, and Ralph demonstrated the proper way to curry a horse, great clouds of dust and dandruff rising from my coat as he did so, for I had received no care of this kind for twenty years, until at last Ralph handed the currycomb and brush to Master and told him to follow his, Ralph's, example, and said that if he, Master, did not work up a more than visible sweat in the process, then he had learned nothing and was not doing his job.

Timorously yet eagerly Master set to, dutifully though weakly circling my matted and itching hide with the curry, periodically banging the teeth of the curry against the wooden back of the brush. However, and despite myself, as soon as Master raised high his arm and attempted to clean and stimulate that part of my neck closest to the base of my bony head, inadvertently I stepped to the side, pinned back my ears, jerked round my head before either one of us could so much as blink, and snapped at Master as at a nagging fly, whereupon Master dropped brush and curry and leapt away.

"Ralph," said Master incredulously, "he tried to bite me!"

"So he did," said Ralph, "the bugger," and did the obvious, which was to step forward swiftly and strike the side of my head as so many down the years had done before him. But to tell the truth, I cared not a jot for the blow that Ralph had given me, though it was a good one, a fast one, a blow that was much more than a cuff to my jaw. However, I did regret having frightened Master, who now, in response to Ralph's rough demand, once more took up his work, though in a still more gingerly fashion than when he had started.

On it went, as Master struggled to comb my matted and tangled tail, holding it at arm's length and clearly attempting to keep himself as far as he could from my hind legs and hooves and out of harm's way, and summoned the courage to attempt to brush my ears with the soft brush—another snap of my jaws, another blow and muttered curse from Ralph—until, quite suddenly, Master dropped his arms and turned to Ralph, as if my grooming had simply fled his mind.

"What now?" said Ralph. "You're not concentrating. And you haven't even begun to work up a sweat."

"Ralph," said Master slowly, "I have just heard in my head the glorious and obvious ring of this horse's name!"

"His name?" said Ralph. "He's already got a name, as you were told by that woman who only yesterday took you to the cleaners, as you Americans say, when she sold you this worthless horse."

"No, no, Ralph," said Master, excitement evident now in his voice. "I mean his new name. His real name. The name that most befits his character. I'm surprised that I didn't know this horse's name the moment I saw him! I should have, Ralph. I should have!"

"I see that I shall be able to teach you nothing," said Ralph, a new and weary disinterest dulling his brogue. As for myself, however, suddenly I remembered the promise that Master had made to Josephine only the day before and stiffened, waited, knowing that for me this moment, this day, this hour, was about to become momentous. Nothing less than the restoration of my dignity was in store for me—and for this I waited as I had waited for nothing at all in my entire life.

The comely immaculate barn was warm and bright and peaceful, and could hardly be more conducive to contentment and a sense of well-being, thanks to the Indian summer sun that was now at its height and hence suffused the place with the fullness of life itself. Ralph, who in but moments had become increasingly if not thoroughly bored, lounged against one of the uprights and held in his thick athletic arms his favorite cat, a great orange long-haired beast called Fuzzy, who, from what I had seen of him the night before, could break a rat's neck with the merest blink of his shrewd and bloodshot eyes and toss a five-pound rodent, broken neck and all, up to the heights of the barn's freshly white-washed ceiling with not much more than a nod of his lazy vicious head—a head more appropriate to a miniature lion than to a cat, no matter the size and fierceness of the cat. Fuzzy was the only male cat on the farm and thus spent most of his waking hours killing rats or crushing beneath him one after another and as swiftly as he possibly could, this yowling female cat or that one, since there were so many female cats on Ralph's farm that one of them was always in heat for Fuzzy. What I thought of that pampered uncastrated cat is clear enough. Yet now, in the aisleway, he filled Ralph's arms like some overblown sleeping infant, orange tail limp and fat face the most odious possible image of self-contentment—though I knew that in this suddenly timeless and tranquil scene, one of that cat's eyes was slit just enough to keep me steadily in full view and that his lazy grinning mouth was as filled with wicked little teeth as a box with pins.

Sun in the barn, cat in Ralph's arms, the distant sound of breeze and creek and Clover whinnying from somewhere in the large pasture into which Ralph had turned her out as soon as she had finished her morning's hay and feed. But into this stilled moment Master leaned, expectantly, eyes wide and throat muscles already in motion, on the verge, obviously, of making his pronouncement. And into this moment I too leaned, listening, waiting, trying to ignore the favored cat.

"Ralph," said Master finally, and not in the eagerness of an aged child but in tone and cadence appropriate to an old man presenting a silent crowd with a declaration of immense magnitude. "Ralph, this horse's name is Petrarch!"

Silence. Cat shifting and yawning in Ralph's arms. Ralph leaning back with half-closed eyes and staring upward as if for some sign of the latest acrobatics of one of Fuzzy's half-dead rats.

"Do you hear, Ralph? Petrarch!"

"Ah yes," said Ralph with a sigh, "I know it well. Famous old County Kildare name."

"Ralph!" exclaimed Master and laughed like a kindly old lecturer high on a podium in a drafty hall filled with dunces. "Don't be absurd. Francesco Petrarch was a fourteenth-century poet. He was born in Italy, Ralph, not Ireland. He was a cleric and a great classical scholar, as well as the author of the *Rime sparse,* which immortalizes his beloved Laura."

"Clerics," said Ralph, now cradling Fuzzy in one arm and stroking the cat behind its ears. "I've no use for clerics. In every pub in the world—in my country, that is—you'll find one pious cleric who after a single glass of red wine, while the rest of us drink one frothy pint of beer, naturally, steals every lass in the place right out from under the noses of us honest lads."

More silence. Cat staring at me with wide-open eyes. Master wringing his hands and beginning, at last, to sweat, as if from the grooming that he had quite forgotten.

"Besides," said Ralph, "I know nothing whatsoever about verse and could care less."

"Poetry, Ralph, poetry!" exclaimed Master, as I, attempting as best I could to ignore the fat cat and the Irish groom, waited to learn more about this mysterious figure whose name was as of this very moment mine.

"Songs, now," said Ralph, tweaking one of the little pointed red and orange ears, "songs are something else again. I've got quite a voice, you know."

"Conceits," said Master, standing taller and once more finding the pleasure with which he had begun his disquisition on my namesake, "and wit, cleverness, disputations, and scholastic precision. Allegory, personification, self-accusation, wooing, outcry,

self-blame, self-praise, repentance, and farewell to love—there
you have him, Ralph, this poet of obsessive yearning and lovesick-
ness, frustration, and a belief in the lady of his life as miraculous
and destined for an early death. He invented the sonnet sequence,
Ralph, and, to his beloved Laura, wrote some of the greatest love
lyrics of all time."

"Well," said Ralph, yawning, as the cat opened wide his mouth
and gave me, so to speak, one terrible sight of the pins and needles
massed therein, "perhaps you should tell me about this Laura."

"Ralph," said Master patiently, "you miss the point entirely.
Petrarch thought of his beloved Laura as a laurel—as a tree, that
is—"

"Poor fool," said Ralph, as the cat, no longer languid, began
to squirm in his arms and to look about the barn with a suddenly
serious and unmistakable gleam in his fiery eyes.

"Purity, Ralph, purity!" exclaimed Master. "Petrarch believed
in writing the page of eternity! He believed that the eternal poem
is achieved only at the cost of the poet's own natural life. The
poet's vitality must be metamorphosed into words. To put it more
simply, just as Petrarch transformed Laura into the ever-living
tree that bears her name—or perhaps it was vice versa—so the
poet both dies and lives in the poem he writes! And thereby lives
on in eternity!"

"I see," said Ralph, and without warning dropped the cat, who
was off like a shot and in another moment causing a yowling
ruckus of desire and conquest I hardly heard, so fixed was I on
Ralph and Master and the discussion that I did not as yet believe
was meant entirely for me or my extolling. "And you want to
name this very horse after such a man? If man he was and if he
did in fact exist!"

"Oh, he existed," said Master with a smile, "though to be
honest, we are not so sure about Laura."

"But we're quite certain about the tree," said Ralph, wiping his
hands as if to rid them of the wet smell of the cat.

"Of course, Ralph," said Master sadly.

"Now as I understand it," said Ralph in a new and stronger tone of voice, "if this ungainly horse is your versifier Petrarch—"

"Poet, Ralph . . ."

"—then you, as prospective rider, are this horse's verse!"

"Why, Ralph," said Master, happiness momentarily restored, "I hadn't thought of that!"

"Which is to say," continued Ralph, glancing again toward the rafters overhead, a sly look beginning to mold the puffy features of his heavy face, "which is to say that this horse is going to give his life for your fulfillment—"

"Wait, Ralph—" Master interrupted with a mild frown but was himself interrupted as Ralph talked on and a second yowling suddenly commenced.

"By analogy," said Ralph, "as we lads used to say down at the Old Tank and Tit—short for Old Tankard and Titmouse, for your edification—this beloved horse of yours is going to die for you if not, in fact, from under you!"

"Oh, Ralph," said Master.

"Or," said Ralph, his voice containing veritable forests and fields and hillocks of emerald green trees and grass and ferns, "to simply reverse the analogy for the sake of the argument, we may say that from your point of view, riding is nothing more or less than writing poetry . . ."

Master for an instant looked relieved.

"Which," finished Ralph with a flourish, "is to say that riding shall be the death of you! And," said Ralph after a pause, his voice descending to its clearest tone of menace and satisfaction, "if that's what riding means to you, then ride you shall!"

"When?" said Master eagerly and without a moment's thought.

"This very day," said Ralph, "or else I'll treat you to a little bit of the Old Tank and Tit, if you follow my meaning. But there's one last thing," said Ralph, turning and with a mean eye looking toward Fuzzy and his by now third willing victim of the hour. "If you insist on calling this owlhead—which for your information is a horse that can't be trained—if you insist on naming this owl-head of a horse Petrarch, as you say you will, then I tell you this: I myself shall never call this animal anything but Pete!"

"No you shan't, Ralph," answered Master, laughing and stooping for brush and currycomb, "for you must remember that Petrarch was an aristocrat, Ralph. An aristocrat! And Petrarch is my horse's name!"

And there I had it, full understanding of Master's wisdom, and dignity restored to me along with the very aristocracy that was mine by birth, and that same aristocracy not only acknowledged but declared and allowed and inscribed forever, like script on a stone, in my new name. Goodbye, Sweet William! Goodbye, Old Horse! Petrarch I was and always would be!

However, and unfortunately for me, on the very aristocracy of my new name there hung, confoundedly, my second disgrace of that strange day. For in my excitement and there and then, while Ralph moved once more as if to take the air outside the barn, and Fuzzy's victim caterwauled in pain and ecstasy, and Master turned and proudly laid one of his long thin parchment-covered hands upon my neck, suddenly and helplessly my tail rose and swung aside and before I could so much as shut my jaws the inevitable occurred, and behind me and flat on the aisleway lay my relief and pleasure in a sweet steaming heap. My only consolation was that Clover was not present to witness my body's dreadful timing. Master, of course, had no consolation at all, as he awaited another burst of wrath from Ralph, as fresh as my manure. But no wrath was forthcoming.

"At least," said Ralph instead, turning again and standing with his hands on his hips, "at least it's not diarrhea. And now you shall have the opportunity of learning how to clean up after your obviously incontinent horse. But here"—another pause, another yowl as faint as a whisper—"here is my final thought of the day. I want you to be absolutely sure—do you understand?—that when you remove that pile there"—indicating my droppings with a single caustic nod of his massive head—"you do not—I say not—deposit those droppings on the mound of manure already

seasoning beside my garden, but rather—rather, do you understand?—start your own quite separate little heap of your horse's
waste. I shall not have your horse's waste contaminating the
compost for my garden, of which, in case you have not already
noticed, I am quite proud."

Whereupon Ralph and Fuzzy strolled out of the barn together,
leaving me to ponder my pleasure and shame and Master to cope
as best he could with his newest problem.

This problem, baffling as it was, was followed swiftly by another,
as is usually the case in the world of the horse. For no sooner had
he managed to discover the large long-handled shovel and to
remove my droppings by use of a spurred and booted foot and a
hand as well, stooping and complaining to himself the while, as
I could plainly see by swinging round my head, than Master, upon
returning to the barn and so propping the shovel against the
nearest wall so that someone—horse or man—was sure to trip
over it, found himself suddenly and confoundedly alone with me.

The noon hour was settling down upon Ralph's place. There
was stillness everywhere and not a cat to be seen, including Fuzzy.
From the apartment above there came the smoky inviting smell of
burning charcoal and blackening meat, and the faint tones of
Ralph humming one of his Irish ditties, as he called them.

And here alone stood Master and I, my head still loosely
trapped between the crossties, my body as tall as ever and quite
free, Master standing before me and again wringing his hands.

"What shall I do?" he asked me in a hopeless whisper, looking
at me with a beseeching eye while standing far enough away from
my long bony face to avoid me, should I choose to thrust forward
suddenly my long thin jaws and rheumy nose.

Naturally I could not answer his question, which was serious
and not at all rhetorical, but instead made a short minimal sound
in my throat, which, misinterpreted as it clearly was, only added
to poor Master's distress.

He stepped back, I advanced, he attempted to move to one side
and, at an angle that could not have been more awkward or

precarious, to lean in my direction so as to study how the crosstie descending from the upright beam nearest him was affixed to my halter. But that sagging length of rope ended in a metal device that hooked, in some fashion that Master could not understand, to a little square of brass in the side of my halter. Master, as I could tell at a glance, knew only one thing about that crosstie—that it could not be unfastened, so far, at least, as he could see.

So there we were.

Finally, in obvious desperation, while pressing himself back against the wooden wall and once again beginning to perspire, Master slowly reached out one long thin arm and hand and extended fingers—for what reason I was sure again that he did not know. But so many brutish young men had thrust their careless hands toward me at the Metacomet Ranch that my reflex—a sudden snapping motion of my jaws at the tips of Master's fingers—was something that as yet I could not avoid, despite my immediate regret and even mortification.

Master stifled his frightened cry and drew back his hand.

Then after a moment, and raising his wolfish face toward the rooms above, "Ralph?" he called. "Ralph? Can you come here?"

Still the lively ditty and the headier smell of smoke and meat.

Master waited and then called again, this time in a voice that was clearly heard above, despite the ring and clatter of cooking and the jaunty dips and dives of Ralph's ditty—heard, as Master and I knew together, because the singing if not the sizzling stopped.

"What on earth do you want?" Ralph shouted down at last.

"I need you, Ralph."

"Whatever for?"

"Why, I simply cannot free my Petrarch from these infernal ropes!"

"For the love of God," shouted Ralph, "throw that animal into his stall and come up here directly or you'll get no lunch!"

"I cannot do it, Ralph," called Master in a voice that was both firm and miserable. "I simply cannot do it."

"Very well," shouted Ralph. "Stay where you are, for all I care!"

"Petrarch," said poor Master then, speaking to me in a soft and sorry voice, "he's not very generous, that man. Or gentlemanly either."

So Master did indeed miss his lunch, as Ralph had promised he would, and passed the time devoted to Ralph's lunch—a long event of great satisfaction, as we could hear—by hefting in either hand the brushes, the currycomb, and once or twice attempting to press one or the other against my coat, an effort that he soon gave up, thanks to my reflexes.

Then the sound of whistling. Then boots clumping down the outside stair. Then the return of the man without whom, sad to tell, neither Master nor myself could get along.

"Now then," said Ralph, "if you'll just open that stall door, we'll just put away this horse of yours until we're ready for him. Next time, or I miss my guess, you'll have learned the rudiments of self-reliance. You know that the noonday meal is the best I cook."

"But, Ralph . . . ," Master began.

"Never mind," said Ralph quickly, his good humor floating on the surface of his full stomach. "You'll get the hang of it soon enough. But as a matter of fact," he continued, unsnapping the crossties and returning me to my stall, "you did exactly the right thing, given the circumstances of your helpless ignorance. That is, we never leave a horse alone for long on the crossties. It's all too easy for such a horse to panic, you see, and to begin to heave himself about or even throw himself down on his haunches like a sitting dog and then, since his head is caught high in the air and his rear end is dragging itself this way and that on the aisleway floor, to break his neck—which I have chanced to see more than once in the home country. There are stupid children everywhere, not just in this great and happy land that's yours. . . ."

"But, Ralph," said Master, risking a modicum of self-assertiveness, "you know my forebears. . . ."

"That's enough!" said Ralph. "I don't want to hear about it. Now then, let's see if we can find your Petrarch"—the *trarch* of my name extended and harshened so that it was a match indeed for the *churl* and *surly* in "Sir"—"a fine big saddle and handsome bridle. Come along!"

Off they went together to the other barn, and back they came, Master struggling to carry in both arms a large dusty English saddle unlike any I had ever seen, and Ralph humming to himself and swinging a bridle as old and dusty and cracked as the saddle.

Back to the crossties. Saddle placed upon my back in much the way that Josephine used to roughly weigh me down with the monstrous Mexican saddle that was once—but never again—the bane of my life.

"But, Ralph," said Master, as Ralph slipped the stiff leather reins over my head and removed my halter and began to draw toward my mouth the thick and ugly-looking bit, "aren't you afraid of him? We know he bites. . . ."

"Afraid of him!" shouted Ralph, whereupon I shied and showed him the whites of my eyes. "This horse knows as well as he knows anything that if he makes one move against my person, I shall kill him!"

"Oh, Ralph," said Master, "you are such a violent man!"

"All depends," said Ralph. "But let's get on with it. I'll teach you the names of the various parts of this fine bridle and saddle another time, as well as how to fit them to Petrarch, here, and to do them up. Of course I might add that I have indeed known a man or two in my life who was afraid of horses. One dandy lad from near my village, and a splendid rider otherwise, was absolutely phobic about walking behind a horse. Got himself kicked to death for his fear. Another lad I remember was forever telling me that he had nightmares every night about his horse tearing a huge chunk from his cheek. Even when he stopped riding, for soon he did, the nightmares, as he used to confess in the Tank and Tit, continued. Served him right. But I'm confident that you're not this kind of man. Besides, and as everyone knows, if a person entertains even the faintest thought of fear in the presence of a horse, that fear will smell as strong to that horse as a full privy would smell to yourself at the height of summer—and naturally such a horse will sooner or later hurt or even maim for life a man who carries about with him such a foul smell. No, better to keep away from fear of horses, Harry Sir."

"But they're so big," said Master.

"A man like yourself," said Ralph, "needs a big horse. Now then . . ."

Midafternoon. The paddock. The soft warm sun going its way. Not a hint of Clover to my eye or nose. And in the middle of the paddock the three of us—Ralph, who now wore his hat, adorned with the dead poppy, Master, and I, equally afraid of each other, though for different reasons, and of the entire procedure that was about to commence. Beside me was a wooden apple crate, intended to help Master raise himself to my back. At my head stood Ralph, holding me, while farther off stood Master, clutching his bone-handled whip and smiling, despite his fear, and awaiting Ralph's first word of instruction. At least the footing in Ralph's paddock was soft and moderately free of pebbles and small rocks, and for a moment longer I was aware of the clear sky overhead, the scent of fading flowers and summer on the air, the gentle landscape all around us, varied and natural, marred only by the sight of the old horse trailers and of Ralph's shirts, still on the line.

"First of all," said Ralph, in tones that were not unkindly, "you may put down your whip and, even more important, remove your spurs."

"But they belonged to my grandfather, as I have told you, Ralph."

"I'll not say it again. Rid yourself of your whip and spurs!"

"But why, Ralph? I have expected all along to be able to ride as I wish."

"Do you want to be killed?" said Ralph, patience all but gone. "If we even get you upon this horse's back we'll be lucky. But should you so much as touch him with that pathetic whip or those spurs that were obviously forged in the Middle Ages, that horse would be off and away and over the fence for all I know, despite his lameness, and you'd be flat on your back and fortunate to be alive, if alive you were, and with God knows what broken hip or leg. And do you know what a single fall like that would do to me? Raise my insurance rates, that's what! Or perhaps make me lose my insurance completely. And where would I be then?"

"Ralph," said Master, as he dropped the whip and knelt—clearly a painful move—and unfastened his ungainly spurs, "with my own eyes I have seen my grandfather mounted and carrying this whip and wearing these spurs. And sooner or later I shall do the same!"

"With your own eyes, eh?"

"That's right, Ralph. It was my grandfather's Golden Wedding anniversary, for which the entire family gathered, even from as far away as America. My grandfather was ninety-two years old at the time, while I was only a shy boy of seventeen."

"Seventeen?" said Ralph. "I suppose you had yourself a pretty good time with our young Irish serving girls."

"Ralph," said Master, climbing awkwardly again to his full height, "this day is so important to me that I don't mind confiding in you a fact of my life. Which is this—that I have yet to know a woman, as I believe the Biblical expression goes."

"Yet to what?" said Ralph in feigned disbelief. "I would never have believed that of you, Harry Sir! But," with a pause, a swipe of his free hand across his thick moist lips, "perhaps I can help you to remedy that sorry condition. If all goes well."

"Oh, but Ralph," said Master, smiling, "I don't mind my 'sorry' condition, as you call it. Not at all!"

"Amazing!" said Ralph. "And to think that I myself was handed my manhood on a platter, so to speak, when I was a mere lad of nine—and by my own sister at that!"

"Your own sister!" exclaimed Master.

"Aye, she was a wicked child, my sister was," said Ralph with a laugh and a new sweet thickening of his brogue, "and a wicked girl and wicked woman after that! I loved her dearly."

"But, Ralph," said Master incredulously, "that's incest!"

"Oh," said Ralph, smiling off toward the horizon, "she never invited me to the final plunge, so to speak, though I dare say she would have if she'd only thought of it. Why, my sister, Carrie, had such a bag of tricks, even when she was a skinny twelve to my remarkably well-developed nine, that when she first opened that lovely sack to my greedy eyes, neither one of us knew then or after what was happening, until all at once she abandoned me for much older lads and full-grown men. Even at twelve she had dandy little freckled breasts—"

"Ralph," Master interrupted with an attempt at sternness, "if you must speak of a woman in this disrespectful fashion, at least you might use the proper word, which is *bosoms.*"

"You do seem a bit obsessed with words," said Ralph. "But bosoms to you, tits to me, there's no joy in the world compared with fondling them!"

"Ralph," said Master faintly, "am I not to ride?"

"Oh, my Carrie was a wicked one," continued Ralph. "She had no use for our parents, but she thought the world of me. Imagine, there was my da, a splendid man weighing a full fourteen stone, and my ma, a tiny thing and given to moping and weeping a great deal, though in my eyes she was the most beautiful woman in the world—except for Carrie, of course. My da and ma were Patrick and Maureen, two lovelier names you could never find in the land of peat bogs and fairies. And do you know that Carrie had no use for these parents of ours, the man and woman of all the men and women in Ireland who brought two such unusual children as Carrie and yours truly into the world? She actually went so far, even before the age of twelve, as to ridicule them—my da and ma—in any and every way she could. She taunted Da and flaunted at poor Da her bosoms, as you call them, while she openly scorned and laughed at Ma, even when that poor little woman was sunk in a corner of the room and weeping. Think of it! As for their names, to their very faces she called them not Father and Mother or Patrick and Maureen but—would you believe it?— Dippy and Mippy of all things! Of course it's perfectly true that Da was a little daft from the Great War, while Ma's moping could get on the nerves, even my own, once in a while, and Carrie thought that Mippy was a better word than Mopey. As you can see, Harry Sir, you're not the only one in this life with an ear and an eye for words!"

"Oh, Ralph," said Master, "I've not yet made a single claim in favor of myself in all the days we've been together!"

"I beg to disagree," said Ralph. "At any rate, those names, Dippy and Mippy, were the only thing I could not forgive of my wonderful wicked sister."

By now I had all but lost sight of the sky above and the day that was passing and the fact that I longed for at least a sign of Clover's whereabouts, so caught up was I in the speeches of these two men and so puzzled by them, though in all they said I had begun to detect an undercurrent that made me think of the hated Fuzzy, who, had he been a horse, would have been known as full, which is to say an uncastrated male horse, which in turn made me more aware than ever that I was anything but full, no matter my love of Clover or how much she aroused sensations I had never thought to feel again. This particular rumination of mine was short-lived, for suddenly I realized that Ralph and Master had fallen silent, as if other and yet related ruminations had possessed them too. Then Master spoke.

"Ralph," he said, "one detail in all you've said seems incomprehensible to me. I hope you don't mind my saying so," he continued with embarrassment, "but I believe that freckles are by definition orange in color. And a woman with black hair and orange freckles is simply an impossibility!"

"Who said that Carrie's hair was black?" answered Ralph with an abrupt return to meanness.

"You didn't, Ralph. But it is common knowledge that every Irish woman's hair is black. It's the black hair that accounts in part for their famous beauty!"

"What!" cried Ralph. "Are you trying to tell me that a man of your learning and gentility and broad-mindedness is still one of those who, in the most bigoted possible fashion, can only conceive of the Irish as stereotypical mockeries? Is that what you mean? To insult my native land and its people? My sister in particular?"

"Oh no, Ralph," Master hastened to say, "and I do apologize if I have offended you. I was merely asking about"—a pause, another pause, eyes averted—"the freckles you happened to mention."

"Can't get my sister's speckled breasts out of your mind, eh?"

"Not at all, Ralph, that's not what I mean. . . ."

"And can you not see my hair? Has the splendid color of my red hair managed to escape your attention?"

"Of course not, Ralph."

"And do you for one moment consider me a stereotypical representative of Irish manhood? Do you?"

Here Master merely shook his head in the negative.

"Well," said Ralph, "if you had merely used a little imagination you would have known that my sister's hair was as red as mine—redder in fact. More fiery, more tinged with gold, and wild—do you hear that word?—wild as my own hair could never be."

"I'm beginning to see her, Ralph. Believe me."

"I should think so," said Ralph, only slightly mollified. "But to be perfectly honest, you could never in a million years see or imagine her white skin, the freckles that spread down her fair thin chest to envelop, finally, her tits. Do you hear? Tits, I say, that were like white eggs speckled but with that irresistible orange color in the nest of her blouse. Oh, the hands that ached for Carrie, but never for long, because she could not tolerate such aching in her brother or any other man, except Dippy, of course, so no sooner did she detect that male aching than she dispelled it, along with her own aching, or I miss my guess. And sing? Why, Carrie could sing like a choirboy, except for the words, of course, which were enough to bring to crumbling ruins any church in Ireland at the first clear note she struck. And do you know from whence came that high clear sound of Carrie's voice engaged in song?"

No answer, though now Master appeared to be suffering again yet to be avidly interested as well.

"From her mouth, of course," said Ralph.

Master nodded.

"But also, astoundingly enough, from between her legs!"

"Ralph!" cried Master, anger and disbelief turning his long face to chalk.

"It's true," said Ralph. "Gloriously true. Or perhaps I should simply say that whatever the origins of Carrie's singing voice, that voice came from the sweetest spot in all the land of Ireland—and was the sweet spot of woman herself."

"But that's vulgar, Ralph! Just vulgar!"

"By God," said Ralph, "you've no ear for poetry, that's all. But if you think Carrie's singing voice was vulgar—"

"No, Ralph, only what you said about it . . ."

"—then I suppose the sight of my sister sitting in the Tank and Tit at a round table with a dozen lads and a log as big as a hog smoking on the hearth and blinding all to everything and everyone except Carrie herself, who was drinking from her tankard like the six poor lads who were beside themselves with the ache that I have tried to describe, would strike you as downright obscene!"

"Ralph," Master tried again, "this is the hour of my first lesson!"

"And a damned good one it is too. But you know, there was a cleric in the room that day, one of the men in black with skirts to his ankles and who had not seen Carrie before in his life, and obviously to all concerned he was struck, yes, struck, even as I stood at the bar and watched, with a lust for my sister as strong as his lust for the Virgin herself. And Carrie was no virgin—"

"I'll not hear it, Ralph. I won't!"

"And do you know that I could have killed that cleric with one good smack to his conceited face but did nothing but laugh and watch how Carrie handled the situation? And do you know that that black devil had the effrontery to think that he could best six Irish lads and steal my very sister from beneath their noses? And what do you think Carrie did about this unknown cleric presuming to insult both her friends and her virtue? Why, slowly as you please she simply set down her tankard and rose from the table. One by one she led off each lad to a little store-room she was privileged to use how and when she wished, until she had gone through the lot of them—it took about three hours—while that poor black-gowned cleric watched and suffered, though obviously he thought that he'd yet have his turn at the end. At last all six lads were again seated round the table, whereupon Carrie, still standing, smiled at the miserable cleric and in her sweet voice said, "Father, perhaps you'll hear my confession tomorrow," and turned and took up her hat and coat and strolled out of the pub. My eyes were smarting that day, I'll tell you, but never have I laughed so hard inside myself. And the lads, I might add, cheered when Carrie started out the door."

"Vulgarity, Ralph," Master managed to say, "and now disrespect for religion."

"I'll tell you what," Ralph said after a pause. "There was no girl in the world more religious than my Carrie. It's just that she hated clerics, despised them, and had long before determined that clerics were the only men in the world to whom she would not give herself. But I'll tell you this too. From my da I learned to ride. From my ma I learned to respect and even to acquire the tenderness of a woman. And from my sister, my dearest sister, I learned what it is to be a man. Now come over here and get on this horse!"

"Ralph," said Master weakly, "I don't believe I can."

"Of course you can," Ralph shouted, and he laughed. "You've a perfect body for riding a horse. So summon your courage, Harry Sir, and do as I say."

Had the moment come? Apparently it had, as Master, who must have remembered again the anticipation that had been his from the hour of dawn, began to smile and stepped forward.

I swung my head, receiving for my curiosity another cuffing to my nose—gentler, to be sure, than I might have expected—and watched my rider approaching me at last. His steps were uneven, his smile faint, his forehead wetter than it had been in the barn or all the while that Ralph had reminisced about his sister.

"Come along," said Ralph in a voice that was almost kindly, and Master obeyed, raising puffs of dusty earth as he did so and, with one unsteady hand, attempted to settle more firmly upon his head the outlandish black velvet helmet. In the center of all the stillness that stretched far and wide around us, we stood to-gether—one horse, two men—in a fateful tableau of three so gathered and grouped as if for some portentous event, as indeed it was. Not so much as the song of a single bird intruded through that motionless Indian summer air, no figure strode across the slopes of the far pasture.

The moment of mounting. The irreversible union of horse and man. At last.

Encouraging words from Ralph, a helping hand extended. Delaying argument from Master. Fear swimming mutely in the sound of his voice.

Master standing atop the wobbling box. Master taking up the stiffened reins. Master thrusting one foot—the wrong one, ini-tially—into a stirrup.

"That's it," said Ralph. "Well done. Now swing your other leg over, and there you are. But mind you don't come down too heavy on his back. His back hurts, you know. And think how it would be if you were out here on all fours and suddenly some great weight came crashing down on your back. Wouldn't like it much, would you?"

But obviously Master was not listening, for all at once, with an abrupt expulsion of breath—immense risk, determined man—he flung his free leg over and came down upon my back like a blade in a stump or a body dropped to the back of an ass. It was a weight I had not expected, a sharp and heavy weight belied by the frailness of Master's looks. He landed, I flinched, he leaned for-ward and clutched the reins—bit jerking backward, bit stretching wide the corners of my mouth—and at the same time jabbed his heels into the hollow tenderness of my gaunt sides.

"Splendid!" exclaimed Ralph, letting go of my reins as I shied and started forward at a stiff and skittery trot, a half-blind jog.

"I'm falling!" came Master's anguished cry from above and behind my upflung head.

"You're nothing of the sort!" cried Ralph in return and laughed.

"I am! I am!" called Master, bouncing atop my back and gripping my sides with thin legs surprisingly strong, and swaying this way and that, and thus causing me to sway and waver correspondingly on my forward path.

"Now you see what I meant about those spurs!" came the sound of Ralph's voice, more faintly with each step I took.

It was then that I reached the fence. It was then that I stopped, of course, and stood as quietly as I could. Still agitated. Breath deep and as sporadic as had been my pace from crate to fence. At least the burden weighting down my back was less painful now than when we had been in motion, though Master was still digging his heels into me and clutching the reins. And at least, I told myself as sense returned and I grew more accustomed to the dead weight I had hopelessly tried to escape, at least Master had had his way and ridden me, while I had carried him, no matter our first brief tribulations together. Thus I stood and collected myself, and felt Master's weight settling down and into me, or so I thought, for Master was by no means balanced or affixed atop me, as things turned out.

"Oh, Ralph," called Master then, weakly but in a voice quite loud enough and piercing enough to alarm even the Irish groom. "I'm falling!"

"You're not!" shouted Ralph, starting in our direction at a run. "The horse has stopped!"

In this instance, and to my bewilderment, both men were right. Ralph drew closer, Master flung free the reins and began to list, first to one side and then to the other, until the old man's upper body finally agreed with itself, apparently, that the left-hand side was to be the side toward which and into which my old rider was to fall. And so it was.

"Hang on to his mane!" shouted Ralph.

But Master had not the slightest interest in saving himself. Instead, and in total contrariness, he began to slide.

"Harry Sir . . . !" shouted Ralph in a final threatening effort. "You are not to allow yourself to go off that horse!"

No use. No use at all. The old man's sliding had begun.

Again I swung my head and watched, and I stared at Master toppling, at Master leaning out and over, squeezing shut his eyes and sliding, beginning his long slow unnecessary descent from my high back to the ground. The waiting ground. Oh, we might have been traveling at full tilt, thumping and thundering across some dangerous field newly plowed, perhaps, or filled with naturally created holes, horse frightened and rider frightened too, horse and rider both vaguely anticipating and hence preparing for the inevitable, yet horse and rider separating, coming unstuck as it were, horse and rider both unbalanced and already going their separate ways! Oh, indeed I might have been running away, though obviously I could not run as fast as I had run in my youth, and I might well have despaired for Master's safety and he for mine as we charged against the wind and together and yet not together leapt or dodged small obstacles—a brook, a ditch—while stands of threatening trees and flights of startled birds flew past.

But it was not so, and we were only an old horse and an old man at a standstill within the safety of a fenced-in ring. And yet in the time it took Master to kick his booted feet out of the stirrups—at least he had sense enough to do so—and to turn his sliding into the genuine descent of a fall, I might indeed have regained a shade of my youth and run away in open country and carried Master many a heartsick mile before dislodging him.

So in my head I leapt a final barrier and then gave it up and returned to myself and quivered, took one step to the side and away from what before my eyes became the fallen heap that was Master. Somehow, in his determination to experience peril rather than pleasure in his first ride, he had managed even to knock loose his helmet, which had come to rest upside down and inert within hand's reach if he had a thought for reaching, which he did not, allowing himself to remain where he was, holding his hands over his uncovered head and groaning, and leaving the helmet for Ralph to retrieve, as in another moment Ralph did, in obvious disgust.

"Get up," said Ralph, stooping for the helmet and grunting. "Now we must do the whole thing over again."

"I can't," came the muffled voice. "I think I've broken something."

A robin piping. The sun once more in motion. Not a sign of Clover.

"I shall not tell you again," said Ralph. "Get up. I shall have no shamming or malingering on my farm."

"Give me a hand," said Master weakly, and thrust up from the tangle of boots and twisted torso and all the ungainly rest of him one arm and one white hand, blindly groping. "I cannot rise alone. I cannot. Falling off is a serious thing, Ralph."

"When you're ready!" came the Irish groom's reply—hearty all at once, filled with the booming timbre of his change in mood—as he caught hold of my loosely hanging reins and turned and, dragging me behind him, stalked back to the center of the ring.

So at last and with much complaining, Master rose of his own accord and, completing our second tableau, mounted me, with no help from Ralph, who this time, however, did not let go of me but tugged on the reins and struck me and spoke sharply to me and thus kept me still while Master sat astride me and smiled, as I could feel, and without moving a single step enjoyed his ride.

Clover's return. End of day. Dusk descending. Clover and I once more in our adjacent box stalls. The evening feed. From above us the childish sounds of Master re-creating for Ralph the elation of his first ride. Ralph—at the stove, from the smells that drifted down to us—singing a ballad about a young man in an older woman's kitchen. Clover agreeing that my day's journey had been as far as hers, though she had grazed for miles while I, in fact, had gone nowhere.

Night. Another sleepless night for Clover and me, our second night of nickering, touching, murmuring to each other, indifferent to the hisses that the watchful Fuzzy, crouched on high in the darkness, showered down on the pure sentiment of our communing.

CHAPTER SEVEN

•

A HOUSE GUEST, A BARN GUEST. A WINTRY
INTERLUDE

It snowed, as it will in winter.

For the old horse nothing is more comforting or more pleasing than the warmth to be found in a well-built, well-run stable of a winter's night. On such a night we are heavily blanketed, our barn doors are securely closed, the darkness that stretches far and wide around us is all the silkier, all the more profound, for being cold and presses so vastly upon the stable protecting us that even the cold air within turns warm and sheltering. We see little, we hear nothing except the sounds of ourselves and the creaking of the timbers that support our barn. Our body heat grows warmer, we hardly move, our frosty breaths are slow and peaceful. Here we have the long winter's night that exists mainly for the old horse and will never end. If all this is true, as I assert it is, then how much more intense the pleasure of a winter's night if on such a night it snows.

As indeed it did.

Clover stirred, I stirred, her haunch thumped the cold wood

between us, I raised my head. I listened, as did she, and yes, sure enough, we heard a steady telltale whispering outside that told us unmistakably that it had begun to snow. There was no wind, no breeze, only the faint determination heard in the steady snowfall that has already become a storm. Not a tumultuous snowstorm of the kind that sends frozen limbs crashing from trees and causes barn roofs to sag, not one of your blinding, swirling, uproarious winter storms, but a massive snowfall nonetheless. A large storm, a quiet storm, for the old horse strange and familiar all at once, freighted as it is with the shapes and shadows of recovered youth. Yet sinister in its steadiness, its resolution, its promise that it might not stop until the lot of us—horses, cats, men, barns—have been effaced in nothing less than total obliteration.

Drowsiness fell away from Clover and me, we grew attentive to the menacing nostalgic whiteness spreading far and wide beyond our barn.

There came a footstep on the outside stair. A tentative crunching muffled footstep as of a boot sinking deep into the fresh snow in which the stair was buried. Another cautious footstep, another, the sound of Master coming down to us—it could be no other, since in all the months that had passed, Ralph had taught Master how to care for us and now relied almost entirely on Master to attend to our needs and to do the work formerly done by Ralph himself.

The barn door began to move, we heard a sound as of a great horse-drawn sleigh gliding across the countryside on its long and nearly silent runners, though this was only the sound of the barn door moving, and the first startling shaft of winter light gave way to a welcome appearance—Master and the falling snow framed together in the open doorway. In addition to the riding boots and britches that he claimed to have salvaged from his by now historical past, and which he refused to abandon no matter how slight the protection they afforded him in this wintry season, Master wore a shabby mammoth sheepskin vest that had belonged to Ralph and hence was much too large for Master. Furthermore and typically enough, Master wore this discarded garment inside out, which is to say that instead of wearing the vest with the curly yellowish fleece turned in and against himself, thus providing maximum warmth against the winter cold, thanks to some quirk of vanity he wore the vest in opposite fashion, skin in, fleece out, with the result that he was forever shivering on these winter morns.

"Snow!" he said aloud, smiling and entering the barn. "How glorious!"

Down the wide aisleway he came, stopping to pat Clover's nose and mine, or trying to, since hunger caused both of us to jerk away from his touch as off he proceeded to fetch our hay, talking or whistling to himself, as he was wont to do when working.

We awaited our hay, which in due time arrived—the best of hay, composed almost entirely of timothy and alfalfa—and stared at the falling snow that filled the barn doorway and by now hid from sight the rusting horse trailers, the paddock, the trees, the second barn. The sweetness and pungency of the smells that arose around us where we stood in our stalls were all the keener thanks to the contrast of the cold wet smell of the falling snow, while the dawn light inside the barn was muted by the snow, yet brighter too.

"My dears," said Master, for thus he usually addressed Clover and me when he was alone with us, "I believe I remember this kind of snowfall from the time of my earliest boyhood! What a curious joy it was!"

He flung our hay, he entered our stalls and gave us fresh water, clearing the ice from our buckets with his long bare hands, and then reluctantly he set out food for Fuzzy and the other cats, for whom he had no fondness.

"Why," said Master, ceasing to sweep the aisleway and leaning thoughtfully on the broom, "I do recall a small blue sleigh, large enough for two persons, and a pony. It was a small fat pony of your own black and white colorings, dear Clover, and there was a storm like this one, and myself, and a driver, and a rug that covered our laps and legs. Along the road we went, immense trees growing suddenly distinct, then fading. How cold I was, yet warm! How indefatigable was that fat pony, how steady his pace! Think of it—a happy little boy with teeth chattering, a little boy bewitched and benumbed with snow in his face, and everywhere the winter cold. Isn't that a peculiar memory?"

The morning increased, we savored our hay, Master finished his sweeping just as Ralph summoned him above to breakfast. And still the barn door was a square of whiteness, impenetrable whenever we raised our heads, though in fact we could also see the individual flakes coming down, while the aisleway around the open door was growing wet.

At last, with much stamping and blowing of breath, Ralph himself came down the stairs accompanied of course by Master, who immediately set himself to preparing our morning feed, while Ralph, appropriately clothed in heavy trousers and one of his many checked caps and a woolen jacket with the collar up, lounged in the barn door, where Fuzzy crouched and rubbed himself against and in between Ralph's fat leather boots, laced up with thongs.

"Well," said Ralph, "we shall have to hook up that plow I bought from old man Fletcher as soon as it stops."

"I hope it lasts a goodly while, Ralph," said Master. "Don't you?"

"Harry Sir," said Ralph, giving Fuzzy a thoughtless nudge with a snow-encrusted boot, "you're a romantic. That you are."

Master smiled and nodded, and readied himself with pitchfork and shovel and wheelbarrow to do our stalls. Then, "I do like the snow," he said simply. "Why, Ralph, I'm sure you've never seen the snow from a longboat off the coast of Ireland!"

"I have not indeed," said Ralph. "And can't imagine wanting to."

"In Ireland," said Master, pausing to recollect with pleasure the story he was about to tell, "in Ireland, for the Golden Wedding, I was informed by the Old Gentleman himself that I had no aptitude for riding horses. I was sorely crestfallen the day he forbade me to join the hunt and said that if I was to see it, I could do so only with the women, from a little two-wheeled carriage drawn by a pony. How well and sadly I remember it!"

"But, Harry Sir, that was your chance!"

"They were older women, Ralph. My dear grandmother and my two maiden aunts."

"I see," said Ralph.

"But my grandfather," continued Master, "had been told that I was a fine shot, which I was. So considering that he thought me at seventeen too old to learn riding, and having already perceived my fear of horses though not my love of them, he offered me another sport, which he said was just as thrilling as riding to the hounds. And that was shooting doves from the rough seas below the cliffs not far to the south of my grandfather's estate, which was the original Hidden Hall, of course."

"I've never been much for hunting with a gun," said Ralph. "Hounds and horses are quite another thing."

"Oh," exclaimed Master, standing beside my stall and caressing my neck and looking where I looked outward into the falling snow, "I loved to shoot! And what could have been more amazing to the young man that I was at the time of the Golden Wedding than to shoot doves from the prow of a longboat manned by six oarsmen and a man at the helm? The Old Gentleman himself put the boat and men at my disposal. Oh," cried Master again, peering off into the snow that concealed the past as well as the future, "surely it was the next best thing to riding! Those black seas were as high as a house, Ralph, the cliffs were sheer and rose straight up for hundreds of feet, as ominous as anything I had ever seen or have seen since, yet providing in their crevices the nesting places for the sweet doves that I meant to shoot. To complete the picture, around the base of those cliffs were strewn an eruption of jagged rocks and boulders that could destroy a longboat in a minute. This, Ralph, was the idea: We launched the boat from a bit of beach, and no sooner had I leapt to the bow and the men to their places than we were carried roughly and swiftly out with that fierce tide, the longboat sitting atop the waves like a mere

cork in a splashing pool. Then, after that vast tide reversed itself
and carried us back toward shore, and just as it became apparent
that the swell was readying to pitch us forward and fling us
against the cliffs or onto the rocks, just at that crucial moment
Derek the helmsman steered with his critical eye and the oarsmen
bent their backs and pulled on the oars, exerting themselves
against that pull of the tide and stopping us just short of swift and
briny destruction. It was in that moment that I, one foot in the
brackish water sloshing in the bottom of the boat and the other
propped up on the very prow, had my one and only chance to
raise my gun—one of my grandfather's prized shotguns—and aim
and fire, bringing down one of the little birds flying out from its
nest in the cliffs, before we were carried just as suddenly back out
to sea. That, you understand, was the idea."

"Well," said Ralph, scowling and attempting to stop the flow
of Master's tale, "I think the snow's letting up. Time for the
plow."

"It's worse if anything," said Master quickly and continued on.
"The point of my story, Ralph, is this: That on the very first
occasion that I went shooting with Derek the helmsman and his
half-dozen men, and the very first time that I stood in the prow
of that blackish salt-smelling boat—"

"Risking your neck for nothing," said Ralph, attempting again
to interrupt, but failing.

"—and felt us rushing backward out to sea, the longboat
perched on the very tiptop of a giant wave and my stomach going
down to the depths of the sea and the glorious dark wind full in
my face—why, as soon as I prepared to raise my gun, fighting for
balance all the while, what did I find myself staring into but a
curtain of snow! I tell you, Ralph, I could see nothing! And if I
could not see, neither then could the men on whom our fate
depended! Well, there I was, a mere boy of seventeen and standing
bravely in the prow of a longboat in the face of the first snow
squall of the year! Oh, what delight I felt and terror too when,
blinded as were Derek and all his men by that curtain of snow,
suddenly I felt the longboat, atop the brutal crest of a mighty

wave, change its direction and begin its sickening plunge toward the rocks and cliffs! Downward we went, shoreward we swept, and what splintering of planks and flaying of arms of drowning men and boy lay mere moments ahead of us, thanks to that sheet of snow! How could we possibly survive? How could Derek know what course to steer and so avert that certain tragedy of death and wreckage? But still I waited, proud and confident—"

Here Ralph groaned and with his impatient boot sent the indignant Fuzzy skulking back down the aisleway and into the darkness of one of the empty stalls.

"—heroic, certainly, with my leg propped up, gun at the ready, determination filling the tall and reedy figure that I was. Well, just as doom was preparing to swallow the lot of us—boat and crew and hunter as well—suddenly a single dove appeared miraculously through a rent in the snow. In an instant I raised my grandfather's prized shotgun and sighted at the dove and fired! And at that moment, as if my shot was the very signal that Derek and his men had awaited, blindly against the momentum of the seas those oarsmen pulled and bent their backs as they had never bent them before, and with a single tremendous heave stayed our course, stopped us dead, then sent us seaward once again! So we were saved, Ralph, saved! Isn't that some story? Suffice it to say that I shot nearly a dozen doves that day, no sooner had the snow squall passed, which it did immediately, bringing down one of the lovely creatures each time the longboat swooped toward shore. Suffice it to say that all dozen birds were served up that night at my grandfather's table, to much applause and embarrassing commendations of my skill and bravery. At any rate, Ralph, I cannot think of snow, let alone see it, without recalling the sport I so much enjoyed off the coast of Ireland."

"Well now, if it's snow you want, and a good story," said Ralph at once and in an unnecessarily loud voice, while Master had barely time to catch his breath and clear his head of the visions he saw concealed in the storm that surrounded us, "let me tell you about the morning I went for an innocent ride down the main street of our village on the only horse I was allowed to ride in those days, an immense peace-loving brute by the name of Dapple Dandy, Dan for short. As you might imagine, he was a dapple gray, but as you could not imagine—not even in all your long life, Harry Sir—he was also the biggest horse ever seen in our village or the farms around it, pure shire as far as anyone could tell and a ton if he was half a stone. A mighty beast and like a kitten, with feathers around his massive fetlocks as long and thick as those of Mippy's feather duster. I trust you remember who Mippy was?"

"I remember, Ralph," said Master, turning away from the sight of the snow and staring at Ralph and inadvertently letting fall the shovel, without seeming to know what he had done. And then, "Ralph," he said quietly, "have you no comment on the story I have just told?"

"Oh, let me talk, will you?" said Ralph. "And pick up the shovel while you're about it."

"Whatever you say, Ralph."

"The cardinal rule," Ralph answered, "is never on any condition to interrupt my train of thought. Now where was I?"

"Dapple Dandy," said Master, sighing and resigning himself once more to the callow ways of his instructor.

"Ah yes," said Ralph, "old Dan. Well, oddly enough, I didn't like him, you see? At the time of which I am speaking, when I was still a mere lad of ten or so, which would have made my sister Carrie about thirteen or so, Dan was the only horse that my da would let me ride, and as I say, I had no use for Dan at all. It was his size, I think, that filled me with such an aversion for that ungodly beast. Remember that my da, a big fellow to start with, had over the years acquired a most unlikely weight or, to be blunt about it, fatness. And remember that I too was big beyond my years, and though my deceptive size gave me a certain advantage in maturity when it came to Carrie, nonetheless I was not happy to be a mere lad, as I knew I was, going about in the bulk of a man's body. I was self-conscious, you see. Mortified at my very self, Carrie or no Carrie. In fact not a day went by that I was not overcome with shame at the feel of my tight clothes on my body or at what I saw of myself in Ma's glass. So it is understandable, perhaps, that I found old Dan's immensity nothing less than a grotesque and downright insulting reflection of the genetic burden that had come down to me from Da. But of course I was an Irish lad, and like all the Irish lads that ever were or will be, I loved horses and was naturally endowed with an ability to ride and had my da to perfect my talents when the time came—"

"Oh, Ralph," Master interjected here, looking sadly into the whiteness beyond, "how I envy you!"

"Are you interrupting? Again?"

"No, Ralph, I'm not."

"Harry Sir, you're a vexing man. Now will you or will you not be quiet?"

Silence. Master appealing as it were to the hidden mysteries of the day outside, Ralph scowling at Master and then glancing once more and with complete indifference at the falling snow. Until he was reassured, apparently, and again amused at what he was remembering this wintry day.

"Very well," he said at last and grinned. "I'm sure you understand that in actuality Dapple Dandy was a fine specimen of a horse, a perfect example of his mighty breed. If I were to see him now, this moment, I would view him with the admiration that would be his due. But back then was another story. After all, Da owned a couple of passable riding horses, which, in comparison to Dan, I thought quite elegant. But would Da let me ride either one of them? He would not, he said, until the proper day arrived. He was stubborn, Da was, despite all my begging, and quite wrong in his approach to my training. So it was Dan for me, though I considered him a terrible nightmare of what a horse should be, and could only tack him up and seat myself on his fat back by the use of a ladder. Irish lads are vainer than most, you know, and I was no exception. The curious thing about Dapple Dandy is that despite his size—he'd hardly fit through the barn door—and for all the contempt I felt for him, still he'd follow you around the barnyard like a household pet. A frightening sight to the uninitiated, perhaps, but sweetness itself, that horse.

"Well, the particular story I have in mind is this: In the middle of one winter night it snowed, a rare thing for the countryside around our village, and when I awoke on my cot beneath the eaves and peered out of my little window I saw a bright day turned completely white, with all the world given over to the deep fresh snow and the morning sun. Before I even sat myself at Ma's table and ate my porridge, I knew what I was going to do that day—ride Dan in the snow! And more than that, ride him down the center of our village street through the virgin snow. Well, Harry Sir, that's what I did. Finished my milk, finished my detestable porridge, then out to the barn for Dan. And picked his hooves, that were like tree stumps, and gave him a hasty brushing—as much of him as I could reach—and climbed the ladder and got the bridle in place on his mammoth head and affixed the old saddle upon his back and climbed aboard.

"Then out we went into that bright and by now lively morning, Dan moving like a ship, you know, his great hooves thumping slowly and steadily through the deep and pristine snow that buried our village street as never before. It was cold, as you might imagine, and yet I sat up there on Dan bareheaded and open-shirted and merely smiled my widest smile and stared ahead at the blinding snow and paid as little attention as I could to the light that flashed off the shop windows and the windows of our poor cottages. Men and women were out and about and laughed and waved when they saw me coming down the middle of the street on Dan. But I did not wave back, happy for once to be making such a spectacle of myself and our old shire, with the snow flying up around his thumping hooves like spray from the waves and his grand size dwarfing the very village itself. What a sight we must have made, a fat young lad with his tousled red hair blazing and his chin raised, proud as you please on one of the Great Horses, as they are called, that come down to us from the Middle Ages.

"Now as you know, there was not a horse in the world more tractable than Dan. He was not slow-witted, as I sometimes thought, but simply devoted, as we might say, to obedience itself. And strong? Why, there was no horse stronger! Well, then, what on earth was old Dan doing, veering off course the way he was about midway down that village street? For that's exactly what was happening, as all at once I realized, first to my surprise and then to my horror. Yes, one moment I was rocking on high to old Dan's regal trot, sending him straight through the snow in utter confidence, the next I felt his tremendous weight shifting away from me as if all at once that paragon of pliancy had found a will of his own! Well, I gave him a little kick, a little tug on the reins, then pulled more frantically as Dapple Dandy swerved off the center of our path and in slow motion aimed himself directly at the gleaming plate-glass window of a shop called Mrs. Simon's Corsets, which was the very shop where Carrie herself was Mrs. Simon's salesgirl. There it was, the expanse of glass, the blinding light, the row of corsets on display behind the glass—as plump and filled out as they would have been by the torsos of living women!—and there too and staring out at me from between the corsets was none other than the face of Mrs. Simon, the proprietor, gone white with shock, and beside it the grinning features of my own most wicked sister. On we plunged, no matter how I pulled and kicked, heading toward the disaster that was by now inevitable. What leviathan was I astride! What leviathan that I could not for the life of me keep from disgrace and destruction on that magical morning while pedestrians turned and watched and behind the plate-glass window Mrs. Simon shook her fist at Dan and me and then leapt out of the way, and just in time as I can tell you.

"Then the crash! The splintering and shattering of glass! I ducked down and crossed my arms to save my face as best I could and heard that dreadful splintering as Dan, quite unaware of what was happening as far as I could tell, and without slackening his pace, moved right on through the blasted glass and into the shop as if he meant to crash right out the other side. Which he could not, of course. Not even Dan could go through a solid wall.

"Well, Harry Sir, there were corsets flying everywhere, and brassieres and panties too, for Mrs. Simon sold ladies' modern-day lingerie as well as the old-style undergarments of stays and laces. All this while Mrs. Simon darted about, screaming in fear and fury as Dan, now showing unmistakable signs of bafflement, crashed in circles inside the shop, sending display racks to the floor and bringing down the counters. Forward and backward and round and round lumbered Dan, apparently in search of a way out, and in his efforts accruing on his nose and neck and ears various items of the lingerie he had so thoughtlessly displaced and deflowered. And Carrie? Laughing, of course. I caught sight of her as I struggled to turn Dan amidst Mrs. Simon's shrieking and the brutal crunching of glass beneath Dan's hooves. I saw my sister standing there with her gorgeous freckles and her unruly red hair tied up in a green velvet ribbon, her black eyes fierce with amusement and her lovely white teeth gleaming. I knew that she detested Mrs. Simon almost as much as she did the clerics, and even amidst my struggling understood the pleasure Carrie took in the chaos I had introduced into the otherwise well-ordered secret world of female underclothing as found in Mrs. Simon's shop. No Actaeon could have been bolder than I had been on my thundering horse! No Artemis could have outdone Mrs. Simon's wrath! I tell you, by the time old Dan in his crashing and turning once more found himself face-to-face with the great and jagged hole in the glass by which we had entered, Mrs. Simon was crying and cursing too into her dainty handkerchief. As for Carrie, the last I saw of her that morning, when I gave one last fearful glance over my shoulder just as Dan began his desperate exit through the shattered glass and out toward the sun and snow and gathered crowd, she was blowing me the most good-humored and yet lascivious kisses that any boy or man could ever hope to see in all his days. Those kisses, and the sight of Carrie drawing up her blouse on her shoulder in a gesture of the sweetest modesty you'd want to see, were what nearly sent me off the horse for sure—and into the waiting arms of my poor wrathful da!

"Now, Harry Sir, how's that for an Irish tale? And a true one too."

A pause. A snowy pause. A considered pause while the ever-present snow came down. Then Master spoke.

"Well, Ralph," he said, "you know I don't like your off-color stories. But on the other hand"—and here his voice resumed its usual tone of cheerfulness—"I had no idea that you were versed in the classics! And for that I am pleased!"

"Ah, you'd best leave my education alone," answered Ralph with a smile.

"But, Ralph," persisted Master, "the difference between your people and mine, or between the commoners and the landed gentry, lies precisely in the classics. Surely you'll agree to that!"

"Harry Sir," Ralph then exclaimed, "you crack me up!—to use a vulgarism of this land of yours." So saying, and standing squarely in the barn door, with his back to the barn's other occupants, he threw back his head and laughed as if the full-chested sounds of one Irishman's self-enjoyment could stop the very fall of the snow.

It was then and swift on the heels of Ralph's aggressive laughter, and as if in response to it, that there came through the snow a sound so unexpected and so inappropriate to this strange wintry day that even Ralph was caught off guard, while Master could only shiver and stare apprehensively toward what he could not see. Again it came, a loud triple-noted blasting that set both Clover and myself to circling in our stalls and whinnying. It was an imperative sound, an erratic sound, a loud unmusical chorus of sounds announcing who could say what intrusion into the snowbound world of Ralph's farm. Closer it came, unrhythmic, peremptory, shaking the cold glassy cobwebs above our heads and sending Fuzzy and his consorts scampering and leaping to the rafters.

"What have we now?" murmured Ralph to himself. "That road's impassable!"

But even as Ralph spoke the boisterous honking began taking shape before our eyes. The broad snout of some huge motor vehicle. The hood. A black and shiny fender. A swath of wind-shield swept barely free of snow by the action of the wipers, longer than a man's arm. A truck, and listing from side to side, and screeching its great black tires and bearing slowly down upon us like some tall engine never seen before by horse or man. Behind it came a horse trailer as large and intimidating as the truck that pulled it. And then stopping, slowing to a halt at last as the horn fell dead and the driver swung down from the cab, calling Ralph's name and waving.

"Well, just look at her!" said Ralph, still as if to himself and smiling.

"But who is she?" asked Master, for our visitor was in fact a woman.

"Why, that's Cory herself!" answered Ralph softly, his eyes shrewd and his plump face red and wet with pleasure. "Coreen Mulcahy, that is, but Cory for short. She may be just what you need, Harry Sir. She's a fancy rider and a substantial girl, as you can see. In fact she's the only girl I've ever met who's as easygoing and as wicked as was my sister!"

"But what could she possibly be doing here?" asked Master.

"That we'll know in a moment, Harry Sir," said Ralph, and stepped out into the snow and in short fat strides plowed his way toward our visitor, who now—without coat or hat—was laughing and stumbling forward into Ralph's embrace.

Where for an unnaturally long while she remained. How they clasped and hugged each other, laughing and crying aloud each other's names, the two of them protracting this performance out there veiled by the falling snow and yet in full view of us who watched and waited inside the barn. At last they separated and, holding each other at arm's length, fell to conferring with a seriousness as suddenly intense as the joy they had at first expressed in their embraces. Then back to it they went, laughing and hugging, while Master groaned softly at the sight of them and we horses stirred. Until at long last Ralph turned and, seizing her hand, drew the enlivened woman at a clumsy frolicsome run in our direction.

Arrival. Much stamping and heavy breathing. Ralph brushing the snow from the woman and she from him. Snow-covered and red-cheeked, both of them. Woman exclaiming at the attractiveness of Ralph's barn, which she had all but forgotten. Woman inspecting horses with great enthusiasm, though pausing, I thought, and allowing a quizzical expression to cross her face, I thought, at her brief sight of me.

"Ah now, Cory, my dear," said Ralph grandly, "I'd like you to meet the man I mentioned. And, Harry Sir," he continued, arm around the woman's waist but facing Master, "I am pleased to present my dear friend Coreen Mulcahy."

Master nodded and tried to smile, the woman seized one of Master's hands in both of hers and, full-lipped and bright of eye, looked up at his long sallow face and forthrightly, alarmingly, attempted to dispel his obvious discomfort.

"Hi . . . !" she exclaimed, as Master stiffened, and I too stiffened suddenly and felt my ears pinned flat to my head. For what I had heard was an adult's voice but a young girl's lighthearted diction, and I had heard that womanly-girlish voice before and heard it now with sensations of both fear and distant longing. But then, and before this person could so much as address another word to Master, Ralph erupted into unseemly speech.

"Give her a smack on the bottom, Harry Sir!" he cried. "We'll not stand on formalities in any barn of mine!" So saying, Ralph withdrew his arm from around our new arrival's waist and drew back his arm and with the flat of his hand demonstrated what he meant by giving her a resounding blow. It was a hard blow, a wet blow, for the woman was of substantial build, as Ralph had said, and against the weather was clothed from neck to ankle in a shiny dark blue garment stretched tight to her body and still glistening, like her mass of black curly hair, with the melted snow.

A pause. A moment of shock most plainly seen on Master's long unhappy face. Sensations of uneasiness expressed by Clover and me. Ralph's face all aglow with his pure Irishman's pleasure at what he had just done. As for his victim, she gave no little jump of surprise, failed to lose either poise or balance, showed no flicker of anger or embarrassment. Instead she merely stood where she was as if nothing at all had happened.

"Ralph's a card," was her only comment, though it was enough to momentarily deflate Ralph's impropriety. "But anyhow," she continued, "accept my apologies for a fellow countryman."

"Apologies!" shouted Ralph, having quickly recovered. "There'll be no apologies in my barn! Harry Sir, tell the lady you're not offended!"

"Of course he's offended," said the woman, laughing and looking up at Master warmly. "He's not like you, Ralph!"

Whereupon Master managed to withdraw his hand from the woman's doubly effusive grasp and to step backward and, despite the apparent dryness of his mouth, to give voice to a clear rejoinder to both Ralph and the woman. How tall he towered in all his dignity, how miserably he stood inside the vastness of his sheepskin vest!

"Vulgar speech is one thing, Ralph," he said. "Vulgar behavior is another. I do not approve of the liberty you have taken with Miss Mulcahy."

"Wet seals!" cried Ralph in return, his hilarity and brogue as thick and compacted as the man himself. "That's what your Miss Mulcahy's bottom felt like and sounded like as well, as you could plainly hear!"

"Oh, cut it out, Ralph," said that person, still smiling at Master. "You're not funny."

"Ralph," said Master, attempting to avert his gaze from the young woman's upturned face, "I should think that you might be less rather than more uncouth in Miss Mulcahy's presence."

Another pause, a sudden gesture of mock capitulation on Ralph's part. "As you will," he said abruptly, "as you will. I am all sobriety. But now, Cory, my dear, to what, as they say, do we owe the pleasure?"

"Oh," replied the young woman, once more gazing in curiously distracted fashion around the barn, letting her eyes again rest for an extra moment, as I thought, on me. "I've missed you, Ralph. How's Fuzzy?"

Here Ralph waited, his round face and Irish eyes alert with friendly skepticism.

And then, "So you were just driving by in a snowstorm, Cory?"

"I'm visiting," was her reply.

"Ah hah," said Ralph. "For long?"

"That depends," said the young woman.

"And where do you propose to stay? At the usual?"

"It's closed, Ralph."

"Ah hah," said Ralph thoughtfully. "A problem, then."

"No, Ralph," said the young woman, who was taller than Ralph and better shaped, and whose voice and figure now filled our wintry barn with an unfamiliar vigor. "This time I'm moving in. For as long as I want, Ralph."

"Impossible," said Ralph. "Why, I would not allow Captain Kelly's mistress herself to set foot in my rooms, as you well know!"

"Oh, you're no match for me, Ralph!" cried the young woman then, and so saying and to Master's obvious horror, with the flat of her hand and with considerable strength and swiftness, suddenly she returned the unseemly blow that Ralph had given her but moments before. "Now, Ralph, wait until you see my Skibbereen!" she added with a girlish laugh and strode out of the barn and back into the falling snow.

Another and much longer pause. Ralph standing in the doorway, hands on hips and staring after the already invisible young woman. Master brooding, Clover sharing my own puzzlement and apprehension, if not those alternating sensations of serenity and rage that still came and went inside me, oh so unaccountably—now one, now the other—like hot and cold.

"Ralph," said Master as last, "does that young woman actually intend to stay the night?"

"So she says," said Ralph, his squat back yet turned to us. "Maybe longer."

"I cannot allow it, Ralph."

"And what do you propose to do?"

"Ralph, you must send her off!"

"Easier said than done. She appears quite determined."

"Could she really be so unreasonable?"

"Well, Harry Sir, I'm surprised myself. She's not the Cory I used to know."

"Can you not exert your authority?"

"I'm not so sure, Harry Sir. I expect she's got quite a temper."

Master dismayed, Master struggling to find his way. Both men at the mercy, or so it seemed to me, of the snow as well as the young woman. Then after that ensuing pause, for it was a morning of strange pauses and confrontations, in which all of us were in danger of drifting to who knows what end, Master made up his mind and spoke.

"If she stays," he said quietly, "then I shall go."

"As bad as that," said Ralph, in his most hypocritically lilting brogue.

Master nodded.

"But consider, Harry Sir. Why, exactly, are you so adamant? If I am willing to take her in, then why not you? After all, I am more finicky than you about where and how I live, and have even made an exception for yourself, to tell the truth. As for women, even Irish women, it's my unalterable principle to forbid them my rooms. No girl or woman has any business in a man's rooms. At least in mine. But in this case I am willing to make an exception and to bow to greater forces, as you might say. Why not you?"

"No, Ralph. I will not."

"Can we not risk a little disarrangement of our things? Can we not tolerate a very special girl who is, I assure you, of Irish descent? She's a gorgeous girl, Harry Sir, and as innocent in the true meaning of the word and as lively as was my sister. Merely to look at her is to smell the burning peat and the unmistakable flow of Irish blood—in a female, that is. In this case it's best for all concerned that we both make an exception."

Silence. Master's lofty visage sealed.

"I tell you," said Ralph then, "there is always a bed for Cory Mulcahy in my rooms! And what have you to lose compared with me? And I tell you"—here his voice softening—"what I mean by innocence in a girl is generosity. Do you understand? Allow the three of us one nightfall, and you'll be convinced!"

"Ralph!" Master exclaimed then. "I shall not be part of it!"

"Anyway," Ralph answered, "I won't deny her. And I want no row!"

"Of course not, Ralph."

"And what do you propose to do? Where shall you go?"

"Why, Ralph, I shall stay right here."

"Here?" cried Ralph. "I don't follow you, that I don't!"

"I mean," said Master slowly, "that I shall remain down here with the horses."

"No!" cried Ralph, his delight and manliness fairly bursting at this turn of events. "Not even you could want to live in a barn!"

"It is what I intend," said Master simply. "I am steadfast, Ralph. I know myself."

"I suppose you do. And I confess I've wondered sometimes whether or not you'd rather be a horse than a man."

"It's possible, Ralph," said Master thoughtfully. "You may be right."

It was at this juncture that from the snow there loomed a shape, a force, more improbable even than the truck that had carried its disruptive presence into our midst. And this darkening figure that loomed ever closer was, as we immediately discovered, Miss Mulcahy's horse, approaching at a massive trot, with its owner laughing and running in a valiant struggle to keep pace with him.

"You see, Ralph," called the breathless young woman, "isn't he wonderful?"

"For the love of Carrie!" muttered Ralph, pushing back his cap and scratching one red ear. "Will you look at that? Dapple Dandy all over again, except for the color!"

"A monster," replied Master.

"A genuine beauty," said Ralph as to himself.

"A dreadnought," said Master.

"Now listen to me!" said Ralph over his shoulder. "You know nothing whatsoever about that horse! He's a Hanoverian with a pinch of Percheron and a pinch of Irish Thoroughbred. Just a pinch. I've never seen a horse like him."

"But, Ralph," persisted Master, "he doesn't even look like a horse! An animal that large is an aberration!"

"Be quiet!" said Ralph then. "I'll hear no more!"

In another moment our commodious little barn shook to the immensity of the big black horse. There was a great deal of tugging on the part of Miss Mulcahy and considerable straining on the horse's part to slow himself to a walk and then a stop, and even he evinced surprise when at last he stood among us at a standstill, his jet coat shining and dripping with wet snow, his great head as high as the rafters, and his flaring nostrils as large as teacups. For that moment, and that moment only, I pitied the poor creature lost and uncertain in his new surroundings.

"Well," said Miss Mulcahy, tipping her head and looking up proudly at the startling height of her horse, "how do you like him?"

"Yes indeed," said Ralph in unfeigned admiration.

"Prix Saint Georges," said Miss Mulcahy.

"Ah yes," said Ralph with pleasure.

"And gosh, Ralph, you wouldn't believe how sweet he is!"

"Cory, my dear," said Ralph, "any horse of yours is bound to be sweet!"

On they went, exclaiming over the new horse while Master stood by sadly watching and Clover, to my alarm, defended the sympathy that she felt for the immense black horse with the Irish name—for Skibbereen was the name of an Irish village, as Ralph later said—and chided me for my envy of a horse so obviously young and agreeably disposed. But envious I was and consumed with an instantaneous dislike of him, and not only because the new arrival was taller than myself by far, and by all appearances fit only for the most arrogant of riders, for he was indeed young as well and of my own gender. How not dislike this horse who had already prompted Clover—my Clover!—to recall and reveal in all her sweet shyness the barn of her foaling and the names of her first owners? How swift their intimacy, how contemptible my rage!

But distraction then, a flurry of fresh activity as Ralph and the exuberant young woman maneuvered our new stablemate into his stall, no easy task and one requiring much laughing and pushing since it could only be accomplished by turning Skibbereen and ascertaining that he fit well and comfortably into a space that was none too large, despite the goodly proportions of the stalls in Ralph's barn. Next the young woman must make three trips back into the snow in order to fetch her saddles, black shiny things of the highest quality, the likes of which I had never seen, along with her oaken tack trunk, which Ralph assisted her in carrying, man and woman displaying great fondness for each other in the process. By now the much-admired horse across the aisleway was staring at Clover in frank delight while conveying that he was one of those young horses most attracted to the older mare. How happily surprised he must have been to find himself so warmly welcomed!

It was then and there that Miss Mulcahy energetically proposed that she and Ralph and Master retire to the rooms above. Whereupon Master grew still more solemn and Ralph, summoning a diplomacy of which he had but little, indicated as best he could and in his most soothing Irish tones the change in plan, which brought an expression of pained concern to Miss Mulcahy's ordinarily open and receptive features.

"Gosh," she said to Master, "you're moving out? Because of me?"

Master nodded. Ralph offered further explanation.

"But that's terrible!" exclaimed Miss Mulcahy. "And anyway, we don't want you living down here and getting pneumonia or something."

Master demurred.

"Well, I'm not convinced," said Miss Mulcahy, looking from one to the other and finally settling her eyes on Ralph, and smiling.

"Oh, but you must think nothing of it," said Ralph quickly. "We must never stand in the way of a moral principle!"

"I guess not," said Miss Mulcahy brightly, her wholesomeness thus speedily relieved of uncertainty.

So without a moment's more hesitation Ralph and the young woman retreated as swiftly as they could to the privacy above, from which Ralph alone descended, briskly and irritably, slipping audibly on the snow-covered stairs, to bring down an armful of blankets and an unruly cot, which with a great show of impatience he set up in the otherwise empty box stall directly across the aisleway from mine and next to that of Skibby, as his enthusiastic owner called him.

"Thank you, Ralph," said Master.

"You'll freeze," answered Ralph. "But that's no concern of mine, Harry Sir."

Darkness. Silence. Dark of the night. Dark of the snow—still falling. Silence in which the shouts and shrieks, groans and giggles that had assaulted us throughout the daylight hours and on into the gloaming now lay at rest—at last.

But then?

A shuffling sound, a creeping sound. Sighing and moaning. The latch of my stall door rattling. Someone—Master of course, who else?—entering my stall in silence. Searching for refuge from the night? the snow? the cold?

"Petrarch," he said behind me and in a voice that only I could hear, "I do not like him, Petrarch."

Slowly and in a wide arc I swung round my head and in the silvery darkness stared at Master. No horse easily allows the presence of man or woman in his stall, and for months now, and no matter the contentment that had become mine at last, whenever I was not watching or listening to the activity that Ralph and Master shared in the aisleway, I stood, according to my newly acquired habit, with my tail and haunches—my skinny butt, as Ralph always said—facing my stall door and my head hanging as far as possible away from the sight of men. "Ah, look at him," Ralph was forever saying, "showing his skinny old backside to the world at large!" And so I was, and with reason as well as preference. That is, I was interested in the fact that Master had by and large overcome his fear of me, and I tolerated him as best I could when perforce his daily barn work brought him inside my stall even when that stall was occupied by me. And I took a reluctant spectator's interest in the life around me, as I say. Nonetheless my natural newfound stance in my stall—and for how many years had I lived in no stall at all?—was backward, for the sake of my buckets and to put me into a position to—exactly!—kick. Yes, my impulse was to reject all men, even Master, and to offer anyone opening my stall door the threat of my all but uncontrollable hind legs and hooves.

In he came with a checkered horse blanket draped over his head and hiding most of his long stooped shivering figure and most of his face as well. Hooded specter! And afraid? No. Sensible? Not at all. The opposite, in fact. For what did he do, even while I watched him, but stand directly behind me and cross his forearms and rest his arms and forehead directly and as high as possible upon my croup! Foolish, trusting old man, as if I were not a living unpredictable horse! As if I could not kick with the best of them!

"Petrarch," he said again, "I do not like him. In fact I cannot sleep in a stall next to Skibbereen's. He is too large and too ungainly. He moves about in the darkness, Petrarch, he breathes so heavily that I cannot sleep. Even at night he refuses to relinquish his self-satisfaction! And, Petrarch, I fear he likes our own Clover, which is why he is wakeful and which distresses me no end. . . ."

Jealousy revived! Muscles tightening! But just in time, and before I could do Master any harm, suddenly I was possessed by a new thought, an abrupt and unmistakable cause for alarm. If Master could not sleep because of Skibby . . . if he had abandoned his cot in the stall adjacent to the lovesick Hanoverian's . . . if there was nowhere else for Master to spend the night, as indeed there was not . . . could he mean . . . ? did he intend . . . ? Yes!

it came to me. Exactly! But how, I asked myself, as fully awake as I would ever be in the dead of night, how could a man lie down with a horse? How could man and horse share the same stall, the same bedding of glossy straw and scattered hay? Would I not step on him? Injure Master inadvertently or otherwise in this long winter's night that was never meant to be?

Yet no sooner did the thought occur to me than Master withdrew himself from behind me, sighed, and the next thing I knew was lying curled and inert and barely discernible in a far corner of my stall. A thin elongated human heap thoroughly concealed beneath the horse blanket in which he was loosely wrapped. An old man curled up in the stall that was mine and already shivering and moaning in the depths of sleep. No thought of risk, no thought of me! No thought of the scattered fresh manure in which he lay. So I had no alternative but to stand as far from his prostrate figure as I could and maintain consciousness and wait out the night. By now I had lost interest in both Clover and the maddening Skibbereen. Let him spend the hours of darkness pursuing Clover, so to speak, let her grow increasingly receptive. In my stall there lay a man—unthinkable—for whom responsibility was undeniably mine. At least he slept, at least I stood irritably and drowsily in silence—except for the creaking of the timbers, the ominous sloughing sound of the snow, the sounds of the young Hanoverian's tireless desire. How peaceful a barn on a winter's night, how often the unreasonable occurs!

And then? Exactly. For just when it seemed that all concerned were settling down to night and snow, just when I thought I might be spared further disturbances and aggravations, up rose Master with a loud moan and, wraithlike, unerringly, found me out in the darkness, glided from his corner of my stall to where I stood and put his hand to my withers, leaned against me, rested his cold cheek against my shoulder, and began to talk. Would I never, ever be free of him?

"Petrarch," he said, as softly and lucidly as if he had not that very moment risen up from the dregs of some deep dreams, "make no mistake, Petrarch. He has offended me.

"Yes, Petrarch, so he has, and sorely. I am well aware of what he has done. I too have feelings. Yet who is the better off? In the question there is consolation. After all, to lie abed with that blameless woman—for she is blameless, Petrarch—and thereby exclude me from my rightful place, in which my role is Master and his the groom, our only subject being the horse, is exactly what we should expect of that commoner, though to say the truth, Petrarch, I never thought he would go this far. On the other hand and as for me, who can say that I have not already bested him? Mine was the moral choice, for no man consumed by interest in a woman can think of his horse! And do I not already ride as well as he, or better? Fall fewer times a day? Look with steadier eyes between your ears? Oh, such is my ambition, Petrarch—to best the very person who is making me your fit companion! And why is it essential that I be a true horseman and nothing else? To ride with a skill that even he has not yet attained? Or at least with an honorable intensity that he has never known and never will? For only one reason, Petrarch, only for the sake of Hidden Hall, about which I say little but which I always seek. Not the original Hidden Hall, of course, not the Hidden Hall of Golden Wedding fame. But that other Hidden Hall on our side of the waters and of which I am Master. Oh, find that second Hidden Hall again I must! And shall—through my horse! Through you, Petrarch . . ."

Here and to my unimaginable relief he broke off his ravings, for ravings they surely were, no matter how softly voiced or with what apparent calm and reason, and fell to fumbling beneath his blanket until he brought forth what I had been smelling all the while and which I now smelled so strongly that I could not help but crave. Crab apples. Crab apples in the middle of the night. And though I wanted nothing more than to be left in peace, now I was helpless—and surely this is the curse of the horse!—helpless but to swing down my head, to thrust at him my expanded nostrils and waiting jaws, to thrust at his clothing, to beg from his hand—horse fully grown and more and now become the victim of a crab apple!—and could not rest until he had proffered me a palm full of the little dried-up droppings from one of Ralph's withered trees and stuffed them into my mouth and his own as well. Horse and man eating crab apples together of a winter's night, and I perforce made Master's captive by instinct alone! How I deplored the power of this gnarled wormy fruit, how I resented having to eat out of Master's hand! In passing I realized that this was how Master intended to subsist while denying himself the companionship of Ralph and Miss Mulcahy—by eating the crab apples that half filled a small nail keg that Ralph kept handy in the aisleway and with which Master had already crammed his pockets.

On went the crunching of Master's teeth, the grinding of mine. Then swift as a bird Master stopped his eating, took hold of my head, put his nose to mine, and—oh rage and shame!—drew into his lungs loud expressive breaths of the very air that I was exhaling. But not for long, for no sooner did Master thus destroy my simple pleasure than I jerked away, yanked up my head. Stood fuming. Quivering. Had I no right even to this purest of the natural functions? Was my very breath not mine? Justified was my anger now, and not easily appeased.

"You see, Petrarch," Master said to himself in the darkness, "the crab apple that you have eaten is the crab apple that I love best! The sweetest scent is carried on the horse's breath!"

And turned without a further word and glided away—far it seemed though only a few steps in fact—and flopped down in the dark hollow he had left in the straw. Thus I was again left to stand alone with an ignominious hunger for crab apples, which I could not quench. But was he asleep? Might I now have a few moments of what might pass for peace? Guardedly I relaxed into that possibility. The barn was not entirely quiet; I caught a soft fragment of Clover's past, that which she had first revealed to my ears alone, and heard a youthful snorting of delight and encouragement from my rival across the aisleway. Far beyond us owls were attendant on the falling snow from within their black holes in trees now thickening to white. No rails or fence posts visible, if we had been free to look. Countryside transformed, and still the interminable storm did not, could not, conclude itself. Where I stood I listened a moment for signs of life from Master—brief span of moaning, a muffled word, occasionally my name, nothing to fear—and gave myself over to the night that was not passing, so it seemed.

And . . . ? Exactly! Jerked again to consciousness and just in time! For up he started and, horse blanket slipping loose, hanging down from a shoulder, long thin graying face exposed, again he found me in the darkness and flung himself upon me, groaned pathetically, dropped his arms from around my neck, leaned against me. Sleepwalking? Drugged in the depths of his dream? Perhaps. Yet when he once more began to talk, for talk he did, Master's tone of voice was that of a kindly old man speaking to an attentive child.

"I have seen his sort before," he said, "though in a different form. Oh yes, Petrarch, I am a more experienced person than thinks my Irish groom. And the offense to which I am referring was, if anything, greater than his, though at the time I was merely privy to it whereas now I have become its brunt and challenger."

He paused, propped himself comfortably against me—I could not move, had not the heart to move—and from his entire person emitted a smell of uncleanness, a smell of great age, which now quite overcame the smell of the few crab apples still bulging his pocket.

"Who would have believed that Henry himself was the perpetrator of that offense? You must understand, Petrarch, that Henry not only was my grandfather's coachman but was older even than my grandfather at the time of the Golden Wedding—above ninety years old, as I was told one day by a little serving girl, who was, as it so happened, my favorite among all the serving girls and women in my grandmother's charge. Now, at the height of the Golden Wedding, when the entire assembly, of which I was a member at the young age of seventeen, shared in a mood that could not have been more festive, suddenly Grandfather let Henry go! Dismissed him, without a word of warning. And why? Wait, Petrarch, and you shall hear."

That I would and so resigned myself to another and still longer siege of Master's storytelling.

"Well," he said, "the news spread, and we celebrants became alarmed since, after all, Henry had been with Grandfather for fifty years, or from the time when my grandfather walked through the rain toward the parish church where he took his wife-to-be in marriage. For fifty years, then, Henry had been entrusted to work in my grandfather's stable until, as I say, he became Grandfather's coachman, which was an exalted position to say the least. And now, while the Golden Wedding was in full swing—I confess that's how I thought of it when I was seventeen!—dismissed! A faithful old retainer for fifty years—and given one hour, exactly, to gather together his scant belongings and leave. And why? Because of impertinence, Petrarch! But how that impertinence burned the ears of all of us who heard it!"

A sigh, a shaking of Master's head so that for the instant I thought and hoped that he had lost the thread of his memory and hence would return to his corner and spare me the rest of his story. But no, for without a word of warning he resumed it precisely where he had let it drop.

"Well, Petrarch," he said, "you must know that the manor house in which my grandfather had been born, as had his father before him and his before him and so on down a line that had no verifiable beginning, so far back it reached in history, was a place of great size and countless rooms arranged about a central hall from which there extended north and south two enormous wings that contained the bedchambers. Ivy covered that Irish manor house, its roof was of slate, a forest of chimneys rose in a smoky tangle above the whole. Space, Petrarch, grandeur! Quite enough to beguile the young person that I was then, especially since the stables and kennels were appropriately imposing for such a lordly dwelling. Many a night for the months devoted to the Golden Wedding did I lie awake and listen to the muted kicking of Grandfather's horses or the squeals and whimperings of his famous hounds.

"Now, as every member of the family knew, and friends and servants as well though they thought nothing of the matter, Grandfather and Grandmother chose to occupy separate bed-chambers in that old manor house, his in the north wing, hers in the south, with their nine sons scattered about in bedchambers in between. So the story is this. That one late frosty afternoon Henry came upon a group of momentarily idle serving girls, who happened to include my favorite. And what must Henry do but, thinking to entertain those young women with their pretty figures and lively Irish brogues, yes, Henry must tell them what turned out to be a rude impertinence. That is, he told them that it was not my grandfather who visited Grandmother's bedchamber those fifty years of wintry nights, and so gave my grandmother all nine of her sons, but Zeus who came down from the cold heavens in a shower of gold and lay with Grandmother while Grandfather dreamt, as he did each night, of the glories of the hunting field. To which the eldest serving girl replied—according to my little favor-ite, who told me this tale with soft and furious blushes—'Oh Lor', sir, that's what all the girls and ladies say. If it's not the husband, then Lor', sir, it's that shower of gold!' To which that immodest group fell to laughing and giggling, while Henry, despite his ninety years, made free with the eldest girl, who had answered him in such a brazen way.

"Well, Petrarch, the disrespectful story spread, as such stories will. Inevitably it reached my grandfather's ears, and when it did he acted. He simply called Henry into his study and let him go, as I have said. But according to my little dark-eyed informant, what most hurt and angered my grandfather was not the crude presumption of his trusted coachman, and not the eldest serving girl's complicity in the matter, but the fact that he himself had introduced his coachman to the classics.

"Oh, make no mistake, Petrarch! My grandfather was not the man to tolerate a coachman's trifling with the sexes! Nor am I . . . !"

With which Master once more stopped talking—from exhaustion, as I rightly thought, and by that exhaustion was swiftly carried back to his corner, into which he fell without a further word or sound. But not for long, since before I was able to do so much as heed and nurse my own exhaustion, which by now was considerable, up he leapt, his indefatigable mind a-working, and leaned against me as against a post and started in as he had before, his voice as bright and energetic as it had been when first he fumbled his way to me and spoke.

"What is a man's place of habitation," he said, "if not a reflection of his stable? Or better still, what is a man's stable if not a true likeness of the dwelling in which its owner lives? And what is the stable if not the measure of that man's character? Decaying stable, immoral man—of that you may be sure, Petrarch! And pristine stable, man of virtue, though it saddens me to say that my Irish groom does not quite hold to the rule. But in truth, Petrarch, I did indeed find my grandfather's stables even more glorious than Hidden Hall itself, and this despite that manor house's crowning position atop a hill from which there was a view of the country-side for miles round, and despite the storks that nested in its forest of chimneys. Oh, my grandfather's Irish dwelling place could not help but engage the imagination of the seventeen-year-old that I was then. But oh, how much more I loved his stables, how keen I was to visit them! And do you know that my grandfather, kindest and most sensible of men, asked me to avoid the stables and to limit my activities to tramping the countryside or to shoot-ing doves? Just as he denied me the opportunity to learn to ride and join the hunt when off it went on those brisk mornings, so he feared that I would be in the way inside the stables or might alarm the horses with my awkwardness or do myself some injury in their midst. It was a cruel kindness, Petrarch! And on that matter alone I disobeyed my grandfather, and to this day do not regret my willfulness—though I adored my grandfather and wanted nothing more than to grow in his image, as I have done.

"The stables, then, were as large as the manor house and in design and construction resembled a temple. Think of it, Petrarch, a temple! How long it was, how rectangular, how rounded on the long sides up to its vaulted roof, which was slate-covered, you may be sure. It was dark and cool and orderly within, and though there were stalls, still the horses were free to roam about that immense interior as they wished, careful to avoid the languid dogs and fearless chickens that lay or moved about randomly underfoot. But the triumph of that stable was its ceiling, for it had been painted a pale blue color on which a smattering of stars was fading! The sky, Petrarch! A rounded summer sky high overhead—was that not a marvel? Day after day I hid myself straight as a soldier in the shadows of that lavish barn and smelled the horses, watched them drifting perilously close to where I stood, and every now and again I leaned back and looked above me, delighting in that illusionary sky forever protecting the wise obedient horses down below.

"I was no trouble to horse or man in that stable, Petrarch. How wrong of my grandfather to judge me so mistakenly!"

A pause. A breath. Then on he went, emotion overcome, tone reestablished.

"On one particular afternoon," he said, "there came the vision—yes, vision—in which I still live. As usual I slipped inside that temple devoted to the horse, as usual took my place well out of harm's way, a lanky youthful figure all but invisible, or so I thought. But there was a difference this afternoon. Yes, I noted as usual the bulky harnesses coming down from their hooks, and the young boys with their forks and barrows, and as usual I saw how the rays of the sun came through the narrow windows to warm the hay in all the wooden hayracks in those silent stalls. Grooms bent to their silent tasks, pigeons fluttered below the artificial sky. The grain in the ancient bins smelled as sweet as if it were still growing in the fields. All was as it should be—but with a difference. For there in the very center of that stable were three horses already saddled, and three riders already sitting on the horses. Two black horses and a bay, riders sitting sidesaddle and dressed in long black riding costumes such as were worn by females who in those days chose to ride. They were smiling, all three, and they were young, hardly more than girls, really, yet perched atop their mounts in that strange position, on the left side only, with their

wide skirts flowing down and their shoulders back, their slim
torsos straight—how regal they were, how balanced, how supple!
Riders, their stately little figures proclaimed, yet mere girls as
well. Capable of jumping over fences taller than the tallest man,
and pursuing foxes with the best of men—yet as slight as they
were formidable, ephemeral somehow and yet enduring, never to
be denied the field, the fence, the flight of their horses. How I
envied them! How I wanted to help them to climb atop their
stately mounts or help them down! How I wanted to ride with
those three young women dressed in black!

"But as if this were not amazement enough, Petrarch, suddenly
I came to my wits and saw that the young woman mounted on the
tall bay horse was none other than my favorite serving girl! Impossible, I told myself, domestics were not allowed to learn the art
of equitation. But there she was, beyond a doubt, glorious on the
shining long-legged bay, who, from my present vantage point,
was very like yourself, Petrarch. An unmistakable likeness—how
did I not think of it until now?

"Of course I had no eyes for the other two young women and
their black horses, but only for that endearing girl I recognized.
And was she not searching me out where I stood in the shadows
and in shyness that was all but self-consuming and desire as pure
as the smile on that young rider's face? She was, and undeniably.
For then, her young eyes fixed on mine, she spoke. 'I am riding
your horse!' she called. 'Do I not ride him well?' Then before I
could so much as smile and return her wave, off they went in
single file, riding out of Grandfather's stable forever.

"There you have it, Petrarch," he said after a heavy silence in
which he had drifted far from me and then come back. "Was she
and is she not irresistible? Once seen, could any boy or man
recover himself from the power of that slim creature, hardly more
than a child, who so erectly sat her horse that day in my grandfather's stable? I glimpsed her, I must glimpse her again, and shall.
How like I am to your namesake, Petrarch! And mark me—no
man may respect a woman, young or old, unless he respects his
horse. . . ."

A final note, a final declaration. Whereupon he stopped his talking, for good or at least for the rest of the night as I was now convinced, and took himself back to his corner and collapsed, fell immediately into a loud sleep from which, I was as sure as I could be, he would not soon awake. But little did I benefit from the certainty that he had talked himself into an oblivion of sorts and thus freed me, at last, to pass the few remaining hours of darkness as I pleased, so long as I kept my sharp hooves away from that corner where he lay wrapped and completely covered in his blanket like a corpse. For even this brief privacy was not to be mine, as I knew in my cold bones and as, in no time at all, proved to be the case.

Because it was dawn, suddenly, and still snowing. And what now but another visitation, and one that I half expected and that was by far the more disturbing to me than had been Master's irrepressible discourse? Exactly. I was in fact listening for the faint footsteps when I heard them, was already watching the barn door when I saw it move. Who now if not Miss Mulcahy herself? Just as I thought. There was a scraping, then the sound of her breath, and then the barn door opened barely enough to admit that early-rising woman along with a heap of snow that spilled into the barn and onto the aisleway behind her. Skibby turned his attention away from my dozing Clover and made a soft sound of surprise and welcome, but perhaps for the first time in his life he was ignored. For Miss Mulcahy made straight for me.

I saw the falling snow, heard it, suspiciously I watched Miss Mulcahy as she stopped at my stall door, unlatched it, entered my stall without so much as acknowledging what should have been, to her, the shocking presence of Master moaning and sleeping in the corner.

"Hi there," she said in a voice that only I could hear, and that made me draw back in alarm, but in joy as well. She stopped, put her hands on her hips, smiled up at me. Her tight blue winter garment was but slackly zippered, her eyes were red, her hair rumpled, her white face puffy, as were her lips, the lower of which, I noted, was more swollen than the upper and sorely bruised.

"Hi there, big boy!" she said, and reached for my nose just as recollection, stronger than the invitational smell of a standing mare, swept over me from head to tail so that I both recoiled yet lowered my cold nose to her hand. Millbank! I thought. Home! I thought. The nameless girl who had subjected me to the sight of my sire mounting the long-forgotten Kate. That presumptuous girl, this immodest woman! Oh, but she had no right to reappear to me in this fashion, no right to provoke my anger and nostalgia in the same wet breath. Yet here she was, grown woman more intrusively familiar than had been the girl.

"Hey," she said softly, "I remember you, big boy. I thought I did. And wasn't that sire of yours a sight? Remember?"

I did; my anger grew. Openly she faced me, widely she smiled despite her injured lip. And was she as fearless of me now as when a girl? Had she learned nothing, though horsewoman she had obviously become? Could she not see that aside from age, aside from gelding, still in one essential way I did not resemble the young horse that this woman as a girl had once offended, intentionally or not?

Beware of the horse.

And then? Then she stirred my uncertainty to rage and dared to do again what she had done before. Even as I watched in horror, powerless to draw away, so swift and unexpected was her gesture, Miss Mulcahy reached out both hands and, placing them on either side of my long nose, drew down my nose and puckered her swollen lips and, yes, kissed my broad flat nose!

But what swift retribution that kiss incurred! For then it was that the kiss with which she had offended me in her girlhood flashed to mind, and Master groaned. In the instant and out from the depths of my tall and bony frame there leapt the misanthropic horse I truly was! And? Exactly. Before the smile could begin to fade from Miss Mulcahy's ravaged lips, before incomprehension could widen her eyes, before I could consider what I was doing and attempt to stop myself—yes, in utter thoughtlessness I snapped my jaws and with a tug as swift as a flick of my tail tore open Miss Mulcahy's cheek.

Up went her hand, out shot the blood. But if I had astonished her, as I surely had, so she astonished me in turn. For in silence she raised one hand and held the side of her face and stood where she was and merely stared up at me with a quizzical look in her eyes the like of which I had never seen. Had it come to her that I would brook no teasing? Did she see in my own proud eyes a reflection of the calm in hers? Suffice it to say that in that cold hour and bound together as we were in this icy incident, suddenly I saw understanding in Miss Mulcahy's eyes and was overcome— yes, it was my turn to be overcome!—by her presence of mind. Slowly she began to move, hand still tightly pressed to her cheek, and slowly backed away from me, clear eyes fixed on mine the while, and stepped out of my stall and with the other hand latched my stall door. And did I then admire Miss Mulcahy? I did. And was it possible that she admired me as well? So said the hard yet gentle look in her eyes, still fixed on me from where she stood holding her cheek in the aisleway.

Then she screamed.

And what a commotion followed! Up leapt Master, hugging the blanket about him and calling my name, as with a dreadful crashing and yelling Ralph came down to us and Skibby trumpeted in fierce alarm and Clover let her fear be known. On went Miss Mulcahy with her screaming, refusing help, refusing explanation, no matter how Ralph shouted and demanded to know what had happened. She would not say, she would not for so much as a moment interrupt her preparations for departure—for that's what she meant to do, to leave us all and as speedily as she could load her tack and the distraught Hanoverian into her trailer, with or without Ralph's help.

"But, Cory," he cried, "you're hurt! You can't go like this!"

No answer. Only her furious single-minded exertions.

"But the snow, Cory, the snow! It's impassable!"

Helplessly Ralph and Master watched as on she went, indifferent to pain, indifferent to the blood that should have been its measure, determined only to quit Ralph's barn, rushing directly to her purpose with a strength and certainty that left Ralph sullen and Master shivering. Not one sound of her affliction followed her first prolonged burst of screaming, not a word did she utter, except for what she said in departure.

"See you, Ralph," she managed to say, and then was gone into the snow, into the roar of the diesel engine that condemned us all like some monster that filled the dawn until, at last, it faded into the falling snow.

"You bastard!" Ralph shouted then, turning and making for my stall door, his fist raised, his checkered shirttails flapping, his boots unlaced, his unruly red hair glistening. "Drive away a pretty woman like my Cory, would you!"

"But, Ralph," said Master, himself once more and speaking in his calmest voice, "surely you don't suspect Petrarch of causing this trouble, do you?"

"Petrarch!" shouted Ralph in scorn. "And who or what if not this useless horse of yours? That lovely woman was bitten, was she not? Her own well-mannered Hanoverian would not have done such a thing, would he now? And obviously my own sweet Clover"—here I flinched—"would not so much as hurt the hair on a child's head. Agreed? Who then if not this mean, foul, untrustworthy horse, this skinny animal I told you not to acquire in the first place? I'll kill him, that I will! Or beat him until he drops and then call for the knacker!"

"Hold, Ralph," said Master calmly, "stay your hand. He is my horse and hence my responsibility. It is for me to determine whether or not he injured Miss Mulcahy, and for me to reprimand him if I must."

"Rot!" said Ralph in disgust. "Irish horseshit, Harry Sir!"

Here I felt true apprehension, for Ralph was a threat that I could tolerate, whereas if Master raised his hand against me, startle I would and kick him I would, unavoidably, and hurting Master in any way was the one thing I now wanted most of all to avoid. But to my great relief he merely entered my stall and, while I held myself in readiness, searched me from head to tail with a stern, judicious, but harmless eye, the while keeping his hands safely occupied with holding his blanket.

"No, Ralph," he pronounced at last. "It was not Petrarch."

Whereupon Ralph grunted, stared, then suddenly began to laugh, and the two returned together to the rooms upstairs, from which the smells of cooking soon descended.

For now I had but one concern remaining, but even Clover gave me her forgiveness. She waited, in silence she conveyed her disapproval of what I had done, then once again approaching the partition between us, she expressed in her quiet way great surprise that I could be so violent. But then she supposed that I was more finely tuned and also less tolerant of teasing than most horses were, and recalled other Thoroughbreds with tempers as short as mine. To all this, and after an embarrassed pause, she admitted that she had found the forward manner of the newly arrived and newly departed Hanoverian too brash and too self-confident for her liking.

Thus in one of the simplest recourses left to the horse—biting—I revenged an old injury, routed my rival, regained my companion, remembered the past, rid my stall of Master, and restored him to the rooms above, where he belonged.

End of snowstorm. End of winter. No need for Mr. Fletcher's plow.

CHAPTER EIGHT

•

INFESTATION. BEFORE. AFTER. IN WHICH I HAVE A PREMONITION OF THE BEND IN THE ROAD

One day—and how often does this expression appear in every horse's history, as it now does in mine?—one day, then, when Ralph and Master were hacking at a slow walk down one of our many country lanes in spring—for it was spring—enjoying a pleasure that would not have been possible without the dutiful cooperation of Clover and me, all at once Master broke the silence that this day hung most unusually between himself and Ralph and us horses on whom they rode. There were woods in the distance and fields of light, the promise of warmth to come and rivulets of remaining snow and glittering combs of ice lying here and there in cold pockets in the reviving grass or at the base of wet and shiny boulders. How clear it was with a fresh chill in the air and winter gone and summer on its way. What brisk contentment we horses and our riders knew that day, until Master broke the silence that reached us from far and wide as on we walked. As follows.

"Ralph," said Master thoughtfully, his disembodied voice adrift somewhere above and behind my nodding head and flickering ears, "I have been thinking about your sister's antipathy toward men of the cloth, as my grandfather of Golden Wedding fame used to call them."

"Ah," said Ralph, his Irish voice more real this day than the man himself, "and what is your determination, Harry Sir? Your final word?"

"That I share your sister's sentiments," said Master without a moment's pause. "Completely."

"Harry Sir," said Ralph, his amusement and disbelief as frothy and audible as an urgent stream on a spring day, "I'm happy to hear it. But surprised as well, as you can understand."

"Yes," said Master. "The world at large respects men of the cloth, naturally. Most people, and from all walks of life, would find your sister's attitude toward men of the cloth objectionable, to say the least."

"True enough," said Ralph. "She was no ordinary lass, my sister. Especially when it came to clerics."

"Generally," said Master in his same thoughtful tone, "I too respect the church and clergy and subscribe to our family motto, *Ne quid nimis,* as did my grandfather. With your training in the classics, Ralph, you will comprehend immediately: *Nothing too much.*"

"Of course," said Ralph with a laugh. "An excellent family motto, Harry Sir. But a bit ambiguous?"

"Yes," said Master. "Grandfather discussed that problem with me more than once. He told me that only the black sheep of the family chose to believe that our family motto gave them the license to pursue and attain the unattainable, no matter the cost to themselves or others. Whereas the family at large did nothing, thought nothing, said nothing in or to excess, which is the other meaning of our motto. Grandfather told me that I too must avoid excess. And so I have."

"Excellent advice," said Ralph.

"Yes," said Master. "My grandfather was a man of mildest manner. Not once in his life did he raise his voice, not even when dismissing Henry, the family coachman of fifty years, or when discussing the often emotional subject of religion, which infrequently he did. More than once he warned me to avoid, in my life to come, the three inflammatory topics as he called them: money, religion, and womanhood. And yet, Ralph, even my grandfather expressed to me his disapproval of the clergy. The Catholic clergy, as of course he meant."

"Protestant, then, your grandfather?"

"Indeed he was, Ralph. Exactly."

"No use for Catholics, eh?"

"Exactly, Ralph. He told me in his mild way that members of the Catholic clergy were unclean."

"Unclean," said Ralph, who at that moment drew the ambling Clover to a standstill, while I, though feeling nothing of Master's hand on my rein, nonetheless followed my beloved Clover's example and halted and, taking advantage of our situation, turned my head and touched my nose to hers.

"Why, yes, Ralph. I hope I haven't said anything offensive. . . ."

"Not at all," said Ralph, jerking Clover's head away from mine with a tug that was unnecessarily severe, "though in my youth, Harry Sir, not a day went by but what my da and ma knelt side by side at the communion rail of our little drafty village church and side by side, Harry Sir, took the sacraments like the good Irish Catholics that they were!"

"But, Ralph . . . ," said Master, as Clover pulled against Ralph's hand and returned her nose to mine and Ralph gave her another hurtful tug, "I'm sure you know I didn't mean . . ."

"It's nothing!" cried Ralph in a louder, gruffer voice. "Think nothing of it, Harry Sir!"

"I only meant to say," said Master sadly, "that if I did not share my grandfather's view of those of the Catholic faith, at least not entirely, nonetheless I am on your sister's side when it comes to men of the cloth. Catholic men of the cloth, that is."

"Harry Sir," said Ralph, clearly mollified and enjoying himself on this spring day, "I never thought to hear you in such a pickle!"

"Not at all," said Master, applying his legs to my sides though

I did not move. "Your sister was offended by the unseemliness of men who denied their manhood while indulging it under the table, so to speak. Or trying to."

"Manhood!" cried Ralph, laughing and once more sending Clover forward at a brisk walk, in which I promptly joined her, though Master had ceased pressing me with his lanky legs. "Wonderful! I never thought to hear that word cross your lips, Harry Sir! And no thanks to your grandfather, I dare say."

"Beg pardon, Ralph?"

"Too inflammatory, I expect!" cried Ralph with a laugh, quickening Clover's walk still more and hence mine as well.

"I've lost you, Ralph," said Master simply.

"Oh never mind!" cried Ralph, laughing the louder. "It's of little consequence."

So on we rode, men silent, hooves of their mounts pocking and pucking agreeably on the rutted surface of the country lane. Now and again our shoulders bumped while our heads nodded in unison and our noses brushed. To one side of us there stretched a field of pale lemon-colored grasses, to the other the embankment sloped down steeply to a narrow strip of sandy marsh across which new currents of frothy water rushed or collected in shallow pools. What a pleasure it was to amble along with my beloved Clover, admiring afresh her shiny coat of pinkish white and rippling black, and trusting in the day and hour to spare us further tribulations from within or without. Oh foolish trust! Surely I of all horses knew better than to trust in anything, but there it was and worth its brief savoring.

"But speaking of Irish manhood," said Ralph then, as a cold cloud crossed the sun, "let me tell you about poor Carrie's ultimate encounter with that phenomenon."

" 'Irish,' Ralph?"

"There is no other, Harry Sir. Believe me. Where are you going to find true manhood except in my native land of the enticing green? We Irish lads are famous for leading the pack when it comes to manhood. But as I was saying," Ralph continued, "Carrie's confrontation with the man who stood at the top of the heap of Irish men was legendary in our county and counties round."

"I am uncomfortable already, Ralph."

"Harry Sir, just enjoy the hour, enjoy your horsemanship, and listen. I am only telling you how poor Carrie fell in love."

"Ralph," said Master brightly, "that's better!"

"It occurred," said Ralph portentously, "on an afternoon as fine as this one. We were gathered as usual in the Tank and Tit, Carrie and her half-dozen expectant lads and yours truly. She was a mere fifteen years of age that afternoon, my sister was, but ripeness never sat more resplendent on any farm wife wanting a man."

Here there was an indication that Master might interrupt, but Ralph pushed on quickly, making it clear that he would brook no interference in the rhythm of his tale.

"She was laughing, to be sure, and fidgeting, as if she knew what was to come, and all her faithful lads were more beside themselves than usual. The old green stump was smoking fiercely on the hearth of the Tank and Tit, all eyes were red, and the first signs of spring were in the blood, that's for sure. Well, suddenly the door flings open, and in strides a young man—note the respectful phrasing, Harry Sir—the likes of which had never before been seen in our village, or county for that matter, let alone in the Tank and Tit. Heads turn, silence falls, in strides our visitor, leaving the door for someone else to close, and makes straight for the bar, where he stops and turns and, resting his elbows on the bar, surveys that silent smoky room and smiles. He was tall, was Kevin, for such was his name, with his head of tousled hair as high as the rafters, or so it seemed, and he was large and well proportioned. Mind you, it was a chilly day, yet here was Kevin dressed only in a thin gray shirt open halfway down his naked chest, and trousers offering no more protection from the chill and rain, for it had just been raining, than the shirt. No cap for Kevin, no jacket. And what do you know but what the sleeves of his shirt were rolled up, while from the knees down the trousers and boots were as thick and black with wet and muck as if he'd been striding for miles through fens and bogs, which as it turned out he had. Now, Harry Sir, you must remember that in the Tank and Tit that day the air was thick and acrid with smoke but, more than that, with the full-blooded breath of hops and the sweet smell of whiskey in the stoppered bottles. All afternoon Carrie had been delaying her desire, and round that old wooden table not one of the lads had yet been invited into the back room. Why, the Tank and Tit that afternoon was as filled with unrelieved desire as an unwed mother's breasts with milk—"

"Ralph . . . ," Master interrupted weakly, yet said no more as off in the distance a small bird newly arrived began to sing and flutter in an unleafed birch and the sun once more appeared.

"So as I was saying," said Ralph, "there was Kevin, as we would come to know him, but a stranger for now, resting as casually as you please against the bar in that hot and chilly room in which my sister and her faithful and deserving lads could hardly contain themselves. What pain, Harry Sir! What restlessness unnaturally constrained! It was like the stillness that precedes the first burst of an Irish song, or the promise plain for all to see in the silence of enraptured eyes. Manhood, Harry Sir, is a matter of unspoken words!"

"I am listening, Ralph," said Master, as against his will.

"Well then," said Ralph, "Kevin waited, sensible lad that he was, and smiled round the room and ignored the glass of whiskey that Old John had in all deference placed at his elbow. Kevin might have walked a hundred miles that day, so burned and ruddy he looked, especially in comparison to all of Carrie's sallow helpless lads, who were now shifting their eyes from lass to stranger and stranger to lass and worrying, as well they might have, about what was to become of their own promised turns with Carrie that day, for by now the poor lass was so distracted that we hardly knew her for the wicked Carrie that she was. But Kevin made no acknowledgment of Old John's whiskey, no matter how manly his need of that Irish replenishment. He merely bided his time, basking in his own good nature, until the lass at the table, my own dear sister, hardly more than a child in age but a woman to be sure in mind and body, no matter the fulsome scrawny look to her, could bear no more and pushed back her chair and faced the waiting stranger and—would you believe it, Harry Sir?—allowed her face to color and her little bosom to heave for all the world like any lovesick lass at a garden gate, which was hardly what you would expect from this tender wily carefree creature who enjoyed the men, as she herself was wont to say in deliberate understatement that most of those same men and boys did not find amusing. So here she was, robbed of speech and near powerless in the throes of her submission to Kevin at the bar. Could she even walk? Her poor lads must have wondered, suffering for Carrie's sake as well as their own. For a time interminable it appeared that she could not, so that in the smoky silence a new and terrible uneasiness was felt round the table where the stout was warming in the tankards and not a soul stirred, for not one of those good lads would ever have wanted to bring Carrie low or to cause her suffering. Yes, Harry Sir, the mood was in danger of turning ugly until Carrie herself saved the day and turned the attention of all back to the drama they expected and even wanted to unfold.

"Yes, Harry Sir, Carrie tugged up her blouse at the shoulder and opened it a notch at the throat and, with more strength than any lass should ever have been called upon to muster, began to move—and oh, how unsteadily!—until she stood before the awesome stranger and then, with a little gasp, courage and strength collapsing, sank down to her bare knees at Kevin's feet. Here was submission for sure, Harry Sir, and not a lad in the Tank and Tit who did not hold his breath at the sight of it. Old John ceased his wiping the bar in midstroke, while I from my dark corner leaned forward and stared in boyish disbelief at my sister all but prostrating herself before this stranger and in total disregard of all who watched. Why, she might have been stark naked and Kevin might have had his trousers down, such was the electrifying effect of what we saw, Harry Sir. . . ."

"Please, Ralph," said Master in a voice that died even while he spoke and to which Ralph paid not the slightest attention, as the small bird preened itself and the cold day grew brighter.

"Well then, Kevin deigned pleasantly to look down at this slight female groveling there on her bare knees, unheard of in an Irish pub, while my sister leaned back her head and stared up at Kevin in mute appeal with her eyes filming over and her pale red hair reflecting the color of her cheeks and freckled bosom, which by now she had managed to bare another notch or two. Oh, weren't her knees spread far apart for balance barely preserved, and weren't her poor hands resting for steadiness on her thin thighs plainly outlined beneath her threadbare skirt, and wasn't she leaning by agonizing degrees ever more closely to Kevin's lower half with a hapless smile on her blushing face and a faint wordless sound now evident in her fragile pulsing throat? She was, Harry Sir, she was. And the sight of her couldn't have been more provocative or discomfiting either to all who witnessed this extraordinary spectacle that day.

"But then Old John, hand and rag still arrested on the bar, suddenly found it in him to clear his throat and speak out into that Dionysian discomfort that filled his pub. 'Dick,' he said, addressing one of the younger lads at the table and struggling to overcome his own self-consciousness, 'how's your mother?' That's all, but quite enough. All eyes, except those of Kevin and Carrie, of course, turned to Old John in unison, and filled they were with relief you may be sure, while in the ensuing moment Carrie let out a little playful laugh and broke the spell of her rapture and discovered anew the self-sufficient lass that she was.

"For what did that clever sister of mine do next but attack not Kevin's trousers, as it appeared she would, but his boots. Yes, Harry Sir, at the sound of Old John's homely question Carrie simply came to herself and, laughing, as I have said, looked down and began to tug this way and that on the laces of Kevin's muddy boots. Obviously she meant to remove the stranger's boots then and there, and obviously would not be deterred from what she intended.

"So she did, as Kevin himself began to laugh and the lads to grin, until Carrie stood up quite unassisted and, clutching those great muddy boots to her slight bosom, embracing so to speak the stench and distance of all the fens and bogs her grand stranger had crossed that day, seized the mysterious Kevin by the hand and pulled him barefooted around the table and through the door to the back room that was Carrie's own, thanks to the generosity of Old John.

"And then? Then Old John filled afresh the tankards with cold stout and served up to one and all, myself included, his famous pork pies, and though the lads round the table began to stuff themselves, as did I, nonetheless the main occupation of everyone in the Tank and Tit that fading afternoon was not eating and drinking but eavesdropping. And unfaltering were the sounds that came to us from the back room that afternoon from the moment the door closed until it opened again about fourteen hours later, when the two of them emerged at last and Kevin's boots were dry.

"Ah, but Harry Sir, I believe you've never heard such sounds," said Ralph then, an edge of humorous challenge in his voice, and paused, clearly expecting a response from Master.

Pock and *pock* came the sounds of Clover's hooves, *puck* and *puck* came mine, Clover's silky tail brushing my flanks and my stiff bristling tail brushing hers. The country road stretched on and away for us alone, for which we were grateful, amused and baffled though we were that the men on our backs were capable of riding us peacefully into the very day that spring had forced, like a new bud, through the last of winter, and still do nothing more than talk and listen instead of devoting themselves to their horses, ambling, as it were, down the garden path. Of course, we agreed, poor Master had no choice, unwilling accomplice that he was to Ralph's storytelling. So at last Master shook my reins, betraying his discomfort to me but not to Ralph, and spoke.

"I have indeed heard the sounds you refer to, Ralph," he said quietly. "I am not a child."

"No, no," said Ralph in a hearty voice. "I hadn't meant to imply you were!"

"I am glad for that," said Master. "And I must tell you, Ralph, that I was pleased once more to hear you making a classical allusion, though Dionysus is not one of my favorite gods."

"Well now," said Ralph, "there is more to come regarding Kevin and Carrie, for I've saved the surprise of their lives to the end. First of all, they could not hasten quickly enough to our village church and marry, according to all the rites and rituals of the Blessed Virgin's Faith—"

"Marry!" interjected Master, the happiest I'd heard him since our ride began. "But, Ralph, that's wonderful! I had not expected such a satisfying conclusion to your sister's story! And in time to come they had children?"

"Oh yes," said Ralph, "kiddies galore, though it was not long after the ceremony that my sister's marriage was annulled by that great Church of ours and poor Kevin was excommunicated in the same breath."

"Annulled?" exclaimed Master weakly. "Excommunicated?"

"To be sure," said Ralph, now relishing his every word. "The very morning after their day in church the word was out. Before the two of them could even bring themselves to quit the nuptial couch, in one of the rooms, I might add, above the Tank and Tit, Kevin made his announcement. He was a cleric, you see—"

"But, Ralph," exclaimed Master, "surely that's impossible!"

"Not at all," said Ralph. "Until he heard of my wicked sister, Kevin was one of the best-loved clerics ever sent to a poor dreary village to the West, a little place much in need of someone to restore the Faith in that cold parish. Kevin was their man, of course, a young and stalwart priest the women could love and the men respect. His celibacy was founded on the rock of manhood, which was plain to see; he was a true man in all his unwavering devotion to the Church. Yes, it was that manhood, along with his Irish humor and his ability to sing, that did the trick. Oh, he was on his way to being canonized, was Kevin, or so said his flock. But then he heard of my wicked sister and her contempt for the clergy, and you know the rest."

"But they stayed together, Ralph?"

"Could they have had all those kiddies had they not?" said Ralph in a sly and sour tone of voice. "But here is a nice question for you, Harry Sir. Was it the clergy that vanquished my poor sister in the end, or Carrie who corrupted for once and all the clergy? The lads she abandoned argued that one for years to come, you may be sure."

"What a terrible question," said Master softly.

"Oh, take heart, Harry Sir! You've only to keep in mind that Eve herself was from the West of Ireland, and proud of it!"

Whereupon Ralph let out a loud and lascivious laugh, and Master, as if to protect himself from flights of confusion, suddenly changed his mood as swiftly as it was Ralph's wont to do, and cried aloud in an eager jovial manner that could not have been more antithetical to the fragile thoughtful man he was.

"Look down there, Ralph!" he cried. "A path! I'll lead the way!"

"No!" shouted Ralph in unmistakable alarm, which he had never before expressed either to Master or to me. "Stay on the road!"

But all the fear and authority in barns the world over could not have deterred Master on that spring day, determined as he was to flee Ralph's stories and assert a boldness that in mere moments proved to be nothing other than wrongheadedness, and of a disastrous kind as well, which I might have expected from poor Master.

"Follow me!" he shouted in timorous delight, and before I could resist him or disobey him, which in fact I had not done so far, over the embankment we went and down, slipping and sliding the entire way. How I struggled to keep my balance, how I struggled to save myself from the panic that was rising up to us before my very eyes. As for Master, I marveled that he stayed on my back, as he somehow managed to do, and yet could only wish that he had fallen off me with our first lurch down. But then we landed on the wintry sandy floor that lay between the embankment and a nearby stand of young birches. From high above, Clover whinnied and Ralph tried once more to save Master if not Master's horse.

"Jump!" he shouted. "Jump!"

But we were already firmly on the bottom and I was still

upright on my four legs and Master was still in the saddle and laughing, childish foolish man that he was. Little did he know what lay in store for him. Little more did I.

"Look, Petrarch," said Master, clearly pleased with himself and straightening as best he could in the saddle, "do you see the path? It promises to be a pleasant path through those birches. Walk on!"

So saying, he gave me several sharp kicks and shook the reins, uselessly as he did not yet know. As for me, I diverted my attention from our plight long enough to see that of course there was no path through the trees, as Master, typically enough, had thought.

In that instant and from above came Clover's uncontrollable sounds of warning, for by now she was much distressed, and similar shouts of alarm from Ralph.

"Jump!" he cried again in a final effort to save the day. "For God's sake, Harry Sir, jump off!"

But Master, who had thoughts only of the nonexistent path and of displaying his leadership to Ralph, paid no attention to the Irish groom, or to Clover's most atypical squeals of pain and frustration, but instead continued to address himself in blithe self-confidence to me.

"Petrarch," he said, "walk on, I say. Whatever is the matter with you?" And then, over his shoulder, "Ralph," he called, "he seems to be stuck! He will not move!"

And stuck I was, and worse. For from the moment that I had found myself still standing on that deceptive bed, sand and marsh grass newly exposed from beneath the snow and water spread here and there across the sand, I knew that I was not standing at all, correctly speaking, but was sinking. Motionless though I was, controlled though I was, attempting not to make matters worse by stirring muddy waters, so to speak, nonetheless I had been mired from the start above the ankles and now was sinking down so smoothly that it took all the strength I had to keep from floundering. And now I was sunken above my knees, so that

Master's feet were suddenly and remarkably close to the surface, which at last he perceived.

"Ralph . . . !" he called, as the path faded before his eyes and the truth of our dreadful plight engulfed him.

"Christ!" shouted Ralph in return. "Kick away the stirrups!" which Master had presence of mind to do.

I waited for my sinking hooves to rest suddenly on solid ground, knowing that this was not to be, while all about this quiet place spring shimmered in the harsh light and was reflected from the skin-deep pools of water and, closer at hand, the newly arrived young bird sounded his melody.

What now?

With Master astride me the end was clear, for burdened with his extra weight I could not hope to save either one of us. Down we must go, together. Whereas if I were free of Master, at least I might be able to wrench myself from a doom as ugly as it was inevitable. But if I could free myself from the old man whose devotion to me I could not deny, he too might manage to keep himself alive.

And then?

Then I of all horses did not accept without a twitch or tremor my approaching end. I did not capitulate. I did not go down without a struggle. Far from it. Instead, and with but one purpose in mind, even as my own chest neared the surface, I gathered myself and in utter silence bucked. Yes, I bucked as I had never bucked before, with all my strength, with all the energy inspired by my inborn misanthropy and my recognition of the fate that was mine to fight, and in that single mighty heave of my back I flung Master high in the air and off. No sooner done than in the same motion I began at last to flounder. I scrabbled thickly against the soupy stuff that sucked me down, I heaved, I heaved again—vainglorious effort—and wishing no more than to keep my nose, my frantic nostrils in the air, tore myself upward from the perilous pit and, yes, lumbered free. *Molly-Long-Legs*, I thought in the midst of my awkwardness, *London Bobby*. Then those two spectral horses fled again and abruptly, for it was my own life that I had saved—and wanted nothing more than that.

Now, free of the grip of nature's treachery, now I gave way to a fear more lively than that I had felt in my desperate struggle. Dripping long gouts and fingers of muck and sand, trembling and all but sightless at my near loss of life and the sickening exertions of self-preservation, but now on solid ground at last, I had no thought but to reach the road and my beloved Clover above me. I struck out, I whirled, still fearful lest the horse gods pitch me into yet another illusory hole, from which I would not a second time escape, and bolted first one step, then another, toward the embankment, but what . . . ! what now? For there in my very path lay Master, facedown, spread-eagle, and with his hands covering his bare head—the black velvet hunting helmet that had survived long generations of deadly mishaps was nowhere in sight—and I was upon him and must surely trample him underfoot, whether he was dead or alive, as I did not know. But I could not, must not, and so gave a final leap of charity, avoiding him, and in fear and ignominy scrambled up the embankment. At least I had that much to my credit, I thought, gasping and pressing myself to Clover as Ralph slipped and slid down the incline to the prostrate figure that looked as if it would never move again.

"Harry Sir!" said Ralph in a frightened voice and stooping over Master. "Are you alive?"

"I am alive," came Master's rueful reply, "but I have lost my grandfather's famous hunting helmet."

"Oh, bugger your grandfather's helmet!" said Ralph, reverting in his relief to anger.

"And, Ralph," continued Master, while Clover and I watched and listened, "I believe that I have lost a tooth as well."

"No doubt you have," said Ralph, "if blood is any indication."

"Oh, it's gone, Ralph. I can feel the space."

"The question, Harry Sir, is can you stand on your feet?"

"I believe so, Ralph," said Master, in an oddly muffled breath, and slowly, bone by bone, limb by limb, he gathered himself onto hands and knees as tentatively as if each movement must produce this stabbing pain or that, until at last he rose to his full but now shattered height. From the top of his bare head to the toes of his boots he was covered in rivulets of sand and slime, his long narrow face was as white as his sideburns, from his sorry open mouth he was bleeding.

"I'll tell you one thing," said Ralph, surveying Master up and down, "you're fortunate to be alive."

"But, Ralph, Petrarch must have kicked me—and in the face, Ralph!"

"Oh, kick in the face be buggered," said Ralph. "It's thanks to that horse of yours that you're not drowned and down to China by now. It wouldn't have been a fit burial for Harry of Hidden Hall, Harry Sir!"

"And Petrarch saved me, Ralph?"

"He did," said Ralph, "though it pains me to say so."

"Well," said Master happily, trying to stanch the flow of blood with his hands, "help me up the embankment, will you, Ralph?"

Thus on that spring day I earned Ralph's praise, while the adventure of which he himself had been the cause ended without the calamity it had promised. Despite Ralph's urging, Master refused to mount me for our return to the barn, so that Ralph had little choice but to accompany Master on foot as they led their docile mounts toward home. Ralph upbraided Master most of the way, forcing Master into renewed humility and promises of faithful subservience to his own groom, though as Ralph's farm came closer, Ralph relented and assured Master that a man could not be a horseman without the occasional broken rib or leg or worse, so that the missing tooth and the kick that had dislodged it marked Master's progress from beginner to intermediate rider, which pleased Master as much as the new esteem in which I was now held by Ralph.

As we were thus proceeding, and the reluctant sun was warming every thistle in sight, and the remnants of near catastrophe were falling from the four of us, though Master's mouth was bleeding as profusely as ever, suddenly Ralph's barns rose distantly to view and we heard a soft and unfamiliar sound and saw an instability in the scene before us and stopped—to a man, to a horse. Oh, what new woe was this? Why the bristling in Clover's coat and mine and our reluctance—no, our near refusal—to walk on? Something was undeniably wrong and was made worse by Master's sudden forgetfulness of me and Ralph's of Clover, quite as if we horses had disappeared for good from our owners' lives.

"Ralph," said Master softly, his speech thoroughly impeded, "what is it?"

"Rats," said Ralph.

"How's that, Ralph? Rats?"

"Harry Sir," said Ralph distinctly, "you must not repeat everything I say. We have got a problem, a very serious problem, with rats."

"But how do you know, Ralph?"

"Just listen," said Ralph. "Use your eyes."

"But what about Fuzzy and the others, Ralph?"

"Ah, Harry Sir," said Ralph, the anger in his voice as frightening now as what we could but barely see and hear in the distance. "Now you've touched on the mystery."

"But if your cats cannot handle the problem, Ralph . . . ," said Master, his voice trailing off and his misery deepening, "what then?"

Here Ralph made no answer but simply grunted, tugged his tweed cap more tightly down on his head, and jerked on Clover and set off, dragging our entourage once more down the road. We were a silent troop, a fearful troop, except for Ralph, whose every plodding step increased his belligerence. And the closer we got to the barns, the greater our apprehension, for now the sound we heard was a distinct whispering, a sound of squealing and scampering that came and went like a malevolent breeze, while by now the rats that Ralph had identified so readily were visible and swarming everywhere like a black carpet.

"Why, Ralph," cried Master through his fear and pain, "there is a horde of them!"

"I can see well enough," said Ralph, and filled himself with deep puffs of anger and more staunchly than ever led us on toward the invaders.

"But, Ralph," cried Master, determined as usual to express himself, "they are even on the rooftops of both our barns! You cannot do battle with them up there! Oh, what an ugly sight they are. . . ."

"Big buggers," muttered Ralph, striding on as Clover and I did our best to hang back. "Black rats by the look of them, ship rats or roof rats as they are also called. Black as sin and longer than fifteen inches, excluding their naked tails. And you may be sure that they are gorging themselves in the feed bins and pissing on the remaining grain they've yet to eat. Filthy buggers. I've warned Old Fletcher a hundred times if I've warned him once."

"Old man Fletcher, Ralph?"

"The buggers must have a source, Harry Sir. Old Fletcher used to run a pig farm on that place of his, until one day he fell into a rage and slaughtered the lot of them, piglets or aged sows, it didn't matter to Old Fletcher, and flung them to rot in the muddy yard of their own former wallowing. And not only that, but he took his dozer and knocked down their filthy barn right on top of the muddy yard where lay the lifeless carcasses—and left the lot of them. Out of sight, out of mind, for Old Fletcher, except for the stench, which even to this day you can smell if the wind's right. But what does a mass of dead pigs yield but a breeding ground for rats? So here without the slightest bit of effort he's bred up this whole community of black rats to come down here bespoiling my property. Infectious jaundice! Salmonellosis! Rat-bite fever! Murine typhus! Not to mention the human plague as carriers of which they're justly famous—"

"But, Ralph," interrupted Master, "how is it that you are so well versed in these repulsive matters?"

"Happened before," said Ralph. "Hence the cats. But this time, Harry Sir, you may be sure that I shall take legal action. Why, this time I shall drive Old Fletcher well out of the region once and for all. After I square off with the rats, that is."

"But what do you propose to do, Ralph?"

"Go after them," said Ralph, "with the back of a shovel. Of course I would get more personal satisfaction out of impaling the buggers on the tines of a pitchfork, but I shall stick to the shovel. More practical. And you may be sure that I shall squash a goodly number of the buggers before I'm done."

"Well, Ralph," said Master slowly, "I too can wield a shovel. I'll join you."

"Ah, Harry Sir," answered Ralph, "it's best that you remain right here with the horses."

So saying, off strode Ralph, while Master, holding Clover's reins and mine in one limp hand and stroking us with the other, spoke reassuringly first to Clover and then to me, the while disregarding the blood that had slowed to a trickle but nonetheless continued to drench his shirt and the front of his ancient riding coat.

"Clover, my dear," he murmured, "it is a sorry day when our tidy barn is invaded by such carriers of filth. And though I do not know it for a fact, I must assume that these pestilential creatures are not beyond biting horses—heaven forbid! As for you, Petrarch," he continued, "at least you are in no way to blame for this calamity. But surely Ralph's own natural Irish ferocity will win back our barn. At least we must trust in Ralph, my dears."

But hardly had those kindly optimistic words left Master's bleeding mouth than suddenly Clover and I fell back as one, jerking to free ourselves from Master and turn and flee, for in this moment the squealing inside our barn rose to a fearsome defiant pitch, while simultaneously there came to us a single shout of rage and pain louder than any I had ever heard. More squealing, another shout, even louder and more agonized than the first.

"Ralph!" shouted Master at the top of his voice, bleeding and trembling and exerting all his energy to prevent our escape. "What's wrong?"

"Fuzzy!" came the delayed reply, Ralph's voice swelling and then cracking with grief. "He's beneath a pile of them, Harry Sir.

They've outnumbered him. Oh, there's hardly a scrap left of my Fuzzy—the buggers!"

The cursing. A barrage of cursing. And the back of the shovel thumping and thwacking in every direction, as far as we could hear. A random tireless attack, a running savage commentary, which, this chaos heard but not seen, was proving all but unbearable to Clover and me. The smell of the battered rats, crushed dead or dragging themselves about the aisleway on their bellies, along with the sound of their frustrated cowardly squealing and the now incomprehensible words of their grief-stricken opponent, were more abrasive to our senses than would have been a clear view of the battle raging inside the barn. How different were our own squeals of alarm from the sickening screeches of the surviving rats! How valorous was Master, who held us fast where we stood and waited together at the edge of the invisible fray. "Oh, Ralph," he called in his next breath as the determined groom emerged from the barn, frowning and glowering, "is it over? Have you routed them, Ralph?"

"I am Irish enough to know when I have been licked," called Ralph, who then flung down his shovel and began to climb the stairway to the rooms above.

"But may I return the horses to the stalls?"

"You may not! Can't you spare me your lack of common sense on this day of days?"

"But, Ralph," called Master, his voice quavering, "what are we to do?"

"We shall move to another barn, of course. Temporarily. And in less than an hour a professional shall drive up this road with his traps and poisons and give these little buggers the what-for."

"Poor Fuzzy," said Master to himself, and let Clover's reins and mine go slack so that we might lower our heads to the stubble and graze, which, calmed as we now were, we did. From the rooms above our stalls there came a sudden last burst of shouting and a brief clattering of pots and pans, and then a silence followed by Ralph's loud voice making our arrangements.

The breeze increased, the sun shone, a shadow of premonition crossed my path. But Master, ever confident of the future, wondered happily aloud about the new barn that awaited us around the bend in the road.

CHAPTER NINE

•

OF THE SURPRISING EVENTS THAT FOLLOWED OUR FLIGHT FROM THE RATS, AND OF OUR BLINDNESS TO THE END IN SIGHT

"Ralph!" cried Master. "Do you know where we are?"

"I should think so," answered Ralph.

"Oh, Ralph!" cried Master, "you are deceived!"

"What," answered Ralph, "not Millie Gordon's place?"

"Hidden Hall, Ralph! Hidden Hall!"

"Well, Harry Sir, I am amazed," said Ralph in a voice that could not have more denied amazement, and proceeded matter-of-factly to the unloading of Clover and me from the rusty black horse trailer in which we had been carried away from Ralph's infested barn.

"But it's true, Ralph! I am not mistaken!"

"This farm," said Ralph with an ill-tempered laugh, "has been in the Gordon family for years."

Surprise. First surprise of a surprising day. Shock, silence, disbelief. Had Ralph indeed said Gordon? The Gordon family? Was he in fact referring to the Gordon girls? The Millie Gordon of my birth, my youth? Most cherished name that obviously meant nothing to Ralph yet everything to me? Even as I doubted what I had heard, for doubt I must, Clover, quick-witted Clover, with the keenest possible memory of all I had told her during our long nights in adjoining stalls, now looked wonderingly at me and whinnied and so confirmed that she too had heard what my disbelief would both admit and deny.

"Oh, Ralph," cried Master as first Clover and then I clattered down the lowered ramp and together stopped and surveyed the scene before us, "I am astounded, Ralph! How can it be? This same Hidden Hall built and named in honor of my own grandfather's vast estate across the waters? The same, Ralph, the same! Here I was born and raised, there I was privileged to attend the Golden Wedding! How can it be?"

"A miracle for sure," said Ralph. "But look now, Harry Sir, you're exciting the horses!"

As was the case. For what I saw all around me, and what Clover recognized from my descriptions, was Millbank—beyond a doubt. The low house with its wide encircling veranda, the gabled barn, the enormous carriage horse still stretched in his eternal gallop atop the cupola, and most of all the mulberry tree—all there, unchanged, except, and here was an "except" that left me stunned where I stood, except that Millbank, my own Millbank, was now a mere ruin of what it once had been. The house, the outbuildings, which in my suddenly awakened memory gleamed with fresh coats of thick white paint, had turned to weathered graying wood. So too the vistas of white fencing before my eyes, unpainted, poorly repaired with mismatched boards. Weeds and high grass everywhere, from lawns to fields, unmowed, untended. Oh, there were broken slats in the cupola, and the ominous sight of wasp nests everywhere. And was that not Jim's tractor of old gone to rust? It was. And on the veranda, under its sloping roof, what was that strange chair with wheels? Why was it there? Emptiness personified, abandon. Yes, I was horrified by the sight of the gloomy chair yet could hardly put it out of mind.

Joy of return, despair of dereliction. What catastrophe had all but destroyed the seemly character of this place of my birth and youth? But if a horse could be racked with age—and was I not so racked?—why not the farm of his birth? In the very instant of my arrival, then, I was doubly if not triply stunned. And yet in that same instant Clover made me know that she understood both my pleasure and my confounding, while Master became ever more rapturous in the sound of his speech and the look in his eye.

"You must know, Ralph," he cried, "that I remember this Hidden Hall of the new world as well as I do my grandfather's Hidden Hall of the old! Oh, but I cannot believe my good fortune!"

"Nor can I," said Ralph.

"Is it not a glorious sight?"

"With work, perhaps," said Ralph. "Millie can't manage the place alone."

"I know that house, Ralph! And that large barn with its commodious box stalls! Many a night I sat at my mother's knee before the bright hearth while the gales blew and the snow fell. Many a morning as a small boy I swept the aisleway inside that barn. . . ."

"The devil you did!" said Ralph with a laugh.

"It is a brick aisleway, Ralph. You may see for yourself. Now you surely must admit that I come from a long line of horse people. What a pity that I was never allowed to do so much as sit on a horse in my childhood. My health was poor, but it was a mistake to deny me the only pleasure for which I yearned—riding, that is."

"Well, Harry Sir, you have surely made up for the sins of the past!"

"Thank you, Ralph," said Master after a considered pause.

Then, as if our arrival at Millbank (to me) or Hidden Hall (to Master) was not already fraught with incongruity, suddenly there came into our midst a strange and desperate cry. A piercing cry, a hopeless cry, not of bird or small animal, as the next moment demonstrated, but of a young and inconsolable infant. A tiny infant newly born, as it seemed to me, and riding high on its mother's back in a little blue canvas device from which it could not escape, as apparently it wished to do.

"Ralph!" Master had barely time to exclaim. "A baby!" When out of the barn came the waving mother and her scant burden, to which, as they approached us, she paid not the slightest attention.

"Millie!" called Ralph, returning her wave.

"Hello," answered the young woman in that sweetest, most boyish voice I had ever heard, could not forget, yet had never expected to hear again, no matter my dim hopes of returning full circle to my lost beginnings. Yes, she was none other than Millicent Gordon, my own Millie, no longer a girl but fleshed in the spirit and self-confidence of a mature woman. She was smiling, she was dressed in an overly large man's shirt with collar open, sleeves rolled, shirttails tied high on her midriff so as to bare her waist, and dressed too in faded shorts and canvas shoes. She was as small as ever, as freckled as ever, yet nothing at all like the girl who had drawn me from my dam on the day of my birth and had loved me from that day forward. In all surprise and shyness, sensations I was not accustomed to, I saw that not only had she cropped her wild black head of hair but she had acquired muscles more visible, skin more weathered, dusty even, and walked differently, smiled differently, was shaped by all that could not be shed—age and the infant screaming from where it rode on her back. Small mother, tiny child, and equally undaunted, as said the cries of the one and the composure of the other.

"Having a bad time, is he?" said Ralph. "Wants what they all want, I suppose. Ma's milk."

Mother apparently deaf to Ralph's comment. So too the child.

And then, "You're Harry,' said Millie Gordon, with a glance at Clover, a glance at me.

". . . of Hidden Hall," stammered Master.

"I know," said Millicent Gordon, her hand thrust out, small face turned up to Master, smiling as at the same time and with a quick jerk of her narrow shoulders she shifted her burden. Sunlight on the dusty peach-colored face of the mother. Infant, in response to new position, screaming the louder. Master fully costumed in usual regalia of hunting field, sporting proudly new black helmet provided by resourceful Ralph. Master alarmed by irate infant, Master's attention torn from panoramic perusal of Hidden Hall by handshake he could not avoid. Ralph amused. Horses mere fixtures in unexpected tableau.

"Shouldn't you do something?" Master managed to say at last, seizing and quickly dropping the proffered hand.

"It's not time for his lunch," said the woman, who was my own Millicent transformed. "But we'll give him a ride on your horse. That'll stop him!"

"Oh my," answered Master. "Petrarch is very skittish."

"Freddie likes tall horses, and there's not a single one on the place. Only ponies. He won't sit on ponies."

"Smart lad," said Ralph, grinning and interrupting from where he lolled in evident amusement against the black trailer.

"But he's a mere infant!" exclaimed Master. "Surely such a tiny infant can neither walk nor sit on a horse?"

"Oh, Freddie's nine months old," said Millicent Gordon. "He's pretty good at both."

"Well," said Master, delaying as long as he could the imminent unnatural disaster he so obviously feared, "does your husband approve? Of your little child riding, that is?"

"Harry Sir," said Ralph promptly, "this gorgeous young woman is a widow! At her young age!"

"Oh dear," said Master, coloring. "I had no idea. . . ."

"Never mind," said Millie, disengaging one arm and then the other and so swinging free the infant and then kneeling, gently lifting infant from blue device. "I was extremely young."

"What's that . . . ?" said Master, frowning anew.

"Exactly!" said Ralph. "Married as a mere slip of a lass to a mere slip of a lad!"

"In fact," added Millie of Millbank as if to reassure poor Master, "we were underage at the time."

"And no sooner hitched," said Ralph, "against the wishes of the parents, naturally, than the mere slip of a lad gets himself pitched off and all but killed!"

"The wheelchair," added Millie, gesturing behind her back to the veranda, "was his."

"Until the poor lad's courage failed him," said Ralph, "as how should it not? A young and even reckless sportsman confined to that ugly thing for life!"

"You mean . . . ?" said Master. And then, more softly, "Good heavens!"

An abrupt pause. A long pause. Child beside himself, even in mother's arms. Child as shrill as a teakettle. Master frowning. Master uncertain which way to turn. Ralph enjoying Master's helplessness.

"But then," said Master finally, frowning more deeply yet speaking so as to encourage an affirmative reply, "you remarried . . . ?"

"Harry Sir," said Ralph in a blustering authoritative voice, "she did not!"

"But this child . . . ?" said Master.

"Ah," said Ralph. And then, pursuing his tone of triumph, "Harry Sir," he said, "in this world there are those few accidents that are meant to be!"

Master dismayed. Infant enraged. Mother nonplussed.

"Freddie's a good baby," she said, speaking directly to Master and as if oblivious to Ralph, "when he's not hungry."

"I am sure he is," said Master weakly.

"Unlike his da!" said Ralph. "Regular scamp, his da! A terrible scamp with the women! Is it not so, Millie?"

No answer. No change in situation. Infant squalling. Mother proud of squalling infant. Mother as deaf to infant as to neighbor Ralph. Mother preparing infant to ride tall horse—myself! Master abject. Tall horse, myself, alarmed.

"Harry," said Millie then, already standing to her full height, which brought her head to my shoulder, and thrusting up her infant into Master's arms, "where did you get this horse?"

"A long story!" murmured Ralph with a laugh.

"Because," Millie continued brightly, "this horse was born on this very farm! I grew up with him; he was my first love back in the days of my girlhood. And look at him now, Harry. Poor Sweet William!"

"No," said Master, suddenly revived. "His name is Petrarch."

"Pe-trarch," repeated Ralph under his breath.

"Of course," said Millie. "But his original and registered name was Sweet William. How pathetic it is to see him broken down this way!"

"What did I tell you, Harry Sir!"

"Naturally I would recognize him anywhere, anytime. . . ."

"To my eye," Master interrupted firmly, attempting to speak above the intolerable sound of the tempestuous infant he himself was now holding, "Petrarch has come back nicely. It has taken time and patience. But he has gained weight and grown obedient, though he behaves like a Thoroughbred, as we must expect. All in all, and thinking of what my illustrious grandfather would have thought of him now, I am quite satisfied."

Respectful pause. Thoughtful pause. Then, "Harry," said Millicent Gordon, "I'll take him, and you put Freddie up on him. Ralph," she said as afterthought, "there's a half jar in the fridge. And bring a spoon."

Small woman's voice vigorous with pleasure. Irish sentiments suppressed. Irish presence withdrawn. Temporarily. Panic coursing through old man holding infant. Clover admonishing tall horse to docility. Unabating sounds of infant as unsettling to tall horse as prospect of bearing infant on tall horse's back. Scene set. Scene all at once resounding with authority of small woman in charge.

Except for a short and unexpected interlude. A moment's interlude shared only by small woman and tall horse. Intimacy unobserved by old man preoccupied with infant or even tall horse's consort. A few words whispered but to me. A gesture meant for me alone. The words? *Welcome back, Willy, where you belong! Good boy!* The gesture? A pat on my shoulder.

Thus, in a moment, Millicent Gordon drained me of resistance and brought me to submission—to her—as the best of the past shone through the present like sun through mist. But the consequence? The consequence was that I found myself, as I well deserved, walking in placid abysmal circles with her infant perched on my back. Thoroughbred, racehorse, noble malcontent, prideful dangerous instincts preserved intact, yet brought to this—bearing Millicent Gordon's infant round and round as if I were but some half-dead pony in a park!

"Millie!" said Master through my glum obedience, and in a voice of softest disbelief. "He has stopped crying!"

So he had, I realized, but at my expense. Though even I acknowledged to myself, as I listened to my own footfalls, the relief of the silence that had been returned to us.

Silence restored. Infant once more in Master's arms. Silence once more shattered but in a different voice and from another quarter.

"Look at you!" shouted Ralph, returning. "Harry Sir, I had not thought to see this paternal streak! Downright domesticity! Most becoming!"

"Thank you, Ralph," said Master for the second time that day. "Our arrival couldn't be more auspicious!"

At which Millicent Gordon of Millbank laughed and, slapping Clover's rump and then slapping mine, sent us trotting off through dead knee-high grass toward the distant array of stunted apple trees. The last human voice we heard until darkness began to fall was Ralph's.

"Ah," he said, from where he sat on an old mounting block, infant cradled in the crook of an arm, a silhouetted lonely pair, "how the little bugger eats!"

The number of days-of-days in a horse's life is sorely limited, and had I but known, mine were now reduced to a mere several, of which the first was none other than this very day of my homecoming. How swiftly this day progressed, how amazingly, and, as befits a day-of-days, how blazingly its end was heralded. For no sooner had Clover and I set off in the all but overgrown direction

to and through the orchards beyond which my innocent youth
had ended, than on the top of a little rise there appeared a sight
that arrested us abruptly in the high grass concealing the path
we'd no other choice but to take. Around us insects puffed upward in transparent clouds, the air ran sweet, we could not
move—two old horses held mysteriously in thrall but by what? A
trick of light? An unheard-of natural apparition composed of light
yet sickening? At first we did not know what we looked upon,
Clover and I: some creature of majestic splendor—for creature he
was and four-legged, though not a horse or a pony either—or
again some strange emblematic showing forth of nature's darker
art quite the opposite of glorious? We looked, he gathered to
himself in myriad shafts the last of the sun's rays. And in that light
he appeared to be covered by nuggets of gold shining fiercely from
where they lay embedded in his long silvery hair. He was large,
he carried atop his head one fragment of curving golden horn, in
that compacting of light he was like nothing I had ever seen in all
the days or dreams of my life. Clover pressed herself to me, as I
to her. Together we stared amazedly, uneasily, at this gold-stud-
ded enigma confronting us. But in the next breath the sun shifted,
dusk came upon us. Suddenly our living enigma was revealed for
what he was.

Exactly! What else? A goat, of course.

Only a goat, an old goat, as in that gray light we saw immediately, and weak, enfeebled, declining through his final hours, as
could not have been more apparent despite his size, for he was
large and once, by the look of him, had been the possessor of a
pride to match his immensity. But no more. Not a shred of pride
remaining to poor Chester, as his name soon proved to be. And
silvery hair? Nothing other than hair long stiffened by the foul
color of old age. And what we had mistaken for golden nuggets?
Mere eruptions! Pustules! Sorry signs of what poor Chester carried deep within him and of which, as he himself said, he was
dying. And his golden horn? Only a wrinkled brother to that other
horn he had long ago broken off and lost, though he remembered
nothing of the incident.

Not only a goat, then, but a dying goat. But one who nonetheless, and for the little time we knew him, retained about himself some shade of the golden aura in which he had initially appeared to us.

Clover, no mare ever more compassionate, trotted forward immediately to join the suffering goat. I followed. Soon we were listening to Chester's story, which he embarked upon with no reluctance, no hesitation, there in the last of the light and while old memories swarmed about us like the newly risen insects. With his head lowered and his rheumy eyes upraised, Chester recalled the goat farm of his birth and the time of his frolicking, one small goat in a herd of goats. With weary pleasure he dwelt upon that sunny afternoon when he, a carefree kid, had been recognized for what he had been born to be—one whose very presence in the long-haired multitude calms distempers, inspires tranquillity instead of rage. Was it fair, he asked us then, that for such a singular ability he must spend his life not among his beloved goats but among horses? So it had been, he went on hastily, enumerating the years of peace he had brought to this horse or that, and to their owners as well, naturally, until at last he had found himself in the stall of Zulu, none other than the favorite horse of the young rider Millie Gordon married. In this way, Chester said, he had arrived at Millbank and instilled a deceptive calm—yes, deceptive—in that tall black dangerous horse who was known, said Chester forlornly, for finding no peace in life except in the company of one pacifying goat or another. Oh, said Chester, he had done his best, enveloping the unpredictable Zulu in his own rare temperament. But it had not been enough. Chester himself, he said, was no match for such a pair—the vicious red-eyed horse, the excessively self-confident young rider. So it was, said Chester dismally, and thus he had been the only witness to that accident. Zulu berserk. Young rider flung to rocky earth and crippled. But so it had been, so he had failed.

The rest, according to Chester, was slow decline, increasing age, the loss of his horn—somewhere, somehow—the worst of it being, as dilapidation possessed Millie Gordon's farm, that he himself, as he knew full well, was kept on the premises only because of Millie Gordon's loyalty to the past—to the dead horse, to the reckless man, both of whom survived in a sense in the now dying goat.

Nothing was left to Chester, he assured us there in the gloaming, except the kindness of Millie Gordon and the sure knowledge that he himself had brought rack and ruin on Millbank, the proof of which were the sores blistering his body as visibly as the deterioration encroaching day by day on the farm. His final understanding, which he bemoaned in the gathering dusk, was that a goat had no business on a horse farm, so that his deepest regret, one that he hesitated to confess even to such sympathetic listeners as Clover and me, was that he had been born only an awkward and ugly-looking goat and not a horse.

Silence. Deepening silence. Until hunger awakened Clover and me and Chester as well. Back we went toward the gate where Master and Millie would find us and lead us to the safety and sustenance of the once proud massive barn, now sagging. In the sweetness of dusk Clover, and hence myself, restrained our appetites and energies so as to keep pace with the failing goat.

That night, and no matter the disagreeable smell of the goat, which found us from where he stood in the darkness, I realized anew that I was home, temporarily or not, and still joined by faithful Clover, in what she now referred to as her adoptive home.

Later, much later that same night, we heard the far-off squalling of the infant, but it was a faint sound and intruded only momentarily on our drowsing.

New birch trees, for surely there had not been a birch on all the extent of Millbank when I had spent the timeless time of my youth on that flourishing farm—new birch trees, then, were already in leaf while preserving, in the brightness of brittle bark, the color of winter. The oaks, the very oaks that had once sheltered the mares and colts and fillies atop the knoll when I had been one of those newborn horses with neither hint nor premonition of what lay ahead—these same massive oaks were still atop that knoll and thickly enough in leaf to protect us all from any downpouring of late spring or early summer rain, no matter how mighty. Except that there were no horses, nor goat either, beneath those oaks, for none of us, including the ponies, were drawn to those trees, that place. And the mulberry tree, as I have mentioned, was larger, more fully in leafy coverage than I remembered it, quite conccaling what Chester knew nothing of and Clover and I held in common regard but ignored. As for flowers, none bordered any longer the path to the house, and yet, though no plantings were cultivated about the place, random bursts of wildflowers grew everywhere.

Millbank familiar, then. But nothing the same. Thriving, dying. To a horse such as myself, what could have been more foreign than nostalgia? And so it was. For every morning Chester was more blistered than the night before, and yet Clover would by no means allow any shunning of the old goat. And there was Millie. Small woman laden with buckets of fresh water. Tossing hay. Heaping high the wheelbarrow with new manure and wet bedding from stalls of ponies and visiting horses alike, as well as the foul nest of the old creature who was not one of us. Or Millie in repose in the sunlight, dressed in familiar shorts and shirt and canvas shoes, but wearing on her head and in decorous incongruity a deep-dish-shaped bonnet of faded straw with a black band. Bonnet from another era. Reposing woman, wasps emerging anew from above her head. From the cupola. From heavy muddy lumps beneath the eaves.

Nostalgia as seen through a misanthropic eye. Awake in sleep. Waxing. Waning.

"Millie!" exclaimed Ralph, sunlight glazing his red hair to a bright orange. "You must put him down! Have you no regard for the health of these horses? No concern at least for this babe in my arms?"

No answer. Shocked unhappy look on Master's face. Millie ruddier than ever. Infant guzzling his bottle.

"Well then . . ." Bottle thoughtlessly withdrawn. Howl from

the infant. Bottle hastily returned. "We shall have an illustrative story—"

"Perhaps this is not the time for a story, Ralph?"

"Wrong again," said Ralph. "Well, as I was saying, when I was a member of the Irish Fusiliers, on foreign soil, you understand, and in the thick of things, my assignment was to our company padre's staff. There's irony for you. It was a staff of one, mind you, and so I must drive the padre's jeep and clean his boots and help him serve the Mass every Sunday morning. Me, of all people. It might have been a good job to have in a war, except that the padre was a gung-ho old gent who thought that those most deserving of the Mass and most in need of it were those lads who were the most forward. So of course the padre and I were forever moving from one all but gutted farmhouse to another and serving the bread and wine to three or four poor muddy lads each Sunday—from a purple cloth spread on some peasant's kitchen table, mind you—and comforting their comrades at all hours of the day and night. The padre wouldn't allow their weapons inside the House of God, as he called whichever wreck of a farmhouse we were inhabiting at the time, the poor old misguided soul—"

"Ralph," Master interrupted, "I had not known you were in the fighting forces. But Millie is trying to work, you must see that."

"And I am trying to teach that very same Millie a lesson," answered Ralph. "And so I will. . . ."

"Even while you are feeding her baby, Ralph?"

"Now early one Sunday morning," said Ralph, disregarding Master altogether, "the padre and I awoke in the farmhouse we had occupied but late the night before, when, what do you know, the padre insists we must take a look outside. Much to my disapproval, you understand. Small-gun fire perfectly audible from surrounding woods. But of course the sweet old padre must have his way, so out we went into a brilliant sunlit early dawn—it had been raining for weeks on end—and there, in the nearest empty field, was a sight to me abhorrent but to the padre as significant

as the Mystery itself made manifest. 'Why, look at that, McCue,'
said the padre, shielding his eyes and smiling. 'Yes, sir,' I answered, 'a dead cow.' 'Ah, look again,' said the padre. 'That is not
a cow, McCue, it is a horse.' 'That may be, sir,' I said and held
my tongue. 'But, McCue,' said the padre, 'do you see nothing
unusual about it? Nothing that quickens your spirit?' 'Well, sir, it
is a dead animal for sure. And bloated as big as a petrol tank on
the back of a lorry. You can smell it from here.' 'I am not talking
about the smell,' said the padre, a little miffed. 'Follow me.'

"And so I did, having no choice in the matter. And to tell the
truth, the closer we got to the horse—naturally I had known it
was a horse all along—the more I had to admit to myself that it
was a peculiar sight. 'Do you see, McCue? Look at the color.
Have you ever seen such a vision of pure gold?' At which I had
to confess that I had not. 'And do you see how the gold that is
blanketing the poor creature is moving? Shifting ever so slightly
in waves and currents across the swollen remains of that white
horse?' Here I said nothing but saw that what the padre said was
true. The wretched horse was alive with golden flecks. For the
moment even I was taken in by the glorious look of the thing, as
on we trudged through that muddy field toward the dazzling sight
of the horse. 'I want you to understand, McCue,' said the padre,
as if I were no more than a child, 'that no one has ever seen what
we are seeing. A poor abandoned horse destroyed in a field by
random fire and now blinding as a glory we cannot hope to
explain.' 'Ah, sir,' I answered, 'I am not so sure about that.' For
now we were within a couple of yards of that carcass and the
answer was clear enough for one of Blackpool's blind to see. I
nearly laughed.

" 'What do you mean, McCue,' said the padre then, who appeared to be quite immune to the atrocious smell.

" 'Maggots, sir,' I said. 'That's all.'

" 'Maggots, McCue?'

" 'Well, yes, sir. Now that we're this close to the carcass, and
have got the sun behind our backs, it's quite plain to see that this

rotting carcass is crawling with maggots. They are inside the carcass and on the surface as well. Alive, sir, which accounts for the fact that the golden light we saw was moving.'

" 'McCue,' replied the padre then, 'I will not say that you are hopeless, but you are nearly so. The point is that what we saw at first is the truth. The maggots, mortally unpleasant when seen through eyes such as yours, will return this white horse to the very earth he lies upon. The maggots are sacred, McCue. No matter how dead white they may now look to you, they are still as golden as they first looked to us both.'

" 'Perhaps, sir,' I answered in all deference. 'But this rotting meat is dangerous to human life. Our medical officer will tell you as much. I should not approach too close to it, sir, if I were you. If you will allow the opinion, sir.'

" 'McCue,' said the padre then, exasperation edging his voice despite his kind nature, 'when I give you the Holy Communion this morning, I want you to concentrate on the beauty of God's maggots. Do you understand?'

" 'I. do, sir,' I said, and back we went to set up the padre's makeshift altar for the men."

A pause. Long overdue. Ralph catching his breath, casting a most meaningful glance in Millie's direction. Then a disdainful glance at Chester, where the all but outcast goat stood fearfully not far from Clover and me, helpless but to stare at Ralph between the fence rails over which we hung our heads, Clover and me, also helpless but to stare at Ralph and listen.

"Ralph," said Master at last, "is that story true?"

"Oh," said Millie with a slight unpleasant laugh, "the Irish are notorious, aren't they, for their inability to tell the truth! It's a national if not congenital flaw—in the men at least."

"If you are saying," said Ralph stiffly, "that my countrymen are liars, to mince no words, then of course I stand by my countrymen. However, and despite present accusations to the contrary, it is a true story. My sister Carrie loved it. And just to prove that I was right, and that that rotting horse was the worst of all possible omens, and of deadly implications to the lot of us, the very next day the poor well-meaning padre was shot dead at my side in the jeep as I was driving at breakneck speed for cover. And I want you to know, Millie," continued Ralph, slowing the rhythm of his speech for emphasis, "that that old goat of yours is already dead, no matter that he still stands and breathes. Dead inside, Millie. Rotting from the inside out. A source of contagion beyond belief. Maggots? Why, that goat's blisters put the padre's holy maggots to shame. And there's nothing holy about maggots—or blisters either.

"Millie," continued Ralph in a calmer voice, as all three of us on our side of the fence, horses and goat as well, stared in disbelief and waited, "you must put that goat down! And," more softly, "you may take your child. You can see that I have gotten him to sleep for you."

Silence. Profound uneasiness. And then, in a vacant musing tone, "I believe my grandfather served in the war," said Master. "He was called, as I remember, a brevet colonel."

"I am sure he was," said Ralph in his most sarcastic voice.

CHAPTER TEN

•

SURPRISING EVENTS CONCLUDED

"Jenny?"
     Millie's voice. Millie softly calling child through dimness inside our cavernous barn.

"How are you doing, Jenny?"

"I've done three of them, ma'am. Four ponies left. Then I must do Trishy, ma'am. And the two chestnuts. And the bay. They're all very tall for me."

"You must stand on a box, then. As I am, this moment."

"Nevertheless, ma'am, it's hard for me to reach them. And to tell the truth, I am very sleepy, ma'am. I nearly fell asleep over Buster's back."

"I'm tired too. It's a hard night's work."

"And there's something else."

"Oh?"

"I do not feel comfortable in this barn."

"Whatever do you mean, Jenny?"

"I am being treated like a child, ma'am."

"Oh, Jenn, that can't be true."

"*You* treat me like a child. . . ."

Weary softly piping voice. Child's misery. Child's indignation. Same child summoning courage to speak out. Horses drowsing. Horses restless. Clover and I among them. One of us—myself—suspicious. Puzzled. Faintly, darkly puzzled. Then the sound of Millicent's voice, close by.

"Jenny," she said, "you work as hard as I do! And you are an excellent rider for your age!"

"That's what I mean, ma'am."

"I'm sure I talk to you as I would to a woman!"

"You may think you do, but you don't, ma'am. And I am not as good a rider as I want to be!"

"No one is, Jenny."

On they went, talking across and through the darkness as they worked. Millie and the unhappy child. And now and then another and still another unformed child's voice speaking up and out from a different corner of the barn, chatting, eager, querulous, comparing problems of the horses that they would ride the morrow. And what were they doing, these small female shadows in the half-lit darkness of our cavernous barn? Braiding manes, as Clover had told me it was called. And what did braiding manes entail? Dividing portions of our manes into sets of separate strands and tying them into odd-looking clumps or knobs with short lengths of yarn, black or green. And why were these girls, these young women, these girl-children, along with Millie herself—and including the sadly complaining Jenn, of course—engaged in this curious labor that would take them most of the long night to finish? Because, Clover explained, a braided mane was thought to enhance the looks of a horse about to be displayed in public. And were we, Clover and I, about to be so displayed on the day that would soon arrive? Clover was not. I was. Because Ralph had refused to allow his horse, my own Clover, to appear in any "schooling show," as he called it, as sloppy and unprofessional as Millie's schooling shows were known to be. And because Master's eagerness was of a greater force than Ralph's common sense and sense in general. And so my Clover was to be spared. And I was not.

"Oh, ma'am, I cannot go on!"

"But you must, Jenny!"

"I am the only child here who works for her lessons, don't you see?"

"There is no life in a barn without work, Jenn."

"Oh, but I am weeping all the time with the unfairness! I can't help it! And I am tired, ma'am. Too tired for a girl my age."

"Now, Jenny, don't forget that I am allowing you to ride Gerald in the show. Isn't that privilege enough?"

"But Gerald is old, ma'am. And fat. And he is not well trained."

"He is always in the ribbons, Jenn."

"But he rolls over, ma'am! Whenever he wishes!"

"You have never ridden that pony, Jenn!"

"Last year he kept rolling over on the girl riding him. I saw him do it, ma'am."

"That girl was just a beginner. Besides, she hopped out of his way easily enough, didn't she?"

"I suppose so, ma'am."

"Well, there you are. If you keep him going you will have no trouble. It's only when he stops that he rolls over."

"Oh, ma'am, I don't trust him!"

"You must remember that Gerald is the best pony in the barn. Except for that one bad habit."

"But I am still a beginner, ma'am. Like that other girl."

"Oh no, Jenn. You're much more advanced."

"Are you sure, ma'am?"

No answer from reassuring woman. Silent child struggling with doubt. Woman approaching. Woman—Millie Gordon—humming to herself in the darkness. And entering my stall, which I should have welcomed but did not. Millie patting my nose and neck and placing a wooden milk crate beside me. Then mounting wooden crate, suddenly tugging a sharp-toothed little comb through my unruly mane. Then pathetic child's voice, of which we had not yet heard the last.

"Ma'am?"

"Jenny?"

"I cannot do it! I cannot be in the show!"

"What now, Jenny?"

"I have no boots! I have only rubber boots."

"No one will notice, Jenn."

"The other girls have leather."

"Rubber boots shine up nicely with Vaseline. You'll see."

"They're too big around the tops!"

"It doesn't matter, Jenn."

"I will be too embarrassed, ma'am!! Please!"

"Jenny!" No answer. "Jenny. Go back to work!"

Tugging sharper than before. Less gentle. Tall horse offering brief resistance. But controlling himself, though increasingly suspicious of what lay ahead. More humiliation akin to that experienced the day before? Young girls less tolerable than infant boy? So I thought by the echoing rise of excited high-pitched voices that grated on my growing defensiveness and obliterated the uncertainties of the worried child. Which was just as well.

For what did I know about the event now imminent? Nothing! And was I fit in any way for this unfamiliar experience, no matter how well my Clover had described it early in the now fading night? I was not. And training, since even the anguished child was aware of training or lack thereof? No training. Could I then anticipate a successful performance in this venture? I could not. What then? A quandary. And all this while night was changing to dawn inside our once palatial barn. Milky light. Pink light. Orange light. Then the welcome ordinary light of the day I feared.

"Willy!" said Millicent Gordon, gathering her yarn and little steel comb and stepping down from her box. "How handsome you look with a braided mane!"

Clover, peering over the top of the partition dividing us, concurred. I was not convinced.

There were horse trailers. Half a dozen horse trailers, more or less. Battered. Newly arrived. Soon to disappear, with the end of that long day. And there were ponies. A handful of ponies large and small, held by riders—little vixens, as Ralph said behind his hand—or held by those responsible for riders—women, not men. And there were horses. Not many. Two in particular. Myself in fact, and another. An Arabian. A small Arabian. A chestnut. More orange in color than Ralph's hair. Female. None prouder. Owned and ridden, or to be ridden, by the only child outgrowing childhood that day. Distinguished from the others by poise as well as height. Taller by half. Old enough to drive her own motor vehicle. Illegally, as Ralph said. This person smartly dressed in black and white, unlike the smaller children, on whom such clothes were ill-fitting. As for the little Arabian, she wore a bit of red ribbon tied to her tail, which signified a horse who kicks, as Clover had already explained. Don't get too close. Tall rider similarly disposed, as Ralph said behind his hand. A fancy pair. Stay off.

How long we waited, how irritating I found my braided mane, how patiently Master walked me up and down beside the dusty ring in which the competition was both confined and continuous! From dawn to dusk, it seemed, as Millie stood in the center of that ring calling out instructions and dispensing ribbons.

"There you have it, Harry Sir. The end of the sport!"

"Beg pardon, Ralph?"

"No laddies, Harry Sir! There is not a single laddie in that ring, nor waiting to enter!"

"Why, Ralph, how right you are."

"Even in my day it was a man's sport. And now? Now the women have quite driven us from the field."

"Strange, Ralph, I had not noticed."

"It has become the sport of vixens, nothing less!"

"But they are only children, Ralph!"

"Of course I would have it no other way. They are all Corys and Carries in the budding. As attested, Harry Sir, by that tall young lady brushing down that little purebred Arabian of hers. A pretty sight, though I don't know what on earth she is doing in a show as miserable as this one is bound to be."

"You may find it curious, Ralph, but all these young people look alike to me. Except for that small girl on the big sloe-eyed pony—just there. She stands out. She has a sweet round face, quite to my liking."

"Just as I might have expected, Harry Sir! Of the pathetic handful of contestants here today, Jenny is the least talented. She is one of those inept self-pitying children quite demoralizing to all the rest, who are keeping to the right track and advancing. I don't see how Millie puts up with a child like that."

"Oh, Ralph, you are very harsh."

"That I am, Harry Sir. And with reason."

Dogs running in and out of dusty ring. Women, gathered at the rail, staring severely at mounted children—their own. Children growing wet with effort. Children scowling fiercely at other children or ignoring same. Children falling. Picking themselves up. Millie, straw hat on head, bare of leg, calling out names, pinning—as Clover said it is called—pinning coveted ribbons to bridles or passing this red ribbon or that white one into this or that pudgy possessive hand.

Day waning. Ripples of clapping at the rail. Women venting anger at unsuccessful charges sniveling, hanging heads. Or women hugging offspring baffled by the glory to be found in winning.

Throughout the day. The entire day.

Until of a sudden I knew that Ralph would speak, as speak he did in his most jovial alarming tone so far.

"You're up!" he cried.

"What, Ralph, is it time?"

"That it is, Harry Sir. 'Open Command Horse' is next!"

"Perhaps it is not too late for me to withdraw, Ralph?"

"Withdraw? Withdraw, you say? Do you mean to tell me, Harry Sir, that you want to scratch?"

"If that is what it is called, Ralph."

"Well, you may not. You have waited the day long for this opportunity. And you shall not pass it by!"

"I believe I cannot do it, Ralph. I am terrified!"

"You must, I say. I am your coach. And no rider of mine has ever scratched merely because of a case of nerves. Now I tell you what. Just pause a moment and think. Breathe deeply and think of your grandfather. Think of the Old Gentleman. Are you not already calm?"

"But, Ralph," in a softer voice, "I have forgotten what I am supposed to do. . . ."

"Listen to Millie! Trust your horse! Above all, simply follow the others. Now up you go, Harry Sir. Give me your leg . . . !"

A grunting, a slipping, a tugging, a long leg snaking up and across me, and once again Master's bony weight on my back. Rigid burden. Rigidity passed on to horse. Unavoidably. Rider's invisible face gone white. My own blood draining. A few horse trailers already inching off noisily, disappearing past the long-abandoned covering yard. Gone. For good. But oh, the last of the loyal or determined women were at the rail, and Millie stood awaiting us in the center of the ring, and Ralph was leaning at the opposite side of the ring from the last of the women. Ralph alone. Gate open.

So it began.

One by one the contestants, including Master's favorite, the child personifying dismay and lack of ease, entered the ring and in orderly procession and in single file commenced to circle the rail at a slow walk. In they went, interminably, until only two pairs of us remained. Master and myself, of course. Young Lady on the Arab, of course. Arriving at the gate together. Bumping, Master yawing on my bit, mumbling deferentially, attempting to hold me back. Arab and Thoroughbred side by side, at a standstill. Locked in the opening through the rails. Impasse. Young Lady glaring, sitting taller yet in the saddle, then driving on the Arab with a contemptuous kick of her heels. Minor mishap. Easily repaired as Master and I took our place behind the little Arab and her rider. Little disdainful horse sweat-colored in the last of the sun, Young Lady as perfectly disdainful as her horse. None prouder.

Ralph then closed the gate, resumed his position beside it. "Sit up!" he said under his breath as we started off.

"Working walk!" called Millie from the center of the ring, and there was a bustling around the circle of contestants, of which I was one, a shortening of reins and straightening of backs and application of little legs, resulting in a change of pace, a livelier turning of our circle, except for myself, of course, who understood no more of Millie's first command than did Master, but was nonetheless swept along, as was he, of course, the two of us following the Young Lady inseparable from her glistening mare. The dust rose, one of the women offered a brief hissing of advice, ignored by embarrassed child to whom addressed, and our circle turned, the light faded, two of the playful dogs scampered off toward the apple orchard and the shadowy solitude to be found therein.

"Rising trot!" called Millie, and there was a lurching, a catching of breaths, a sudden escalation of desperate effort firing from rider to rider, horse to horse, and accompanied by a more violent kicking of little booted legs, a sudden application of springy whips, and directly ahead of Master and me the Young Lady, so handsomely attired, youthfully composed in fresh womanhood all but hers, floated off—updown updown—on her little responsive mare, whose tapering tail, near the tip of which was tied the fatal red ribbon, flicked suddenly, sharply upward and backward in my direction.

"Heels down!" commanded Ralph in exasperation as we passed him, even as Master jammed down his heels, attempting to obey Ralph's inadmissible instruction, and even as I fell forward and struggled to imitate the floating gait of the little chestnut, which finally I did after a fashion, throwing myself up and into a hopeless wooden simulacrum of the little mare so close yet far—trot *trot* trot *trot*—as her neatly tied red ribbon swished in my face. Thus awkwardness pushed on roughly in pursuit of grace.

The dogs returned, sat side by side outside our ring, panting, watching. Birds gathering overhead. Pinkish light of dawn reappearing as the cloak of dusk. Women at the rail showing signs of fatigue. Horses and riders still bobbing upward, downward, round the never-ending ring, myself among them, Master as well, sitting when he should have been rising and vice versa, yet still aboard me, as Ralph expressed it a few moments thence, bouncing bravely round the ring, expelling great painful puffs of breath that caused the loyal female spectators to turn heads and follow progress of old horse and rider with scowls and grimaces, which contributed to Master's anguish but not to mine, newly and sorely preoccupied as I already was.

"Relax!" cried Ralph in muffled fury as again we passed. "Enjoy yourself!"

"But, Ralph . . . !" came poor Master's voice above me, no sooner spoken than lost to further breathlessness as round we went and round in the misery of that relentless trot. Would it never end? Would Millie never order us back to the walk and hence relief? Yet even as Master thumped and swayed upon me and clutched at the painfully tight braids in my mane, and even as I thought I must drop, exhausted in the grip of that mocking rhythm—trot *trot* trot *trot*—which meant, it seemed, to crack my bones, from flattened hooves to hocks to knees to shoulders, suddenly I found that I had gained on the Arab or that she had slowed, expecting me to fill the space between us, as I had done. And the red ribbon? Before my eyes the little mare's red ribbon was changing shape, swelling, ballooning, growing as large as the slender billowing tail itself! Oh, I was awash in that red film, engulfed, and there was more, as redness and beckoning tail rose to greet my hopelessly extended face, nose, eyes—for what accompanied that cloudy redness? None other than the wafting of the all too familiar scent of—yes—pheromones! For unbeknownst to anyone, owner included, the little Arab had timed herself so that there and then she was ready, as so many other mares had in the past been ready, for me and me alone! So quite naturally I thrust still more forward my expectant nose. In a word managed an extra stride and plunged ahead and found awaiting me no kick but quite the opposite.

Whereupon the Young Lady, who sat her little Arab with nothing less than classical handsomeness, narrow shoulders straight, bun of copper-colored hair tucked up beneath rim of black helmet, long back descending to tapered waist, dash of white posterior revealed through vents in black jacket with every tight effortless rise and fall of upper body—this person, then, turned round her head and briefly displayed to Master the perfection of her expressionless face, and spoke—not to me but to Master.

"Get off my tail," she said, "you old fart!" and crisply and in the same breath turned back to her riding.

Oh, but little did the well-schooled Young Lady know how great was the humiliation taking place for all to see—all, that is, except for Master and the Young Lady herself, who rode on blindly secure, as she thought, in girlish dignity. Nor could I see what was so horribly displayed before the eyes of the distracted matrons at the rail, as well as those of Ralph himself. And Millie. See, no. Feel, yes. Was I never to be spared my recurring past? Had I not enjoyed enough and suffered enough those various cycles of the male horse? Must I remember youth? Must my sad figure again play host to a final intrusion of brash youth? Must best-forgotten mares return for a last time? Must Honey herself—

even as her name returned to me in a flood of joy? And all because of one small unscrupulous Arabian mare still leading me on? Oh, the answer was apparent in what I could not see but feel.

Yes, letting down! Yes, I was once more letting down, as it is called in horse parlance, and for all the world to see, such as it was.

A sensation, then. A feeling. The return of that phenomenon I had long accepted as forever lost to my past, and rightly so. A heaviness. An increasing presence I could not deny. And now, when all but impossible? When least wanted? Why, even Clover had never so aroused me and never in the midst of motion and situation as inappropriate as these.

Trot *trot* thump *thump* I went, aghast at so new and ugly an impediment, which with every stride impaired further a gait I was already at my wit's end to maintain, inching ever closer the while to the little silky mare and abandoning dismay, ridding myself of reason, determining that the travesty approaching could not be helped—why try?—and so gathering myself to become once again that mighty agent of mortification I once had been. Oh, little did Master and Young Lady and snickering or angry women know what awaited them—unless? But surely by now I could not be stopped.

Unless?

"Walk!" cried Millie. "Change direction!"

Confusion. Wheeling and bumping. Pushing and shoving. Direction finally changed as ordered, in blinding dust and failing light. Which meant that suddenly the little Arabian was to my rear and I in the lead. Thwarted! Saved! Reverse sensation in loins! Rapid retreat! Retraction!

"Canter!" cried Millie. "Gallop!" And off we went, charging and frantic, as I searched in vain and foolishly for the Arab and Master rocked so violently atop me that with every bound, I thought, he must go off. But where was the Arab? Gone. And directly ahead? Nothing! Only a small black shaggy pony and his little feverish rider, whom I was now forced to follow—in pain, exhaustion, disappointment, relief.

"Halt!" cried Millie. "Line up!"

And so we did. And so, docilely, I stood old and towering in that weary elated line of mean ponies and little girls, having already forgotten the trial I had just undergone, the calamity that had not occurred.

Settling dust. Heavy breathing. All eyes on Millie, who was glancing at notes and holding a placard to which were affixed the bright ribbons she would now award. Six ribbons, as Clover had explained to me the night before, eight pairs of us in that expectant line.

"First Place," called Millie, and then a name. Young Lady, of course. Little Arabian, of course. Blue ribbon fluttering as big as a flag from bridle. Then flouncing off. Gone. Good riddance.

"Second Place," called Millie, and so on down through the ranks of achievement until five ponies and five children had accepted recognition and departed the ring. Leaving behind? Exactly. The last three sorry pairs of us. Master and myself. In the middle. Towering. Flanked on one side by small black shaggy pony—the same—and hard-faced child determined to have sixth and final place, at any cost. Flanked on the other side by large gray pony and bleak bewildered child. As expected.

"And now," called Millie, and held aloft the coveted color, announced the name that caused a surge of blackness, an expression of spite and triumph too large for that small face, and off they dashed and disappeared with appropriate parent.

No women lining the rail. No birds overhead. No dogs. Blue light descending. Last two pairs of competitors side by side, together, powerless to move, saving a day that had not been theirs.

"Next time, Jenny," said Master, leaning forward to pat my neck and straightening, "next time we shall do better."

The child's face that was round. The child's face that glistened in the blue light. The smile that appeared. And grew. And took possession of child's face. Bright smile on field of grief. More grateful than grieving. But not for long. Only long enough, in fact, for alarm to reappear and smile to vanish.

"Oh, sir," she suddenly exclaimed in a faint voice, "stop him, sir . . . !" Head hanging? Eyes shut? Legs buckling? No to each!

"Oh, sir! I knew he would . . . !"

Was he swaying, then? Gone limp? Some other indication of collapsing? No again.

"Oh, sir! He will roll over now! He will roll over *me* . . . !"

Any sign of same? No. A fair warning? No. Did he then sink at last to the dusty sand and roll? He did not. Nothing at all, then, to justify her apprehension? Nothing.

"Jenny," said Master after a suitable pause and in his most kindly voice, "you had best hop off your horse now and cool him out. I shall do the same."

But when he finally led me back to the barn, did he notice that I was weak and overly tired and fretful? He did not. Did he notice that my ankles were wobbling and that I could hardly walk? He did not. And therein lay the danger that he should have seen and I admitted. But did not.

CHAPTER ELEVEN

•

IN WHICH RALPH SINGS

A new day. Another day. The next day, perhaps, or the following. One or the other. And still the sun shone and the breeze blew and the carriage horse atop our barn turned slowly, stopped, turned again, settled on his chosen path and, stationary as he always was, sped on. I too was stationary. But differently, beyond a doubt. Without the benefit of breeze or storm. Fixed in sunlight at the end of a sagging lead rein held by

Master, who, seduced by the indolence of this season, as all of Millbank was so seduced, had determined to groom me more thoroughly than he had ever groomed me until this day. And now, jacketless and bareheaded, though still garbed in customary boots and britches, was happily occupied in same. And there was Millie Gordon, seated on the mounting block, cleaning tack. As for Clover, she was comfortably as near at hand as ever, lingering a scant few paces beyond the fence that set us apart. She grazed, but pickily, as I saw, now and again raising her head and looking at me with worrisome concern, newly acquired.

There was a breeze, then. There was sunlight. But no infant or any sign or sound of him. And no children. No ponies in view. Wasps, yes. Horseflies, yes, though flying randomly, keeping their distance. Thus we stood or sat, variously, when Ralph emerged from the house—quietly, for him—and started down the path—casually, for him—and whistled—softly, for him—and so with a suspicious lack of purpose thrust himself into our midst, quite as if we had nothing at all to fear from him.

"Well, Harry Sir, is he still off?"

"How's that, Ralph?"

"Lame! Is he still lame? Your horse, that is."

"Oh, I think not, Ralph. Petrarch is quite sound."

"Thanks be," said Ralph. "I'm glad to hear it. And is the poor goat out of his misery yet?"

No answer. Silence. Tip of a dark wing descending. Casting its shadow suddenly. On us. On auditors increasingly uneasy. As usual. Except for dear Millie, bent to her work and untouched, self-sufficient. As usual.

"Well now, Harry Sir, I have news. Good news!"

First hint of exuberance to come. Or mischief. Checkered cap on back of head, face flushed, eyes bright, red hair damp and flaming, in need of shears. Or clippers. Or both. And shirt tight. Britches tighter. Boots tighter still, all but impossible to remove. Man himself fresh from customary shower. Pleased as such. Less than ever to be trusted.

"News, Ralph?"

"Ah, to be sure. I have just spoken with Fitch and Fitch."

Sun shining between his words, breeze blowing between each of the words he said as he waited, swelled, allowed tightening to appear in his eyes. Ready at any moment to pounce and crush.

"Fitch and Fitch?"

"The exterminators, Harry Sir! Have you forgotten?"

"Perhaps I have, Ralph. I think I have."

"The barn! The rats!"

"What about them, Ralph?"

"Well now. Is it possible that we are not of one mind?"

"I thought we were. I'm sure that we were. . . ."

"Well then. The point is this. I have just been informed by Fitch and Fitch that they have done their job." Pause. "Our barn is clean, you see! And safe! There is not one single bugger dead or alive on our premises! Our barn awaits us, Harry Sir! We are free to return!"

Pause. The grand gesture. Ralph at his best. Smiling, challenging, all the time in the world to wait.

"Oh dear . . ." Baffled casting about for help. No help in sight. "But whatever shall we do now, Ralph?"

Another pause. Pause of a different quality. Softer, slower voice. Less threatening, as it seemed. Condescending, but only well intentioned. As it seemed. Quizzical, but of an amused and friendly nature. As it seemed. While Millicent worked and Master gradually accepted the fact that he had nowhere to turn, any more than did the horses, we who were not at all sure of outcome but awaited same. With trepidation. Loath to admit what lay so near yet far behind.

"Well, Harry Sir," assuming his most falsely reassuring voice, "I should think that we might pack our gear and load our horses and depart. Is that not what we have been awaiting? Is this not our day?"

Silence. A terrible flurrying and scampering of small creatures in the air, through tall grasses, in the leaves above. For miles around. And here, now, Master frowning. Master gathering himself. For what? Assertion, of course, as foreign as assertion was. Gathering himself. Speaking at last.

"But, Ralph. I cannot return."

Well said! Simply said! Creatures settling back to where they had been and belonged, for miles around. Relief distinctly heard and felt for miles around. Master retaining severity of face and voice. Ralph nodding and allowing himself for once a smile, a true smile, an ingenuous smile. As it appeared.

"Now, Harry Sir," he said, "I must tell you something. I'm duty bound to say it. In truth, I mean to say, I suspected all along that those might be your very sentiments!"

"Is that so, Ralph? Did you really?"

"Harry Sir, I did!"

A gift bestowed. From the short to the tall. The young to old. The fat to thin. The strong to weak. A revelation. A humbling. With predictable effect.

"Thank you, Ralph. I'm glad. Very glad."

Faint smile no match at all for the broad. But preferable.

"And I have not fallen in your estimation? Nor caused you too much inconvenience? You are not offended?"

"Think nothing of it!"

"Then I shall stay and you shall leave?"

"Agreeable to me. And as I understand it, Harry Sir, agreeable to you as well!"

"But what shall you do, Ralph? Resume your career? Ride again? In public?"

"Ah no," with a faint injured inclining of the head, "that I shall not."

"No, Ralph?"

"To put it bluntly, Harry Sir, you have quite broken my spirit. . . ."

"I, Ralph? I . . . ?"

"No blame intended, Harry Sir. But there's the truth of it. I am done with the sport."

"But what then, Ralph? Where shall you turn?"

"To Cory! As I have been wanting to do for some while now. Yes," with a sidelong glance at Millie, "I shall search out my Cory. She'll not pitch me into the fire, Harry Sir, as the saying goes. That she'll not!"

Not at all the response expected. Reserve, or a minimum of same, required.

"She is a nice woman, Ralph."

"None more to my taste!"

"But, Ralph . . . !"

Alarm. A sudden thought. An inappropriate thought intruding. But the right thought? The essential thought? The thought without which the rest was nothing? The vital question stammering at last for asking? Could it be? Had he the courage? But surely Master had learned the Ten Good Rules of the Barn? *If you break it, fix it. If you open it, close it. If your horse makes a mess, clean it up.* And the others, the others. So surely he had learned the most important rule of all? The Golden Rule? *Horses Before People.* Exactly. *Horses Before People,* as every child knows! Surely he would not give me Millbank only to deny me Clover? Surely he would not fail us now, at the last moment?

He would not. He did not.

"Forgive me, Ralph . . ." Now! At last! "But what do you intend to do with Clover? Clover and Petrarch are quite fond of each other, as you've no doubt observed. . . ."

"Take her, Harry Sir, she's yours!"

"A gift, Ralph?"

"Oh, let us say you may have her on indefinite loan, as the old farmer said of his daughter when he gave her away at the altar!"

"I'm grateful, Ralph. She is a sweet horse."

Done! World restored! Breeze blowing through safe pastures! Light of the sun untroubled. A still picture, in which no one moves but Ralph. He inhales, smiles more broadly, looks from one of us to the other, raises a hand as if to the brim of his cap, nods—to no one. Nods again.

"Well, I'll be gone, then," he says. "Goodbye, all!" And off he goes, singing.

> *"The Irish doctor fails, with all his art,*
> *to cure an impression on the Irish heart. . . ."*

CHAPTER TWELVE

•

IN WHICH MILLIE GORDON SPEAKS OUT

A morning feed. An hour of nourishment that might have been like any other but was not. There was darkness, despite the early sunrise, and there was rain, which had begun in the night and would soon stop but for now was falling, softly, warmly, denying the light of the new day but not its heat.

There were other comforting sounds than that of the rain, as there should have been. For there is nothing more reassuring than the sounds we hear in a large barn occupied by horses eating their first feed of the day—the long sounds, the flat sounds, the steady sounds of all of us preoccupied with chewing, grinding, ingesting, when there is nothing to distinguish one of us from the other by the sounds we make, and yet we are most alone, most individual, thanks to the special privacy found in this loud process or in the full grain tub, which we wish and do not wish to empty.

We are feeding, then, launched into that rare yet ordinary activity that is ours alone, as I have said, and that brooks no interruption. Up and down the length of our dark aisleway there came communal yet solitary sounds of munching. From the ponies, including the desultory Gerald, and from Clover, who, invisible in her stall adjoining mine, was eating as any horse should eat except that now and again she paused and listened—to me, as I knew—and then went back to her feed in a dispirited fashion that I did not like to hear.

And myself? Was I too eating my fill as long as I could, until there was nothing left in my tub but the wet smell of sweet feed smudging and smearing its bottom? I was not. For I was off my feed, as Millie had said, and but recently had acquired a way of eating—or of not eating, as was the case—that was so peculiar and unpleasant, even to me, that I longed to stop it, suppress it, overcome it, yet could not. And how did I eat, or appear to eat, for in fact I did nothing of the sort? By scattering my feed! By flinging my generously apportioned feed about my stall! Helplessly, with a violent abandon I could not control! Attacking my feed instead of eating it! What indulgence, what dismay!

Thus I was engaged this morning—a dissident among fellows willing enough to feed—when Millie and Master, contrary to the ways of the barn at feeding time, entered my stall. I saw them, plunged my nose into my feed, jerked up my head, flung up my nose, sent feed showering far and wide. So much for Millie and Master, who had no business being where they were and at this hour.

Together they stood, staring at me, yet seeing, as I thought, not myself, not the guilt I flaunted, but something else.

"There is nothing we can do," she said.

"But, Millicent . . ."

"Don't you see the change in him?"

"Perhaps he is thinner? Perhaps he has lost some of his precious weight?"

"I can't keep it on him. But there's more. His dull coat, his sour contrary attitude. And loss of energy, droopy ears, unsteady stance . . ."

"Oh, Millicent . . . all that?"

"His suspensories are gone. He can't walk. He is unfit for riding. He is in pain. . . ."

"Oh, my dear Millicent, are you sure?"

"If it weren't for the pain, we might just turn him out to spend his days with Clover. . . ."

"We cannot do that, Millicent?"

"He hurts too much."

"But what now . . . ?"

"We can't keep him. We have to put him down."

"You mean we are going to take Petrarch's life?"

"Destroy him. But humanely. Virginia will give him a shot. He won't suffer, he won't know what's happening. Virginia's my vet."

"Poor Petrarch." And then, "But where shall we bury him? On the knoll perhaps?"

"We won't bury him. . . ."

"Millicent! Surely Petrarch deserves to remain in some peaceful place at Hidden Hall, where he belongs? What else could we do with him?"

"It's Holly's business. She'll take him off with Chester. At no charge to us. In fact, I've already arranged for Virginia and Holly to meet us tomorrow. If we wait a day more, Chester might not be able to get to his feet, let alone walk out to Holly's truck. And if we have to put him down in his stall, and drag him out, the whole thing will be worse."

"Drag him . . . !"

"We'd have no choice."

"So Petrarch shall die with a goat. . . ."

"Why not? It's an odd coincidence. But sensible."

"I see."

There it was. Case considered. Final determination made. Did the munching cease, the barn fall silent, the entirety of Millbank take shocked cognizance of what had just occurred? Nothing of the sort. The promise of an everyday event that none acknowledged. But even as Master and Millicent Gordon talked, I changed, became unrecognizable. And how? By giving up. And how? By knocking my feed tub from its ringbolts on the wall—last gesture of a defeated horse, as I thought—and turning away, turning myself into a corner. And drooping. Waiting. At least I would have no more premonitions.

The warm day grew warmer. The sun appeared yet did not rise. The rain stopped but was replaced by mist that lay everywhere, its only purpose being to absorb and shroud the sun. Master walked as slowly as I hobbled when he led me out to the smallest and most confining paddock we had at Millbank, which also was the closest to the great barn and hence the easiest for me to reach and the safest, though I had disliked it from the start, refusing to admit its significance. Here, fellow horses, stands an old Thoroughbred on his last legs!

When, momentarily, Master brought Clover to join me, in silence, without his usual signs or words of affection, he did not merely leave us together, with a happy wave, and seek out Millie to be of what help he could. Instead he stopped, paused, frowned, and then made three trips to the by now near-empty barn. Upon his return from each trip he carried in his arms an old round bushel basket, long forgotten, long ignored, the waste of past harvests, all but dead. One of crab apples that had survived from some winter or another—memory briefly stirred, no more—and one of carrots, similarly old but more bruised than the crab apples, more shrunken, clotted with dried earth turning to powder. And finally a basket of potatoes once fresh but now blackened, soft and pulpy in the last stages of rot. These Master set down in a row before us, and remained with us, now and again offering first Clover, then me, a carrot, potato, crab apple, on an outstretched palm. He said nothing yet stayed with us, watched us, as the day passed. We ate, unable to resist the temptation of even such mean treats as these, dipping our noses into this basket or that. All the while Master's silence grew, until I was aware of nothing else, puzzled, irritable, begrudging him the very mood into which I had sunk.

He was serious, he was somber, distracted, though he looked only at Clover and me, spending his newfound concentration on nothing else. Barn, house, fields, Millie coming from this direction or that, the infant jouncing on her back or soundlessly squalling from where she had propped his pack against the base of a tree—Master saw none of it, heard nothing, had no thought even for Hidden Hall. How could he be this undemonstrative, how concerned only for two horses, one of whom consumed his attention almost as much as the other?

He stood before us, tall and lean, without a hint of grief or his usual innocent self-concern on his narrow face. He did not move, did not cease regarding us, except for his occasional abstracted interference in our eating. It was as if all three of us, horses and man, were held in the same strange protective vacancy that Master himself had imposed on us.

Then all at once there was a change.

He moved, and even as Clover and I turned our heads in unison to watch him, down he stooped and blindly seized not a crab apple, not a carrot, which might have been reasonable enough, perhaps, but one of the runny little potatoes, which he carried to his own mouth, not mine, and, taking one thoughtless bite, began to chew.

Relief! Release! For it was then that I threw off my imminent future, or future that was all but upon me, and reverted to the horse I was and in a few deft choppy kicks, aware of yet indifferent to the pain they caused me, tipped over the three baskets and, joined by Clover, began to eat—ravenously, as had not been the case that day.

"Poor Petrarch!" Master exclaimed, as he had earlier, but with a smile, and thereupon left our paddock.

Dawn. Millie's dawn, Master's dawn, Holly's dawn and Virginia-the-vet's, and Chester's, of course, and mine most importantly. This dawn, then, found me as I had spent the night, pressed tight against the perennial wooden wall between us, just as Clover was so pressed to the other side. We faced in the same direction, our two heads drooped, in silence and through the wood that might just as well not have been there to keep us apart, for in fact we were not apart, each of us felt the quiet entirety of the other. Her warmth I felt as mine, while mine she felt as hers. Alone, as never before, mute with no other need but for ourselves, mute and hence invulnerable to whatever and all activity gathering around us. As gather it did.

The sound of an automobile aggressively but quietly approaching up Millbank's long curving private road. Then swinging into our stable area and halting. Virginia-the-vet on hand, accounted for. And the sound of a multi-animal carrier—old slatted truck, as it turned out, big as an ark—making same sinuous approach but with much clanking, thumping, loud unwholesome noises announcing this aged truck for what it was. Then truck proclaiming its unwholesome presence in our stableyard. And stopping. Truck of abominations on hand and accounted for, along with Holly, whose means of livelihood was all too obvious and unsurprising, gender notwithstanding. At least Master made no comment on the gender of these attendants now arrayed for first work of day.

Light outside. Light within. Amber-colored light arising from pit that was Chester's stall, first light of day stopping short of barn and standing firm, and waiting. New day on hand.

"Harry!" Millie exclaimed in a newly feminine whisper. "What have you done?"

"Nothing that this event does not call for, Millicent."

"But you cannot ride in such clothes!"

"Ah," said Master, "that's perfectly true. I made my decision during the night. I shall not ride again."

"But I've got a new horse coming this afternoon. Elaine's bringing him over, just for you."

"In my life," said Master, "I have ridden but one horse. If I cannot ride Petrarch, then I shall ride no other."

Whispering. Conferring. Holly the dealer in dead horses, and in dead whatever else according to her clients' needs, and Virginia-the-vet talking from where they leaned against the car of one or truck of the other, interrupted sleep and hazy tones of young womanhood still clinging to professional voices that rose and fell, drew near and faded, gave way now and again to soft laughter that only persons of young womanhood could share.

"Very well," said Millicent Gordon, "give him a little loving up, Harry, and bring him out. Virginia and Holly and I will do the rest."

"Oh no," said Master. "I shall be with him. I shall lend whatever assistance I may from first to last."

"It's not pleasant, Harry. I think you can leave it to us."

To which he did not reply, as my keen listening made all too clear, but instead stepped from the light of waiting day into our barn and Chester's light. And into my stall, gaunt Master as resigned as Clover and I to the event in process, or rather to the event he himself was setting in motion. Here he was, and yes, the solution to the brief mystery of his clothing, easily predicted, was just as easily revealed. For yes, here he was in black suit, white shirt, polka-dotted tie, with the tip of a white handkerchief protruding from the breast pocket. Same clothes as when first we met. Same formally attired man. Yet changed. For ill or better I could not tell. And if he had been inappropriately clothed the day he found me and led me away to a new life, or close to it, how much more inappropriately clothed was he now as into my stall he came, my halter in hand, to pat me and lead me out to Millie and Holly and Virginia-the-vet and their grisly but humane collaboration that I could not avoid? Poor Master.

Into the midst of his thoughtlessness and my refusal to raise my head, for so I refused, there came a clumsy melody of speech and effort from across the aisleway, where Chester lay groaning and demanding to be the first of us to be taken out to Holly's truck. By all means, I thought. Whereupon goat noises and human noises became a still louder muddle, filled the aisleway, and then faded progressively until the goat was safely lodged in Holly's truck.

"Petrarch," said Master softly, "raise your head."

No response.

"Petrarch! Raise your head!"

Odds against me. Situation I could not deny. Situation I must not prolong. So I did what he asked and allowed him to slip my halter onto my head, prepared for the inevitable. What else?

"Now, Petrarch, come along."

Tentatively I tried a wobbly step, another, bore as best I could the pain that each such uncertain step now cost me, bore with greater pain the start of my separation from my already grieving companion as the threads and sutures that had stitched and sewn us together through solid wood snapped, ruptured, parted, and step by step I tore myself from her and, with all possible meekness, went limping after Master into the light of day.

Nothing behind me. Nothing ahead. Surrender.

Until I stood drooping at the foot of the massive knotted wooden ramp leading up and into the darkened interior of Holly's truck. It was a gray day, a somber day, there was nothing on the stage of this day except the old truck with its slatted sides and thick slippery bed of straw and cavernous depth all but concealing the goat where he lay, still groaning. Deep inside, invisible from where I stood, were Holly and Virginia-the-vet as well, deep in talk. There was also the smell, which I must not neglect to mention.

"Harry," said Millicent Gordon, "I'll take him."

But Master merely leaned forward into the smell that issued from the mouth of Holly's truck and climbed the ramp, in his best and only suit of clothes, until the lead rope stretched tight between us.

"Petrarch!" he said sharply, tugging and struggling for balance at the top of the ramp. "Come up!"

But I did not. And abruptly and to my surprise there ensued a contest that was long and well fought on both sides. Master tugged, Millicent Gordon pushed, I yielded a step or two up the ramp and then slid back down, and up and down, balking and giving way and thwarting them as I had not planned to do. And why? No answer. And how? By obstinateness. Until Virginia-the-vet came down the ramp and lent her assistance to Millicent, the two young women standing to my rear and pushing this way and that and with more caution for their own persons than I would have thought. Impatient voices! A shoulder here, a shoulder there, leaning into me and leaping away, and a long rein that they held behind my tail, by means of which they tried to launch me up the ramp. How they wanted their way with an old horse who could not have been more enfeebled, how they failed! I started up, came down, then all at once employed to best advantage my weakness, by proceeding slowly up and then allowing a weak hip to sag, a flaming hoof to fall from the edge of the ramp so that in a flurry and clatter of helplessness I once again found the safety of solid ground.

Oh, the delay I caused them! And the anger! Until of a sudden there came the briefest lull in our impossible contest. There was silence. There was cessation. There was a chaos of emotions by no means resolved. Deep breathing. Frustration. But above all silence, which old horse and young women fully intended to destroy one way or another before it could so much as settle, like raging dust, about our feet and ears. But this brief hiatus was all it took, for even as I stood chafing and trembling, and even as the women were once more gathering themselves to unite against me, suddenly I heard the querulous voice of Chester. Yes, Chester.

And what was his appeal? To heed his rights. To be humane! To attend his needs! In a word, as he gave me to understand—for it was to me that his appeal was addressed—to allow the proper proceedings to continue until he, at least, was cold and white of eye and rigid. . . .

But I heard enough! Oh, I had heard enough! Let the goat be lifeless and the horse as well! Whereupon, and meekly, up the ramp I went of my own volition and on my own strength, and thus found myself exactly where I belonged. Standing tall and skinny beside and above the flattened figure of Chester where he lay deep in the bed of wet straw in slatted darkness, slatted light. Then Master and the three women recovered themselves and caught up with me, so to speak, and assumed their prescribed positions in Holly's truck.

Master standing at my head. Millicent at my side. Virginia-the-vet kneeling and preparing to minister to Chester, as he wished. Holly unoccupied for the moment. Watching. And the smell. The heat of the day. Smoldering straw. Ice in the straw. Bars of light, bars of darkness, bathing us all. Virginia-the-vet opening her satchel. Keen expectation. Keen expectation thwarted. Momentarily. As follows.

"Dignity," said Master, and heads turned, frowns appeared, Virginia-the-vet glanced up at Millicent and stayed her hand, and from Chester there came the longest softest wettest coldest sigh I had ever heard, "dignity, my dears, generally meets a harsh end. But at the Golden Wedding, with which you are all familiar, there occurred an event that proved the exception to that cruel rule."

Master's chin was raised, his voice was mild, gently but firmly he meant to talk, no matter the smell in Holly's truck and the destruction—humane or not—soon, if not sooner, to be enacted in that grim space.

"The event I have in mind," said Master into the silence that was like no other, "took place on a Sunday at the midday meal. What a gathering of honored guests! How rich the appointments of that paneled room! We were all in our places, and my beloved grandfather, standing at the head of the table as he always did, was preparing to carve the roast. Once more we waited on his largess, once more we knew the spell of his generosity, which he enjoyed as much as we on whom it would fall. But then, just as he was leaning forward, a gentle smile on his severe countenance—he dearly loved to carve the roast—what should happen but that into that elaborate scene came the unthinkable. An interruption. An intrusion that caused a tremor in the very walls of tradition!

"It was William, a young groom who by his appearance had come directly from one of Grandfather's fields and who by the gravity of his expression made clear that he presumed beyond a doubt his right to enter this great hall and to interrupt the meal just beginning. My grandfather stayed his carving knife, stayed his fork, and inclined his ear to young William, who, cap in hand, spoke briefly and then stood back, awaiting Grandfather's bidding.

" 'Flossy,' said Grandfather to his wife, who was seated at the opposite end of that long table, 'a tragic accident has occurred.'

"Here I should interject that my grandmother's name was Florinda Ann, as she was known and called by friends and family members alike, except for Grandfather, who for all their fifty years together had addressed her as 'Flossy.'

" 'Well, Harry,' my grandmother replied, 'what has happened?'

"Here also I must confess that I cannot remember whether or not I have already conveyed that I am named for my grandfather, so that he was Harry as am I. But such was the case.

" 'Flossy,' said my grandfather, speaking down the length of the table to Grandmother, who sat as straight and tall and deep in her resplendent chair as she sat upon her favorite horse, a lovely dark mare by the name of Meg, 'Flossy, William tells me that Meg is lying in great pain in the back field. She is lying quietly, without the slightest movement, as William says, in an apparent effort to save herself from further harm. But she is beyond saving. We must put her down.'

"Not a guest at that long table spoke. Not a face but did not reflect the seriousness of what was taking place. Slowly Grandfather returned the long bone-handled fork and the still longer knife to their places beside the waiting roast and stared down the length of assembled guests at Grandmother, and she at him.

" 'Very well, Harry,' she said at last, reserving to her deepest self the love she felt for Meg, 'the case is clear. Tell William to put her down and resume your carving.'

" 'But, my dear Flossy,' replied Grandfather, 'surely you must know that I am not the man to allow another man, and a stable-hand at that, to put down my own wife's horse! No, Flossy, I shall attend to this sad matter myself.'

"And so he did, as Grandmother inclined her head and the roast was removed from the table to await my grandfather's return. And do you know," continued Master, "that that very afternoon my grandmother herself supervised the burial of Meg, after which she summoned young William and appointed him to be her private groom thenceforth? And do you know, my dears, that in time to come my grandmother ordered that same William to disinter her favorite horse's head, which thenceforth, plated in silver and mounted on a hardwood plaque, hung on the wall facing her own great bed? It is a strange story, my dears. But I myself can attest to its truth, for I learned it one day from my own mother.

"Well, my dears, have I succeeded in demonstrating that dignity does not always come to a harsh end? I hope I have."

Ride on! Ride on through it!

FOR THE BEST IN PAPERBACKS, LOOK FOR THE 🐧

In every corner of the world, on every subject under the sun, Penguin represents quality and variety—the very best in publishing today.

For complete information about books available from Penguin—including Pelicans, Puffins, Peregrines, and Penguin Classics—and how to order them, write to us at the appropriate address below. Please note that for copyright reasons the selection of books varies from country to country.

In the United Kingdom: For a complete list of books available from Penguin in the U.K., please write to *Dept E.P., Penguin Books Ltd, Harmondsworth, Middlesex, UB7 0DA.*

In the United States: For a complete list of books available from Penguin in the U.S., please write to *Consumer Sales, Penguin USA, P.O. Box 999—Dept. 17109, Bergenfield, New Jersey 07621-0120.* VISA and MasterCard holders call 1-800-253-6476 to order all Penguin titles.

In Canada: For a complete list of books available from Penguin in Canada, please write to *Penguin Books Canada Ltd, 10 Alcorn Avenue, Suite 300, Toronto, Ontario, Canada M4V 3B2.*

In Australia: For a complete list of books available from Penguin in Australia, please write to the *Marketing Department, Penguin Books Ltd, P.O. Box 257, Ringwood, Victoria 3134.*

In New Zealand: For a complete list of books available from Penguin in New Zealand, please write to the *Marketing Department, Penguin Books (NZ) Ltd, Private Bag, Takapuna, Auckland 9.*

In India: For a complete list of books available from Penguin, please write to *Penguin Overseas Ltd, 706 Eros Apartments, 56 Nehru Place, New Delhi, 110019.*

In Holland: For a complete list of books available from Penguin in Holland, please write to *Penguin Books Nederland B.V., Postbus 195, NL-1380AD Weesp, Netherlands.*

In Germany: For a complete list of books available from Penguin, please write to *Penguin Books Ltd, Friedrichstrasse 10-12, D-6000 Frankfurt Main 1, Federal Republic of Germany.*

In Spain: For a complete list of books available from Penguin in Spain, please write to *Longman, Penguin España, Calle San Nicolas 15, E-28013 Madrid, Spain.*

In Japan: For a complete list of books available from Penguin in Japan, please write to *Longman Penguin Japan Co Ltd, Yamaguchi Building, 2-12-9 Kanda Jimbocho, Chiyoda-Ku, Tokyo 101, Japan.*

Firestone Rent-a-Limousine . . . stop/go
The mechanical centipede slowed
By Progress   stop/go
                Business as usual
"¡Hijo, hijo . . . te han asesinado!"[10]
I just tapped him across the . . .
It seems an overdose of . . .
Business as usual . . . stop/go

IV

Look back
Look back Chente . . . si puedes[11]
Remember the Roach Pad hunger
Joys . . . highs, sorrows?
Mission sidewalks (BART raped)
Hum goodbye pa' siempre carnal[12]
But the genocide trail begins su fin[13]
Trembling with the weight of our guns . . ./
Chente 18 brown and dead
In the land of E Pluribus Unum
Dead in the land of the Apollos/
Edsel . . . Titanic . . . U2 and Gary Powers
Mission Hi . . . State College
                and business as usual/

V

Now passing local draft board
Vision of monsoon flies
Bloodsmell cheeks of bronze
Organisms shell-pierced screams of death
Vietnam! Vietnam!
                Chente dies everywhere
                (Blame the reds!)
En los barrios de Guatemala[14]
San Francisco or Mississippi
                (Blame the reds!)

---

[10]Son, son . . . they have assassinated you   [11]if you can   [12]forever brother
[13]its end   [14]In the *barrios* of Guatemala

(Free los 7
    Free los 7)

raz lives

rdman)

VI

Holy Cross . . . silent in wait
Lágrimas de madre[15] soak black lace
   Hijo. Hijo no te vayas[16]
    Wife wails ripped/soul fright
        alone now . . .
Chente flows into open wound
In earth . . . magic dance of
Mayan ancestors . . . tears
Silent war drums sound
Chente killed by the Guardians
     of Enterprise
Their red white and blue
phallic symbols thrust deep
      in our throats . . .
Moist dirt falls . . . covers
Ashes to ashes . . . peace brother
Peace . . .   business as usual

"Blame it on reds!"

Elegy Pa Gringolandia in 13

It seems . . . just the other day
Acid/Guru/Dr Leary tuned into his local W
Turned on to a million micrograms of Mar
And dropped out of Apathy (Tune in
        Turn on
         Drop out?

It seems . . . just the other day
Brother Hendrix Dreamt
Of Decibels . . . Glowing ebony
holes in the air-Nirvahna (and the wind
      cries
       Mary . . .)

[15]Tears of a mother   [16]Son. Son don't go

It seems . . . just the other day
6 million Chicanos offed their cactus
And cried chale[6] no we won't go
The Álamo is alive and falling
In L.A. Remember the Salazars
And Chente . . . (Chicano Power
        Chicano Power)

It seems . . . just the other day
Los Siete[7] played Latino[8] musical chairs
all the witnesses in Amerikka
(Bound by oath) Hollered! Desafinado!
They all look alike
Maybe They're from L.A.
While my brothers mambo softly
In their minds/Mambo, Qué Rico[9] El Mambo

It seems . . . just the other day
Brother Victor Cruz changed his
Channel . . . again . . . took another sip
Of his Margarita sucked smoke
From fine cigar and sang Poems
For liberation (Papo got
        his
        gun
         SNAP!)

It seems . . . just the other day
Mohawk brave Oakes packed
Wife/child/friends into beat up
Silver Buffalo . . . bus to rediscover Life
Squaw teepees feathers y Indo-América (Alca
        no

[6]hell   [7]The Seven   [8]Latin   [9]how pleasing the mambo is

It seems . . . just the other day
The Wall Street Journal (His Master's voice)
Chanted extreme Unction rites
To the tinkle of a no-sale cash register
In the belly of the Stock-Exchange
Amerikka Hemorrhaged internally
And died . . . Of an overdose of Hate
(Did they blame it on reds?) (O say
                              can you
                                see . . .)

It seems . . . just the other day
A new world . . . began . . . again
Chepito in Nicaraguan natural
Sticking life to drumskin
Splashing Tim-Timbale voodoo
On Santana's Mayan/pocho[10]/Afro
Sinconia (Jungo-Jingova)
And today the new children
Are STONED on Liberation
                    and love . . . (At the risk
                                      of seeming
                                    Ridiculous . . .)

Primer Canto[1]

Homenaje a la tercera marcha de Delano.
Manifestación contra la uva gorda y blanca.[2]
Domingo 8 de Septiembre, 1968
San Francisco, California

Domingo . . .[3]
En el sol del medio día[4]
Old prayers chant to notes
of New Guitar Strings

[10]a Mexican
[1]First Song   [2]Homage to the third march from Delano. Declaration against the fat, white grape.   [3]Sunday   [4]In the sun of the mid-day

Air . . . Heavy incense
Proud Sonrisas[5] of Young Brown Berets
Adding to the richness and splendor
De este Domingo[6]
En el sol del medio día/[7]

The "Huelga"[8] Banners (Black and Red)
Point silent proud fingers
To the witness clouds . . .
That softly glance by

Picket signs que reclaman[9]
El espectacular silencio de las injusticias[10]
A nuestra RAZA[11] . . . on this Domingo
Y miles y miles pasados[12]

5000 Bodies melting in human ether
singing/breathing/dancing of oneness
5000 Minds crying . . . of truth and lies
            crying . . . of death and rebirth
            crying . . . of newfound awareness

5000 heartbeats marching death
                        to the American Dream
5000 Guides marching in
                  the new order of consciousness

FEET STEP FEET STEP
EYES MEET EYES THEY KNOW
                        THEY KNOW

        Vanguard of Proud Blacks/on chrome and
        iron camels roaring in the lead
        they know . . . Goddamn they know

Gentle fluttering Indio Feathers
Dancing Red in Sunday unison

·[5]Smiles   [6]of this Sunday   [7]In the sun of the mid-day   [8]Strike
[9]that reclaim   [10]The spectacular silence of the injustices   [11]to our RACE
[12]And millions and millions past

Dancing away forked tongues
and BROKEN TREATY/PROMISES
Heralding the Coming of the Buffalo
They know . . . verdad[13] . . . they know

Asian Brothers and Sisters
in Half somber songstep;
keeping cadence
With Hiroshima thoughts
in their hearts and wise eyes
And they know . . . por Dios[14] . . . they know

BEN LUNA

In Days of Wine

In days of wine
and machine gun bullets bouncing off walls
where young men got their quick
and justly deserved fate
There is no one to speak above the screaming
of idiots waving
their country's flag
in streets littered with
disappointments
and yesterday's empty promises
And in their minds everyone is convinced
that "Little Beaver"
was a punk or else "Red Rider" was not as white as he made
believe
The question is why did the Cisco Kid have it made
when all the rest of us greasers are suspected of being subversive?
All the while
out in "La Puandtea"
Juan is trying hard to prove
that he is as good a racist american
as any blue-eyed wonder
And in my heart i know Juan's right.

[13]true [14]by God

JOSÉ RENDÓN

José's Lament

Morning hits me
like eyeballs
poked
from their sockets
and tipless tongues
sing my song in silent
despair.
Where is the blood
that gift from Cuahtemoc?[1]
Is the general's head
really in pieces
between
tortillas at taco bell?
I refuse to believe
the death of Mexico is by accident.
The sun can't be meant only to color
pale skin.
I'll push aside this madness
known as America
and find truth
in flowers
on grandfather's grave.
I
jump from my bed
at the treetops
and wade through the slime
to murder my fish.
How poetic
to be insane beyond the reach
of those madmen.

[1]young Aztec prince who fought against the Spaniards in the early sixteenth century

Ernesto, Emiliano, y Doroteo

Ernesto, Emiliano, y Doroteo
foreign to an english mouth
but not my half-bastard tongue

these lyrics glide past it
with the ease of a machete through caña

Images that I see by these sacred words
live in my soul
                buried deep
                never to be destroyed by white-wash

Images running through me
                        taking the place of mortal blood
leaving me inhuman strength
bestowing upon me a frame of mind
that will conquer a sick earth
                        and be gentle to children y abuelitas[1]

Ernesto, Emiliano, y Doroteo
your hand will steady my gun
your eyes will re-enforce mine
                        guide my bullets at white oinkers
you will teach me to hide, teach me to become rivers,
trees and mountains, teach me to fight with the fury
of a mother protecting her young, and with skill only you can possess
                teach me to be brave
                teach me to have respect
                teach me to be loyal
                teach me to be loved
                teach me to be you

[1]grandmothers

JOSÉ ÁNGEL GUTÍERREZ

22 Miles

From 22 I see my first 8 weren't.
  Around the 9th, I was called "meskin."
    By the 10th, I knew and believed I was.
      I found out what it meant to know, to believe . . . before my 13th.

Through brown eyes, seeing only brown colors and feeling only
brown feelings . . . I saw . . . I felt . . . I hated . . . I cried . . . I tried
. . . I didn't understand during these 4.
      I rested by just giving up.

While, on the side . . . I realized I BELIEVED in
  white as pretty,
    my being governor,
      blond blue-eyed baby Jesus,
        cokes and hamburgers,
          equality for all regardless of race, creed, or color,
            Mr. Williams, our banker.
      I had to!
    That was all I had.
  Beans and Communism were bad.
        Past the weeds, atop the hill, I looked back.

Pretty people, combed and squeaky clean, on arrowlike roads.
Pregnant girls, ragged brats, swarthy machos, rosary beads,
and friends waddle clumsily over and across hills, each other,
mud, cold, and woods on caliche ruts.
At the 19th mile, I fought blindly at everything and anything.
  Not knowing, Not caring about WHY, WHEN, or FOR WHAT.
    I fought. And fought.
      By the 21st, I was tired and tried.

        But now . . .
I've been told that I am dangerous.
That is because I am good at not being a Mexican.
That is because I know now that I have been cheated.
That is because I hate circumstances and love choices.

Reprinted by permission of José Ángel Gutíerrez from *La Raza*, Vol. I, No. 4 (Fall 1971), p. 46.

You know . . . chorizo tacos y tortillas ARE good, even at school.
Speaking Spanish is a talent.
Being Mexican IS as good as Rainbow bread.
And without looking back, I know that there are still too many . . .
   brown babies,
     pregnant girls,
       old 25-year-old women,
         drunks,
           who should have lived but didn't,
            on those caliche ruts.

       It is tragic that my problems during these past 21 miles
   were/are/might be . . .
      looking into blue eyes,
     wanting to touch a gringuita,
    ashamed of being Mexican,
   believing I could not make it at college,
pretending that I liked my side of town,

     remembering the Alamo,
  speaking Spanish in school bathrooms only,
and knowing that Mexico's prostitutes like Americans better.

At 22, my problems are still the same but now I know I am your
problem.
That farm boys, Mexicans and Negro boys are in Vietnam is but one
thing I think about:
        Crystal City, Texas 78839
        The migrant worker;
        The good gringo:

Staying Mexican enough;
Helping;
Looking at the world from the back of a truck.

The stoop labor with high school rings on their fingers;
The Anglo cemetery,
Joe the different Mexican,

       Damn.
       Damn.
       Damn.

Fiction

AMÉRICO PAREDES

The Legend of Gregorio Cortez

They still sing of him—in the *cantinas* and the country stores, in the ranches when men gather at night to talk in the cool dark, sitting in a circle, smoking and listening to the old songs and the tales of other days. Then the *guitarreros* sing of the border raids and the skirmishes, of the men who lived by the phrase, "I will break before I bend."

They sing with deadly serious faces, throwing out the words of the song like a challenge, tearing savagely with their stiff, callused fingers at the strings of the guitars.

And that is how, in the dark quiet of the ranches, in the lighted noise of the saloons, they sing of Gregorio Cortez.

After the song is sung there is a lull. Then the old men, who have lived long and seen almost everything, tell their stories. And when they tell about Gregorio Cortez, the telling goes like this:

HOW GREGORIO CORTEZ CAME TO BE IN THE COUNTY OF EL CARMEN

That was good singing, and a good song; give the man a drink. Not like these pachucos nowadays, mumbling damn-foolishness into a microphone; it is not done that way. Men should sing with their heads thrown back, with their mouths wide open and their eyes shut. Fill your lungs, so they can hear you at the pasture's farther end. And when you sing, sing songs like *El Corrido de Gregorio Cortez*. There's a song that makes the hackles rise. You can almost see him there—Gregorio Cortez, with his pistol in his hand.

He was a man, a Border man. What did he look like? Well, that is hard to tell. Some say he was short and some say he was tall; some say he was Indian brown and some say he was blond like a newborn cockroach. But I'd say he was not too dark and not too fair, not too thin and not too fat, not too short and not too tall: and he looked just a little bit like me. But does it matter so much what he looked like? He was a man, very much of a man; and he was a Border man. Some say he was born in Matamoros; some say Reynosa; some

Reprinted by permission from Américo Paredes, "*With His Pistol in His Hand*": *A Border Ballad and Its Hero* (Austin: University of Texas Press, 1958; paper 1971), pp. 33–54.

49

say Hidalgo county on the other side. And I guess others will say other things. But Matamoros, or Reynosa, or Hidalgo, it's all the same Border; and short or tall, dark or fair, it's the man that counts. And that's what he was, a man.

Not a gunman, no, not a bravo. He never came out of a cantina wanting to drink up the sea at one gulp. Not that kind of man, if you can call that kind a man. No, that wasn't Gregorio Cortez at all. He was a peaceful man, a hard-working man like you and me.

He could shoot. Forty-four and thirty-thirty, they were the same to him. He could put five bullets into a piece of board and not make but one hole, and quicker than you could draw a good deep breath. Yes, he could shoot, But he could also work.

He was a vaquero, and a better one there has not ever been from Laredo to the mouth. He could talk to horses, and they would understand. They would follow him around, like dogs, and no man knew a good horse better than Gregorio Cortez. As for cattle, he could set up school for your best caporal. And if an animal was lost, and nobody could pick up a trail, they would send for Gregorio Cortez. He could always find a trail. There was no better tracker in all the Border country, nor a man who could hide his tracks better if he wanted to. That was Gregorio Cortez, the best vaquero and range man that there ever was.

But that is not all. You farmers, do you think that Gregorio Cortez did not know your business too? You could have told him nothing about cotton or beans or corn. He knew it all. He could look into the sky of a morning and smell it, sniff it the way a dog sniffs, and tell you what kind of weather there was going to be. And he would take a piece of dirt in his hands and rub it back and forth between his fingers—to see if the land had reached its point —and you would say he was looking into it. And perhaps he was, for Gregorio Cortez was the seventh son of a seventh son.

You piddling modern farmers, vain of yourselves when you make a bale! You should have seen the crops raised by Gregorio Cortez. And when harvesting came, he was in there with the rest. Was it shucking corn? All you could see was the shucks fly and the pile grow, until you didn't know there was a man behind the pile. But he was even better at cotton-picking time. He would bend down and never raise his head till he came out the other end, and he would be halfway through another row before the next man was through with his. And don't think the row he went through wasn't clean. No flags, no streamers, nothing left behind, nothing but clean, empty burrs where he had passed. It was the same when clearing land. There were men who went ahead of him, cutting fast along their strip in the early morning, but by noontime the man ahead was always Gregorio Cortez, working at his own pace, talking little and not singing very much, and never acting up.

For Gregorio Cortez was not of your noisy, hell-raising type. That was not his way. He always spoke low, and he was always polite, whoever he was speaking to. And when he spoke to men older than himself he took off his hat and held it over his heart. A man who never raised his voice to parent or elder brother, and never disobeyed. That was Gregorio Cortez, and that was the way men were in this country along the river. That was the way they were before these modern times came, and God went away.

He should have stayed on the Border; he should not have gone up above, into the North. But it was going to be that way, and that was the way it was. Each man has a certain lot in life, and no other thing but that will be his share. People were always coming down from places in the North, from Dallas and San Antonio and Corpus and Foro West. And they would say, "Gregorio Cortez, why don't you go north? There is much money to be made. Stop eating beans and tortillas and that rubbery jerked beef. One of these days you're going to pull out one of your eyes, pull and pull with your teeth on that stuff and it suddenly lets go. It's a wonder all you Border people are not one-eyed. Come up above with us, where you can eat white bread and ham."

But Gregorio Cortez would only smile, because he was a peaceful man and did not take offense. He did not like white bread and ham; it makes people flatulent and dull. And he liked it where he was. So he always said, "I like this country. I will stay here."

But Gregorio Cortez had a brother, a younger brother named Román. Now Román was just like the young men of today, loud-mouthed and discontented. He was never happy where he was, and to make it worse he loved a joke more than any other thing. He would think nothing of playing a joke on a person twice his age. He had no respect for anyone, and that is why he ended like he did. But that is yet to tell.

Román talked to Gregorio and begged him that they should move away from the river and go up above, where there was much money to be made. And he talked and begged so, that finally Gregorio Cortez said he would go with his brother Román, and they saddled their horses and rode north.

Well, they did not grow rich, though things went well with them because they were good workers. Sometimes they picked cotton: sometimes they were vaqueros, and sometimes they cleared land for the Germans. Finally they came to a place called El Carmen, and there they settled down and farmed. And that was how Gregorio Cortez came to be in the county of El Carmen, where the tragedy took place.

ROMÁN'S HORSE TRADE AND WHAT CAME OF IT

Román owned two horses, two beautiful sorrels that were just alike, the same color, the same markings, and the same size. You could not have told them apart, except that one of them was lame. There was an American who owned a little sorrel mare. This man was dying to get Román's sorrel—the good one—and every time they met he would offer to swap the mare for the horse. But Román did not think much of the mare. He did not like it when the American kept trying to make him trade.

"I wonder what this Gringo thinks," Román said to himself. "He takes me for a fool. But I'm going to make him such a trade that he will remember me forever."

And Román laughed a big-mouthed laugh. He thought it would be a fine joke, besides being a good trade. There were mornings when the American went to town in his buggy along a narrow road. So Román saddled the lame sorrel, led him a little way along the road, and stopped under a big mesquite that bordered on the fence. He fixed it so the spavined side was against the mesquite. Román waited a little while, and soon he heard the buggy coming along the road. Then he got in the saddle and began picking mesquites off the tree and eating them. When the American came around the bend, there was Román on his sorrel horse. The American stopped his buggy beside Román and looked at the horse with much admiration. It was a fine animal, exactly like the other one, but the American could not see the spavined leg.

"Changed your mind?" the American said.

Román stopped chewing on a mesquite and said, "Changed my mind about what?"

"About trading that horse for my mare."

"You're dead set on trading your mare for this horse of mine?" Román said.

"You know I am," the American said. "Are you ready to come around?"

"I'm in a trading mood," said Román. "With just a little arguing you might convince me to trade this horse for that worthless mare of yours. But I don't know: you might go back on the deal later on."

"I never go back on my word," the American said. "What do you think I am, a Mexican?"

"We'll see, we'll see," said Román. "How much are you willing to give in hand?"

"Enough to give you the first square meal you've had in your life," the American said.

Román just laughed, and it was all he could do to keep from guffawing. He knew who was getting the best of things.

So they made the deal, with Román still sitting on his spavined horse under the tree, chewing on mesquites.

"Where's the mare?" Román said.

"She's in my yard," said the American, "hung to a tree. You go get her and leave the horse there for me because I'm in a hurry to get to town."

That was how Román had figured it, so he said, "All right, I'll do it, but when I finish with these mesquites."

"Be sure you do, then," the American said.

"Sure, sure," said Román. "No hurry about it, is there?"

"All right," the American said, "take your time." And he drove off leaving Román still sitting on his horse under the mesquite, and as he drove off the American said, "Now isn't that just like a Mexican. He takes his time."

Román waited until the American was gone, and then he stopped eating mesquites. He got off and led the horse down the road to the American's yard and left him there in place of the little sorrel mare. On the way home Román almost fell off his saddle a couple of times, just laughing and laughing to think of the sort of face the American would pull when he came home that night.

The next morning, when Gregorio Cortez got up he said to his brother Román, "Something is going to happen today."

"Why do you say that?" asked Román.

"I don't know," said Gregorio Cortez. "I just know that something is going to happen today. I feel it. Last night my wife began to sigh for no reason at all. She kept sighing and sighing half the night, and she didn't know why. Her heart was telling her something, and I know some unlucky thing will happen to us today."

But Román just laughed, and Gregorio went inside the house to shave. Román followed him into the house and stood at the door while Gregorio shaved. It was a door made in two sections; the upper part was open and Román was leaning on the lower part, like a man leaning out of a window or over a fence. Román began to tell Gregorio about the horse trade he had made the day before, and he laughed pretty loud about it, because he thought it was a good joke. Gregorio Cortez just shaved, and he didn't say anything.

When what should pull in at the gate but a buggy, and the American got down, and the Major Sheriff of the county of El Carmen got down too. They came into the yard and up to where Román was leaning over the door, looking out.

The American had a very serious face. "I came for the mare you stole yesterday morning," he said.

Román laughed a big-mouthed laugh. "What did I tell you, Gregorio?" he said. "This Gringo Sanavabiche has backed down on me."

Now there are three saints that the Americans are especially fond of —Santa Anna, San Jacinto, and Sanavabiche—and of the three it is Sanavabiche that they pray to most. Just listen to an American any time. You may not understand anything else he says, but you are sure to hear him say,

"Sanavabiche! Sanavabiche! Sanavabiche!" Every hour of the day. But they'll get very angry if you say it too, perhaps because it is a saint that belongs to them alone.

And so it was with the Major Sheriff of the county of El Carmen. Just as the words "Gringo Sanavabiche" came out of Román's mouth, the sheriff whipped out his pistol and shot Román. He shot Román as he stood there with his head thrown back, laughing at his joke. The sheriff shot him in the face, right in the open mouth, and Román fell away from the door, at the Major Sheriff's feet.

And then Gregorio Cortez stood at the door, where his brother had stood, with his pistol in his hand. Now he and the Major Sheriff met, each one pistol in hand, as men should meet when they fight for what is right. For it is a pretty thing to see, when two men stand up for their right, with their pistols in their hands, front to front and without fear. And so it was, for the Major Sheriff also was a man.

Yes, the Major Sheriff was a man; he was a gamecock that had won in many pits, but in Gregorio Cortez he met a cockerel that pecked his comb. The Major Sheriff shot first, and he missed; and Gregorio Cortez shot next, and he didn't miss. Three times did they shoot, three times did the Major Sheriff miss, and three times did Gregorio Cortez shoot the sheriff of El Carmen. The Major Sheriff fell dead at the feet of Gregorio Cortez, and it was in this way that Gregorio Cortez killed the first sheriff of many that he was to kill.

When the Major Sheriff fell, Gregorio Cortez looked up, and the other American said, "Don't kill me; I am unarmed."

"I will not kill you," said Gregorio Cortez. "But you'd better go away."

So the American went away. He ran into the brush and kept on running until he came to town and told all the other sheriffs that the Major Sheriff was dead.

Meanwhile, Gregorio Cortez knew that he too must go away. He was not afraid of the law; he knew the law, and he knew that he had the right. But if he stayed, the Rangers would come, and the Rangers have no regard for law. You know what kind of men they are. When the Governor of the State wants a new Ranger, he asks his sheriffs, "Bring all the criminals to me." And from the murderers he chooses the Ranger, because no one can be a Ranger who has not killed a man. So Gregorio Cortez knew that the best thing for him was to go away, and his first thought was of the Border, where he had been born. But first he must take care of his brother, so he put Román in the buggy and drove into town, where his mother lived.

Now there was a lot of excitement in town. All the Americans were saddling up and loading rifles and pistols, because they were going out to kill Cortez. When all of a sudden, what should come rolling into town but the buggy, driven by Gregorio Cortez. They met him on the edge of town, armed to the teeth, on horseback and afoot, and he on the buggy, holding the reins lightly in his hands. Román was in the back, shot in the mouth. He could neither speak nor move, but just lay there like one who is dead.

They asked him, "Who are you?"

And he said to them, "I am Gregorio Cortez."

They all looked at him and were afraid of him, because they were only twenty or twenty-five, and they knew that they were not enough. So they stepped aside and let him pass and stood talking among themselves what would be the best thing to do. But Gregorio Cortez just drove ahead, slowly, without seeming to care about the men he left behind. He came to his mother's house, and there he took down his brother and carried him in the house. He stayed there until dawn, and during the night groups of armed men would go by the house and say, "He's in there. He's in there." But none of them ever went in.

At dawn Gregorio Cortez came out of his mother's house. There were armed men outside, but they made no move against him. They just watched as he went down the street, his hands resting on his belt. He went along as if he was taking a walk, and they stood there watching until he reached the brush and he jumped into it and disappeared. And then they started shooting at him with rifles, now that he was out of pistol range.

"I must get me a rifle," said Gregorio Cortez, "a rifle and a horse."

They gathered in a big bunch and started after him in the brush. But they could not catch Gregorio Cortez. No man was ever as good as him in hiding his own tracks, and he soon had them going around in circles, while he doubled back and headed for home to get himself a rifle and a horse.

HOW GREGORIO CORTEZ RODE THE LITTLE SORREL MARE ALL OF FIVE HUNDRED MILES

He went in and got his thirty-thirty, and then he looked around for the best horse he had. It is a long way from El Carmen to the Border, all of five hundred miles. The first thing he saw in the corral was the little sorrel mare. Gregorio Cortez took a good look at her, and he knew she was no ordinary mare.

"You're worth a dozen horses," said Gregorio Cortez, and he saddled the little mare.

But by then the whole wasp's nest was beginning to buzz. The President of the United States offered a thousand dollars for him, and many men went out to get Gregorio Cortez. The Major Sheriffs of the counties and all their sheriffs were out. There were Rangers from the counties, armed to the teeth, and the King Ranch Rangers from the Capital, the meanest of them all, all armed and looking for Cortez. Every road was blocked and every bridge guarded. There were trackers out with those dogs they call hounds, that can follow a track better than the best tracker. They had railroad cars loaded with guns and ammunition and with men, moving up and down trying to head him off. The women and children stayed in the houses, behind locked doors, such was the fear they all had of Gregorio Cortez. Every town from the Capital to the Border was watching out for him. The brush and the fields were full of men, trying to pick up his trail. And Gregorio Cortez rode out for the Border, through brush and fields and barbed wire fences, on his little sorrel mare.

He rode and rode until he came to a great broad plain, and he started to ride across. But just as he did, one of the sheriffs saw him. The sheriff saw him, but he hid behind a bush, because he was afraid to take him on alone. So he called the other sheriffs together and all the Rangers he could find, and they went off after Gregorio Cortez just as he came out upon the plain.

Gregorio Cortez looked back and saw them coming. There were three hundred of them.

"We'll run them a little race," said Gregorio Cortez.

Away went the mare, as if she had been shot from a gun, and behind her came the sheriffs and the Rangers, all shooting and riding hard. And so they rode across the plain, until one by one their horses foundered and fell to the ground and died. But still the little mare ran on, as fresh as a lettuce leaf, and pretty soon she was running all alone.

"They'll never catch me like that," said Gregorio Cortez, "not even with those dogs called hounds."

Another big bunch of sheriffs rode up, and they chased him to the edge of the plain, and into the brush went Cortez, with the trackers after him, but they did not chase him long. One moment there was a trail to follow, and next moment there was none. And the dogs called hounds sat down and howled, and the men scratched their heads and went about in circles looking for the trail. And Gregorio Cortez went on, leaving no trail, so that people thought he was riding through the air.

There were armed men everywhere, and he could not stop to eat or drink, because wherever he tried to stop armed men were there before him. So he had to ride on and on. Now they saw him, now they lost him, and so the chase went on. Many more horses foundered, but the mare still ran, and Gregorio Cortez rode on and on, pursued by hundreds and fighting hundreds every place he went.

"So many mounted Rangers," said Gregorio Cortez, "to catch just one Mexican."

It was from the big bunches that he ran. Now and again he would run into little ones of ten or a dozen men, and they were so scared of him that they would let him pass. Then, when he was out of range they would shoot at him, and he would shoot back at them once or twice, so they could go back and say, "We met up with Gregorio Cortez, and we traded shots with him." But from the big ones he had to run. And it was the little sorrel mare that took him safe away, over the open spaces and into the brush, and once in the brush, they might as well have been following a star.

So it went for a day, and when night fell Cortez arrived at a place named Los Fresnos and called at a Mexican house. When the man of the house came out, Cortez told him, "I am Gregorio Cortez."

That was all he had to say. He was given to eat and drink, and the man of the house offered Gregorio Cortez his own horse and his rifle and his saddle. But Cortez would not take them. He thanked the man, but he would not give up his little sorrel mare. Cortez was sitting there, drinking a cup of coffee, when the Major Sheriff of Los Fresnos came up with his three hundred men. All the other people ran out of the house and hid, and no one was left in the house, only Gregorio Cortez, with his pistol in his hand.

Then the Major Sheriff called out, in a weepy voice, as the corrido says. He sounded as if he wanted to cry, but it was all done to deceive Gregorio Cortez.

"Cortez," the Major Sheriff said, "hand over your weapons. I did not come to kill you. I am your friend."

"If you come as my friend," said Gregorio Cortez, "why did you bring three hundred men? Why have you made me a corral?"

The Major Sheriff knew that he had been caught in a lie, and the fighting began. He killed the Major Sheriff and the second sheriff under him, and he killed many sheriffs more. Some of the sheriffs got weak in the knees, and many ran away.

"Don't go away," said Gregorio Cortez. "I am the man you are looking for. I am Gregorio Cortez."

They were more than three hundred, but he jumped their corral, and he rode away again, and those three hundred did not chase him any more.

He rode on and on, until he came to a river called the San Antonio. It is not much of a river, but the banks are steep and high, and he could not find a ford. So he rode to a ranch house nearby, where they were holding a baile because the youngest child of the house had been baptized that day, and he asked the man of the house about a ford.

"There are only two fords," the man said. "One is seven miles upstream and the other is seven miles down."

"I will take another look at the river," said Gregorio Cortez. He left the baile and rode slowly to the river. It was steep, and far below he could see the water flowing; he could barely see it because it was so dark. He stood there thinking, trying to figure out a way, when he heard the music at the baile stop.

He knew the Rangers were at the baile now. So he leaned over in his saddle and whispered in the mare's ear. He talked to her, and she understood. She came to the edge of the bank, with soft little steps, because she was afraid. But Gregorio Cortez kept talking to her and talking to her, and finally she jumped. She jumped far out and into the dark water below, she and Gregorio Cortez.

The other bank was not so high, but it was just as steep. Gregorio Cortez took out his reata, and he lassoed a stump high on the bank. He climbed up the rope and got a stick, and with the stick he worked on the bank as fast as he could, for he could hear the racket of the dogs. The ground was soft, and he knocked off part of the top, until he made something like a slope. Then he pulled and talked until the mare struggled up the bank to where he was. After that they rested up a bit and waited for the Rangers. Up they came with their dogs, to the spot where the mare had jumped. When they came up to the river's edge, Cortez fired a shot in the air and yelled at them, "I am Gregorio Cortez!"

Then he rode away, leaving them standing there on the other side, because none of them was brave enough to do what Cortez had done.

He rode on and on, and sometimes they chased him and sometimes he stood and fought. And every time he fought he would kill them a Ranger or two. They chased him across the Arroyo del Cíbolo and into the oak grove, and there they made him a corral. Then they sent the dogs away and sat down to wait, for they wanted to catch him asleep. Gregorio Cortez thought for a little while what he should do. Then he made his mare lie down on the ground, so she would not be hurt. After that Gregorio Cortez began talking to himself and answering himself in different voices, as if he had many men. This made the Rangers say to one another, "There is a whole army of men with Gregorio Cortez." So they broke up their corral and went away, because they did not think there were enough of them to fight Gregorio Cortez and all the men he had. And Gregorio Cortez rode away, laughing to himself.

He kept riding on and on, by day and by night, and if he slept the mare stood guard and she would wake him up when she heard a noise. He had no food or cigarettes, and his ammunition was running low. He was going along a narrow trail with a high barbed wire fence on one side and a nopal thicket on the other, and right before he hit a turn he heard horses ahead. The first man that came around the turn ran into Gregorio Cortez, with his pistol in his hand. There was a whole line of others behind the first, all armed with rifles, but they had to put the rifles away. Then Gregorio Cortez knocked over a tall nopal plant with his stirrup and made just enough room for his mare to back into while the Rangers filed by. He stopped the last one and took away his tobacco, matches, and ammunition. And then he rode away.

He rode on to La Grulla, and he was very thirsty, because he had not had water in a long time, and the mare was thirsty too. Near La Grulla there was a dam where the vaqueros watered their stock. But when Gregorio Cortez got there, he saw twenty armed men resting under the trees that grew close to the water. Gregorio Cortez stopped and thought what he could do. Then he went back into the brush and began rounding up cattle, for this was cattle country and steers were everywhere. Pretty soon he had two hundred head, and he drove them to water and while the cattle drank he and the mare drank too. After he had finished, some of the Rangers that were resting under the trees came over and helped him get the herd together again, and Gregorio Cortez rode off with the herd, laughing to himself.

He rode on and on, and by now he knew that the Río Grande was near. He rode till he came to Cotulla, and there he was chased again. The little mare was tired, and now she began to limp. She had cut her leg and it was swelling up. Gregorio Cortez rode her into a thicket, and the Rangers made him a corral. But once in the brush, Gregorio Cortez led the mare to a coma tree and tied her there. He unsaddled her and hung the saddle to the tree, and he patted her and talked to her for a long while. Then he slipped out of the thicket, and the Rangers didn't see him because they were waiting for him to ride out. They waited for three days and finally they crept in and found only the mare and the saddle.

HOW EL TECO SOLD GREGORIO CORTEZ FOR A MORRAL FULL OF SILVER DOLLARS

Gregorio Cortez was gone. While all the armed men were guarding the thicket where the mare was tied, he walked into Cotulla itself. He walked into town and mixed with the Mexicans there. He sat on the station platform and listened to other men while they talked of all the things that Gregorio Cortez had done. Then he went to a store and bought himself new clothes and walked out of the town. He went to the river and took a bath and then swam across, because the bridge was guarded. That sort of man was Gregorio Cortez. They don't make them like him any more.

He had only three cartridges left, one for one pistol and two for the other, and he had left his rifle with the mare. But he was very near the Río Grande, and he expected to cross it soon. Still he needed ammunition, so he walked into El Sauz and tried to buy some, but they did not sell cartridges in that town. Then he thought of trying some of the houses, and chose one in which there was a pretty girl at the door because he knew it would be easier if he talked to a girl. There was not a woman that did not like Gregorio Cortez.

The girl was alone, and she invited him into the house. When he asked for ammunition, she told him she had none.

"My father has taken it all," she said. "He is out looking for a man named Gregorio Cortez."

Gregorio Cortez was embarrassed because he could see that the girl knew who he was. But she did not let on and neither did he. He stayed at the house for a while, and when he left she told him how to get to the Río Grande by the quickest way.

Now all the people along the river knew that Gregorio Cortez was on the Border, and that he would soon cross, but no one told the sheriffs what they knew. And Gregorio Cortez walked on, in his new clothes, with his pistols in a morral, looking like an ordinary man, but the people he met knew that he was Gregorio Cortez. And he began to talk to people along the way.

Soon he met a man who told him, "You'll be on the other side of the river tonight, Gregorio Cortez."

"I think I will," he said.

"You'll be all right then," said the man.

"I guess so," said Gregorio Cortez.

"But your brother won't," the man said. "He died in the jail last night."

"He was badly wounded," said Gregorio Cortez. "It was his lot to die, but I have avenged his death."

"They beat him before he died," the man said. "The Rangers came to the jail and beat him to make him talk."

This was the first news that Gregorio Cortez had heard, and it made him thoughtful.

He walked on, and he met another man who said, "Your mother is in the jail, Gregorio Cortez."

"Why?" said Gregorio Cortez. "Why should the sheriffs do that to her?"

"Because she is your mother," the man said. "That's why. Your wife is there too, and so are your little sons."

Gregorio Cortez thought this over, and he walked on. Pretty soon he met another man who said, "Gregorio Cortez, your own people are suffering, and all because of you."

"Why should my people suffer?" said Cortez. "What have I done to them?"

"You have killed many sheriffs, Gregorio Cortez," said the man. "The Rangers cannot catch you, so they take it out on other people like you. Every man that's given you a glass of water has been beaten and thrown in jail. Every man who has fed you has been hanged from a tree branch, up and down, up and down, to make him tell where you went, and some have died rather than tell. Lots of people have been shot and beaten because they were your people. But you will be safe, Gregorio Cortez; you will cross the river tonight."

"I did not know these things," said Gregorio Cortez.

And he decided to turn back, and to give himself up to the Governor of the State so that his own people would not suffer because of him.

He turned and walked back until he came to a place called Goliad, where he met eleven Mexicans, and among them there was one that called himself his friend. This man was a vaquero named El Teco, but Judas should have been his name. Gregorio Cortez was thirsty, and he came up to the eleven Mexicans to ask for water, and when El Teco saw Gregorio Cortez he thought how good it would be if he could get the thousand-dollar reward. So he walked up to Cortez and shook his hand and told the others, "Get some water for my friend Gregorio Cortez."

Then El Teco asked Gregorio Cortez to let him see the pistols he had, and that he would get him some ammunition. Gregorio Cortez smiled, because he knew. But he handed over the guns to El Teco, and El Teco looked at them and put them in his own morral. Then El Teco called the sheriffs to come and get Gregorio Cortez.

When Gregorio Cortez saw what El Teco had done, he smiled again and said to him, "Teco, a man can only be what God made him. May you enjoy your reward."

But El Teco did not enjoy the reward, though the sheriffs gave him the money, one thousand dollars in silver, more than a morral could hold. He did not enjoy it because he could not spend it anywhere. If he went to buy a taco at the market place, the taco vendor would tell him that tacos were worth two thousand dollars gold that day. People cursed him in the streets and wished that he would be killed or die. So El Teco became very much afraid. He buried the money and never spent it, and he never knew peace until he died.

HOW GREGORIO CORTEZ WENT TO PRISON, BUT NOT FOR KILLING THE SHERIFFS

When the sheriffs came to arrest Gregorio Cortez, he spoke to them and said, "I am not your prisoner yet. I will be the prisoner only of the Governor of the State. I was going to the Capital to give myself up, and that is where I'll go."

The sheriffs saw that he was in the right, so they went with him all the way to the Capital, and Cortez surrendered himself to the Governor of the State.

Then they put Cortez in jail, and all the Americans were glad, because they no longer were afraid. They got together, and they tried to lynch him. Three times they tried, but they could not lynch Gregorio Cortez.

And pretty soon all the people began to see that Gregorio Cortez was in the right, and they did not want to lynch him any more. They brought him gifts to the jail, and one day one of the judges came and shook the hand of Gregorio Cortez and said to him, "I would have done the same."

But Gregorio Cortez had many enemies, for he had killed many men, and they wanted to see him hanged. So they brought him to trial for killing the Major Sheriff of the county of El Carmen. The lawyer that was against him got up and told the judges that Cortez should die, because he had killed a man. Then Gregorio Cortez got up, and he spoke to them.

"Self-defense is allowed to any man," said Gregorio Cortez. "It is in your own law, and by your own law do I defend myself. I killed the sheriff, and I am not sorry, for he killed my brother. He spilled my brother's blood, which was also my blood. And he tried to kill me too. I killed the Major Sheriff defending my right."

And Gregorio Cortez talked for a long time to the judges, telling them about their own law. When he finished even the lawyer who was against him at the start was now for him. And all the judges came down from their benches and shook hands with Gregorio Cortez.

The judges said, "We cannot kill this man."

They took Gregorio Cortez all over the State, from town to town, and in each town he was tried before the court for the killing of a man. But in every court it was the same. Gregorio Cortez spoke to the judges, and he told them about the law, and he proved that he had the right. And each time the judges said, "This man was defending his right. Tell the sheriffs to set him free."

And so it was that Gregorio Cortez was not found guilty of any wrong because of the sheriffs he had killed. And he killed many of them, there is no room for doubt. No man has killed more sheriffs than did Gregorio Cortez, and he always fought alone. For that is the way the real men fight, always on their own. There are young men around here today, who think that they are brave. Dangerous men they call themselves, and it takes five or six of them to jump a fellow and slash him in the arm. Or they hide in the brush and fill him full of buckshot as he goes by. They are not men. But that was not the way with Gregorio Cortez, for he was a real man.

Now the enemies of Gregorio Cortez got together and said to each other, "What are we going to do? This man is going free after killing so many of our friends. Shall we kill him ourselves? But we would have to catch him asleep, or shoot him in the back, because if we meet him face to face there will be few of us left."

Then one of them thought of the little sorrel mare, and there they had a plan to get Gregorio Cortez. They brought him back to court, and the lawyer who was against him asked, "Gregorio Cortez, do you recognize this mare?"

"I do," said Gregorio Cortez. "And a better little mare there never was."

Then the lawyer asked him, "Have you ridden this mare?"

And Gregorio Cortez answered, "She carried me all the way from El Carmen to the Border, a distance of five hundred miles."

Then the lawyer asked him, "Is this mare yours?"

And Gregorio Cortez saw that they had him, but there was nothing he could do, because he was an honest man and he felt that he must tell the truth. He said no, the mare did not belong to him.

Then the judges asked Gregorio Cortez, "Is this true, Gregorio Cortez? Did you take this mare that did not belong to you?"

And Gregorio Cortez had to say that the thing was true.

So they sentenced Gregorio Cortez, but not for killing the sheriffs, as some fools will tell you even now, when they ought to know better. No, not for killing the sheriffs but for stealing the little sorrel mare. The judge sentenced him to ninety-nine years and a day. And the enemies of Gregorio Cortez were happy then, because they thought Cortez would be in prison for the rest of his life.

HOW PRESIDENT LINCOLN'S DAUGHTER FREED GREGORIO CORTEZ, AND HOW HE WAS POISONED AND DIED

But Gregorio Cortez did not stay in prison long. Inside of a year he was free and this is the way it came about. Every year at Christmastime, a pretty girl can come to the Governor of the State and ask him to give her a prisoner as a Christmas present. And the Governor then has to set the prisoner free and give him to the girl. So it happened to Cortez. One day President Lincoln's daughter visited the prison, and she saw Gregorio Cortez. As soon as she saw him she went up and spoke to him.

"I am in love with you, Gregorio Cortez," President Lincoln's daughter said, "and if you promise to marry me I will go to the Governor next Christmas and tell him to give you to me."

Gregorio Cortez looked at President Lincoln's daughter, and he saw how beautiful she was. It made him thoughtful, and he did not know what to say.

"I have many rich farms," President Lincoln's daughter said. "They are all my own. Marry me and we will farm together."

Gregorio Cortez thought about that. He could see himself already like a German, sitting on the gallery, full of ham and beer, and belching and breaking wind while a half-dozen little blond cockroaches played in the yard. And he was tempted. But then he said to himself, "I can't marry a Gringo girl. We would not make a matching pair."

So he decided that President Lincoln's daughter was not the woman for him, and he told her, "I thank you very much, but I cannot marry you at all."

But President Lincoln's daughter would not take his no. She went to the Governor and said, "I would like to have a prisoner for Christmas."

And the Governor looked at her and saw she was a pretty girl, so he said, "Your wish is granted. What prisoner do you want?"

And President Lincoln's daughter said, "I want Gregorio Cortez."

The Governor thought for a little while and then he said, "That's a man you cannot have. He's the best prisoner I got."

But President Lincoln's daughter shook her head and said, "Don't forget that you gave your word."

"So I did," the Governor said, "and I cannot go back on it."

And that was how Gregorio Cortez got out of prison, where he had been sentenced to ninety-nine years and a day, not for killing the sheriffs, as some fools will tell you, but for stealing the little sorrel mare. Gregorio Cortez kept his word, and he did not marry President Lincoln's daughter, and when at last she lost her hopes she went away to the north.

Still, the enemies of Gregorio Cortez did not give up. When they heard that he was getting out of prison they were scared and angry, and they started thinking of ways to get revenge. They got a lot of money together and gave it to a man who worked in the prison, and this man gave Cortez a slow poison just before Gregorio Cortez got out of jail.

And that was how he came to die, within a year from the day he got out of jail. As soon as he came out and his friends saw him, they said to each other, "This man is sick. This man will not last the year."

And so it was. He did not last the year. He died of the slow poison they gave him just before he was let out, because his enemies did not want to see him free.

And that was how Gregorio Cortez came to die. He's buried in Laredo some place, or maybe it's Brownsville, or Matamoros, or somewhere up above. To tell the truth, I don't know. I don't know the place where he is buried any more than the place where he was born. But he was born and lived and died, that I do know. And a lot of Rangers could also tell you that.

So does the corrido; it tells about Gregorio Cortez and who he was. They started singing the corrido soon after he went to jail, and there was a time when it was forbidden in all the United States, by order of the President himself. Men sometimes got killed or lost their jobs because they sang *El Corrido de Gregorio Cortez*. But everybody sang it just the same, because it spoke about things that were true.

Now it is all right to sing *El Corrido de Gregorio Cortez*, but not everybody knows it any more. And they don't sing it as it used to be sung. These new singers change all the old songs a lot. But even so, people still remember Gregorio Cortez. And when a good singer sings the song—good and loud and clear—you can feel your neck-feathers rise, and you can see him standing there, with his pistol in his hand.

ALFREDO OTERO Y HERRERA

"And Man Was Made WORD": *Chicano Genesis*

The brown leather jacket was too small for him, pulling his shoulders up at the armpits. And its zipper did not work. His small, red, chapped hands clutched the front of the jacket, hugging it to his skinny body. He stood at the entrance to the alley in the cold winter air that parted at random his thick black hair, watching the group of boys all larger than he. They milled, shouting, around the shed of rusted corrugated iron that jutted out behind the newspaper plant. Their white breath stabbing the cold air, they stamped their feet on the hard ground. He watched them for a few minutes; then, before walking in their direction, he shivered, not from the cold, but from fear. To keep the sole of his right shoe from flapping, he approached slowly toward the group to the steps that led to the office at the back of the print shop. As he reached them, they fell silent and spread apart to let him pass. Suddenly, a tall red-haired boy pushed him against a thin blond whose face and neck were scabbed with acne.

"Look where you're going, you little spic!" spat the blond, grabbing his jacket and jerking him violently.

"I didn't do it! He pushed me!" Ralphie replied, clutching the front of his jacket once more.

"Well, if it ain't little Ralphie All-Manure," mockingly whined the redhead.

"My name's Almansur. And leave me alone. Please." he choked, scrambling up the dried splintered steps. At the top he turned to look back at them. They stood hooting with laughter, some with hands thrust in back pockets, others smoking, each spitting now and then his own special way.

"Come on down here, you sissy greaser! You afraid of us?" sneered a fat blond with a broken front tooth.

"Yeah, you little Mex. What you doing here? You think you're going to sell papers?" shouted a younger boy from the rear of the group, looking around at the reaction of the others.

The tall redhead pointed at Ralphie's pants, laughing, "Hey, lookie! Ralphie's got on girls' bloomers!"

He started up the steps. "Let's pants him! I'd like to have those for my sister."

Ralphie opened the door and rushed into the office marked "Circulation." He hurriedly made his way among the neat stacks of newspapers to the desk by the gas heater. A tall, long-necked girl with jet-black hair and a pock-marked face heavily made up sat counting change that she had spread out over the desk top.

"Hello," he said.

"What do you want?" she asked, writing figures in a spiral notebook that lay beside the coins.

"I'm the new paper boy."

"Oh, yes. That's right. What's your name?"

"Rafael. I mean, Ralphie Almansur."

"Spell it."

"A-L-M-A-N-S-U-R."

"How many papers do you want to start with?"

"I don't know. How many do the other boys take?"

"It all depends. Some take thirty. Some forty. It all depends on how many customers you have. Do you have any customers?"

"No. At least, I don't think so," he replied, adding, "How do you get customers?"

"How should I know?" she said, shrugging her shoulders. "Ask the other boys. They know."

She opened the drawer of her desk and pulled out a black notebook and wrote down his name.

"How old are you, Ralphie?"

"Ten."

"Where do you live?"

"In the Y of the tracks. Mr. Jones, the plumber, lives next door."

"No! No! I mean . . . What's the street and number of your house?"

"We don't have a number; but Mother says that we might get one this year. But the nearest street is Eighth."

She carefully wrote down his street and age, then asked, "What does your father do?"

"My father's dead."

"Where does your mother work?"

"At home. She takes in washing."

"All right," she said, closing the notebook and throwing it back into the drawer. "How many papers do you want this week?"

"Do you think ten will be enough?"

"We'll see. If you need more, we'll give you more next week."

"Thank you very much," he said warmly.

The girl stood up, smoothed the back of her black wool skirt, hiked and knotted her rayon stockings just above the knee to keep them from slipping. Touching her hair lightly in the back with both hands, she walked out of the office in the direction of the roar of the presses.

Ralphie sat on the floor next to the heater. The heat burned into the side of him, but he did not move. He looked at his pants. They weren't Levi's, but they looked like them. They were some off brand that the Welfare Department had given his mother for him. They were too big, too, and he had had to fold them over in the front, fastening them tightly with a safety pin to keep them up. He had known that someone would make fun of him and his pants, but then, he had no choice. He had nothing else to wear. Unconsciously, he shifted to let his other side face the heater and when settled, decided to wait there until the papers came out. He had been happy when he had told his mother that he had gotten the job. She had smiled and said that it was wonderful and that she was proud of her new man of the house. His brother had been eager to know how he had gotten the job and asked him if he was not afraid to sell papers because of the Stableford brothers. He had told him that he wasn't afraid of anything. But he was afraid and now was planning that if he were to stay in the office until the papers came out, he could make it all right.

The girl came back into the office.

"Do you want something else, Ralphie?"

"No, thank you."

"Well then, you'll have to get outside with the others."

"I just wanted to get warm."

"So do the other boys, but they have to stay outside."

He got up to go; then, turning to smile at her, said, "The doctor said that I had to keep warm."

"I can't help that. Outside!"

He started once more toward the door, counting stacks of papers on the floor, stalling.

"Golly, did you have to count all these papers?"

"Most of them."

"I'll bet you did them all."

She started to answer him impatiently; but he interrupted her.

"You know my mother said to me when she found out that I was going to sell papers here that you had the prettiest black hair in the world," adding quickly, "and she said that you probably used Drene Shampoo on it to make it shine like it does. I'll bet you use Drene!"

"Yes, as a matter of fact, I do."

"She's saving her money so as she can buy a bottle of it before the Elks' Christmas Tree Party."

He started moving back to the heater when the back door burst open and Dickie Stableford, the tall redhead who had pushed him, came in.

"Hey, Cleo! When are the papers going to come out?"

"Not for another half hour."

"Hi, Dickie," offered Ralphie, forcing a smile. "How many papers are you going to sell?"

Dickie did not answer. Ralphie wished that someone would help him, yet he knew, too, that no one would.

Dickie was now at Cleo's desk, asking, "Who gets their papers first tonight?"

"Let me see," she said, checking the list. "Your brother Bobby. No. Wait a minute. Ralphie here gets his papers first."

"How come?"

"You know darn well, Dickie, that when a new boy comes on, he gets his papers first the first time."

"Yeah. But he'll probably steal our customers. He'll be the first one out on the street and we'll have all had to wait our turn. How come he can't?"

"That's the rule, Dickie. You got to go first when you started."

"Aw, come on, Cleo. Let Bobby get his turn."

"You heard me, Dickie! Now get outside! And you too, Ralphie!"

"Yeah. You too, Ralphie All-Manure! Come on outside with the boys!" said Dickie, imitating Cleo's voice.

Dickie grabbed Ralphie by the arm and jerked him toward the door. Ralphie tried to free himself, but Dickie pulled him past the stacks of papers, out of the door and onto the top step.

"Lookie who I have here. The little greaser, Ralphie All-Manure!"

Ralphie looked out, terrified. He knew every one of the faces that sneered up at him. They were all older than he. And bigger. Too old and too big for him. And too many.

"Hey! Guess what? All-Manure's going to get his papers first today! Isn't that something?" jeered Dickie.

"Hey! I'm supposed to get mine first today!" shouted Bobby. "I've had to wait ten weeks! What the hell are you trying to pull, All-Manure?"

"Nothing," stammered Ralphie, shrinking back against the door.

Bobby leaped up the steps and helped Dickie drag him down.

"Let's pants him and throw them into Nita Shanks' yard and see how big his thing is. If he has one!"

"*Suelta. ¡Déjame, pendejo!*"[1] Ralphie shouted, jerking himself free.

Swinging his arms wildly at the faces and hands that grabbed at him, he headed out of the alley, his face twisted, on the verge of tears. He kept expecting to be knocked down, and then the horrible shame to be pantsed, especially since he had no underwear on. He ran until, amazed, he realized that no one was chasing him, daring only then to turn around. They were picking up rocks. Gasping for breath, he ran faster to get out of their throwing range in the direction of his house.

When he entered the kitchen, he found his mother at the drain board cleaning beans. Looking up in surprise, she asked, "*Rafael, ¿qué haces por aquí?*[2] I thought you were going to sell papers."

---

[1]Let go. Stupid, leave me alone!   [2]What are you doing here?

Trying to catch his breath, he replied, "I was, Mother, but Cleo, you know, the girl with black hair, said that I couldn't have the job as I was too young. All the other boys are older. She said I couldn't handle it."

"*Ay, ¡Dios mío!* Now what are we going to do for school money?" she asked in disgust, putting her hands on her hips as she turned to glare at him.

Without answering or returning her gaze, he wiped his nose, which was running uncontrollably, on his jacket sleeve and moved toward the space between the wood and coal range and the wall. He did not care now that the sole of his shoe had been bent off almost completely in flight, making him walk as if he were crippled. Sitting down in the space half-occupied by a hot-water tank, he leaned against the heat-blistered wall and closed his eyes, the blood thumping in his temples.

"Oh no, you don't, *flojo!*[3] Don't think that you're going to sit there! How many times do I have to tell you and Leopoldo to stay outside! Besides, it wouldn't hurt you to chop some more kindling for the living-room stove!"

Ralphie opened his eyes and glanced up at his mother who stood over him. Silently, he scrambled to his feet. The sole of his shoe flapping, he made his way across the kitchen, out the back porch to the wood shed situated beside an old umbrella tree, its leafless branches heavy with wrinkled yellow berries moving stiffly in the chilling wind. He entered the shed, looking around for the hatchet. It lay upon a dust-covered cardboard box filled with old books and *Liberty* magazines to the right. As his hand moved to its handle, his eye caught the title of the book on the top, *The Dobbs at the Seashore.* He flipped up the cover. The title page had been torn out. He read instead, through scribblings of blue crayon, the title of the first chapter, "Daddy Surprises the Boys." His finger tracing the lines, Ralphie heard Mrs. Dobbs call gaily to her boys playing in a sun-drenched garden that their daddy would be home soon and that they must hurry to eat their lunch of all sorts of good things before they piled happily into their motor car and set out with shouts of glee for the white cottage with green shutters at the seashore. Ralphie picked up the book and sat down on the chip-covered dirt floor in the light of the doorway. Continuing to trace the lines slowly over the pages, Ralphie forgot the hatchet. A warm, happy feeling came creeping up from deep inside.

[3]lazy

Drama

RICARDO JUAN DURÁN

Dos Vatos

An Animated Television Play

VIDEO	AUDIO
Sunny morning—kitchen window, two flies, MOSES and FREDDY, on window pane	MOSES Tune in to El Jefito Sol,[1] Freddy . . . It sure feels good, carnal.[2]
	FREDDY Sure does, carnal.
[Close-up of MOSES—one leg is crippled he is hairy; has black, beady eyes and a Zapata moustache.] MOSES is rubbing his butt up against the window glass.	MOSES Hmmm . . . a toda madre . . .[3]
[Close-up of FREDDY—looks like MOSES, but no moustache or bad leg.] FREDDY stands on window sill, sniffing the air. [Air has wavy lines representing aroma.]	FREDDY [*Sniffing*] Híjola mano[4]— I smell all kinds of refín[5] ésta mañana.[6] [*Slight pause*] I think I'll take a spin around . . . ¿Vamos?[7]
Close-up of MOSES	MOSES [*Con tristeza*][8] Órale, carnal[9]—I'll bug you later, ese.
Close-up of FREDDY	FREDDY If I find some fresh frijoles,[10] I'll let you know.
	MOSES Ándale,[11] I want to stay here with El Jefito![12]
FREDDY takes off.	[*Sound accelerates.*] BzzzZZZ
FREDDY a la volada[13]	

[1]Father Sun [2]brother [3]real cool [4]Gee whiz [5]food [6]this morning
[7]Let's go? [8]With sadness [9]Say, brother [10]beans [11]Hurry up [12]Father
[13]swiftly

71

VIDEO	AUDIO
Close-up of FREDDY a la volada, thinking to himself	FREDDY Pobre carnalio, ya ni la chinga[14] . . . qué surra![15] He sure makes it hard on himself.
	ZZZZZ
FREDDY a la volada	He should get around with the plebe[16] and make some pedo[17] once in a while . . . at least tirar chingasos de vez en cuando[18] . . . wow! How can there be anything better than this pinche casa?[19]
	ZZZZZ
MOSES—still against the window, but not rubbing	MOSES Gracias, Jefito[20] [*to the sun, seriously*], para darnos todo.[21]
MOSES, crippled, walks to edge of window sill, dragging leg.	Chingao[22]—this leg sure hurts. That gringo[23] fly swatter—ya mero me mandaba.[24]
MOSES at edge of window sill— black, hairy body—crippled leg colgando[25]	My jefita[26] always used to tell me, "No te acerques con esos gachos gabachos,"[27] she used to say . . . She was right, chingao! Que aguitado y gacho me siento.[28] Esta pierna ya ni sirve.[29]
FREDDY a la volada	FREDDY Híjole[30]—I think I got some fresh frijoles on my sniffer . . . Que Mo tá tapado[31]—with all this good refin and smells, who has got time to think? We may not be here tomorrow— today is *it*.
FREDDY a la volada[32] into the bathroom	La vida te da en la madre.[33] I got no time to be aguitado[34] about nothing . . . trying to figure that pedo[35] out. ¡Ya estubo![36]

[14]Poor little brother, it's a bitch   [15]what a drag!   [16]peer group   [17]fart   [18]throw blows once in a while   [19]goddamn house   [20]Thank you, Father   [21]for giving us everything   [22]Goddamn   [23]Anglo   [24]he almost sent me   [25]hanging   [26]mother [27]Don't get near those lousy Anglos   [28]How depressed and lousy I feel.   [29]This leg is of no use.   [30]Wow   [31]That Moses is out of it   [32]swiftly   [33]I throw myself at life. [34] pissed off   [35]fart   [36]That's it!

VIDEO	AUDIO
FREDDY almost at toilet [direct flight line from FREDDY to toilet]	When we get here . . . pues aquí no más,[37] and tomorrow—los estiramos and more vatos[38] will be around here taking our places, cantoniando y refinando donde pueden.[39] ¡Qué vida tan aquellas![40]
FREDDY rockets in on toilet seat.	Zzzzzz
FREDDY standing on toilet-seat edge, looking in	Wow—look at all the refín . . . I better bug Moses.
FREDDY "revs" wings.	[*Accelerating*] zzzzZZZ
MOSES at edge of window sill	Zzzay, carnal, zzzezzta la cozza zz . . .[41]
MOSES tunes into buzz. [Wings of blue-green and body black velvet]	
MOSES "revs" wings.	
MOSES flying into bzzz	
MOSES lands on toilet seat next to FREDDY.	[*Anxious*] Órale, carnal, te esperé.[42]
	MOSES Wow, ese[43]—look at it all.
	FREDDY C'mon, carnal—let's go. Last one in don't get shit!
Shot of toilet seat [MOSES and FREDDY are gone.]	[*Voice sounds as if it is coming from a deep well.*] Wow! Look at it all, carnal . . . How could there be anything better? We sure got it made here . . . right, Moses?
Toilet seat, with HOUSEWIFE's hand about to flush	HOUSEWIFE [*Upset*] Homer! You dun forgot to flush yor droppings agin.
	MOSES [*Voice sounds as if it is coming from a deep well.*] Trucha, carnal[44] . . . [*With fear*] ¡La Mano Blanca!

[37]well, I'm just existing   [38]we'll die and more guys   [39]living and eating where they can
[40]What a far-out life!   [41]Say, brother, check the thing   [42]Say, brother, I waited.   [43]dude
[44]Careful, brother

VIDEO	AUDIO
	[*Flushing sound*]
	FREDDY Vamos a la volada. ZZZZ
MOSES and FREDDY flying away from toilet.	MOSES Ya mero mano, ya mero La Mano Blanca ya mero nos mandaba.[45]
	FREDDY Híjole,[46] just when I was really getting into it. I ate so fast I feel kinda sick.
An odor [wavy lines] comes at MOSES and FREDDY while they are flying.	Hey, carnal, smell that smog?
	MOSES Yeah—it's some of that rancid bacon que a La Mano Blanca le gusta tanto.[47]
Close-up of MOSES and FREDDY flying	FREDDY Qué gacho[48]—I can't take it—está podrido.[49]
	MOSES Órale,[50] let's dive down for fresh air.
MOSES and FREDDY dive down below a table.	Órale, carnal—mira allí en el techo de la mesa[51]—está lleno de chicle.[52]
MOSES and FREDDY each on a mound of gum under table [lots of gum]	FREDDY Wow! Tengo[53] Juicy Fruit. What you got, Mo?
	MOSES Es Spearmint, carnal. ¿Todavía te sientes mal?[54]
	FREDDY A little bit. Why?
	MOSES Ven aquí pues[55]—este Spearmint tiene hierba buena y te arregla.[56]
	FREDDY Órale, allí vengo.[57]

[45]Almost, buddy, the White Hand was almost sending us.   [46]Wow   [47]that the White Hand likes so much   [48]How crummy   [49]it's rotten   [50]O.K.   [51]Say, brother—look look on the roof of the table   [52]it's full of gum   [53]I have   [54]Do you still feel bad?   [55]Come here then   [56]This Spearmint has good weed and will fix you.   [57]O.K., here I come.

VIDEO	AUDIO
MOSES and FREDDY on Spearmint mound	Hey, I feel better already, carnal. How did you know about this?
	MOSES Abuelita me lo enseñó.[58]
Darken	NARRATOR For the rest of the day Freddy and Moses waited out the rancid bacon smog alert under the table. [*Pause*]
Sunset at kitchen window	The sun began to set and the coolness of the evening wrapped around the house and crept in.
	The cold made the wood creak and made the other moscas[59] fly a little faster to keep warm.
	[*Buzzing sound*]
	Only the noise of buzzing moscas broke the silence of the afternoon. [*Pause*]
	MOSES Oye,[60] Freddy ya se va el jefito. Hay que ir a la ventana.[61]
	FREDDY Vamos.[62]
Close-up of MOSES and FREDDY flying	Check it out, Mo, allí está toda la RAZA[63] giving thanks to jefito.
Kitchen sill—lots of moscas sunning and cleaning themselves	MOSES Everybody's taking their sunset bath—we're just in time.
Close-up of FREDDY and MOSES [rubbing legs and cleaning face]	VOICES [*All appreciating sun's last rays*] Órale, Jefito—gracias. ¡Qué suave![64]
	MOSES Sure feels good, huh, carnal?
	FREDDY So good it almost puts me to sleep. [*Shouts*] Trucha— ¡La Mano Blanca![65]

[58]Grandmother showed it to me.   [59]flies   [60]Say   [61]the sun is going down. We should go to the window.   [62]Let's go.   [63]there is all the RACE   [64]Say, Sun—thanks. How good.   [65]Be careful—the White Hand!

VIDEO	AUDIO
A hand with fly swatter	HOUSEWIFE You damn, dirty, lazy, good-for-nothing . . .
Kitchen window scene—fly swatter hits—flies scatter.	VOICES Trucha — cuidado, carnal.[66] Watch out—La Mano Blanca El Kookooy.[67]
MOSES and FREDDY a la volada	MOSES Follow me, carnal, I know where it's safe.
	FREDDY Let's go, Mo . . .
MOSES and FREDDY change course and fly up.	MOSES Para 'cá[68] . . . zzzz
MOSES and FREDDY on ceiling near light bulb	Aquí sí, ese,[69] we can sleep here.
	FREDDY Yeah, we're safe here . . . and warm, too.
	MOSES It's not the same as the jefito, pero[70] it'll keep us warm.
	FREDDY Yeah, I'm tired anyway.
	MOSES Duérmete, carnal. Aquí no llega La Mano Blanca.[71]
	NARRATOR And so Freddy and Moses went to sleep, feeling safe from danger so high in the sky . . . awaiting their jefito, who would bring them the holy warmth of new life in a new day.
	[*Pause*]
Close-up of MOSES and FREDDY, sleeping on ceiling [It is morning.]	[*Swatting noise—"explosion"—far off*]
Close-up of MOSES and FREDDY— they open their eyes.	[*"Explosion" closer—with hissing from spray can*]
MOSES flies off, FREDDY still hangs on.	MOSES Trucha, carnal, allí viene La Mano Blanca con su Black Flag.[72]

---

[66]Look out—careful, brother.   [67]the Spooky White Hand   [68]i.e., *Para acá* (Over here)   [69]Right here, guy   [70]but   [71]Sleep, brother. The White Hand won't reach here.   [72]Be careful, brother, here comes the White Hand with its Black Flag.

VIDEO	AUDIO
HOUSEWIFE with spray can of Black Flag in one hand and fly swatter in the other, swinging it	HOUSEWIFE You dang, lazy, good-for-nothing, dark, dirty things! Take that! [*Swat. Splat.*]
FREDDY on ceiling, with fumes coming up	FREDDY Gas . . . [*coughs*] I gotta get away— [*Swatting sounds getting closer*]
MOSES on light bulb	MOSES Acá, Freddy— ¡acá! Vente para 'cá, carnal, ¡ándale!⁷³ They got Louie!
FREDDY falls from ceiling.	FREDDY Ya me cagaron el palo mano . . .⁷⁴
FREDDY flying dizzily toward the light coming from the kitchen window	Híjole, estoy bombo.⁷⁵ Mo, ¿dónde estás, Mo? No puedo ver.⁷⁶ Jefito—¿dónde estás, Jefito?⁷⁷ I can't see.
MOSES on light bulb	MOSES Apúrate, Freddy. Apúrate. Para 'cá carnal, pa' cá.⁷⁸
FREDDY flying dizzily toward light coming from kitchen window	FREDDY [*Singing, drunk*] La vida no vale nada⁷⁹ . . . [*Pause*] No vale nada la vida.
MOSES on light bulb	MOSES Cuidado, Freddy— ¡allí viene La Mano Blanca!⁸⁰
FREDDY smashes into middle of kitchen window.	FREDDY [*Drunk*] Jefito! Ay⁸¹ ay ay, you feel so good, jefito.
MOSES on light bulb	MOSES Over here, Freddy, hurry. Allí viene El Kookooy.
	FREDDY [*Drunk and singing loudly*] No vale nada la vida . . .
MOSES crawling up the light cord toward the ceiling—fumes are getting close.	MOSES [*Coughing*] Ándale, Freddy, póngase trucha.⁸² Hurry before they give you a chingaso, vato.⁸³

---

⁷³Here, Freddy—here! Come over here, brother, hurry!   ⁷⁴They shitted my stick, friend
⁷⁵Wow, I'm drunk.   ⁷⁶Moses, where are you, Moses? I can't see.   ⁷⁷Sun—where are
you, Sun?   ⁷⁸Hurry, Freddy. Hurry. Over here, brother, this way. ⁷⁹Life isn't worth anything.
⁸⁰Careful, Freddy—here comes the White Hand.   ⁸¹Oh   ⁸²wise up, be alert   ⁸³blow, guy

VIDEO	AUDIO
	[*Swat.*]
MOSES on ceiling where light cord goes into small hole. He is looking down at FREDDY.	MOSES Freddy! [*Shouts*] Carnal!
FREDDY is smeared—spread-winged against the glass, the golden rays of sunrise filtering through his wings in orange, yellow, green, and turquoise. A rainbow forms between his wings.	HOUSEWIFE That'll teach ya, ya good-for-nothing, lazy . . .
Close-up of MOSES at hole in ceiling—tears are rolling down his face.	MOSES [*Sadly*] Carnal. Ya,[84] carnal, es verdad—la vida no vale nada. ¡Cuidado, jefito! ¡Cuidado![85]
MOSES halfway through the hole—rear-end shot	Órale—where am I? Hey! There's jefito's light. Por allí me voy.[86]
All dark except for a ray of light coming from a crack in the roof	¡Híjole![87] That Black Flag is getting to me. I gotta hurry. It sure is dark in here!
MOSES coming out through the roof	¡Híjole! Look at all this. ¿Dónde estoy?[88] ¿Es un mundo nuevo?[89]
MOSES flying high—house and countryside below	Me la rayo.[90] This is it—AZTLÁN. Mi abuelita[91] used to tell me about it but I never really believed it.
MOSES flying over completely natural scene—no evidence of man is visible.	I remember abuelita used to say how this is where the mero moscos chingones[92] live—Aztlán. You could get lost just looking everywhere . . . and the air, so pure and fresh . . . no more rancid bacon, no more Black Flag or gacho gavacho con su mano blanca.[93]

[84]O.K. (it's all right)   [85]it's true—life isn't worth anything. Be careful, old man! Be careful!
[86]That's how I'll go.   [87]Wow   [88]Where am I?   [89]Is it a new world?   [90]Right on.
[91]My grandmother   [92]the most heavy flies   [93]lousy Anglo with his white hand

VIDEO	AUDIO
MOSES flying back toward the house	Pobre carnal,[94] he never knew. This is where it's at, this is where we belong—not in that gava[95] house. Pobre Freddy.
The window, with FREDDY pasted to it in two huge streaks which resemble a huge *Chicano* face, smiling, in rainbows	Wow, qué vato—se aventó[96] to the end. He was happy in that place, pero now—now it's my turn in mi tierra Aztlán.[97]
MOSES flying toward sunrise and countryside	Me la rayo, con razón[98] I was always aguitado.[99] Pobre carnal . . . Es verdad[100] . . . la vida no vale nada, vale todo.[101]

LUIS VALDÉZ

The Dark Root of a Scream

CHARACTERS

LIZARD	GATO	DALIA
CONEJO	MADRE	PRIEST

SETTING

[*The scene is a collage of myth and reality. It forms, in fact, a pyramid with the most real artifacts of* barrio *life at the broad base and an abstract mythical-religious peak at the top. The lighting follows the same pyramidal pattern, from bright at the bottom to dark at the top.*

[*The bottom part of the set consists of two scenes blending into each other. On the right there is a street corner, a brick wall covered with* Chicano *writings in* pachuco *script. Three* vatos locos—LIZARD, CONEJO, *and* GATO—*are huddled against the wall. On the left there is an interior scene showing a* velorio, *a wake, in someone's living room.* MADRE, DALIA, *and the* PRIEST *are entering through a curtained doorway. Inside the room is a metallic black coffin draped with an American flag.*

[94]Poor brother   [95]i.e., *gavacho* (Anglo)   [96]What a guy—he enjoyed himself   [97]my land Aztlán   [98]Right on, with reason   [99]pissed off   [100]It's true   [101]Life isn't worth anything, because it's worth everything.

[*Above these scenes the images blend one into the other to form the upper part of the structure. Some are made of iron and the hard steel of modern civilization—guns, knives, automobile parts; others reveal a less violent, more spiritual origin—molcajetes, rebozos, crucifixes, etc. Finally, the very top of the pyramid is dominated by ancient indio images: conches, jade, the sun stone, feathered serpent heads.*]

I

LIZARD   Come on, ese, let's toke up.

[CONEJO *lights a leno.*]

Man, you sure sucking on that thing.

CONEJO [*Holding his breath*]   I awready had a lotta practice wis Indio.

LIZARD   Every night?

[CONEJO *passes the joint to* GATO.]

CONEJO   Sometimes.

LIZARD   No wonder the vato used to like you so much, ese. I bet you can open your mouth without showing your teeth, huh? Watcha. [LIZARD *does it, sucks his own tongue.*]

CONEJO [*Realizing*]   ¡Toma![1] [*Gives him the finger.*]

LIZARD [*Laughs*]   Chale,[2] man. No te aguites.[3] Indio's dead anyway. [*He gets the leno.*]

GATO [*Holding his breath*]   Heh, Funnybunny, is your carnala[4] going to the wake?

CONEJO   I don't know.

GATO   Don't act stupid, ese!

LIZARD   Take it easy, man! Poor Funnybunny don't know nothing. Besides, you already know she's going to be there. She was Indio's ruca.[5]

II

[*The action at the street corner freezes. There is movement at the coffin. The* MADRE *comes forward, held by* DALIA, *then the* PRIEST.]

PRIEST   That's it, easy does it, Señora Gonzáles. No sense in getting hysterical about these things.

[*The* MADRE *kneels at the coffin.*]

---

[1]Here!   [2]Hell   [3]Don't get mad.   [4]sister   [5]woman

No, not there, madre. You are supposed to sit over there. On the chair.

DALIA She'll be all right here.

PRIEST Yes, you're right. Of course. Then I guess you and I can sit over here.

[DALIA *and the* PRIEST *sit on the chairs.*]

Terrible thing this war. ¡Ojalá que se acabe pronto con la ayuda de Díos! Tú fuiste la prometida de Indio, ¿qué no?[6]

[DALIA *looks at him blankly.*]

Shall I say it in English?

DALIA I can speak Spanish, father.

PRIEST Entonces puedes contestarme la pregunta, ¿no?[7]

DALIA Sí. Indio and I were engaged.

III

[*Action freezes at wake. Movement at street corner.*]

CONEJO Man, it's hard to think of Indio dead, you know?

GATO He never done us no favors.

CONEJO You don' care he's dead?

GATO [*Shrugs*] I din' ask him to join the pinche[8] army.

CONEJO He din' join. They draft him.

LIZARD Símon, it was you that try to join, ese.

GATO Órale, but what happen? [*To* CONEJO] We walk into that place and tell 'em we want to join up, you know? The púto[9] sergeant laughed at us, man. "You?" he said. "Son, you guys have records longer than your greasy arms. You been shooting too much smack to let you shoot the gooks." Huh! I coulda give it to the cabrón right in the mother! Split his white gavacho belly like a fat pig! Pinche buey.[10]

LIZARD [*Laughs*] You shoulda cut out his pecker, ese.

IV

[*Action freezes at street corner. Movement at the wake.* MADRE *makes a choked sound. She is leaning forward, touching the place where the flag*

[6]Hope that it ends quickly with the help of God. You were the one promised to Indio, weren't you? [7]Then you can answer the question, can't you? [8]damn [9]queer [10]Damn guy.

sweeps the floor. The PRIEST *goes forward and sweeps his hand over the same spot. His hand picks up a red stain.*]

MADRE   Sangre.

PRIEST [*Realization hits him.*]   Oh my God!

MADRE   ¡Su sangre . . . se está saliendo de la caja! ¡Mijo está vivo! ¡Todavía está vivo!¹¹

PRIEST   Now, madre, calm down.

MADRE   ¡Es su sangre, padre!

PRIEST   No, señora, creo qué no.¹²

MADRE [*To the coffin*]   ¡Mijito, mijito de mi vida, estás perdiendo tu sangre!¹³

PRIEST   Madre, why don't you sit—

MADRE [*Starting to get hysterical*]   ¡No! ¡No me quiten de mijo! ¡Tengo que verlo! ¡Tengo que verlo!¹⁴ [*She tries to open coffin.*]

MADRE   ¡Ayyyyyyy! ¡Mijo! ¡Mijito de mi alma! ¡Estás muerto y se te está perdiendo la sangre! ¡Ayyyyy, corazón de tu madre, te mataron y nunca te volví a ver! ¡No me dejes, hijo! ¡No dejes a tu madre!¹⁵ [*She faints.*]

[PRIEST *holds* MADRE *and with the help of* DALIA *moves her over to a chair.* MADRE *is moaning with grief. A medal falls from her hand.*]

DALIA ¿Doña Rosa?

PRIEST ¿SEÑORA? ¡Señora Gonzáles!

DALIA   I'll get some alcohol. [*She goes out.*]

PRIEST [*Looks down at stain on floor*]   Bendito sea Dios.¹⁶

V

CONEJO   You think they gonna open Indio's coffin?

LIZARD   Chale, not a chance. They get him wis a grenade, and I bet you coulda put the pieces in a shoebox. By now he probably look like a rotten enchilada.

CONEJO   I don' like to talk like that.

---

¹¹His blood . . . is coming out of the box! My son is alive! He is still alive!   ¹²No, señora, I believe it isn't.   ¹³My little son, my little son of my life, you are losing your blood! ¹⁴Don't! Don't take me from my son! I have to see him! I have to see him!   ¹⁵My son! My little son of my soul! You're dead and you are losing your blood! Ayyyyy, heart of your mother, they killed you and never again did I see you! Don't leave me, son! Don't leave your mother!   ¹⁶Blessed be God

GATO   You vatos shoulda seen a dead cousin I had once. He was knife in Phoenix, and they ship him out here by train after two weeks, you know? My tía open up the lid to look at him. His hair was black still, but his skin was yellow like pus and the wax in his eyes was melting, and the smell of death was coming through his mouth.

LIZARD   Man, and you look at that? [*Spits*] Smell is right.

GATO   I bet Indio smells like that.

[DALIA *returns to the room on the opposite side with a bottle of alcohol and a cloth. She drenches the cloth. The* PRIEST *takes it.*]

PRIEST   Here, madre, smell this.

[*The* MADRE *moans.*]

DALIA [*Putting alcohol on the* MADRE'S *neck*] ¿Doña Rosa? Soy yo, señora,[17] Dalia. I think she's waking up.

PRIEST   We'd better clean that up before she—

[MADRE *moans in half-conscious grief.*]

Ya, madre, no llore. Aquí estoy contigo.[18] Do you have a mop?

[DALIA *nods, then looks at the stain on the floor.*]

Don't you be silly now. It's not what you think it is.

[MADRE *moans—it is almost a cry.*]

Get the mop.

[DALIA *exits.* PRIEST *prays.*]

Padre nuestro que estás en los cielos, santificado sea tu nombre . . .[19]

VI

GATO [*Passing the cigarette*]   Aquí te vas, loco.[20]

LIZARD   Órale. Dumb-ass vato.

GATO   Who?

LIZARD   Indio. I told him not to go in the army.

CONEJO   He had to go.

LIZARD   Shit, man. Then what was all this pedo[21] about Chicano power and snuffing gavachos? Some Chicano leader he turned out to be.

---

[17]It's me, señora   [18]There, Mother, don't cry. Here I am with you.   [19]Our Father Who art in Heaven, hallowed be Thy name . . .   [20]Here you go, crazy.   [21]ruckus

CONEJO   If he din't go, they would put him in the pinta.

LIZARD   Who says? You remember La Mula? He was drafted a couple of years ago, and the vato's still on the street. Símon,[22] he just took a little vacation in Mexicali, and that was it, man. Indio knew about it, too. If you ask me, that vato just like to be out front talking like he was a heavy dude. Now look where he's at.

CONEJO   They give him a Congressional Medal.

LIZARD [*To* GATO]   Este vato,[23] man.

VII

[DALIA *has entered and the* PRIEST *mops the stain on the floor. He picks up the medal.*]

PRIEST   There, you see? All wiped up. It must have been the dye from the flag.

[*The* MADRE *revives.*]

DALIA   Señora, ¿cómo se siente?[24]

PRIEST   You're going to be all right, madre. You fainted. I think you'd better go lie down for a while.

DALIA   Véngase al cuarto para que descanse, señora.[25]

MADRE   No—

PRIEST   Vale más que vaya.[26] I'll call you when we start the prayers. Here you dropped this. [*Gives her the medal*] In spite of your grief, you can be very proud of your son. The Congressional Medal of Honor is the highest award his country could give him.

MADRE   La medalla. Ya van tres.[27]

PRIEST   ¿Tres?

DALIA   That's right, father. She has three. One for her oldest boy killed in France, another killed in Korea, and now Indio.

PRIEST   I didn't know! Madre, you should be taken to see the President. El Presidente, usted debe ir a conocerlo.[28]

MADRE   Cuauhtemoc, Nezahualcoytl, Quetzalcóatl.

PRIEST   Perdóname, no entiendo. Otra vez más despacio por favor.[29]

---

[22]Yes   [23]This dude   [24]Señora, how do you feel?   [25]Come to the room so you can rest, señora.   [26]You'd better go.   [27]The medal. That makes three.   [28]The President, you should go meet him.   [29]Pardon me, I don't understand. Another time, this time more slowly, please.

MADRE   Cuauhtemoc, Nezahualcoytl, Quetzalcóatl.

PRIEST   I'm sorry. Did you get that? My Spanish isn't bad, but that—

DALIA   It isn't Spanish, father. Those are the Indian names of her three sons.

[DALIA *exits with* MADRE.]

PRIEST   Ah.

VIII

GATO   Hah! So that's it for Indio, vatos. A medal for your honor and a stinking box. Old chickenshit Gonzáles! Or whatever his name was.

CONEJO   It was Quetzalcóatl.

LIZARD   Quetza—what?

CONEJO   Quetzalcóatl, the feathered serpent.

PRIEST   Quetzalcóatl Gonzáles. What a name for an American soldier. I wonder what it means? The first part, of course. Everyone knows what Gonzáles means.

CONEJO   Quetzal means a green bird and cóatl means serpent. Bird-serpent. Quetzalcóatl. Feathered-serpent.

LIZARD   You're fulla shit.

[DALIA *re-enters alone.*]

IX

PRIEST   How did Indio come to have a name like that?

CONEJO   His father name him that.

PRIEST   Oh yes, his father. How did his father—?

DALIA   He was a teacher in Mexico.

CONEJO   His name was Mixcóatl—Cloud-serpent.

PRIEST   I see. A nationalist, eh?

LIZARD   So what, man? Over here he was a wetback, a farm laborer just like everybody else.

PRIEST   A political exile, no doubt.

CONEJO   He knew a lot about Mexican history. Quetzalcóatl used to be a god for the Indians a long time ago.

LIZARD   Sure, man, the Apaches.

CONEJO   Chale, indios mexicanos. Like us, we got Aztec blood.

PRIEST   Is that how Indio learned about the Aztecs? From his father?

DALIA   Just at first. He died when Indio was eight.

PRIEST   And left his son misguided. Full of hate.

CONEJO   Indio used to say a Chicano is an indio with a white man's name.

LIZARD   Like what?

CONEJO   Gonzáles.

GATO   Bullshit, that ain't white.

CONEJO   It's Spanish. They're white.

GATO   Who says?

CONEJO   Indio used to.

X

PRIEST   That's the only thing that bothers me about this Chicano thing: the racism. Indio was a racist, you know.

DALIA   Why? Because he taught Chicanos to be proud of what they have— their culture, their heritage?

CONEJO   Símon, he used to say to be proud of our nonwhite heritage.

LIZARD   Listen to this vato, ese. What did you say, Funnybunny?

CONEJO   I don' know. Heritage?

PRIEST   What heritage is that—human sacrifice?

LIZARD   Símon.

CONEJO   Like Quetzalcóatl. He put a stop to human sacrifice.

PRIEST   I'm sure Indio didn't mean that.

DALIA   How do you know?

PRIEST   Because the true facts are not very inspiring at all, Dalia. As a matter of fact, I've studied the subject with a great deal of interest.

GATO   Big deal.

PRIEST   The Indians of Mexico practiced ritualistic cannibalism and human sacrifice.

CONEJO·   They used to take these vatos up to a pyramid, you know? Then they put 'em on a big stone—like this, watcha—then wis a big knife—

GATO   A filero?[30]

PRIEST   They would tear the living heart out of the bodies of their victims and offer them to their merciless sun god!

LIZARD   ¡En la madre![31]

GATO   Who did they sacrifice, ese?

CONEJO   Oh, sometimes virgins.

LIZARD   They cut off a chichi to get to the heart, ese.

CONEJO   Most of the time it was prisoners from the wars.

PRIEST   They'd have wars especially to capture sacrificial victims.

CONEJO   They used to call 'em Wars of the Flowers, because nobody was supposed to get kill. Only take prisoners.

PRIEST   Some of the captives even considered it an honor to be sacrificed.

CONEJO   They used to take 'em beans and chocolate to fatten them, you know? Then they bring in rucas[32] for 'em and pulque.[33]

LIZARD   ¿Pulque?

CONEJO   Pisto.[34]

GATO   No shit?

CONEJO   Simon.

PRIEST   Then after the victims were sufficiently fattened on cactus wine and half-naked Indian women, they would be taken to the pyramid of the Sun or Moon or Corn God or any of their thousand gods, and there they would undergo bloody sacrifice. All in the name of religion.

XI

CONEJO   And that's the way it was until Quetzalcóatl become the chief. He put a stop to all that.

LIZARD   Nel, he din't.

CONEJO   Símon. After that he only allowed them to sacrifice monkeys and rocks.

LIZARD   No more rucas or pisto?

CONEJO   Chale.[35]

---

[30]knife   [31]Oh, wow!   [32]women   [33]a type of drink   [34]Liquor.   [35]Hell.

GATO   Din' I tell you, man? Chickenshit Gonzáles all over again! Pura périca[36] and no action.

LIZARD   So how come this Quetzalcóatl was so hot? He din' do madre.

CONEJO   That's what you think. He made miracles and change the indio civilization all around.

XII

DALIA   I don't think you understand what Indio was trying to do, father.

LIZARD   So what he do?

CONEJO   He built great pyramids.

DALIA   He wanted the Raza to be close to God.

CONEJO   He give the indios corn and fire.

DALIA   He wanted our people to have enough to eat.

CONEJO   He show 'em how to make pottery and paint and write books.

DALIA   He wanted Chicanos to express and educate themselves.

CONEJO   He teach 'em how to make their own government.

DALIA   He wanted us to live free and equal.

CONEJO   He was against all the wars.

DALIA   He didn't want his carnales to die uselessly.

CONEJO   He was the God of Civilization.

DALIA   He was a beautiful nuevo hombre.[37]

CONEJO   He was a vato de aquellos.[38]

XIII

LIZARD   ¿Sabes qué?[39] There's only one thing I don't understand, ese. If this Quetzalcóatl was so great, what happen to him?

CONEJO   The priests got rid of him.

LIZARD   What priests?

CONEJO   The Aztec priests. They wanted war and human sacrifice.

DALIA   Why were you against Indio, father?

---

[36]Pure talk   [37]new man   [38]one of those far-out guys   [39]You know what?

PRIEST   I wasn't against him!

DALIA   Then why didn't you loan him the church hall for meetings?

PRIEST   My Dalia, Indio's meetings were violently political. It's not the business of the Church to get involved in such matters.

DALIA   Some priests do.

PRIEST   And they must answer to their bishops. Besides, Indio was politically naive.

GATO   I remember Indio talking all that shit at meetings. He was full of it.

PRIEST   If you must know, it was some of your own Raza, some Chicanos in the parish, that kept me from loaning Indio the hall. They didn't like what he had to say. What could I do?

DALIA   You could have done anything, father. You're barrio priest.

LIZARD   Tell me something, ese. If Quetzalcóatl was a god, how could the priests put him down?

CONEJO   They call in his brother who was a evil god, Tezcatlípoca. He give 'em a mirror and told them to give it to Quetzalcóatl for a present.

LIZARD   A mirror?

CONEJO   Símon, then when Quetzalcóatl see himself in it, he got all scared. Se escamó.[40]

LIZARD   What did he see?

CONEJO   I don't know. But he ask the priests to hide him. So they give him pulque[41] and honey and got him drunk. Then they brought in a ruca for him.

LIZARD   ¡Hay te llevo! ¿Y se la dejó—?[42]

CONEJO   Símon, only he wasn' supposed to because he was a god. After that his people turned against him, so he sailed off into the sea on a raft of serpents, telling everybody he was coming back someday.

LIZARD   ¿Y qué?   Did he?

CONEJO   I don' know.

LIZARD   ¡Este vato, man! How did you learn all this shit, Funnybunny?

CONEJO   [*Shrugs*]   Maybe I'm pendejo[43] like everybody says, but I learn something from Indio. Now he's dead.

---

[40]He got scared.   [41]a type of drink   [42]That's really together! And he left her—?
[43]stupid

XIV

PRIEST   All I can do now is pray for his immortal soul that God might forgive him.

DALIA   For what?

PRIEST   Sus pecados, mujer.[44] Or do you believe he was beyond mortal sin?

GATO   Chale, man! You vatos got me up to here with Indio. If he was so smart, he wouldn't be lying over at the wake stiff like he is.

PRIEST   In the final analysis, he was just a boy. Filled with anxiety, uncertainty, fear.

GATO   All that cuacha[45] he used to say din't mean nothing.

PRIEST   He came to see me, you know, shortly after he received his draft notice.

GATO   He rapped against the war, but his time came and he had to go a huevo[46] just like everybody else.

PRIEST   He was concerned what the barrio would think if he refused induction.

GATO   If he'd gone to the pinta instead of the army, all the barrio would have said he was chicken.

PRIEST   He was considering fleeing the country, but he knew he'd never be able to return as a community leader.

GATO   Big community leader. That draft notice showed him to his face who he was, like a mirror.

PRIEST   He was caught. He'd been playing at revolución, but the draft letter snapped him back to reality. He wasn't Zapata or Ché Guevara or even Quetzalcóatl, really. He was just Indio—and as Indio, he knew he had no choice, so he went.

GATO   He tried to play the odds and make it out alive. He lost.

XV

DALIA   You're wrong, father. Indio *was* Quetzalcóatl. You just can't see it, because you're racist.

PRIEST   [*Pause*]   You hurt me deeply, Dalia. I've always loved your people. I've always felt God had a special place for them.

---

[44]His sins, women.   [45]bullshit   [46]by force

DALIA   Where, at the bottom of society?

PRIEST   This is precisely the kind of talk that turned many of your people against Indio!

DALIA   He knew that. Our people have loved your God very much. We've brought little things to him—candles, oraciones, devotions—all that we have, even our blood in penance. Or in war. We've loved him because we saw him nailed to a cross, suffering and bleeding like us. Every time we've been cheated, worked like animals, had our lands stolen—we've cried out and prayed to him to help us. ¡Jesucristo! Nothing has happened. But we still go on believing in him like faithful indios.

PRIEST   Do you still believe in him, Dalia? [*Pause*] Do you?

DALIA   I don't know. Indio was Quetzalcóatl, and—

PRIEST   Quetzalcóatl is dead! Remember your commandments? I will not have false Gods before me.

DALIA   He said he was coming back! [*She weeps.*] Indio!

PRIEST [*Embracing her*]   Padre nuestro, ayudanos a olvidar a este hombre.[47]

XVI

LIZARD   Yeah, that Indio was one vato I'll never forget.

CONEJO   A lotta Chicanos learned from him.

GATO   Who's that, you?

CONEJO   Nel, lots of raza in the barrio.

GATO   Oh, símon, I forgot. He was a Chicano leader. Shit, man! What about that last parranda[48] he took after the army call him? Cagó la estaca,[49] man! He was pedo[50] for two weeks and even showed up drunk at a picket line. Then he split with your carnala.[51] I bet your jefitos[52] aren't gonna forget Indio.

PRIEST   Is your family coming?

[DALIA *shakes her head no.*]

LIZARD [*To* CONEJO]   How does your sister feel, ese?

GATO   That depends, man. You mean how she feels or how she *feels*.

CONEJO   Oh, she's okay, except she cry a lot when Indio was killed.

GATO   Hah! Listen to this vato, man. You're pretty funny, Funnybunny?

---

[47]Our Father, help us to forget this man.   [48]drunken spree   [49]Shitted the stick
[50]drunk   [51]sister   [52]parents

CONEJO   How come?

GATO   Well, shit, you'd cry too if the vato that was doing it to you got kill.

CONEJO   Indio was't doing it to her!

GATO   He took off for a week and din't do nothing, uh? ¡Madera! He did what he wanted, then dumped her off. Ain't that right, Funnybunny?

CONEJO [*Feigning ignorance*]   What?

GATO   Did Indio pump your carnala?

CONEJO   Dalia?

GATO   I don't mean your old lady.

XVII

[MADRE *re-enters*.]

PRIEST   ¿Se siente mejor, madre?[53]

MADRE   Sí, padre, perdóneme.[54]

PRIEST   No hay que perdonar.[55]

GATO   WELL?

CONEJO   I don' know.

GATO   You're lying, cabrón.[56]

LIZARD   Aw, get off his case, man! You'd like to pump his sister yourself. I seen the way you go around sniffing up her tail like a dog.

GATO   Shut up, Lizard.

LIZARD   You got so much envidia,[57] you wish it was your wake tonight instead of Indio's.

GATO   Shut up, ese!

LIZARD   You're licking up Indio's blood.

GATO [*With sinister malevolence*]   Who's going to lick up yours, púto? You want this filero in your guts?

[*Pulls out knife;* LIZARD *does too*.]

CONEJO   Eh, man, contrólensela![58] Come on, Lizard.

LIZARD   Stay outa this, punk.

CONEJO   Gato, let's go to the wake. It's midnight already.

---

[53]Do you feel better, Mother?   [54]Yes, father, forgive me.   [55] There's nothing to forgive.
[56]bastard   [57]envy   [58]cool it

GATO   Fuck you, Funnybunny. [*To* LIZARD] Some night I'm going to slit your green belly with this.

LIZARD   ¡Pos pónle, ese![59] Órale, try it. Come on.

[*They fight.* GATO *kicks the knife out of* LIZARD'S *hand, and traps him.*]

GATO [*Pause*]   What do you say now, ese?

LIZARD   Me la pelas.[60]

[GATO *pushes* LIZARD'S *face to one side and walks off putting knife away.*]

GATO   Let's go to the fucking wake. [*Exit*]

[CONEJO *follows* GATO, *glancing back at* LIZARD, *who is still on the ground.*]

LIZARD [*Standing up, dusting off*]   Chickenshit!

[*He struts off, chuco style, after* GATO *and* CONEJO.]

XVIII

[*Prayers start at the wake.* PRIEST *kneels facing downstage and toward the women, but addressing heaven.*]

PRIEST   Now we will pray.

[*All cross themselves.*]

En nomine patri, et filio, et spiritu sanctu, amen, amen. Merciful Señor, author of infinite forgiveness, here lies the poor mortal flesh of Quetzalcóatl Gonzáles.

WOMEN [DALIA *and* MADRE]   Bless him, Señor.

PRIEST   Quetzalcóatl, your humble servant, who was named by his pagan father but who was called Indio by his Catholic madre and all who came to love him.

WOMEN   Bless him, Señor.

PRIEST   Quetzalcóatl, your humble—

[GATO, CONEJO, *and* LIZARD *walk in and stand at the door.*]

Please, come in. Pray with us.

[LIZARD *starts to go;* GATO *grabs him.* CONEJO *looks at* LIZARD *then at* DALIA *and shrugs his shoulders. As* CONEJO *tries to kneel beside his sister,* GATO *edges him to one side.* LIZARD *then crowds in next to* GATO. PRIEST *clears his throat.*]

PRIEST   Quetzalcóatl, your humble servant, who was born of the body of

[59]Well, get it on, man!   [60]You got me.

woman and died by the hand of man amid the bloody excrement of war.

WOMEN   Bless him, Señor.

PRIEST [*Whispers to vatos*]   Say "Bless him, Señor." [*Pause*] Go on, say it. The Señor is listening. [*He points heavenward.*]

[CONEJO *and* LIZARD *look up.* LIZARD *is about to laugh and nudges* CONEJO. GATO *looks at* DALIA, *whose head is bowed.*]

Come, come, say it!

VATOS [*Clumsily, overlapping one another*]   Bless him, Señor.

PRIEST   Again.

VATOS [*Still clumsily*]   Bless him, Señor.

PRIEST [*Making a face*]   Try to follow the women, please. [*Clears throat*] Quetzalcóatl, your humble servant, who knew love of God.

ALL [*Clumsily because of boys*]   Bless him, Señor.

PRIEST   Quetzalcóatl, your humble servant, who knew love of church.

ALL   Bless him, Señor.

[GATO'S *hand strokes* DALIA'S *back.*]

PRIEST   Quetzalcóatl, your humble servant, who knew love of madre.

ALL   Bless him, Señor.

PRIEST   Quetzalcóatl, your humble servant, who knew love of country.

ALL   Bless him, Señor.

[DALIA *shakes off* GATO'S *hand.* PRIEST *pauses.*]

PRIEST   Quetzalcóatl, your humble servant, who knew love of flag.

ALL   Bless him, Señor.

PRIEST   Quetzalcóatl, your humble servant, who knew love of obedience.

ALL   Bless him, Señor.

[GATO'S *hand comes up again.*]

PRIEST [*Intoning rhythmically*]   Bless him, Señor. Now he is dead. Quetzalcóatl . . .

WOMEN [*Completing chanted phrases*]   Your humble servant.

PRIEST [*Pause*]   Well, come on, boys. Where's your catechism? Quetzalcóatl . . .

VATOS [*Clumsily*]   Your humble serpent!

PRIEST   WHAT?

VATOS [*Clumsier*]   Your humble serpent!

PRIEST   Again!

VATOS [LIZARD *shouts.*]   Your humble serpent!

XIX

PRIEST [*Standing*]   Serpent! [*Sees* GATO *fooling with* DALIA] What are you doing? Have you no respect for the dead? Stop that!

GATO   Stop what?

PRIEST   Get out of here!

[GATO *and* LIZARD *laugh.*]

My child, call the police.

GATO [*Grabs* DALIA]   No, you don'!

DALIA   Let me go, Gato!

MADRE   ¡Muchachos, por Díos, mijo está muerto y tendido! ¿Cómo pueden hacer esto?[61]

GATO   AAAH, we're not doing nothing.

MADRE   ¡Padrecito, haz algo![62]

[LIZARD *pulls out a knife casually.*]

PRIEST [*Pause*]   I'm going to get help! [*Rushes out*]

LIZARD   Heh, man! [*Runs out after the* PRIEST]

DALIA   Conejo, help me!

CONEJO   Cut it out, Gato.

GATO   Later for you, punk! [*Pushes* CONEJO *away*]

DALIA [*Almost screaming*]   Let me go, let me go! [*Kicks, scratches* GATO]

GATO   Órale, esa, come off it, man! [*Shoves her aside*] What's all the pedo[63] anyway? We don't come for this! That father shouldn't have tell you to call the pigs.

DALIA   Get out of here or I will!

GATO   Órale, and what happen to all the carnalismo?[64] Din't Indio say we gotta unite against the placa?[65]

DALIA   Somebody oughta kill you!

---

[61]Children, for God's sake, my son is dead and lying still! How can you do this?   [62]Dear father, do something!   [63]ruckus   [64]brotherhood   [65]police

XX

GATO   Oh yeah, well who's going to do it? Funnybunny? How about it, Funnybunny? You going to snuff me? Or maybe it's Indio, uh? Símon, the chingón's[66] going to do it. Din't he say he was coming back? Well there he is, ese. He came back. Tell him to get up and snuff me! [*Goes to coffin, bangs on it*] Heh, Indio, it's me, man—Gato! I'm calling you out, ese! I say you're a liar! The Raza's full of shit!

MADRE   [*Bloodchilling wail*]   AYYYYYYYYYYYYYY! [*She attacks* GATO.]

[DALIA *pulls her away.*]

GATO [*Startled*]   Heh, man, cut that out! [*He backs off.*]

MADRE   ¿Señor, Señor, cómo puedes permitir ésto, Díos mío?[67] [*She drops to her knees in front of the coffin. Her voice is a despairing whisper.*] ¡Mijo está muerto y estos canallas siguen viviendo![68]

GATO   Aah, what are you talking, señora? How do you know Indio's in there anyway? You see him? The gavachos send you a stinking coffin; that don't mean Indio's in it.

LIZARD [*Runs in wearing* PRIEST's *cassock*]   Heh, look what I got! Now I'm a priest like I always want to do it. [*Laughs, blesses* CONEJO]

CONEJO   Where's the father?

LIZARD   Running down the street in his shorts. [*He glances at* DALIA *and* MADRE.] Órale, what are they doing?

XXI

[*They turn toward* DALIA *and the* MADRE. *Blood is dripping from flag and coffin again.* CONEJO *goes over to them. The* MADRE *has blood on her hands and is moaning almost inaudibly.*]

CONEJO   ¡Hijo de la chi—![69] Heh, ese, this thing's dripping blood!

LIZARD   Blood!

GATO   You're full of it, Funnybunny.

[LIZARD *and* GATO *see for themselves.*]

LIZARD   It's coming from the flag!

CONEJO   Chale, it's from the box. Watcha! Let's get out of here, man!

---

[66]big shot's   [67]God, God, how can you permit this, my God?   [68]My son is dead and these cowards continue to live!   [69]Son of a bitch!

GATO   Let's open it.

LIZARD   Open what?

GATO   The coffin, pendejo.[70]

LIZARD   'Tás lucas.[71]

GATO   Funnybunny?

CONEJO   Screw you, man, I ain't gonna do nothing.

GATO [*To* LIZARD]   How about it, ese, you chicken to do it?

LIZARD   Nel, but you're crazy. This thing's welded together, man!

GATO   Let's see. [*He pulls off the flag and unsnaps the locks: the coffin snaps open with a thud. The lid is ready to be lifted.*] Okay, which of you vatos is going to help me open it?

XXII

CONEJO   You really going to do it?

GATO   What's it look like, punk? Now come and help me.

DALIA   Don't do it, Conejo! [*She rushes to him.*]

CONEJO   I'm not doing nothing.

GATO   Well, Lizard, what you going to do, vato? It's all set. What's the matter? I cut off your machos[72] back on the street? Come on, ese—it's your big leader waiting for you in there. He promise to come back, din't he? Go look at him!

LIZARD   You go look at him.

GATO   Chale, that's too easy. I'll do it, if you do it.

DALIA [*Glancing toward the coffin*]   ¡Doña Rosa!

XXIII

[*The* MADRE *is at the coffin.* DALIA *rushes to her, then* CONEJO, *then* LIZARD. GATO *stays behind. The others are too late.* MADRE *lifts the lid. Everyone gasps, expecting the worst.*]

CONEJO   It's . . . feathers!

[LIZARD *reaches in and pulls out a brilliant headdress of green feathers and a cloak of Aztec design.*]

---

[70]stupid   [71]You're crazy.   [72]manhood

LIZARD   Man, this is better than this priest thing! [*He puts the cloak and headdress on.*] How do I look, ese?

GATO [*At loss for what to say*]   See? I tell you it wasn't Indio.

[*Drums begin to beat immediately, low and somber and increasingly loud.*]

LIZARD   What's that?

GATO   Sounds like drums.

[*The* MADRE *has found something else in the coffin. She cries with horror. Everyone turns to her.*]

GATO   What?

LIZARD   Something else in there?

[*They approach the coffin and look in.* LIZARD, *in his headdress, is at the center of the group. He reaches in and pulls out something, turning around and holding it up before him. Lights dim.*]

LIZARD [*Screams*]   Indio's heart!

[*The heart gives out light in the descending darkness.*]

[*Curtain*]

PART *II*

MY HOUSE

The selections in Part II, My House, illustrate the Chicano's *search for self-definition, for a definition of his community experience and of his culture, and for an identity. The best of the early literature of most American ethnic groups has frequently been heavily autobiographical, and* Chicano *literature is no exception. The writers of this part look either inward, at their immediate surroundings, or at their collective past in the United States, and out of this material they create a group identity.*

Where the writers of this part explore the past to find heroes, what emerges is not so much the hero who will give them courage for the revolution, but rather a hero such as Valentín Mansera (see "I Love Singing to the Wind"), who is comparable to Anglo heroes such as Billy the Kid and helps to comprise a lore for Chicanos *analogous to Anglo Western lore. But most frequently, the writers of this part are concerned with the immediacy of the* Chicano *experience—with what it means to live* Chicano *in the United States, now. And out of this concern come new voices in literature.*

As these selections illustrate, what it means to live Chicano *at this time in history is to have an intimate knowledge of the* barrio *(see "Los Angeles," "Hickscamp," and "Sparkling Alleys"), which is a source of both strength and weakness, both a home and a prison; it is to have an intimate knowledge of the earth which should put one in touch with miracles (see "I Have Seen"),*

99

but now only puts one in touch with poverty and weariness (see "Grapefields as a Child" and "In a Farmhouse"). This Chicano identity is defined by each brush with the Anglo, which serves to intensify a sense of separateness and bitterness as well as Chicano unity (see "Roberto en Kindergarten" and the excerpt from Vásquez' Chicano). It is defined by the struggle against the shame which is treacherously implanted in the Chicano child (see "Cecilia Rosas" and the excerpt from Villarreal's Pocho) and by a victory over that shame.

The Chicanos in this part are thus often seen in a fighting stance, but they are also seen in quieter, gentler moods (see "When I'm with You" and "Interlude"), and strength is often derived not from challenge and battle, but from love and endurance (see "Esperanza," "My Grandmother Would Rock Quietly and Hum," and "To an Old Woman"). Similarly, the poetry and fiction in My House depict the spectrum of the community—the child in innocence and in terrible knowledge, the young man defeated and in prison or battling in "freedom" to make a place for himself, the old woman as rock and nurturer or as a sad, mortal figure. And out of this spectrum of mood and character and situation comes a cohesive picture of the Chicano experience and of Chicanismo.

Introduction

MARIO SUAREZ

El Hoyo

From the center of downtown Tucson the ground slopes gently away to Main Street, drops a few feet, and then rolls to the banks of the Santa Cruz River. Here lies the section of the city known as El Hoyo. Why it is called El Hoyo is not very clear. In no sense is it a hole as its name would imply; it is simply the river's immediate valley. Its inhabitants are chicanos who raise hell on Saturday night and listen to Padre Estanislao on Sunday morning. While the term chicano is the short way of saying Mexicano, it is not restricted to the paisanos who came from old Mexico with the territory or the last famine to work for the railroad, labor, sing, and go on relief. Chicano is the easy way of referring to everybody. Pablo Gutierrez married the Chinese grocer's daughter and now runs a meat department; his sons are chicanos. So are the sons of Killer Jones who threw a fight in Harlem and fled to El Hoyo to marry Cristina Mendez. And so are all of them. However, it is doubtful that all these spiritual sons of Mexico live in El Hoyo because they love each other—many fight and bicker constantly. It is doubtful they live in El Hoyo because of its scenic beauty—it is everything but beautiful. Its houses are simple affairs of unplastered adobe, wood, and abandoned car parts. Its narrow streets are mostly clearings which have, in time, acquired names. Except for some tall trees which nobody has ever cared to identify, nurse, or destroy, the main things known to grow in the general area are weeds, garbage piles, dark-eyed chavalos, and dogs. And it is doubtful that the chicanos live in El Hoyo because it is safe—many times the Santa Cruz has risen and inundated the area.

In other respects living in El Hoyo has its advantages. If one is born with weakness for acquiring bills, El Hoyo is where the collectors are less likely to find you. If one has acquired the habit of listening to Octavio Perea's Mexican Hour in the wee hours of the morning with the radio on at full blast, El Hoyo is where you are less likely to be reported to the authorities. Besides, Perea is very popular and sooner or later to everyone "Smoke In The Eyes" is dedicated between the pinto beans and white flour commercials. If one, for any reason whatever, comes on an extended period of hard times,

Reprinted by permission from *Arizona Quarterly* (Vol. III, No. 2, Summer 1947), University of Arizona, Tucson, Arizona 85721. Revised by the author.

where, if not in El Hoyo are the neighbors more willing to offer solace? When Teofila Malacara's house burned to the ground with all her belongings and two children, a benevolent gentleman carried through the gesture that made tolerable her burden. He made a list of five hundred names and solicited from each a dollar. At the end of a month he turned over to the tearful but grateful señora one hundred dollars in cold cash and then accompanied her on a short vacation. When the new manager of a local store decided that no more chicanas were to work behind the counters, it was the chicanos of El Hoyo who, on taking their individually small but collectively great buying power elsewhere, drove the manager out and the girls returned to their jobs. When the Mexican Army was en route to Baja California and the chicanos found out that the enlisted men ate only at infrequent intervals, it was El Hoyo's chicanos who crusaded across town with pots of beans and trays of tortillas to meet the train. When someone gets married, celebrating is not restricted to the immediate friends of the couple. Everybody is invited. Anything calls for a celebration and a celebration calls for anything. On Memorial Day there are no less than half a dozen good fights at the Riverside Dance Hall. On Mexican Independence Day more than one flag is sworn allegiance to amid cheers for the queen.

And El Hoyo is something more. It is this something more which brought Felipe Sanchez back from the wars after having killed a score of Vietnamese with his body resembling a patch-work quilt to marry Julia Armijo. It brought Joe Zepeda, a gunner, . . . back to compose boleros. He has a metal plate for a skull. Perhaps El Hoyo is proof that those people exist, and perhaps exist best, who have as yet failed to observe the more popular modes of human conduct. Perhaps the humble appearance of El Hoyo justifies the indifferent shrug of those made aware of its existence. Perhaps El Hoyo's simplicity motivates an occasional chicano to move away from its narrow streets, babbling comadres and shrieking children to deny the bloodwell from which he springs and to claim the blood of a conquistador while his hair is straight and his face beardless. Yet El Hoyo is not an outpost of a few families against the world. It fights for no causes except those which soothe its immediate angers. It laughs and cries with the same amount of passion in times of plenty and of want.

Perhaps El Hoyo, its inhabitants, and its essence can best be explained by telling a bit about a dish called capirotada. Its origin is uncertain. But, according to the time and the circumstance, it is made of old, new or hard bread. It is softened with water and then cooked with peanuts, raisins, onions, cheese, and panocha. It is fired with sherry wine. Then it is served hot, cold, or just "on the weather" as they say in El Hoyo. The Sermeños like it one way, the Garcias another, and the Ortegas still another. While it might differ greatly from one home to another, nevertheless it is still capirotada. And so it is with El Hoyo's chicanos. While being divided from within and from without, like the capirotada, they remain chicanos.

Poetry

BEN LUNA

I Love Singing to the Wind

Suggested by the Mexican ballad "Feria de las Flores"

The bandit Valentín Mansera sings
as he rides along to a country fair.

I love singing to the wind
The wind that scatters my songs
Telling that which I feel
Wherever my songs may roam

I have come across the mountains
To this festival of flowers
I have ridden from afar
I have come to see the flowers

I have come to see the flowers
That are my heart's desires

As I journey across the mountains
The mountains open before me
There's no mountain that can bar
Nor steed that can throw me

I have traveled from afar
Just to come and see the roses
I search for a sullen Rose
That is my heart's desire.

If I find her I will pick her
And take her home to my garden
If someone plucks her before me
She is mine and I will claim her!
If she has another gardener
The pistol at my side will tame him!

I have come to see the flowers
That are my heart's desire.

Los Angeles

A bit of sprawling madness
A bush-land Babylon
A den of thieves . . . once?
                    Still.

The summer nights
            Are pleasant there
On Hammel Street
            Where I was born.
The people dream in Spanish
And live as best they can.

I Have Seen

I have seen corn
I am a Mexican
Maize from Zoogacho
Grained by kneeling women
I was amazed
By what I saw
Brown hands
Brown hands
Graining yellow corn
On black stone

BENJAMIN DURAZO

Grapefields as a Child

Great clouds wired to the ground
            confer and tremble
when a boy, loaded with water, passes
pulling his feet quickly from the smoldering earth.
His family has sent him, the youngest,
        for the gallon jugs, that were of wine,
            now covered with soaked burlap.

The brown skin blotches with the dust
that is everywhere
His father, who is grey, has spotted him but keeps working.
And there are people now, everywhere,
bobbing in and out of the leaves
eating from the clouds
that tug at the ground.

LEONARD ADAMÉ

Esperanza

Friday morning
brothers awake
clothes ironed
tomato-stained
hands making lunch
brushing your hair
you remember the
five and ten dress

Late sun
in the fields
warm tacos
cold sodas
you think
of pay checks
and receptions
The Odd Fellows Hall
(an uncle
passing out in the toilet,
a five-year-old pissing on him)
and tonight's dance there.

Six o'clock
and long day's over
laughing with friends
father comes
your eyes
suddenly tire

he's drunk
your check
sticking out
of his pocket
he says
your mother
needs help
let's go

Half-asleep
on your cot
your brother
rubs his eyes
shakes you gently
and asks
can he work
tomorrow
to help you
buy your dress
and maybe
a hamburger
and a
milkshake too.

The White Theater

Drinking Brewers Best
in the '47 Plymouth
        the ashes of our cigarettes
            fell as easily as the crumbling
                walls of the White Theater

Where once the nudies on
the posters screamed
in our heads and the
        usher's pimpled smirk
            bored through the backs
                of our heads like
                    a weasel through chicken dung.

Parking a block away,
holding back the urge
to piss as we shivered
in the warm night air,
    we talked knowingly of
        the many girls we'd never had
        and believed ourselves
            like runny-nosed kids on
                the lap of J. C. Penney's Santa Claus.

In the half-empty balcony
we forgot each other,
our eyes drawn to
    the different shades
        of pubic hair
            like water into dry sand.

And afterwards, on the
bathroom toilet, I thought
    of the nameless vaginas,
        relief spreading on my face.

Roberto en Kindergarten

    They say you do not understand
that you are quiet.
    They do not hear
        your mother at 5:00 in the morning
            hum the warm song of flour tortillas,
    or the grinding starter motor
    of the '42 Ford pick-up
        in whose bed you've slept.

    Through the morning fog, never losing your way,
only to stumble in the strange light.
    After hundreds of trays,
        nickels and empty Coca-Cola bottles
            counted, you've fallen behind,
    never having seen,
        in a thousand acres of vines,
            picket fences or elm trees.

```
            In our tongue
      you knew you were apart
         and your eyes burned
               through me in asking
                  why . . .
      and mine through you
               while I held your hand
                  and ran.
```

My Grandmother
Would Rock Quietly and Hum

```
    in her house
    she would rock quietly and hum
    until her swelled hands
    calmed

    in summer
    she wore thick stockings
    sweaters
    and grey braids

    (when "el cheque" came
    we went to Payless
    and I laughed greedily
    when given a quarter)

    mornings,
    sunlight barely lit
    the kitchen
    and where
    there were shadows
    it was not cold
```

she quietly rolled
flour tortillas—
the "papas"
cracking in hot lard
would wake me

she had lost her teeth
and when we ate
she had bread
soaked in "café"

always her eyes
were clear
and she could see
as I cannot yet see—
through her eyes
she gave me herself

she would sit
and talk
of her girlhood—
of things strange to me.
    México
    epidemics
    relatives shot
    her father's hopes
    of this country—
how they sank
with cement dust
to his insides

now
when I go
to the old house
the worn spots
by the stove
echo of her shuffling
and
México
still hangs in her
fading
calendar pictures

ENRIQUE RODRÍQUEZ

Hickscamp

My barrio hickscamp
 Small and almost square.
Encircled by a field,
 Railroad tracks, a river,
And one paved street.
 Be careful, wino.
Don't fall into a puddle
 After a rain.
Watch out for the holes
 in the street.
A carro might come
 And run you over.
Go stand by the fire
 With your wino camaradas.
Hurry, it's getting dark.
 Go before kids come out
To play and call you names.
 If you see my father,
Tell him Mom said to save
 six dollars for this month's rent.
This was my world,
My barrio hickscamp.

Ode to My Cane

he pounded you
to show his strength
handed back two pieces
said Goddam it Bob

how bad is it
can I fix you
it's raining tonight
sidewalk outside is slick

we walk together
I'm used to you
carried you a long time
or maybe
you me

now on smelly wet bar
next to my beer
head and body
broken at the neck
Indian face on painted bottom
seems sad and the snake looks dead

amigo cane ahora que
you're my third leg
to help the other weak two
I'm heavy
my belly is big and round
just like that keg

hope I can fix you
with glue and tape
doctors say I'll need you
as they put it
no telling how long

JOSÉ RENDÓN

I Walk on Treetops and Water

I walk on treetops and water
You can't see me

I don't care

I have talked with Ophelia
and Sancho Panza
You haven't even seen your tongue

I have made love to clouds
while
you talk of ionosphere and
barometric pressure

I have talked with Jesus
brother to the earth

I have written dictionaries
of nerves
painted bundles of hemorrhages

I have flown on a mattress
so beautiful
that only a child could see
and a day could hear

What have you to offer?

Home

Night has come through sad eyes
and my mother's broken feet
on the bed
Tío Joe
drowns in his puke

My jefe has a new car
the tires won't roll
but we still make the payments

this city is new again
fresh blood
in all the fountains
I
with the nose of an old man
seek my life
between
the legs of a saint
in missionary apartments
of the dead

Sparkling Alleys

Sparkling alleys have long
            been my school
    here my blood-red
        puffed eyes
have seen the wonders
        of the inside
        of heads
opened with meat cleavers
            and
            garages
    giving comfort to
            fat smelly women
        with 12 men
        here the power of government
            is felt
            coming from both sides
                with piercing lights
                    and leather-covered
                        pieces of steel
            and here also
                our
            identity crisis
            is solved

RICARDO JUAN DURÁN

In My Cell

In my cell,
8 bars, grey and heavy, oppress the blue bright sky.
Smeared fat with lead enamel
and the frustrations of a thousand sweaty hands
they kill the bright blue sky outside.
Out! Out! I cry.
To walk on a hill of wind . . .
To lie in the tall grass and look up at an endless sky.
8 bars
as heavy as any storm
encarcerate my soul.

Everything in this world is behind these 8 bars.
My hands grab them and pull them.
I can feel the fat wall of concrete that anchors them.
Against the sky so clear
a small bird flies near.
My whole body pulls and pulls
until it aches . . .
until it cries . . .

When I'm with You

Querida,[1]
It's like a dream when I'm with you.
A spiraling dream.
We go spinning,
hand in hand,
dizzying ourselves in each other.

When I'm with you,
the whole world is you.
I can't think when I'm with you,
I can't hear!
My eyes are your eyes,
they lose themselves in yours.
The rest of the world floats around us
like an illusion,
always on the periphery,
and when it closes in on me—
I burst into your eyes
hypnotized . . .

A train goes by the rose bush
and I don't hear it.

[1] Lover

RAFAEL JESÚS GONZÁLEZ

To an Old Woman

Come, mother—
   Your rebozo trails a black web
   And your hem catches on your heels.
You lean the burden of your years
On shaky cane, and palsied hand pushes
   Sweat-grimed pennies on the counter.
Can you still see, old woman,
The darting color-trailed needle of your trade?
   The flower you embroider
   With three-for-a-dime threads
Cannot fade as quickly as the leaves of time.

   What things do you remember?
Your mouth seems to be forever tasting
The residue of nectar-hearted years.
Where are the sons you bore?
   Do they speak only English now
   And pass for Spaniards?
Did California lure them
To forget the name of *madre*?
   One day I know you will not come
   And ask for me to pick
   The colors you can no longer see.
I know I'll wait in vain
   For your toothless benediction.
I'll look into the dusty street
Made cool by pigeons' wings
Until a dirty child will nudge me and say:
   "Señor, how much ees thees?"

LUIS OMAR SALINAS

In a Farmhouse

Fifteen miles
out of Robstown
with the Texas sun
fading in the distance
I sit in the bedroom
profoundly,
animated by the day's work
in the cottonfields.

I made two dollars and
thirty cents today
I am eight years old
and I wonder
how the rest of the Mestizos
do not go hungry
and if one were to die
of hunger
what an odd way
to leave for heaven.

From Prison

Mother:
        Please send me a package
of dexadrines
        and a pan to boil
my eggs in
        . . . oh yes also a coat
it's a bit drafty in here.

Jazz through an Open Window

For Carlota

With hate
in the
back room,
children
avoid
silence.

Mestizo
jazz
through
the open window,
cognac and death
. . . a soft woman
blushes
on the street.

Horses pulled
by the wind
display
nobility.

There is noise in
an upper bungalow
in crisis
cheerful
happy bulls
a dancer's night
the plight
of the world
in a song

Walk with me Señorita
I too have
tears in my eyes.

Jazz por una Ventana Abierta

Para Carlota

Con odio
en el cuarto
de atrás,
niños se esconden
del silencio.

Jazz Mestizo
por la ventana
abierta,
cognác . . . y la
muerte
de golondrinas
. . . una mujer
en la calle
se ruboriza.

Ven los caballos
lo agrio del sol
nobles
llenos de amor.

Hay ruido en el cuarto
de arriba
en crisis
alegres toros
es la noche
de la bailarina
el dolor del mundo
en una canción.

Anda conmigo chica
yo también
tengo lágrimas
en los ojos.

Interlude

To an Unknown Maya

Ishlatiya
is it raining
where you are?

Open up, drink.
The donkey's mother
is sleeping.

Ishlatiya
I need you,
Ishlatiya . . .

Canto

A una Maya

Ishlatiya
está lloviendo
¿dónde estás?

Abrete, toma
bebe.
La madre del burro
está durmiendo.

Ishlatiya
te necesito,
Ishlatiya . . .

Fiction

RICHARD VÁSQUEZ

From Chicano

Dear Mr. Sandoval:

It has been several weeks now that Sammy has been in this class and he has shown no inclination to overcome his weaknesses. He is weak in Spelling, Arithmetic and Reading in particular. You must at once help him to catch up to the other students in the class if he is to remain with us.

Miss A. Clark

Minnie read the note and handed it to Pete. They had just finished dinner and Mariana and Sammy were in the living room watching television. Pete called Sammy in.

"Hijo! How come we got a note saying you don't do your school work?"

Sammy shrugged. "It's too hard."

"Too hard? The other kids are doing it, aren't they?"

"Yeah, but . . . I just don't understand it."

"Why not?"

"I just don't know how."

"Okay. Bring me your arithmetic. I'll show you."

Sammy brought his work and laid it on the table. Pete looked it over. "What's this little thing here mean?"

Sammy smiled a little. "That means to divide this number by that number there."

Pete studied the page more. "And this, that little 'X' means that number has to be *times* that one, right?"

"Sí."

"Okay, so what's so hard about that? Let's see you do that now."

"But, papá. I just don't know the times table and the division things. I can't."

"Okay, then, call Mariana. Mariana!"

"Manda, papá," she called.

"Come here to help Sammy with his arithmetic. You can do this stuff easy, can't you?"

Mariana came in. "Sí, papá. But he won't let me help him."

Pete looked at Sammy. "What's this you won't let her help you?"

He was sullen. "I don't want her to teach me."

"That's silly. I never heard of anything like that. Now you let her help you or you'll be sorry. Andale. Now beat it."

The next day the teacher called to him from her desk.

"You turned in a very nice paper, Sammy. You learned quickly, didn't you?"

Sammy nodded.

"Look, class," Miss Clark said, holding the paper aloft. "Sammy did all his work correctly. I'm very impressed. Now Sammy, go to the blackboard and take the chalk."

Sammy was looking directly at her. He didn't move at first. "Come on, Sammy. Go to the board. I'll give you a problem to work."

Sammy went to the board and took the chalk. "Now write these numbers . . ."

He wrote the problem and then stood, back to the class, hands at his sides. And as first the coaxing came, then the demanding, then the ridicule, he stood still, unflinching, until finally he heard, ". . . now take your seat and don't ever try cheating again. It doesn't pay. In this school we don't cheat. You've got to learn to own up to it."

He took his seat near the rear of the class and kept his eyes on the desk.

At recess time he waited to be chosen on one side for a game. When all were chosen but him he quickly set about doing something else. He felt before that he was being left out, now he was sure of it. When school first started he was chosen as much as anybody else, but now it was changing. He decided one of the big differences between this school and the one in Los Angeles was that over there when the teacher got after you, you had buddies. All the other guys she got after met with you at recess and made you feel better. But here it wasn't the case. In Los Angeles the guys who wanted to do everything the teacher said were considered sissies, goody-goody boys. The guy who got left out and bullied the most by the other guys was the best student, always.

He liked the other school better.

A week later his class was reading aloud in turn. He had only been called upon to read once or twice before, and he had stumbled through, self-consciously, knowing he was the only one who talked with an accent. But he tried to read along when others read aloud and was learning to recognize more and more words. This story was about some children watching a repair crew working on the street. "All right, Sammy, your turn," Miss Clark called out.

"The foreman walked to the . . ." he fumbled.

"Excavation," the teacher put in. Sammy skipped it.

". . . and took a . . ." he knew the word wouldn't fit his tongue, "cha-bull." A titter went through the class.

"That word is 'shovel,' Sammy," the teacher said with an air of tolerance. Sammy started on.

"He looked at the . . ." But the teacher cut in.

"Say 'shovel.' I want you to pronounce it."

Sammy hesitated and a little silence developed. "Go on, say it," the teacher coaxed. Sammy twisted his tongue, but the vowels and consonants were too alien to him.

"Chabull," he said again. This time the class, thinking the teacher critical of Sammy, snickered louder.

"Sammy," the teacher said in a tone implying extreme patience, "you must learn to say these words if you want to stay in this grade level. Now say 'sh-sho-vel.' " Sammy retreated. His face went expressionless and he dropped his eyes, aware that every eye in the class was on him. What had she meant by saying if he wanted to stay in this grade level? Was she considering setting him back? With that thought drenching his consciousness he tried to read aloud with a corner of his awareness. Desperately, he tried to put his tongue and lip muscles into the attitude which allowed those words to come out sounding like the white guys' talk. He saw the word "pick" rushing toward him in the sentence he was reading. He knew words containing the vowel as in "pick" were the ones most often seized upon by those who lampooned the Mexican. "Pee-eck," they always said, making their voices drop a little for the last half of the word. Sammy read the word, straining to avoid his natural pronunciation. It came out "peck." Again the teacher stopped him.

"Say 'pick,' Sammy." Sammy was silent, eyes on the book.

"You've got to at least try," the teacher said in a demanding tone. Sammy remained silent. "Now listen," she said, "one of the things you've got to learn is that when we say something, we mean it."

Sammy raised his eyes to her. He understood what she said, although she herself didn't. He knew when she said "we" she meant all the others, the Anglos, the "Americans," and when she said "you" she meant "you people." This was as far as he could reason it out. He could never have put it in words, English or Spanish. He remained silent and the teacher allowed a long silence to develop. "Say the word 'pick,' Sammy," she said sternly. Sammy glanced at the nearby door to the hall. That was the only escape. To run. Solve the problem immediately, for now. Never mind that tomorrow must be dealt with. The teacher, seeing that Sammy might bolt, quickly moved so that she was between him and the door. Feeling trapped, Sammy made a rush to get by her. Miss Clark seized him by the arms and they struggled, Sammy breaking into great uncontrollable sobs. The class was fascinated, motionless.

"Sammy, stop it! Sit down," Miss Clark demanded. By her superior physical strength she managed to force him back into his seat. Still holding his hands, she turned to the boy behind. "Go get Mr. Scott," she ordered. The boy scurried out to the principal's office. In a few moments he returned with the worried-looking principal. Miss Clark was still holding Sammy.

"What's the trouble?" he asked, laying a hand heavily on Sammy's shoulder. In the presence of his greater strength Sammy quit struggling, gave up, sat shuddering, eyes down.

"He refuses to read," Miss Clark reported. "He tried to run away. I don't know what to do with him." The principal looked around at the other children, most of whom sat, mouths agape, watching.

"All right," he said soothingly, "I'll talk to him in my office." He took Sammy firmly by the arm and led him to the door. "Come to my office as soon as the bell rings," he said to Miss Clark.

Walking down the hall, Sammy could feel Mr. Scott's fingers dig into his arm. "You're hurting me," he said in a tiny voice.

"Will you not try to run away if I let you go?" Mr. Scott asked. Sammy nodded. Deep within his chest was a terrible spasmodic jerking. He proceeded down the hall one step in front of Mr. Scott, half-expecting at any moment to be cuffed. But the blow never fell. Mr. Scott's long arm reached in front and took the door knob as they reached the office. Sammy felt he was being herded.

"Sit down, Sammy," Mr. Scott ordered. Sammy took a seat on a couch across from Mr. Scott's desk. His breath was still jerking. Mr. Scott sat down at his desk and looked severely at Sammy. "Now," he said, "tell me what the trouble is." Sammy sat, hands in his lap, eyes down. He shrugged. "Are you unhappy in Miss Clark's class?" Sammy shrugged again, remaining silent. "Very well, then we'll wait 'til Miss Clark gets here."

The boy sat still, listening, while Mr. Scott started going through some papers and books. Sammy could hear the great clock on the wall click twice every minute or so. The school seemed strangely silent. He kept his eyes down. Presently the bell sounded announcing the end of class. For perhaps a half minute the school remained silent, and then sounds began. Just faraway noises at first, doors opening, feet scuffing. Then the sounds of children's voices began rising, a high-pitched chorus of unintelligible syllables. As the halls filled, the sound grew, louder yet muffled. Sammy imagined all the students were discussing his plight. The door opened and Miss Clark entered.

"He just refused to cooperate," she said to Mr. Scott. "It was reading time and he just took it upon himself to be above the others, I guess." She looked at Sammy accusingly. Mr. Scott was also looking at him. Sammy sensed Miss Clark's defensiveness. It puzzled him a little. He had always regarded the school staff as being in unison, collectively united. Now Miss Clark was afraid of Mr. Scott.

"How long has he been acting up?" Mr. Scott asked.

Miss Clark hesitated before answering. "Actually, today was the first time I became aware he was a problem reader. But he's completely unwilling to try. I tried to get him to make an attempt, but he just wanted to walk out of class." They were both looking at him. For a moment Sammy looked up at them, a pleading expression on his face. He wanted desperately to say something, but he knew the words would have a thick accent. He remained silent.

"What do you suggest?" Mr. Scott asked.

"I think, for his own benefit as well as that of the rest of the students, he should go back to third grade and learn the fundamentals of reading a little better."

Mr. Scott regarded Sammy a few moments. "You hear that, Sammy? Miss Clark thinks you ought to be set back a grade. What do you think?"

Sammy thought. Above all, he didn't want to go back into her class again. He nodded.

"All right, Sammy," Mr. Scott said with finality. "But I do want to talk to your parents about it first. I'll give you a note to take home." He wrote a note to Pete and Minnie, and although it was only afternoon recess, he allowed Sammy to go home, knowing it would quite possibly save him embarrassment and perhaps ridicule from the other boys in his class.

That night, after Minnie had read the letter to Pete as he sat soaking up the remaining chili on his plate with a piece of tortilla, Pete grunted.

"Why does he want to see us?"

"I guess like the letter says, to talk about Sammy."

"Doesn't Meester Scott know it's a working day? I can't take off. We got a big pour coming."

"Okay, Pete, okay," Minnie said before he could work himself into a pretended small rage. "I'll go see him. I can handle it."

Pete raised his voice so that Sammy could hear in the next room. "Oye, mijito! Ven aquí." Sammy came in. "Why are you giving trouble to your teacher? Don't you know no better?"

Sammy knew his father's gruffness, when he was stern, was all put on. It was an effort for Pete not to sound like the loving father all the time. Sammy smiled. He had no fear of his father.

"She wanted me to say some words I couldn't."

"What words?"

". . . Pala. Pico. In English."

"Those are easy words. Chawbool and peck. Why didn't you say them?" Sammy shrugged. Pete went on: "Now your mother has to go to school to talk to the principal. Please don't make any more trouble." And he turned to the TV set.

Mr. Scott and Miss Clark appraised Minnie severely when she entered the principal's office the next day leading Sammy. She wore a black taffeta dress with frills and lace, a black bead hat with a heavy veil over her face and white gloves with glass beads. Scott and Miss Clark noticed she was a remarkably attractive woman in spite of the heavy lipstick and volumes of eyeshade and rouge she wore.

"Mrs. Sandoval. Glad you could come. Have you met Miss Clark?" Scott eyed her as he talked. Minnie stepped to Miss Clark and boldly held out her hand, smiling. The scent of her perfume quickly filled the entire room.

"Pleased to meet you," Miss Clark smiled sweetly.

"The same here," Minnie said. She sat down, Sammy beside her.

"Mr. Sandoval was unable to come, I suppose," Mr. Scott said.

"Yes," Minnie answered, "he has to work every day. But he takes his truck. I have the Cadillac." Sammy glanced up and saw Mr. Scott and Miss Clark exchange glances. It troubled him a little that instead of a swell of pride at his mother's mention of the Cadillac, he felt a little ashamed.

"I see," Mr. Scott went on. "As the note said, Sammy seems to be having a little trouble reading at fourth-grade level. Did he tell you about it?"

"No," Minnie said. "I just got the note. But he's always been a fair reader before. We all are. He got some A's in the school in East Los Angeles. His sister—do you know Mariana?—she reads real good."

"You see, Mrs. Sandoval," Miss Clark put in, "we want Sammy to . . ." she chose her words carefully, as though she were trying hard to say it as simply as possible, "be as good a reader as possible. It seems he doesn't grasp the fundamentals . . . the first things he should know about reading. We think perhaps if he continues at this level it would hurt his chances of developing into a fine reader. Perhaps he should go back to some easier reading for a while."

"Okay," Minnie said agreeably. "You want him to start reading easier books?"

Mr. Scott spoke up. "Yes . . . that's it in a way. Miss Clark feels that if we put Sammy back into third grade he would quickly grasp what he lacks."

Minnie looked a little shocked. But she knew she was helpless. She looked down tenderly at her son. Sammy sat still, eyes still down. Once he looked up at her, pleading. She said to him gently, "¿Entiendes tú?"

"Yes, I understand," he answered her in Spanish. "But she just wanted me to say words I couldn't pronounce." They talked at some length in Spanish, much to the annoyance of Mr. Scott and Miss Clark, who were quite sure Sammy was berating them in their presence. Mr. Scott wanted to say, "What are you saying?" But he didn't have the courage. Soon the conversation between Minnie and Sammy ended and Minnie turned to the teacher and the principal.

"He says he will do what you tell him and he will try harder to please you," she said.

Sammy was set back from fourth to third grade. His new teacher was Mrs. Sanford. She listened with practiced patience as Miss Clark explained Sammy's problem and the subsequent official action.

"Take a seat, Sammy," she said in her gentle voice. "As soon as I give the class some assignment I'll have someone show you to the school library. There you can pick out any special books you want to take home tonight."

Sammy felt all eyes on him as he took an empty desk. Mrs. Sanford passed out material and gave instructions to the others.

"Now. Who will show Sammy to the library?" she asked. The children looked a little puzzled. "Who's Sammy?" someone asked. Mrs. Sanford pointed. "The . . . Spanish boy," she said with some difficulty. Sammy felt his face flush. One youngster held up his hand.

"All right, Charles," Mrs. Sanford said. "Take him to the library. Then come right back. Understand?"

Charles took Sammy to the librarian. "This is Sammy, he's supposed to pick some special books to read," Charles recited. Then he added, "He's a Spanish boy." Sammy looked at him, then up at the librarian.

"I am not," he said.

The librarian dismissed Charles with a wave of the hand. "Oh? You're not? I know your sister. I thought you children came from a fine Spanish family."

"We're Mexican," Sammy said almost belligerently.

The librarian winced a little at the word. She groped for the right thing to say. "Well, around here we'll just use the word 'Spanish.' It sounds . . ." she fumbled, trapped, "more . . . accurate."

She showed Sammy where the simpler books were, encouraging him to choose whichever he wanted, yet selecting some which she thought he should read.

Sammy looked over the books. It showed children, about his age, but they didn't look anything like him. They were all light-complexioned. He thumbed through a particular book, noticing all parents represented were nearly identical. They had typical Anglo features. The fathers all wore suits to work and the mothers all were slim and beautiful. He didn't recall seeing any books like these in East Los Angeles. He read carefully, but spent equal time studying the pictures of the family in the book. He saw them getting into their car for an outing. He saw and read how they sat at the dinner table, how they reacted to the visit of the grandparents. It made him somewhat uneasy that he could find nothing to indicate everything wasn't perfect for the family in the book.

"Find something you like?" The librarian surprised him. He nodded. "That's a good series," she told him. "Why don't you take a few of those with you? It's a whole series of books about a lovely family. You have very good taste, to pick out that book, Sammy."

She gave him three books on the family and he returned to his class. Mrs. Sanford smiled when he showed her the books. She explained to him that he didn't have to join in any of the class activities until he felt comfortable. She didn't want him to feel any pressure whatever. "Just spend your time improving yourself until you feel just like you're one of us," she told him.

Within a week Sammy had read the series on the Carter family. He found the world in the book completely foreign to him, and he wondered if the Anglos all secretly tried to be just like the family in the book. He tried other books, but found nothing he could get interested in. The books on adventure, the books on life in general all required a field of common understanding he did not have. Something, he knew, was amiss.

Mariana, in her advanced fourth-grade class, got out of school a half hour later than he did, and that half hour of waiting each day became an ordeal, as his former classmates began tormenting him. He didn't realize that what brought on the teasing and harassing was mostly his timidity and shyness. Soon it became a game for the other boys to trap him, corner him, jerk his books away. "Aw, we read those years ago," they would scoff, throwing the books on the ground. And Mariana would rescue him simply by her presence. They always quit teasing when she came. It really wasn't that important. To them.

One day during one of his free periods in the library at school he happened to pick up a first reader about a Utopian society comprised of small, benevolent, talking animals.

He read about Brer Rabbit living in the briar patch. Brer Rabbit wore only coveralls, no shoes, went fishing when he felt like it, associated with other small, carefree animals such as Bobby Coon, Unc' Billy Possum, Chatterer the Red Squirrel. True, there was an element of danger in the society, primarily from Reddy Fox and the crafty Old Man Coyote, but the more helpless members of the group could invariably forestall personal disaster by telling some outlandish lie to either Reddy Fox or Old Man Coyote, setting the would-be predators on some harmless but effective wild goose chase. The smaller characters had a dauntless if unwitting champion of the oppressed in Bowser the Hound, whose only duty was to chase Old Man Coyote or Brother Fox whenever he saw them. Bowser the Hound belonged to Farmer Brown, a rather obscure human-type, who only infrequently wandered through the plots.

Life among Thornton W. Burgess' little animals of the woods was truly paradise. There was no parental authority, yet there was never the need for parental love. Indeed, there was no moral behavioral problem at all among the little creatures. Each was obviously different from the others, yet all were equal in reasoning power—except, of course, the fox and the coyote. These two could easily be outwitted.

Life in the woods was no struggle. Food grew for the picking. There was no school, no schedule, nothing was expected of anyone except that he be a good friend.

Sammy read the first book with great interest. He was entranced by the simplicity of life in the woods. He grew to know the characters. He was delighted to find the Burgess animal series was almost endless. He began reading more of them. Within a month he had finished all the books on the little animals in the school library. Then he started all over and reread them.

Somehow, when the other boys picked on him now, he didn't seem to mind. He would endure their tormenting until they tired or help came, then he would go home to his room and read about the little animals.

He began daydreaming, interjecting himself into the world of little animals, longing to be able to touch them, talk to them, be a friend among them. He pictured himself seated against a tree in the woods, the little animals in their coveralls gathered about him, looking to him as a friend, knowing Old Man Coyote and Reddy Fox would give them a wide berth with Sammy in their midst.

He lost interest in trying to catch up in his school work and read and reread animal books, then searched for similar books.

"Sammy, this is the third time today I've caught you reading that book. You have to pay attention to what the class is doing," his teacher warned. He tried, but felt he was hopelessly outdistanced by the others. He just wanted to get back to the woods.

"What's the matter with you?" Pete scolded each time Sammy brought a note telling of his unsatisfactory performance at school. "Your sister gets the top grades all the time. You make me ashamed. The neighbors don't want you at their houses anymore. I don't blame them." When Pete said this,

Sammy noticed his father and mother exchanged glances. *They don't want you either,* he said silently to himself, *you think I don't know about those telephone calls and the flat tires when you go out some mornings?*

Since the house had been vandalized that weekend they were away, the family had never gone away overnight. Sammy knew that the worry every time they all left for the store was telling on his parents. One night in bed he heard:

"That damn Nueman. I know it was his boy who put the tacks under the tires this time. He was the only one in the yard. When I told Nueman he got mad and said we should get out."

"That's what Miss Clark said. She called again and said we should take the twins back to Los Angeles to school, or they'll both be flunk-outs." "We've got to go back home." "Yes. Soon."

Good, Sammy thought as he lay back to try to sleep through this night as his sister was doing so easily across the room.

RUDY GALLARDO

The Reflection

The keys are pulled out, jingling, and the door clanks shut behind me. I feel my balding forehead and ask, "Where do I sleep?"

"That's your problem," answers the jailer as he goes down the stairs.

In the big room before me winos are sprawled on the cold concrete. I move looking for a place to sleep, careful not to step on them. On a table against the wall to my left lies a Mexican in dirty slacks and thin-soled pointed shoes. Opposite, on tables against the bars, are a shaggy-haired Okie in faded jeans and a T-shirt, and an Indian with a jagged scar on his cheek, his straight black hair scattered about his head. A Negro, arms crossed on his chest, flapping thick lips as he snores, sleeps on a bench in the center.

The tables and benches are taken. I go to the far right corner, near a shivering old man humped against a garbage can, moaning for a smoke. I search my pockets and pull out a crumpled pack of Pall Malls with two badly shaped cigarettes in it. He eyes them and I offer him one. His shaking hand reaches out for it, grabs it and puts it between his lips. I light it for him and watch him draw with soggy lips. After a few puffs saliva drenches the cigarette and it goes out.

Reprinted by permission from Lillian Faderman and Barbara Bradshaw, *Speaking for Ourselves* (Glenview, Ill.: Scott, Foresman, 1969).

"Mother fuck, a smoke down the drain." I say.

The moaning of the old man starts again but I ignore it. I look at the cell doors on the left and the right of a hallway leading to the shit-house.

"Lucky bastards, those who have bunks," I mutter.

I lower my eyelids, but I can't sleep. Finally I slide down the bars and the concrete sends icy sensations through my body when I sit. I place my head between my knees. A noise makes me lift my eyelids. A Negro and a white come out of the restroom. They stop before different cells.

"Same time tomorrow?" asks the white softly.

"Yes," the Negro answers musically.

"Son of a bitch, if it takes being a punk to get a bunk I'd be one this minute," I mumble.

The fruits wink at each other before they close the doors behind them.

The moaning continues, and out of a small cell, opposite where the tricks went in, comes a short stocky Mexican boy and says, "Damn, old man, stop your noise, you been at it all fuckin' night."

The old man doesn't stop and the kid clenches his fists and walks angrily toward him.

"Are you going to shut up or am I going to have to shut you up?" he says.

I lift my head to see who's doing the threatening.

"Chapo," says the boy as he turns to me. "When did you get here?"

"About forty minutes ago," I reply.

"*Ese*," he says, "Why didn't you come to my room? I could have fixed you up with a place to sleep."

"I didn't know you were here. Where's your brother? I haven't seen him for a while."

"Oh, he's in the big joint again."

"How long you've been here?"

"Too damn long," he answers.

The old man continues the noise.

"Damn, old man, lighten up and let the people sleep. Okay?" says the boy.

"Lighten up on him yourself," I snap.

"The *ruco* shouts like that every night, *ese*," he apologizes.

"Yeah, but you know he's an old *vato*," I reply.

"I'm sorry, but still you can't sleep by this old bastard. Come on," he says.

The boy goes down the hall to his cell. I raise up and, running my hand through my thinning hair, I follow him. Inside it is dark, but two bunk forms can be made out, and between them on what seems to be a box, a Saint Joseph sits, glowing in the dark.

"Damn, this cold draft pities no one. It even put out the candle I lit to keep my saint warm," he says. "Here, strike a match, I've got to get you some blankets."

He gives me two rolled blankets which served as his pillow, and indicates that I can use another that's under the saint. Then he says, "Chapo, is it okay if you sleep under my bed? I'm sorry, but there's no other place."

"Yeah, sure," I answer.

I unfold the blankets, lay them neatly under the bed, crawl underneath it, and stretch. I hope the boy doesn't start a conversation.

The boy moves on the bed and asks, "*Ese*, didn't the damn people know who you are? Stupid bastards, they should know better than to throw you in with the bums. Hell, I bet if they messed with you on the outside, you'd drop them in a minute. Yeah, my *carnal* used to tell me about the times you and him used to clean up; man nobody messed with you.

"You know why they busted me?" he pauses. "The clique and I were *lirando* with some Texas *vatos*."

"Where's the rest?" I ask.

"They all split before the law got there. Only I was doing a job on this dude and it was too good to leave, so here I am."

Then he starts talking of the other times he's been in jail.

My mind swirls to the past.

Brown unpainted houses, chipped sidewalks. I walk on. Home is near and I want to get there and feed my hungry stomach. I see a plain brick house and run towards its broken wooden gate. I smile at the smell of stewing beans. I enter and sit at a table made of Hunt's tomato boxes. My mother silently brings me a plate of cooked beans with sliced onions and chile and a half a dozen tortillas.

She sits next to me and watches me eat. I dip a large spoon into the beans, bring it up to my mouth and, slurping, swallow the stuff on it. A rolled tortilla follows, and munching sounds come from me.

"Chuey is in jail again, and Benjamín fell off the ladder while he was thinning peaches. He won't be able to work for two weeks. Monico wrote and said he would be up before the board soon and hopes they okay his release this time." All this she says while I eat.

I finish eating, get up and eye my confused mother. I pace the small kitchen.

"Were the frijoles and chilito good?" she asks.

"*Sí. Mucho*," I answer.

"I must go sew now," she says as she gets up and goes to her room.

I follow her asking, "Are you okay, Mamá?"

"*Sí, mi hijo*," she answers.

"I'm going to shine shoes," I tell her.

"*Está bueno*," she replies.

I arrive in town, pick up my shine box at the bar and spend the afternoon and part of the night as usual, going in and out of bars saying, "Shine, sir?"

Winos on the beat stop me and ask for change; others, too drunk, just stretch out their hands and make the gesture. The whores toy with my hair as I pass near them. Customers joke about not paying, but I've learned to take it until they have satisfied their need for laughter. Some call just to tease me—to them I give the finger. They never get shines anyway.

Evening. I'm tired and I decide to call it quits. I put the box away and start home from town. A thin man with grey hair, dressed in khaki pants and a short-sleeved shirt, stops me.

"Going home? When I was your age I used to shine shoes too," he says.

"Oh," I reply.

"Yeah, in my young days no one could outshine me."

A cold draft chills my feet and I pull them under the covers and rub them together until they become warm again. Then I turn on my side, face a thick concrete wall, and wish for a bunk.

Saturday morning, behind a dorm building in a boys' correctional school. I lie curled on the grass, elbows tight against my stomach, hands fisted over my face. Shoe toes dig into my ribs and fists bounce off my neck and the unprotected sides of my face.

"Chicken-shit fink! We told you! Maybe this will teach you," they mumble as they bang against me. They warned me about what would happen to a person who was part of the clique and broke its rules.

I grunt softly at the blows. I grunt softly because no one is to hear or know, just the clique. That's the law. A thin whistle is heard. They run.

I moan and stay still. Footsteps vibrate in my ears. Then I crawl towards the nearby building, lean on it.

The supervisor sees me, head between knees, gripping my middle. "What's the matter?" he asks.

"Nothing," I answer.

"What's the reason for being crumpled like that?" he says.

"I little sick," I reply.

"What about?"

"The lousy chow you give here."

"Look, Chapo, who was it?" he asks.

"Was what?"

"Who squared off on you?" he says.

"Look, leave me alone, nobody squared off on me. I'm not doing nothing, just let me be. Okay?"

"All right, suit yourself," he says and walks away.

The draft chills my feet again. I pull my knees close to my stomach and rub my feet against one another.

The company falls into formation; feet make shuffling sounds as they drag forward. The morning is nice, the sun makes droplets of dew glitter against green grass. A breeze unspoiled by the day's activity leaves a good smell of pine. Mornings like these used to leave me in wonderment, but that was a long time ago. Now as I march my thoughts are only of the clique. I'm almost in. Huero has approved of me, but Colorado considers me a punk yet. No sweat though, he'll change.

The formation comes to a halt and the groups separate. I go to the school group. From there I look at the trade group, and my eyes meet those of close friends. We greet each other in comradeship. Then I glance at Huero, standing shoulders hunched, hands gripping one another behind his back. Huero curls his lips downward and nods in recognition. I feel warm and good. The groups move out to begin the morning's activities. We arrive at school. My hands become moist. The warm sensation is gone. I move forward and my walk is unsteady. I enter the hallway, twenty-three, twenty-two and on down, the numbers on the doorways catch the corners of my eyes as I move down the hall. My number is eleven and I look forward to it. As I pass room fourteen a door opens and a dark husky-shouldered kid swaggers out.

He glares at me and bawls, "Did you get the shine?"

Dumbly I walk on.

"*Ese, púto,* I'm talking to you," he says.

I turn and reply, "What did you say?"

He brings his hands up, challenging, and answers, "You heard, punk."

A voice cuts in, "Stop that, you fellows."

It is Mr. Brunk, my teacher. He grips my left elbow and leads me to the classroom. Inside, I sit at my desk, pull out a history book, open it and stare at it. Just when I'm almost in, Nicko has to call me out. I don't want any trouble. What am I doing in this school? God, God please help me. My insides begin to pulse and pain makes me lay my head on the desk. The bell rings for break. Outside I sit away from the crowd. Mosca then comes and tells me Nicko wants to see me at the laundry in the afternoon. I find myself asking Mosca for a smoke before he leaves. I light it and draw on it. The cigarette upsets my stomach, but it is good. This way the mind concentrates on the discomfort.

The break ends and I go back into the classroom. I look at the history book.

Chapter seven, "The Roman Empire," it reads.

In desperation I go to the restroom and play with myself. For a while it feels good, but that is all and it doesn't help. Time passes and the bell for lunch sounds. Chow is hazy. Not until I am back at the cottage area am I able to think clearly. The clique knows of the fight.

George says, "Nicko is going to do you in."

"Yeah, I knew Nicko back at the Flats in L.A. and he can really throw," adds Colorado.

The other boys eye them severely. They aren't following the rules. The clique is supposed to back its members in beefs like these, no matter what. Only in inter-racial fights does one show any favoritism to different cottage cliques.

Huero jumps in "Look, damn it, you aren't back in Flats, you are here and Chapo is of our cottage and you better act like it. If you two think so much of Nicko why don't you transfer to his cottage?"

"Yeah, sure," several others add.

"Well, things better go right," Colorado weakly grumbles.

They turn their attention to me and give me advice.

"Don't forget to kick at the balls," Flucko tells me.

"No," says another, "put soap in a sock and bust his damn head."

One takes off his belt and bangs it against the ground; he huffs, "Use the old buckle on him, *ese*."

I am afraid of Nicko but the boys stimulate me. They're behind me. They've accepted me. The buzzer blares, ending lunch break. Formation is made and the company moves out to the day's remaining activities. I go to my trade, shoeshop, unhappy that the laundry and shoeshop are separated only by a wall. In the shop I heel and sole and shine shoes. The feelings of the morning are gone. I glance at the clock: break is nearing. I must get ready. I sit on a chair near the door leading to the laundry and slowly take my overalls off.

"No weapons, just fists and feet, a clean fight," flashes through my mind. A knock on the door, the signal. I am ready.

I open the door and he glares and nods with his head towards the restroom. I walk down the low stairway and follow him. As he opens the door I hit him with a right on the back of the head. He reels back and I follow through with a kick to his belly. Then I feel a sharp pain on my left jaw and a knuckle on my mouth. He sees my pain and comes swinging wildly at me. I clinch him and spin around, throwing him against the wash basin. We wrestle, pushing each other against the restroom wall. Then he tears loose from my grip and begins striking my face, but his blows don't have the sting of before. Then I measure him with lefts and follow through with rights. I see his face grimacing. He moves slowly now and breathes heavily. Sensing victory, I kick at his nuts to finish him faster. Nicko flops on the floor, and the door opens.

"What's going on in here?" snaps the supervisor.

I am taken outside and a supervisor asks, "Who started it?"

I stutter, "He-he wanted me to steal him some shine from the shoeshop."

Later at the clique's corner in the cottage, I sit in the center telling of the fight. I move my hands wildly, kicking at the space before me and talk very fast, almost sputtering my words, and I beam as I narrate. The boys wince their faces, clinch their fists and tensely sit on their butts as they listen. At the end all of them except Colorado shout congratulations.

Noticing Colorado's silence, the boys look at him.

He says, "Nicko is in segregation. Chapo put the finger on him, told the man why the fight started."

I drop my head and say nothing.

The corner buzzes; the boys want to know when it will be. Huero and Colorado glance at each other. Colorado gets the privilege.

"*Sábado,*" he says.

Slowly I roll to my knees, push against the ground and lift myself to my feet. I lean on a wall and pain is everywhere inside me. What did I do wrong? Why didn't someone tell me what finking was? Back on my block that wasn't finking. Revenge bites, but there are thirteen of them. I must decide. Shall I go back to the clique or go it myself? But then I'll be a stone out. Stone outs have no clique. They sit by themselves, no one wants them. A feeling cuts me. I heave myself from the wall and limp to find the clique.

The cold draft chills my feet again.
The wino yells loudly, "Aah, help me please, somebody!"
The boy arrogantly says, "Help yourself, you old bastard."
"Fool," I mutter.

AMADO MURO

Cecilia Rosas

When I was in the ninth grade at Bowie High School in El Paso, I got a job hanging up women's coats at La Feria Department Store on Saturdays. It wasn't the kind of job that had much appeal for a Mexican boy or for boys of any other nationality, either. But the work wasn't hard, only boring. Wearing a smock, I stood around the Ladies' Wear Department all day long waiting for women customers to finish trying on coats so I could hang them up.

Having to wear a smock was worse than the work itself. It was an agonizing ordeal. To me it was a loathsome stigma of unmanly toil that made an already degrading job even more so. The work itself I looked on as onerous and effeminate for a boy from a family of miners, shepherds, and ditchdiggers.

Reprinted by permission from *New Mexico Quarterly* (Winter 1964). Copyright © 1964 by the University of New Mexico Press.

But working in Ladies' Wear had two compensations: earning three dollars every Saturday was one; being close to the Señorita Cecilia Rosas was the other.

This alluring young woman, the most beautiful I had ever seen, more than made up for my mollycoddle labor and the smock that symbolized it. My chances of looking at her were almost limitless. And like a good Mexican, I made the most of them. But I was only too painfully aware that I wasn't the only one who thought this saleslady gorgeous.

La Feria had water fountains on every one of its eight floors. But men liked best the one on the floor where Miss Rosas worked. So they made special trips to Ladies' Wear all day long to drink water and look at her.

Since I was only fourteen and in love for the first time, I looked at her more chastely than most. The way her romantic lashes fringed her obsidian eyes was especially enthralling to me. Then, too, I never tired of admiring her shining raven hair, her Cupid's-bow lips, the warmth of her gleaming white smile. Her rich olive skin was almost as dark as mine. Sometimes she wore a San Juan rose in her hair. When she did, she looked so very lovely I forgot all about what La Feria was paying me to do and stood gaping at her instead. My admiration was decorous but complete. I admired her hourglass figure as well as her wonderfully radiant face.

Other men admired her too. They inspected her from the water fountain. Some stared at her boldly, watching her trimly rhythmic hips sway. Others, less frank and open, gazed furtively at her swelling bosom or her shapely calves. Their effrontery made me indignant. I, too, looked at these details of Miss Rosas. But I prided myself on doing so more romantically, far more poetically, than they did, with much more love than desire.

Then, too, Miss Rosas was the friendliest as well as the most beautiful saleslady in Ladies' Wear. But the other salesladies, Mexican girls all, didn't like her. She was so nice to them all they were hard put to justify their dislike. They couldn't very well admit they disliked her because she was pretty. So they all said she was haughty and imperious. Their claim was partly true. Her beauty was Miss Rosas' only obvious vanity. But she had still another. She prided herself on being more American than Mexican because she was born in El Paso. And she did her best to act, dress, and talk the way Americans do. She hated to speak Spanish, disliked her Mexican name. She called herself Cecile Roses instead of Cecilia Rosas. This made the other salesladies smile derisively. They called her La Americana or the Gringa from Xochimilco every time they mentioned her name.

Looking at this beautiful girl was more important than money to me. It was my greatest compensation for doing work that I hated. She was so lovely that a glance at her sweetly expressive face was enough to make me forget my shame at wearing a smock and my dislike for my job with its eternal waiting around.

Miss Rosas was an exemplary saleslady. She could be frivolous, serious, or demure, primly efficient too, molding herself to each customer's personality. Her voice matched her exotically mysterious eyes. It was the richest, the softest, I had ever heard. Her husky whisper, gentle as a rain breeze, was like a tender caress. Hearing it made me want to dream, and I did. Romantic thoughts burgeoned up in my mind like rosy billows of hope scented with Miss Rosas' perfume. These thoughts made me so languid at my work that the floor manager, Joe Apple, warned me to show some enthusiasm for it or else suffer the consequences.

But my dreams sapped my will to struggle, making me oblivious to admonitions. I had neither the desire nor the energy to respond to Joe Apple's warnings. Looking at Miss Rosas used up so much of my energy that I had little left for my work. Miss Rosas was twenty, much too old for me, everyone said. But what everyone said didn't matter. So I soldiered on the job and watched her, entranced by her beauty, her grace. While I watched, I dreamed of being a hero. It hurt me to have her see me doing such menial work. But there was no escape from it. I needed the job to stay in school. So more and more I took refuge in dreams.

When I had watched her as much, if not more, than I could safely do without attracting the attention of other alert Mexican salesladies, I slipped out of Ladies' Wear and walked up the stairs to the top floor. There I sat on a window ledge smoking Faro cigarettes, looking down at the city's canyons, and best of all, thinking about Miss Rosas and myself.

They say Chihuahua Mexicans are good at dreaming because the mountains are so gigantic and the horizons so vast in Mexico's biggest state that men don't think pygmy thoughts there. I was no exception. Lolling on the ledge, I became what I wanted to be. And what I wanted to be was a handsome American Miss Rosas could love and marry. The dreams I dreamed were imaginative masterpieces, or so I thought. They transcended the insipid realities of a casual relationship, making it vibrantly thrilling and infinitely more romantic. They transformed me from a colorless Mexican boy who put women's coats away into the debonair American, handsome, dashing, and worldly, that I longed to be for her sake. For the first time in my life I reveled in the magic of fantasy. It brought happiness. Reality didn't.

But my window-ledge reveries left me bewildered and shaken. They had a narcotic quality. The more thrillingly romantic fantasies I created, the more I needed to create. It got so I couldn't get enough dreaming time in Ladies' Wear. My kind of dreaming demanded disciplined concentration. And there was just too much hubbub, too much gossiping, too many coats to be put away there.

So I spent less time in Ladies' Wear. My flights to the window ledge became more recklessly frequent. Sometimes I got tired sitting there. When I did, I took the freight elevator down to the street floor and brazenly walked out of the store without so much as punching a time clock. Walking the streets quickened my imagination, gave form and color to my thoughts. It made my brain glow with impossible hopes that seemed incredibly easy to realize. So absorbed was I in thoughts of Miss Rosas and myself that I bumped into Americans, apologizing mechanically in Spanish instead of English, and wandered down South El Paso Street like a somnambulist, without really seeing its street vendors, cafés and arcades, tattoo shops, and shooting galleries at all.

But if there was confusion in these walks, there was some serenity too. Something good did come from the dreams that prompted them. I found I could tramp the streets with a newly won tranquility, no longer troubled by, or even aware of, girls in tight skirts, overflowing blouses, and drop-stitch stockings. My love for Miss Rosas was my shield against the furtive thoughts and indiscriminate desires that had made me so uneasy for a year or more before I met her.

Then, too, because of her, I no longer looked at the pictures of voluptuous women in the *Vea* and *Vodevil* magazines at Zamora's newsstand. The piquant thoughts Mexicans call *malos deseos* were gone from my mind. I no longer thought about women as I did before I fell in love with Miss Rosas. Instead, I thought about a woman, only one. This clear-cut objective and the serenity that went with it made me understand something of one of the nicest things about love.

I treasured the walks, the window-ledge sittings, and the dreams that I had then. I clung to them just as long as I could. Drab realities closed in on me chokingly just as soon as I gave them up. My future was a time clock with an American Mister telling me what to do, and this I knew only too well. A career as an ice-dock laborer stretched ahead of me. Better said, it dangled over me like a Veracruz machete. My uncle, Rodolfo Avitia, a straw boss on the ice docks, was already training me for it. Every night he took me to the mile-long docks overhanging the Southern Pacific freight yards. There he handed me tongs and made me practice tripping three-hundred-pound ice blocks so I could learn how to unload an entire boxcar of ice blocks myself.

Thinking of this bleak future drove me back into my fantasies, made me want to prolong them forever. My imagination was taxed to the breaking point by the heavy strain I put on it.

I thought about every word Miss Rosas had ever said to me, making myself believe she looked at me with unmistakable tenderness when she said them. When she said, "Amado, please hang up this fur coat," I found special meaning in her tone. It was as though she had said, "Amadito, I love you."

When she gave these orders, I pushed into action like a man blazing with a desire to perform epically heroic feats. At such times I felt capable of putting away not one but a thousand fur coats, and would have done so joyously.

Sometimes on the street I caught myself murmuring, "Cecilia, *linda amorcita*, I love you." When these surges swept over me, I walked down empty streets so I could whisper, "Cecilia, *te quiero con toda mi alma*"* as much as I wanted to and mumble everything else that I felt. And so I emptied my heart on the streets and window ledge while women's coats piled up in Ladies' Wear.

But my absences didn't go unnoticed. Once an executive-looking man, portly, gray, and efficiently brusque, confronted me while I sat on the window ledge with a Faro cigarette pasted to my lips, a cloud of tobacco smoke hanging over my head, and many perfumed dreams inside it. He had a no-nonsense approach that jibed with his austere mien. He asked me what my name was, jotted down my work number, and went off to make a report on what he called "sordid malingering."

Other reports followed his. Gruff warnings, stern admonitions, and blustery tirades developed from them. They came from both major and minor executives. These I was already inured to. They didn't matter anyway. My condition was far too advanced, already much too complex, to be cleared up by mere lectures, fatherly or otherwise. All the threats and rebukes in the world couldn't have made me give up my window-ledge reveries or kept me from roaming city streets with Cecilia Rosas' name on my lips like a prayer.

The reports merely made me more cunning, more doggedly determined to city-slick La Feria out of work hours I owed it. The net result was that I timed my absences more precisely and contrived better lies to explain them. Sometimes I went to the men's room and looked at myself in the mirror for as long as ten minutes at a time. Such self-studies filled me with gloom. The mirror reflected an ordinary Mexican face, more homely than comely. Only my hair gave me hope. It was thick and wavy, deserving a better face to go with it. So I did the best I could with what I had, and combed it over my temples in ringlets just like the poets back in my hometown of Parral, Chihuahua, used to do.

My inefficiency, my dreams, my general lassitude, could have gone on indefinitely, it seemed. My life at the store wavered between bright hope and leaden despair, unrelieved by Miss Rosas' acceptance or rejection of me. Then one day something happened that almost made my overstrained heart stop beating.

It happened on the day Miss Rosas stood behind me while I put a fur coat away. Her heady perfume, the fragrance of her warm healthy body, made me feel faint. She was so close to me I thought about putting my hands around her lissome waist and hugging her as hard as I could. But thoughts of subsequent disgrace deterred me, so instead of hugging her I smiled wanly and asked her in Spanish how she was feeling.

*I love you with all my soul.

"Amado, speak English," she told me. "And pronounce the words slowly and carefully, so you won't sound like a country Mexican."

Then she looked at me in a way that made me the happiest employee who ever punched La Feria's time clock.

"Amadito," she whispered the way I had always dreamed she would.

"Yes, Señorita Cecilia," I said expectantly.

Her smile was warmly intimate. "Amadito, when are you going to take me to the movies?" she asked.

Other salesladies watched us, all smiling. They made me so nervous I couldn't answer.

"Amadito, you haven't answered me," Miss Rosas said teasingly. "Either you're bashful as a village sweetheart, or else you don't like me at all."

In voluble Spanish, I quickly assured her the latter wasn't the case. I was just getting ready to say, "Señorita Cecilia, I more than like you; I love you" when she frowned and told me to speak English. So I slowed down and tried to smooth out my ruffled thoughts.

"Señorita Cecilia," I said. "I'd love to take you to the movies any time."

Miss Rosas smiled and patted my cheek. "Will you buy me candy and popcorn?" she said.

I nodded, putting my hand against the imprint her warm palm had left on my face.

"And hold my hand?"

I said "yes" so enthusiastically it made her laugh. Other salesladies laughed too. Dazed and numb with happiness, I watched Miss Rosas walk away. How proud and confident she was, how wholesomely clean and feminine. Other salesladies were looking at me and laughing.

Miss Sandoval came over to me. "*Ay papacito,*" she said. "With women you're the divine tortilla."

Miss de la Rosa come over too. "When you take the Americana to the movies, remember not to speak Christian," she said. "And be sure you wear the pants that don't have any patches on them."

What they said made me blush and wonder how they knew what we had been talking about. Miss Arroyo came over to join them. So did Miss Torres.

"Amado, remember women are weak and men aren't made of sweet bread," Miss Arroyo said.

This embarrassed me, but it wasn't altogether unpleasant. Miss Sandoval winked at Miss de la Rosa, then looked back at me.

"Don't go too fast with the Americana, Amado," she said. "Remember the procession is long and the candles are small."

They laughed and slapped me on the back. They all wanted to know when I was going to take Miss Rosas to the movies. "She didn't say," I blurted out without thinking.

This brought another burst of laughter. It drove me back up to the window ledge, where I got out my package of Faros and thought about the wonderful thing that had happened. But I was too nervous to stay there. So I went to the men's room and looked at myself in the mirror again, wondering why Miss Rosas liked me so well. The mirror made it brutally clear that my looks hadn't influenced her. So it must have been something else, perhaps character. But that didn't seem likely either. Joe Apple had told me I didn't have much of that. And other store officials had bulwarked his opinion. Still, I had seen homely men walking the streets of El Paso's Little Chihuahua quarter with beautiful Mexican women, and no one could explain that either. Anyway, it was time for another walk. So I took one.

This time I trudged through Little Chihuahua, where both Miss Rosas and I lived. Little Chihuahua looked different to me that day. It was a broken-down Mexican quarter honeycombed with tenements, Mom and Pop groceries, herb shops, cafés, and spindly salt-cedar trees; with howling children running its streets and old Mexican revolutionaries sunning themselves on its curbs like iguanas. But on that clear frosty day it was the world's most romantic place because Cecilia Rosas lived there.

While walking, I reasoned that Miss Rosas might want to go dancing after the movies. So I went to Professor Toribio Ortega's dance studio and made arrangements to take my first lesson. Some neighborhood boys saw me when I came out. They bawled, "*Mariquita*" and made flutteringly effeminate motions, all vulgar if not obscene. It didn't matter. On my lunch hour I went back and took my first lesson anyway. Professor Ortega danced with me. Softened by weeks of dreaming, I went limp in his arms imagining he was Miss Rosas.

The rest of the day was the same as many others before it. As usual I spent most of it stealing glances at Miss Rosas and slipping up to the window ledge. She looked busy, efficient, not like a woman in love. Her many other admirers trooped to the water fountain to look at the way her black silk dress fitted her curves. Their profane admiration made me scowl even more than I usually did at such times.

When the day's work was done, I plodded home from the store just as dreamily as I had gone to it. Since I had no one else to confide in, I invited my oldest sister, Dulce Nombre de María, to go to the movies with me. They were showing Jorge Negrete and María Felix in *El Rapto* at the Colón Theater. It was a romantic movie, just the kind I wanted to see.

After it was over, I bought Dulce Nombre *churros* and hot *champurrado* at the Golden Taco Café. And I told my sister all about what had happened to me. She looked at me thoughtfully, then combed my hair back with her fingertips as though trying to soothe me. "Manito," she said, softly. "I wouldn't. . . ." Then she looked away and shrugged her shoulders.

On Monday I borrowed three dollars from my Uncle Rodolfo without telling him what it was for. Miss Rosas hadn't told me what night she wanted me to take her to the movies. But the way she had looked at me made me think that almost any night would do. So I decided on Friday. Waiting for it to come was hard. But I had to keep my mind occupied. So I went to Zamora's newsstand to get the Alma Norteña songbook. Poring through it for the most romantic song I could find, I decided on "La Cecilia."

All week long I practiced singing it on my way to school and in the shower after basketball practice with the Little Chihuahua Tigers at the Sagrado Corazón gym. But except for singing this song, I tried not to speak Spanish at all. At home I made my mother mad by saying in English, "Please pass the sugar."

My mother looked at me as though she couldn't believe what she had heard. Since my Uncle Rodolfo couldn't say anything more than "hello" and "good-bye" in English, he couldn't tell what I had said. So my sister Consuelo did.

"May the Dark Virgin with the benign look make this boy well enough to speak Christian again," my mother whispered.

This I refused to do. I went on speaking English even though my mother and uncle didn't understand it. This shocked my sisters as well. When they asked me to explain my behavior, I parroted Miss Rosas, saying, "We're living in the United States now."

My rebellion against being a Mexican created an uproar. Such conduct was unorthodox, if not scandalous, in a neighborhood where names like Burciaga, Rodríguez, and Castillo predominated. But it wasn't only the Spanish language that I lashed out against.

"Mother, why do we always have to eat *sopa, frijoles refritos, mondongo,* and *pozole?*" I complained. "Can't we ever eat roast beef or ham and eggs like Americans do?"

My mother didn't speak to me for two days after that. My Uncle Rodolfo grimaced and mumbled something about renegade Mexicans who want to eat ham and eggs even though the Montes Packing Company turned out the best *chorizo* this side of Toluca. My sister Consuelo giggled and called me a Río Grande Irishman, an American Mister, a gringo, and a *bolillo.* Dulce Nombre looked at me worriedly.

Life at home was almost intolerable. Cruel jokes and mocking laughter made it so. I moped around looking sad as a day without bread. My sister Consuelo suggested I go to the courthouse and change my name to Beloved Wall, which is English for Amado Muro. My mother didn't agree. "If *Nuestro Señor* had meant for Amadito to be an American, he would have given him a name like Smeeth or Jonesy," she said. My family was unsympathetic. With a family like mine, how could I ever hope to become an American and win Miss Rosas?

Friday came at last. I put on my only suit, slicked my hair down with liquid vaseline, and doused myself with Dulce Nombre's perfume.

"Amado's going to serenade that pretty girl everyone calls La Americana," my sister Consuelo told my mother and uncle when I sat down to eat. "Then he's going to take her to the movies."

This made my uncle laugh and my mother scowl.

"*¡Qué pantalones tiene!* (what nerve that boy's got)," my uncle said, "to serenade a twenty-year-old woman."

"La Americana," my mother said derisively. "That one's Mexican as *pulque* cured with celery."

They made me so nervous I forgot to take off my cap when I sat down to eat.

"Amado, take off your cap," my mother said. "You're not in La Lagunilla Market."

My uncle frowned. "All this boy thinks about is kissing girls," he said gruffly.

"But my boy's never kissed one," my mother said proudly.

My sister Consuelo laughed. "That's because they won't let him," she said.

This wasn't true. But I couldn't say so in front of my mother. I had already kissed Emalina Uribe from Porfirio Díaz Street not once but twice. Both times I'd kissed her in a darkened doorway less than a block from her home. But the kisses were over so soon we hardly had time to enjoy them. This was because Ema was afraid her big brother, the husky one nicknamed Toro, would see us. But if we'd had more time, it would have been better, I knew.

Along about six o'clock the three musicians who called themselves the Mariachis of Tecalitlán came by and whistled for me, just as they had said they would do. They never looked better than they did on that night. They had on black and silver charro uniforms and big black Zapata sombreros.

My mother shook her head when she saw them. "Son, who ever heard of serenading a girl at six o'clock in the evening," she said. "When your father had the mariachis sing for me, it was always at two o'clock in the morning— the only proper time for a six-song *gallo*."

But I got out my Ramírez guitar anyway. I put on my cap and rushed out to give the mariachis the money without even kissing my mother's hand or waiting for her to bless me. Then we headed for Miss Rosas' home. Some boys and girls I knew were out in the street. This made me uncomfortable. They looked at me wonderingly as I led the mariachi band to Miss Rosas' home.

A block away from Miss Rosas' home I could see her father, a grizzled veteran who fought for Pancho Villa, sitting on the curb reading the Juárez newspaper, *El Fronterizo*.

The sight of him made me slow down for a moment. But I got back in stride when I saw Miss Rosas herself.

She smiled and waved at me. "Hello, Amadito," she said.

"Hello, Señorita Cecilia," I said.

She looked at the mariachis, then back at me.

"*Ay*, Amado, you're going to serenade your girl," she said. I didn't reply right away. Then when I was getting ready to say, "Señorita Cecilia, I came to serenade you," I saw the American man sitting in the sports roadster at the curb.

Miss Rosas turned to him. "I'll be right there, Johnny," she said.

She patted my cheek. "I've got to run now, Amado," she said. "Have a real nice time, darling."

I looked at her silken legs as she got into the car. Everything had happened so fast I was dazed. Broken dreams made my head spin. The contrast between myself and the poised American in the sports roadster was so cruel it made me wince.

She was happy with him. That was obvious. She was smiling and laughing, looking forward to a good time. Why had she asked me to take her to the movies if she already had a boyfriend? Then I remembered how the other salesladies had laughed, how I had wondered why they were laughing when they couldn't even hear what we were saying. And I realized it had all been a joke; everyone had known it but me. Neither Miss Rosas nor the other salesladies had ever dreamed I would think she was serious about wanting me to take her to the movies.

The American and Miss Rosas drove off. Gloomy thoughts oppressed me. They made me want to cry. To get rid of them I thought of going to one of the "bad death" cantinas in Juárez where tequila starts fights and knives finish them. There I could forget her in Jalisco-state style with mariachis and tequila. Then I remembered I was so young that *cantineros* wouldn't serve me tequila.

So I thought some more. Emalina Uribe was the only other alternative. If we went over to Porfirio Díaz Street and serenaded her, I could go back to being a Mexican again. She was just as Mexican as I was, Mexican as *chicharrones*. I thought about smiling, freckle-faced Ema.

Ema wasn't like the Americana at all. She wore wash dresses that fitted loosely and even ate the *melcocha* candies Mexicans like so well on the street. On Sundays she wore a Zamora shawl to church, and her mother wouldn't let her use lipstick or let her put on high heels.

But with a brother like Toro, who didn't like me anyway, such a serenade might be more dangerous than romantic. Besides that, my faith in my looks, my character, or whatever it was that made women fall in love with men, was so undermined I could already picture her getting into a car with a handsome American just like Miss Rosas had done.

The Mariachis of Tecalitlán were getting impatient. They had been paid to sing six songs and they wanted to sing them. But they were all sympathetic. None of them laughed at me.

"Amado, don't look sad as I did the day I learned I'd never be a millionaire," the mariachi captain said, putting his arm around me. "If not that girl, then another."

But without Miss Rosas there was no one we could sing "La Cecilia" to. The street seemed bleak and empty now that she was gone. And I didn't want to serenade Ema Uribe, even though she hadn't been faithless as Miss Rosas had been. It was true she hadn't been faithless, but only lack of opportunity would keep her from getting into a car with an American, I reasoned cynically.

Just about then Miss Rosas' father looked up from his newspaper. He asked the mariachis if they knew how to sing "Cananéa Jail." They told him they did. Then they looked at me. I thought it over for a moment. Then I nodded and started strumming the bass strings of my guitar. What had happened made it only too plain I could never trust Miss Rosas again. So we serenaded her father instead.

JOSÉ ANTONIO VILLARREAL

From Pocho

The world of Richard Rubio was becoming too much for him. He felt that time was going by him in an overly accelerated pace, because he was not aware of days but of weeks and, at times, even months. And he lived in dread that suddenly he should find himself old and ready to die before he could get from life the things it owed him. He was approaching his thirteenth year, and thought of his friend Joe Pete Manõel, though not forgotten, did not hurt as much. For the most part, he lost himself in dreams or spent hours reading everything he could find, indiscriminate in his choice through his persevering desire to learn. Now, after work, he was a familiar figure in the town library, and later, when the vacation ended, he continued the practice, for by then the meager library at school provided little for him. Yet he was disturbed by the thought that now, while he was young and strong in body, his wanderings should be physical. Imagination would do only when he became old and incapable of experiencing actual adventure.

At school, Richard was the favorite of his teachers because his old-country manners made him most courteous in contrast to the other students. He was also a good student, and stood near the top of his class without seemingly trying. His teachers encouraged his reading, but unfortunately did not direct it, and he became increasingly complex in his moods.

It was natural that in his frantic hunger for reading he went through books he did not understand. A friend of his father had a few Spanish novels, and he read a simplified "Quixote" and made several attempts at Ibáñez, but for the first time in his life he found reading to be actual work. So he limited his Spanish reading to the newspaper he received in the mail from Los Angeles. With determination, he followed Tom Jones and Dr. Pangloss through their various complicated adventures. From *Gone with the Wind,* he emerged with tremendous respect and sympathy for the South and its people. And when the Dust Bowl families who had begun trickling into the valley arrived in increasing numbers, he was sad. They represented the South to him, and he mourned that the once proud could come to such decay.

When the boy fell asleep over a book, his father blew out the coal-oil lamp and tenderly put him to bed. Only when riding out in the country lanes was Richard forbidden to read. Twice his father threw his books out the window of the car. "Look!" he would say. "Look at the world around you, burro!" And the boy would think, What a funny one the old man is!

Indeed, the father was a paradox.

Richard went into the barn that was used to house the town's garbage wagons. Today the barn was empty of equipment and full of young guys and a few older people. Over at one end of the building stood a huge ring. It had two ropes, instead of three, and the posts were big iron pipes wrapped in burlap. There were two kids going at it pretty hard, and suddenly one of them put his hands to his mouth and stood transfixed in the center of the ring. The other one jumped around, throwing punches that either missed his opponent completely or landed on his shoulders or the top of his head. The puncher was too anxious, and the one who couldn't believe his mouth was bleeding got away, and then the bell rang.

Two other guys jumped into the ring then, and started dancing around and flexing like professionals, blowing snot all over the place, and then this local guy who was doing pretty good in the game up in the City jumped in there to do the announcing, and another guy who was already in there was the referee.

He noticed that the announcer's face was a little bumpy already, and he was already talking through his nose from fighting pro. He was a little guy and he moved around funny—real jerky, like the old silent movies—and somebody said there goes the next flyweight champ, which meant he would be the Filipino champion, since they were the only flyweights around. Richard could tell already he would not even be champ of Santa Clara, but he did not say anything, because people in small towns are funny about things like that—they think they have the best of everything.

While the two guys were fighting, Thomas Nakano came over to him. He was wearing only pants, and they were rolled up to his knees and he was barefooted.

"You gonna fight, Thomas?" asked Ricky.

"I can't find nobody who's my size and wants to fight me," Thomas said, sounding disappointed.

Richard felt his stomach begin to get funny, because he knew what was coming. "Don't look at me, Punchie," he said, trying to make a little joke out of it, but nobody laughed and it was real quiet.

"Aw, come on, Richard." He was begging him to let him hit him. "Come on, you're just my size. I'll fight anybody, only they won't let ya less'n you're the same size as the other guy."

He said no he would not, but he felt sorry for Thomas because he wanted someone to fight with him so bad. And then the guys were finished in the ring, and somebody called Thomas and asked him if he had a partner yet. He said no, but by then even guys Richard didn't know were trying to talk him into fighting him, and the pro came over, and in the end he was up in the ring shaking, because he didn't want any of these people to see him look bad. He thought back to the pictures in *Ring Magazine* and tried to imitate the poses, but before he could really decide which he liked best, Thomas was all over him. He kind of clinched and said, "What the hell you trying to do, you crazy bastard?" And Thomas said, "Don't worry—I'll take it easy," and Richard felt pretty good about then, because Thomas was his buddy and he would take it easy on him. But as they pulled away from each other, Thomas clouted him on the mouth when he wasn't looking, and Richard's head felt suddenly numb. Then Thomas was hitting him all over the place, like nobody's business—in the ribs, the stomach, and even his back sometimes, and the gloves were feeling like great big pillows on Richard's hands. It was the longest round in the history of boxing, and Thomas pissed him off. *My friend—one of the gang!* So he thought and thought, and finally, when they were apart one time, he dropped his hands and moved toward Thomas, looking real sadlike right into his eyes, as if to say, *Go ahead, kill me.* Thomas stopped also, and a funny what-the-hell's-going-on? look came to his face, and when Richard knew he was relaxed good, he brought one up from the next neighborhood and clipped him good right on the ear. Thomas spun clean around and started to walk away; then he walked in a circle and the son of a bitch was smiling, but he walked right past Richard and around the other side again, and all Richard could do was stand there and look at the crooked little legs that were browner than his. Then he heard everybody hollering for him to go after Thomas, and he thought he might as well, so he followed him around, but Thomas wouldn't stand still. So finally he grabbed him and turned him around, and Thomas stood there grinning, and his eyes were almost closed, because his eyelids were almost together anyway. Richard couldn't hit him when he was smiling at him like that. He smiled back at him, and then the bell rang.

Richard couldn't help laughing at Thomas's grin, but suddenly he stopped, because the bell rang again and he knew he was in for it. Right away, Thomas hit him in the stomach, and Richard bent right over, and there it was—he just kept right on going, and landed on his head and took the count there curled up like a fetus. He didn't have to fight any more, and Thomas was very happy as he helped him up, and Thomas kept saying how he was like Fitzsimmons and that his Sunday punch was a right to the solar plexus. "I hit you in the solar plexus, Richard," he said over and over again, but Richard wasn't really listening to him, because he was sneaking looks at the people, and finally decided he had made it look pretty good.

The referee and the professional came over to see him. "Nice faking, kid," said the referee. "How'd ya like to be a fighter?"

"Uh-uh," he said, pulling at the laces with his teeth. The man took his gloves off.

"You don't know how to fight, but you got a punch for a kid and you're smart," he said.

"I not only can't fight, but I'm scared to fight, so you don't want me," he said.

"How old are ya, kid?"

"I'll be thirteen soon."

"I thought you was older," he said. "But, hell, I can teach ya a lot, and in a year I can put you in smokers. Make five or ten bucks a night that way."

"Not me, Mister. I don't need five or ten bucks."

"How about me?" said Thomas. "I'm the guy that won. You saw me hit him in the solar plexus." Now Richard knew why Thomas had been so anxious to fight.

"Yeah, I can use you, too," said the man, "but I want this other kid."

"Oboyoboy!" said Thomas. He had a trade now.

"How about it, kid?" asked the man. "I'm giving ya the chance of your life—it's the only way people of your nationality can get ahead."

"I'm an American," said Richard.

"All right, you know what I mean. Mexicans don't get too much chance to amount to much. You wanna pick prunes the rest of your life?" Richard didn't say anything, and he said, "Look, I'll go talk it over with your old man, and I'll bet he'll agree with me. I'll bet he knows what's good for you."

"You better not do that, Mister. You don't know my old man. He's already been in jail for knifing three guys."

Richard could tell he was dumb, and, like a lot of people, believed that Mexicans and knives went together. He thought he had finished with him, but the man said, "All right, we won't tell 'im anything, and when you start bringing money home, he'll come and see *me*."

"Listen," Richard said. "He'll come and see you all right, but it won't make any difference. My old man don't feel about money the way some people do. So leave me alone, why don't you?"

But the man kept insisting, and said, "I gotta line up a smoker for the Eagles, and if you and the Jap kid here put 'em on, I'll give ya each a fin. Then, when your old man sees the dough, he'll be in the bag. What do you say?"

"Okay with me, said Thomas, "but don't call me no Jap." Richard was walking away by then, and the man followed him. "I'll give ya seven-fifty and the Jap a fin."

"No, thanks." He kept walking. They would never be able to make him do anything like that. He was sure he could be no more than a punching bag, because, hell, everybody in the neighborhood could beat him, and besides he was afraid.

The guys caught up to him, but he wasn't talking. He thought how funny the guy back there was—the fight manager. He felt that the manager was the kid and he was the grownup. *Amount to something!* Jesus! Everybody was telling him what he should make of himself these days, and they all had the same argument, except that this guy was thinking of himself. At least the little old lady who was so nice and let him read the Horatio Alger books was thinking of him when she told him he should work hard to be a gardener and someday he could work on a rich person's estate; she was sure he would be successful at that because she had known of some Mexicans who held very fine places like that. . . . Funny about her, how the Horatio Alger books meant as much to her as the Bible meant to Protestants. . . . And the adviser in the high school, who had insisted he take autoMechanics or welding or some shop course, so that he could have a trade and be in a position to be a good citizen, because he was Mexican, and when he had insisted on preparing himself for college, she had smiled knowingly and said he could try those courses for a week or so, and she would make an exception and let him change his program to what she knew was better for him. She'd been eating crow ever since. What the hell makes people like that, anyway? Always worried about his being Mexican and he never even thought about it, except sometimes, when he was alone, he got kinda funnyproud about it.

As he walked toward home with the guys, he thought about the things he had just discovered. He would never really be afraid again. Like with hitting

Thomas and ending the fight the way he did; funny he had never thought about that before—the alternative. Everything had another way to it, if only you looked hard enough, and he would never be ashamed again for doing something against the unwritten code of honor. Codes of honor were really stupid—it amazed him that he had just learned this—and what people thought was honorable was not important, because he was the important guy. No matter what he did and who was affected by his actions, in the end it came back to him and his feelings. He was himself, and everything else was there because he was *himself*, and it wouldn't be there if he were not himself, and then, of course, it wouldn't matter to him. He had the feeling that *being* was important, and he *was*—so he knew that he would never succumb to foolish social pressures again. And if he hurt anyone, it would be only if he had no choice, for he did not have it in him to hurt willingly.

He thought of Thomas's face in the ring, and began to laugh at the silliness of his grin, and then he laughed louder and louder, about the fight manager and all the people who tried to tell him how to live the good life, and then laughed about the guys with him, because they were laughing like crazy, too, and the sad bastards did not know what the hell they were laughing about.

The Contributors

Leonard Adamé I was born in the San Joaquin Valley in 1947. Most of my early years were spent in my dad's restaurant, where I grew to hate dishes. I spent a few summers on my uncle's farm and had my first taste of shit. High school was disastrous for me, as it was for most Mexicans who were not "motivated." I remember my grandmother dying at the hospital and the most delicious and tender tortillas she made for me when I was small.

After high school I became a half-ass musician and played in a number of the better run-down west-side clubs. I've toured the United States with rock groups and come to the conclusion that things are generally the same wherever you go.

I'm married and have three beautiful daughters.

My brother and two uncles have muscular dystrophy and are in wheel-chairs. When I feel pompous and depressed, I remember them and kick myself in the ass.

Alfredo Cuéllar Ph.D. candidate in political science at the University of California, Los Angeles; instructor at Claremont College; M.A. from North Texas State University with thesis entitled *A Social and Political History of the Mexican American Population of Texas: 1929-1963* (1969). Contributing editor to *Aztlán: Chicano Journal of the Social Sciences and the Arts.*

Ricardo Juan Durán *Born:* East Los, Califas Aztlán, 33 B.C. (Before Chicanismo). *Education:* Streets of Los, six years at University of Southern California. *Occupation:* Teacher. Calmecac, Universidad de Aztlán (on probation); Estudios de la Raza, Fresno State (fired); Chicano Studies, Fresno City College (fired); Center for Social Action, U.S.C. (fired); Black History, Compton Continuation High School, Watts (fired); Kindergarten, El Monte School District (fired). *Writings:* "Canción de la Raza," first bilingual television series, National Education Television, seventeen shows. *Published Essays:* "Educational Genocide" (*Muhammed Speaks*), "Mis-Education" (*La Raza*), "Education—A Chicano Perspective" (Long Beach State College), "Education as Liberation—Not Domestication" (*Orígenes*). *Novels:* Untold number—all unfinished. *Poetry:* Published—0. Unpublished —two or three hundred.

Benjamin Durazo   Born in Madera, California, in 1951. Raised with eight brothers and sisters. Had a hand in making the San Joaquin Valley for its owners, hope to die making the San Joaquin Valley for its workers.

Look at my poems—aspects of my thoughts. If you recognize these poems, hold and warm them in your hands, give them to your brothers and sisters. Their purpose will then be done. [Ed. note: Ben Durazo died in the summer of 1971 in an accident.]

Rudy Gallardo   Born in Guanajuato, Mexico, in 1940. Went with family in 1944 to California's Imperial Valley, where they worked as migrant farm laborers. Later traveled all over California as farm worker. Years in jails, years in colleges. Now teaching at San Francisco State and writing.

Rafael Jesús González   Born in 1935. Grew up in El Paso, Texas. Attended University of Texas at El Paso—president of the student literary society. Studied at the National University of Mexico. Now teaching English at Laney College in Oakland, California.

José Ángel Gutiérrez   Born in Crystal City, Texas. Attended Southwest Texas Junior College. B.A. from the Texas College of Arts and Industry at the University of Houston. Organizer for La Raza in Crystal City, Texas. Founder of two P A S O chapters and three M.A.Y.O. groups. Member of the Mexican-American Youth Organization and the *Alianza Federal de Tejas*.

Ben Luna   *Born:* East Los, Califas, Aztlán, 31 years old—todo en el barrio. *Education:* sixth-grade dropout. *Occupation:* None. *Life interest:* Painter, poet, lover, revolutionary anarchist. *Writings:* "Flowers for the Dead Kings of Mexico" (unpublished poetry book). Fifty or sixty poems published in the *Chicano* press. Television play for Channel 28, Hollywood. *Paintings:* Eight murals in churches, auditoriums, and wino alleys of East Los. Many paintings given away.

Amado Muro   Born in Parral, Chihuahua. Father was a singer and composer of ballads. Moved to El Paso, Texas, as a child and attended school there. Worked as a field hand and construction worker. Traveled to Europe and South America as a seaman. Published frequently in *Chicano* and Anglo literary magazines. Now living in El Paso.

Alfredo Otero y Herrera   Born in the *barrio* in Jerome, Arizona, in 1932. Grew up in the *barrio*, attended universities in the United States, Spain, and Mexico. Now an associate professor of Hispanic literature at California State University, Los Angeles.

Américo Paredes   Professor of English and anthropology, director of the Center for Mexican American Studies at the University of Texas, Austin. Ph.D. from the University of Texas for doctoral dissertation, *With His Pistol in His Hand*—an exploration of the Gregorio Cortez legend (published 1958). Also author of *Folktales of Mexico* (1970) and numerous short

⎧ries and poems. Editor of *Journal of Mexican American Folklore* and member of the editorial board of *Folklore Américas*.

Armando Rendón Presently head of a *Chicano* consulting firm, A.T.M. Systems, based in Washington, D.C. Past staff member of *Civil Rights Digest*. Author of *Chicano Manifesto* (New York: Macmillan, 1971) and of numerous articles on the *Chicano*.

José Rendón I was born in Laredo, Texas, moved to Detroit that same year. My old man went looking for work. Went to Catholic school, changed my name to Joseph, learned to hate penguins and God. I went to Texas at fourteen and discovered that I wasn't black. Became José again. Ran with my semi-*chuco primos*.

Back to Detroit after two years, learned to dance and discovered the movement, worked for grape boycott and balled white chicks. Came to California to find the answer. Still looking.

Enrique Rodríquez Born in Los Angeles to a poor family, I grew knowing suffering, but even more I learned to see and feel the beauty of life. Even amidst poverty I found beauty in my *barrio*, my *raza*, my *familia*. At 23 I fought with death and almost lost; now you see my limp and cane. No longer can my body run and jump, but my mind and heart can still fly with the wind and I write words.

Luis Omar Salinas
I am Omar, forlorn passenger on a train of somnambular beginnings
who was born in Robstown, Texas, and attended Catholic grammar
school where they taught us to tolerate racial hatred/
after reading Neruda and Baudelaire became antifascist
and worker for La Raza Cósmica/
I put my heart away from American imperialism and wrote poem
for Guevara/renaissance man
taught school at Fresno Chicano Bilingual Creative Writing/
trying to develop young writers/
acted with Teatro Campesino under Luís Valdéz
Wrote "Crazy Gypsy" book of poems.
I love women who tolerate me and my poems/
and walk away from despair when I can
I write poems on walls that crumble and fall
and tell stories to the rabbits of my neighborhood
while walking pigtailed girls to school
learned not to cheat on exams otherwise I might not make West Point/
All of us seem to be caught on a wall of mediocrity
system does not tolerate fuck words or marihuana/
Plan to go to Europe and start serious work on novel/
the one about the supposed sophisticated Chicano
who travels to Europe after suicide of his mother

and his consequent moral corruption in Paris/and salvation
by a girl like his mother from a rich American family/
Novel's title: *Marvelous Mexican in Paris.*
Finally getting money for poems.
Readings so far: St. Paul, Minnesota; Monterrey, México;
Robstown, Texas; University of California at Irvine;
and Stanford University/
Known to drink Mexican liquors and preference for aristocratic
young women been arrested by pigs for drinking with girls
under-age/Never been married/but seduced into bedroom
several times/has known grief in early childhood with death
of his mother . . . never forgot her stoic beauty and intelligence/
known to bum cigarettes in restaurants/has many friends
some real some unreal digs James Bond, Cantinflas and Octavio Paz
(Poet)/
is serious
loves to write
presently in love
and Mexican to the core
lived in Monterrey, Mexico, as a child/caused vast impression
has written for East Los Angeles newspaper
worked as dishwasher construction worker shoe salesman
copy boy and while not working teaches and writes
lives in Sanger, California
where he drinks gallons of coffee
and works in yard . . . listens to music and sometimes
tells it like it is and when he doesn't rarely gets in trouble
except for sometimes starting rumors/
Thinks highly of Women's Lib
would like to travel to Cuba and France Spain
thinks Mexican government uptight
doesn't think much of immortality and rarely goes to church
smokes little cigars.

Mario Suarez   Born in 1925. Grew up in Tucson, Arizona, in the *barrio*. Studied writing and folklore at the University of Arizona. Recipient of the John Hay Whitney Fellowship for creative writing. Now on the faculty of Chicano Studies at California State Polytechnic College in Pomona, California.

Ernesto Trejo   I was born in Fresnillo, a small mining town in central Mexico, in 1950. My family moved to Mexico City when I was two, and I didn't see Fresnillo again until 1967, when I remet my blind grandfather and my insane grandmother. Later we moved to Mexicali, where I grew up and went to school. I recently got a degree in economics. Some people call economics the science of the future, but to me in a sense it has always been the poetry of the masses; but today it is becoming more a political question, more so than in the time of Marx, and I am a political man.

I started to write poetry in winter nights of insomnia, and looking back, the poems show it: They are sleepy, obscure, and incoherent. Writing a poem is a ritual, and one should not fool around with such serious matters in nights of insomnia; so I changed my writing time to more lucid moments of the day, and decided to leave the night to its own rituals: dreaming, love-making, and the anarchy of cows . . .

Luis Valdéz   Began the *Teatro Campesino* in a small shack in Delano, California, in 1965, at the age of 25, after acting with the San Francisco Mime Troupe. Talked with Delores Huerta about the possibility of establishing a farm workers' theater. One night in November 1965 began talking to the *campesinos,* but saw it was useless unless talk could be illustrated. Had a friend make signs: *"huelguista," "patroncito," "esquirole," "campesino."* Hung the signs around some of the *campesinos* and asked one of them to act like an *"esquirole."* Two other *campesinos* began shouting at *"esquirole,"* and by the end of the evening the shack was full. Everyone jumped in and imitated all kinds of things. And so the *"actos"* originated and the *Teatro Campesino* began.

Roberto Enrique Vargas   Born February 24, 1941 (Pisces). Raised in San Francisco Mission District. Graduated Mission High School. Active in Third World Liberation Front at S.F. State College and the world. Teaching creative writing at S.F. State. Working with the Art Commission to develop a truly People's Art Program. Developing Word/Drum Alchemy. Stimulating revolutionary thought/feelings through poetry sung to beat of congas/timbales. Rebirth of Aztlán in our lifetime . . .

Enriqueta Longauex y Vásquez   Born and raised in Colorado. Spent ten years in Denver, one year in Los Angeles. Living in the small mountain village of San Cristobal, New Mexico, with husband and two teenaged children since 1967. Five years of work in legal offices, one year on welfare. Years of living in housing projects. Director of the Skills Bank of Operation —a program to help get jobs for *Chicanos.* Always involved with the *Chicano* community. Now writing a regular column for the movement newspaper, *El Grito del Norte.*

Richard Vásquez   Living in Altadena, California. Frequent contributer to *La Raza,* "brown power" underground newspaper. Professional experience as a newspaperman, publicist, screenwriter. And a native understanding of the streets of the *barrio.* Now working on second novel.

José Antonio Villarreal   Born and raised in California. Traveled in Mexico and eastern United States. Son of a Mexican migrant worker. Four years in the Navy. Degree from the University of California. Married. Father of three children. Author of *Pocho,* the first *Chicano* novel (1959).